Jesse Helms must not read this novel. He'll denounce it from the Senate floor as a threat to Western civilization. And Bill Clinton will probably sue for sexual harrassment.
— Fab Magazine, Toronto

The novel reads like a whirlwind. One has so much fun with this mean-and-lean page-turner that one at first overlooks what a gripping, compelling suspense thriller it is
— on multiple levels.
— Books Today, Atlanta

Savvy, crisp portraits of characters on the make in the fleshpots of "The Last Resort" of Key West.
It ensnares the reader.
— Advance Reviews, New York

There's something for everyone here: Sadists, size queens, romance readers, thrill seekers, Bi's, gossip-mongers, defenders of the paparazzi, and bedmates of Cuban men.
— Siegessaule, Berlin

Hallucinatory entertainment...You'll be hooked by this gut-wrenching and sometimes demonic work. The characters grab you and hold you right from the beginning.
— What's New in Fiction, Boston

Darwin Porter is the Tennessee Williams of today--that is, if "Tom" were born in 1972.
— Nat og Dag, Copenhagen

If Dino and his father, Rafael, are typical of Cuban manhood, book me on the next flight to Havana.
— La Noche, Barcelona

Like the title promises, a dazzling work. We want the movie rights.
– Lothian, Edinburgh

I haven't had so much fun since Margo Channing confronted Eve Harrington in the final reel of All About Evita. Porter redefines the word bitch. Dare we use the C word?
– La Movida, Madrid

I agree with Sherry Kelly. It's the size that counts!
– Munich Found, Munich

After reading Darwin Porter's Razzle-Dazzle, I've decided to come out of the closet. Key West, here I come.
Or is it "kum" in English. You Americans!
– La Trova Roma, Rome

Only Elizabeth Taylor could play the mother, Mia. Only Madonna could play the daughter, Sherry.
Are there any actors in Hollywood big enough for the parts of Rafael and Dino?
– Inferno, Buenos Aires

Who says money can't buy happiness?
– Gab, Frankfurt

If Razzle-Dazzle is ever made into a movie, it should be cast on the couch.
– Hinnerk, Hamburg

I haven't had so much fun since my daddy spanked my bare butt.
– Out! New Zealand

Forget those "coming out" novels. Sherry and her gang long ago "came out." Now they're just coming.
– G-Scene, Brighton

Only the names were changed to protect the guilty. But we know who they are!
— Cruiser, Zurich

With one hand, I kept turning the pages. With the other...
— Queer Biz, Helsinki

Devilishly delicious. Delectable. Desirable. Demented. Devouring. De cream in my coffee or somewhere.
— Angles, Vancouver

Sherry Kelly and her "cunties" bring a hot time to 'ol Key West. Forget South Beach. Take me to "where the boys are."
— Use-it, Amsterdam

I didn't think Darwin Porter could top Butterflies in Heat. But that's before I read Razzle-Dazzle. I'm in love!
— Outrage, Sydney

This is entertainment. Forget MGM. This is comedy! But on the dark side. This kept me so busy all night, I had to turn down Tom Cruise.
— Sortie, Montreal

Razzling, dazzling, truly original, and seductively written. Compellingly suspenseful.
— X-TRA!, Vienna

RAZZLE-DAZZLE

A Novel by
Darwin Porter

STARbooks/FLF
Sarasota, Florida

Also by Darwin Porter

BUTTERFLIES IN HEAT
MARIKA
VENUS

COPYRIGHT 1995 BY DARWIN PORTER
& DANFORTH PRINCE

ALL RIGHTS RESERVED
First Edition Published in the U.S. in February 1998
Library of Congress Card Catalogue No. 97-062287
ISBN No. 1-877978-96-5

Publication made possible in part by a grant from
the Florida Literary Foundation.

Cover design by Scott Sosebee

FOR DANFORTH PRINCE

CHAPTER ONE

April, 1993
Star Island, Florida

Every day a young Dino brings me the supermarket tabloids to see what's been written about me overnight. The whole world's falling apart, but it seems these rags have nothing else to write about but me. Ever since I uncrossed my legs and flashed before millions of film-goers in the movie, "Kinky," I've been hot copy. The stuff of Second Coming headlines.

Last week, to hear the press tell it, I was beamed aboard a flying saucer and raped by six little bug-eyed green men no more than four feet tall. Can you imagine that? Long-limbed me, who likes her men tall in the saddle, as Daddy Kelly used to say. At least six foot three. I insist upon that since I'm not exactly a midget myself.

The week before last, there was a front page photo of blonde Madonna kissing blonde me in a night club. What was I to do? Jump back in horror when Madonna lip-locked with me and started exchanging body fluids? I had to kiss her back. Lesbians are some of my biggest fans, and they like to see me kissing a woman ever so often. They also like to see my tits and ass, just as much as men do, maybe more. I understand more women collected that copy of *Playboy*, in which I bared all, than did men.

Today, I'm in the prime of my life, or so my fat agent tells me. I will not actually give his name in this script, but know that behind his back he's called "The Iguana." The name says it all. Although repulsive, he's occasionally effective in a crude sort of way.

I'm a ripe 36. In spite of the adoring hordes, I know that 36 is a dangerous time for a woman, even though I'm called the reigning goddess of the screen. You'd think I'd have to make a dozen films to be the queen of Hollywood. But everything is speeded up these days.

Marilyn was 36 or some such age when she died. *Marilyn knew*. Those bleached streetwalker sluts get wised up by the time they reach 16. Marilyn knew when to get off the stage

–unlike me who seems to be just making her debut. Why couldn't I have been discovered when I was 20? If things continue their downward trend, they'll be hiring body doubles for me for my next picture.

One of those vicious rags headlined a story last month that I was old enough to be Dino's mother. Tell me about it. The boy is only seventeen, and everybody agrees that he looks much older. He's a dead-ringer for Antonio Sabato Jr. How did I know when I saw him in that Banana Republic ad that he was that young? He told me he was twenty-two, and I believed him.

When I first saw that ad, I knew Dino was hot. I was slightly bothered by the ad, noticing that Dino's beautifully sculpted male hand was pressed against the beautifully sculpted Davidesque chest of another young stud. Yet I had high hopes. There was also a cute girl in the picture, a little too young for my tastes, and her hand was pressed against Dino's, almost urging him to feel the hard chest of his companion even harder. Pictures don't lie. That meant Dino had to be bi-...at least. Hell, it was worth a chance, I told myself. Those models in the Banana Republic ads, male or female, are deliberately chosen to look as if they'd go willingly either way, depending on circumstances.

The next day I called The Iguana. Considering his looks, calling him is better than a face-to-face. I told him to get me the boy's home phone from the modeling agency who arranged the booking. I got immediate protests from The Iguana, a sleaze from Fall River, Massachusetts. As a little boy, he'd actually tossed stones at Lizzie Borden whenever she went to church in a black veil. "Lizzie Borden took an ax, gave her mother forty whacks..." You know that taunting little ditty. I personally think Lizzie Borden was innocent (and should have left Fall River), but that's another story.

This foul-mouth agent of mine, who should have been smothered the moment he popped out of the womb, screamed at me into the phone. "Why do you want to shack up with some stupid kid for? He's probably a fag." This same agent always speaks as if he were Zanuck and we were back in the Hollywood of 1934.

I told him that I wanted Dino and that no other man would do. When I get hung up on a guy, I've got to have him. Even if he's gay, as they so often are these days.

How right I was. Getting fucked by Dino is a celestial experience that every man or woman in America should have, at least once. Getting photographed with seventeen-year-old Dino, however, is hell. No one should match their beauty with his. That's why we don't go out much any more. I'd go out by myself but I don't dare leave Dino alone. He might pick up something he couldn't get rid of, then pass that virus along to me.

Being with Dino most of the time is like living alone. Many days go by when he mutters only three lines. "Wanna fuck?" That invitation is extended when we first wake up, again after lunch, and finally right before we go to sleep.

When the kid's not doing it, he works out. He's got to keep that perfect body in shape in case Banana Republic ever calls him again to pose for one of their ads. When not balling me or lifting weights, he eats yogurt on which he sprinkles wheat germ, a ghastly idea. He also watches films. His favorite movie scene is my legendary crotch shot in "Kinky." Personally, I don't know why he likes to play that scene so much when he can walk into the bedroom and see the real thing, all the way to Honolulu, any time he so desires. Men are beyond my understanding anyway.

It's nearly time for lunch, and I haven't gotten out of bed yet. It's Saturday. A few minutes ago, I heard Dino return. He always drives my Mercedes at eighty miles an hour up the driveway, coming to a crashing halt at the garage doors. I'm too tired or I'd call Barbra or Cher and ask them what they see in younger men.

Even though it's my day off, I still have a wardrobe fitting. Today I'm to pick out the brassiere I'll wear in an important scene in "Butterflies in Heat," my second film, to be shot in Key West. I do the whole take in my bra. At least I don't have to flash like I did in Kinky.

I believe a bra should make a statement, but not steal the picture. I don't want everybody in every movie theater from Nome to Delhi looking at some lingerie when their time might be better spend gaping at me, the star, for Christ's sake.

A woman makes a lot of bad decisions in her life, and I think the first mistake begins when she picks the wrong bra.

. . .

I hear Dino right now in the kitchen ordering the cook how to prepare his breakfast, and I must join him soon, but only after I've had my toilette, and only after I have made myself ready for the bra session this afternoon.

I can also hear the fat Mexican woman yelling at Dino about his latest ridiculous request. Yesterday, he demanded a bean sprout salad with a soy sauce vinaigrette, and that of a woman who knows how to make only tacos or is it tortillas?

After my bath, it was time to face Dino and the Mexican cook's freshly baked bread, the aroma of which was wafting across the house. No sooner had I barged into the kitchen, making a dramatic appearance, than I was completely upstaged by a fight between Dino and the fat Mexican cook. Dino, it seemed, had brutally rejected the cook's freshly baked bread and had insisted instead on a kale milkshake. Health food nuts are the same the world over.

He was parading around the kitchen in a little white sex-hider pouch that was much too small for its ample load. He might as well have been naked. I wonder if kale milkshakes contributed to a body like that. The fat cook was in her usual gray dress uniform, the one with salsa dripped on the front.

Since Dino was on exhibit, I gave him a fast appraisal. Bubble butt, flat washboard stomach, the most perfect shade of olive skin yet invented--not too brown, a golden glow. Jet-black hair, thick and curly, much too long for my tastes, as I fantasize about men with military crew-cuts. In his case, I made an exception because of his other talents. Suffice it to say that he looks one hundred percent more spectacular than your wildest fantasy in an Esquire ad modeling some new Italian men's wear.

"Mama!" Dino called out upon seeing me enter the kitchen. "How's the bush?"

"Some greeting." He is not a boy with a lot of culture. "Yes, everything is just fine down there if you must know. The flavor today is strawberry, but I don't really want to talk about it before breakfast."

"Not talk about it," he said, astonished. "Do you know that right this very minute millions of men around the world--not to mention what else--are dreaming of just one thing: The Golden Honeypot. What a mama and she's all mine!"

"Cafe!" I yelled, turning to the Mexican cook. If you're going to keep a trick like Dino around the house, there are advantages in hiring people who have a limited grasp of English. The cook's entire English vocabulary consists of three words: Money, day-off, and eat.

With the coffee, I had one slice of the cook's freshly baked bread with a patty of real butter. I do not indulge in health foods. I like baked potatoes with sour cream, lobster swimming in real butter, chicken roasted under slabs of bacon fat, and velvety smooth ice cream, banana only. I do not eat yogurt, wheat germ, kale milkshakes, bean sprouts, or squirrel brains.

The bread tasted good, and I savored the strong black Mexican coffee. I drink it black, not with heavy cream, as you might have gathered, based on my previous culinary revelations. I am not always consistent, as Dino keeps pointing out.

Slamming down the coffee, I turned to him. His beautiful brown eyes with their long thick eyelashes gazed lovingly at me. "What's on mama's mind?"

"Stop calling me mama. I'm much too young to be anybody's mama!"

"You're mine and I love you." He scooted his red Valencian chair closer to mine and gently licked my lilywhite neck with that smooth, talented tongue of his.

I backed away, somewhat reluctantly. The Mexican cook might not understand English but she certainly knew a lick when she saw one from a seventeen-year-old Latino boy. I think she dislikes him intensely.

I turned to Dino in my most imperial manner. "Get me those god damn tabloids. That's what I sent you to the market for, and you were gone an awfully long time. One hour and fifteen minutes to be exact. A lot can happen in one hour and fifteen minutes. A seventeen-year-old can father a baby, contact AIDS, get a blow job in the back seat of a car, or exchange some wicked body fluids with God knows who."

"There you go again. Always talking about body fluids."

"Don't you think that's a very legitimate subject to be talking about these days? What do you think people in the Middle

Ages talked about with the Black Death killing off everyone around them? I mean, in the last four months, haven't thirty-six people we know--some friends, most casual acquaintances--died of AIDS?"

He shrugged his shoulders, as if that would keep AIDS from ravaging his beautiful young body. In his heart, I don't think Dino feared AIDS the way I, a mature woman, did. He seemed to feel he was not vulnerable to AIDS, that nothing, not even the passage of time, could ever harm that perfect physique which looked as if it were sculpted by Michelangelo or at least Charlton Heston playing Michelangelo in the movie.

He shoved three tabloids at me. Dressed like a hooker, Cher disgraced the cover of the first one. I tossed that one aside. I already know more about Cher than is good for me. Some alleged indiscretion about Michael Douglas involved with another woman was splashed on the cover of the second rag.

On the third piece of crap we got down to some serious business. Moi. There I was on the most lurid cover of the month. Taking inspiration from one of those quickie exploitation films, The Hand That Rocks the Cradle, the art director ran a picture of me looking like I'd been snapped in some drug rehab center, with my breasts half exposed. I'm leering down at Dino, around whose perfect, angelic body the art director had superimposed a picture of a cradle.

Far from being offended, as I was, Dino seemed overjoyed. "Look at me. Don't I look terrific? I bet I'll get a lot of offers for modeling."

"You'll get a lot of offers," I said sarcastically. "This is shit! Get my lawyer, David Miller, on the phone. I'll sue."

"But it's all true. We're an item."

"When did those rags ever write the truth about anybody?" I turned the pages to read the copy. Even for a sheet that specializes in sensationalism, the story about me was a little raw. A number of my enemies, including the bitch who lost the role of Kinky to me, were quoted – all at my expense.

Get an ear of this:

"Joan Crawford liked to adopt children and beat them with coat hangers. Sherry Kelly likes to adopt children too, and she's putting new meaning into the phrase, 'Tuck them into bed at night.' That's 'tuck,' darlings."

"Sherry Kelly likes them so young she's liable to get arrested for raiding a sperm bank."

"Next thing you'll hear is of Sherry Kelly approaching expectant mothers and asking them if they're about to give birth to a boy or girl. Only those fresh from the womb will satisfy Ms. Kinky."

And this final comment from some producer who wisely preferred not to give his name. "Let's face it, all of us used to molest children in the 70s and 80s when it was the sporting thing to do. But when it became politically incorrect in the 90s we dispensed with this pleasure and took up other activities, like gardening. Sherry Kelly continues in our old but abandoned tradition, putting new meaning into Dan Quayle's family values."

Throwing the rag on the floor, I ran hysterically into the garden in my white see-through gown. I wasn't really crying, although it might appear that I was. A rage engulfed me. I wanted to strike back, but didn't know how. No wonder people feel impotent. I wanted to hire an Arab terrorist to blow up that newspaper office, and God knows those bastards know how to blow up things.

I remember once overhearing talk in a restaurant. "Do you think Sherry Kelly ever lost one night's sleep fretting over what some tabloid wrote about her?"

That anonymous diner didn't know me at all. Sherry Kelly has lost many a night's sleep over what was said about her in the newspaper. I'm very sensitive, and I do have feelings. They can hurt me, but I'll never give them the satisfaction of knowing how much.

I collapsed on a bench and wanted to sob but the sounds seemed clogged in my throat.

In moments, warm, comforting arms were wrapped around me, cuddling me like a baby.

It was Dino. "There, there, mama, it's going to be okay."

. . .

As the time neared for my brassiere wardrobe selection, I stayed alone in the garden to contemplate my breasts after Dino went back inside.Press attacks aside, I had to get back to the business of the day, my tits. What can I say about my breasts that is original, and hasn't been written about by every newspaper in the world, except those aimed directly at the Neo-Nazi radical right, or perhaps the Fundamentalist Islamic gazettes? Suffice to say, these boobs are the stuff of dreams, the most celebrated pair of knockers on the face of the earth. I asked Lloyd's of London to insure each of them for two million dollars and was turned down. Lloyd's isn't what it used to be. I hear they're almost bankrupt anyway.

My mammary revelry was rudely interrupted by the fat Mexican cook yelling at me from across the garden. Who knows what had pressed her hysteria button now? When she shook her tits at me, I finally gathered that my staff had come back home with the selection of brassieres.

Making my way across the garden and into the back den, I noticed that Dino had changed from his see-through sex hider white pouch to a Mesh Thong of light, airy, revealing cotton. He'd chosen the red one, after having rejected, I was certain, the white, beige, green, yellow, black, and purple ones in his collection.

"Dino!" I called out, a little too harshly for a goddess. "You know perfectly well that Ted and Maxie are child molesters. Don't you think a pair of long, loose gym shorts would be better? After all, this summit meeting is about my breasts. You might upstage me – at least with those two!"

"Now, mama, we who have bared all for Playboy can't tell anyone else how to dress. Besides, as you've taught me, it pays to advertise one's assets."

The kid's logic was unassailable. Sighing, I headed for my gigantic living room, there to encounter Ted Hooker, my live-in longtime secretary. Ted's real name was Hooker, even though many people had accused him of making it up. The son of Helen Hooker, Ted doesn't know who his father was. According to Ted, Hooker, his mother's maiden name, aptly described her. Ted's in his 50s now; I suspect near the top of the scale, although he insists he's in the early years. The boy is a definite bottom in my opinion. Before becoming my secretary, he tried for a film career. Who hasn't? His first part was in a Walt Disney movie impersonating a duck. His career as a movie extra went nowhere fast, and by the time he'd turned thirty he'd prematurely wrinkled. Each year of his life, his once naturally red hair got redder or was it a bright pumpkin orange? Ted always quite honestly compared his appearance to Mildred Natwich in drag. No one may know who Mildred Natwich is any more, but if you do, it's a brilliant comparison. Much to the annoyance of my Mommie, Ted always advised me on what to wear. Or, as is so often the case, what not to wear.

He rushed to kiss me. After the obligatory peck on the cheeks, Ted, bundle of hysterical energy that he is, whirled around like a drunken ballerina to make way for his designer friend, Maxwell LaLanne, my live-in stylist. "Maxie," whose face had undoubtedly known the wind, rain, and hail of the 30s, was clad in a white turban, evocative of Lana Turner. Remember her? The blonde MGM movie star of the 40s?

"Why the turban?" I asked.

Maxie looked dumbfounded and just a bit hurt.

Ted interceded. "Maxie had a little struggle last night and this one managed to lose her wig. You know the one. Jet-black. Makes him look like a dead ringer for Bela Lugosi. The turban will have to do until we get across town and get him another one."

It was at that moment that Dino chose to make a guest star appearance in front of our staff. As he entered the room--too bad he didn't have musical accompaniment--I must say he attracted more attention than I did, legend or not. I long ago learned that even if I appeared jaybird-naked in front of certain audiences, Dino in a Mesh Thong would steal the show.

Dino failed to make eye contact with either Ted or Maxie, their gazes focused elsewhere. With a beautiful smile, Dino settled down on the sofa in his most provocative lounge lizard position, exposing his dangling assets to their ample advantage.

It required my most forceful command, but I managed once again to regain the attention of those two.

"Okay, fellas," I said, "down to business. It's audition time. Bring in your bra. It'd better be good and hot." I then proceeded to go into a mock strip routine, tantalizing the audience as I hummed a few words – "A pretty girl is like a melody" – removing my night gown to expose the breasts the world drools over. I'd modestly retained my bikini briefs, although Ted and Maxie had seen the moneymaker so many times they no longer bothered to notice, if they ever did. Perhaps a quick glance to broadcast to friends if I were a natural blonde, and that was it.

Maxie went to get a box he'd left in the rotunda, then returned and carefully opened it, handing me his latest design creation. In spite of the fact he'd probably been born in 1791, he looked amazingly like a thirteen-year-old, bringing home his report card to a stern, witch-burning daddy. He handed me a flesh-colored bra with great delicacy.

"Forget about that bra Howard Hughes allegedly designed for Janie Russell," Maxie said. "Janie denies there ever was such a bra, incidentally." He looked down at his creation, resting in my hand. "This will become the bra to make film history."

Holding the bra up, I carefully inspected it. My deft fingers liked the feel of it, and I tried it on, aided in part by Maxie. Once all of us were convinced that it was firmly in place, I turned to survey my figure in a full-length mirror. Every room in my manse has a full-length mirror. The boys were right. The bra was a sensation. It fitted snugly, holding everything in its proper place. I appeared nude above the waist. Even my nipples showed through in all their glory.

"Oh, mama, talk to me!" Dino yelled from the sofa.

I paraded around the room in Maxie's latest creation. Ted and Maxie were just as delighted with the results as I was. I could have gone on and on and on with my one-woman show had I not noticed activity beginning to occur in Dino's Mesh Thong. Not wanting matters to rise too far, I quickly reached for my robe, concealing myself.

"Gentlemen," I said, turning to Maxie and Ted. "You're absolutely on target. This is the perfect bra."

"It takes the perfect woman to bring out its charms," Maxie admitted.

I walked over and took Maxie's hand and gave him a light brush kiss on his withered cheek. "It's perfect."

He seemed so happy he appeared on the verge of tears. I glided over to Ted, night gown flowing, and took his hand and gave him the same light brush kiss on that Mildred Natwich look-alike cheek. "Once again, you've come through for your favorite star."

With that declaration, I led Ted and Maxie to the patio, with Dino trailing obscenely behind.

The fat Mexican cook had prepared a south-of-the-border luncheon, and we had a lot of gossip to catch up on. It was our Sunday ritual. We were too busy during the week for serious dissing. Ted had news from Key West, news from my Mommie. I feared hearing of her latest escapades.

. . .

The gossip and the margaritas went on for hours until afternoon faded to evening and it was time for the fat cook's Mexican supper. I could tell no difference between lunch and supper. All the dishes tasted the same to me. There was more drinking, more talking, and more indiscreet gossip. Many of the stories I'd already heard, although I pretended to be shocked or horrified at the latest indiscretion of the film world, as seen through the now glassy eyes of Ted and Maxie. In total boredom, Dino had long ago drifted away.

It was only when the gossip had inevitably turned to the subject of Mommie that my interest was truly piqued.

Ted looked hesitant. He usually bit into gossip like he was devouring the contents of a Mesh Thong. Tonight he held back, as if not wanting to divulge something.

"What is it?" I asked with growing alarm. "Mommie isn't sick, is she?"

"No, nothing like that," he said, taking my hand. "Maybe sick in the head. Mia has officially disinherited you and adopted a daughter."

A silence fell over the patio.

I sank back into my chair, hearing but not answering, not wanting to hear. Maxie moved to comfort me, but I brushed him away. A rage growing within me was about to burst forth. "Adopted a daughter? I'm her daughter. What in hell does she need to adopt one for?"

"Beats me," Ted said. "This girl – read that old hag – has exerted some strange influence over Mia. You know how your mother has always taken up with strange creatures. She's moved this latest one into her house in Key West. I hear they spend all their time together."

I yelled at the fat Mexican cook to bring me another margarita, a strong one. "And, if I may be so bold as to ask, who is this strange pussy?"

"Anishi Mishima."

"I know that name. She's that Japanese servant Mia hired a few months ago."

"She's not a servant any more," Ted said.

I stood up and began a slow, deliberate walk around the patio, breathing the night air. "Mommie hires servants. She doesn't adopt them."

"She's gone and done it this time," Maxie chimed in.

"The way I hear it," Ted said, "Anishi got a job in Mia's house as a maid, and then rose through the ranks fast."

"Too damn fast for me," I said, filled with jealousy and fright. "I've been replaced. I know Mia's pissed at me because of Kinky and that centerfold. But this is a bit much."

"You know Mia," Ted said. "She's always flown around the world to get a message from some guru or some fake messiah. Obviously, this Oriental hustler has enthralled her."

"And with what?" I asked. "What could that pathetic Suzie Wong clone give Mommie that I can't?"

"We don't know all the details," Maxie said, "but it seems your Mommie isn't the only rich person that this Mishima creature has ingratiated herself with before. I hear she's quite captivating. She's patented some formula. Calls it an elixir. After a year of injections, it's said to take twenty years off your age. If only I could get it down this tired old gullet."

"The Fountain of Youth," I said, brimming with despair. "Mommie always wanted to find the Fountain of Youth. She once hired men to go through The Bahamas on the trail of Ponce de Leon. Instead of the Fountain of Youth, he found Florida. Mommie always believed that somewhere, he went off course. Those Indians claimed there was a Fountain of Youth somewhere out there, and Mia was determined to find it and bottle it, after saving a cellar of it for herself."

"Mia was just ripe and ready for that little bitch to come along with her injections," Ted said.

An ominous dread came over me. I feared my Mommie was in some sort of trouble. This yellow hooker didn't seem as harmless as others of Mia's gurus, messiahs, and prophets of the past. I had to force Mommie to see me, even though she never accepted my calls and had barred me from setting foot on her property. Of course, until the legal dust settled, we weren't completely sure what was hers and what was mine. Daddy Kelly's will was baffling on some of the finer points. This was one disinherited daughter who was coming home, even if I had to blast my way inside her Key West fortress.

Mommie has more money than the Queen of England; not as much as the Sultan of Brunei, but getting there. So we're talking serious cash here. It's amazing how profitable drugs, gambling, and prostitution were in pre-Castro Cuba. Daddy Kelly was a big player back then.

"No Yoko Ono type is going to move in on my turf and take what's rightfully mine," I said, ostensibly to Maxie and Ted. I was really making a solemn promise to myself. I'd give up my screen career, buy back every copy of Playboy, enter a convent. I'd do anything. I wanted to get back in Mia's good graces, not to mention back in her will.

Up until Ted told me of this little yellow tramp, I'd never taken Mommie's threats seriously. Now I did. In her dotage – Mommie is sixty-one – she's lost sight of what's important. Me, Sherry Kelly, flesh of her loins, that was important. Not some maid, now adopted daughter.

"I've got to get back with Mommie."

Ted stood up, a little drunkenly. "If you need me, I'm always here for you."

"I know, dear, and I desperately need you. Maxie, too. We'll go to Key West."

After the obligatory brush kisses, the final good night, the last-minute comments on the bra, and all their good wishes during the upcoming battle between The West, as represented by Sherry Kelly, and The East, as represented by Anishi Mishima, they left for the cottages in back.

Much later in the evening when I found sleep impossible, I sat alone in my dressing room staring at my image in the mirror. I was still wearing the flesh-tone bra Maxie had designed for me, as if getting used to it before facing the cameras. Dino had insisted that I wear it during our before-bed ritual. I wouldn't be going to Key West just to make a movie, but for war games.

At midnight, a call from California came in from The Iguana. From the tone of his voice, it was apparent he'd finished one of his "safe sex" auditions of new talent. "The shit's about to hit the fan. My office got three calls from some Cuban in Miami. A Rafael Navarro."

"Sounds like he was in silent movies."

"Silent is the way we want to keep him. I took his fourth call myself and spoke to him."

"What's his problem?"

"A long story. Seems he's some sort of political hero to anti-Castro Cubans. Castro was going to kill him. But he hijacked a plane and escaped to a big hero's welcome in Miami."

"If he's trying to sell this to me as a film plot, we'll have to do a little sex-change surgery here. Make the pilot a woman, and I might play it."

"This is no damn movie, this is real life. Navarro claims he's Dino's father. Except it's not Dino. The kid's name is Desiderio."

"Dino's Cuban?" I paused. "Maybe Navarro's a liar. Dino claims he's Italian."

"Maybe. But Navarro could be telling the truth. He could be Dino's father. After all, you don't know anything about the kid's background but what he's told you. From day one, I always said this boy Dino is bad news. I want you to drop this kid at once."

"I can't do that."

"As George Bush would say, you're getting into deep do-do. Deep do-do can turn into a pile of shit. If Navarro's really Dino's daddy, he can make big trouble for you. The kid's a minor, for Christ's sake. Since you're in Miami, I want you to meet this Navarro Spik. With your lawyers, of course. See if you can get him to shut up. With your money, you can buy off anybody--even me should I decide to write a 'tell-all' book."

"Shut-up money? What used to be called hush money?"

"Why not? More rotten publicity is the last thing you need. Through your hot-shot attorney--slash lover boy--David Miller I've already arranged a meeting."

"Okay, I'll meet the guy."

"Call David first thing tomorrow. He will have already grilled this Navarro. If David finds out he's a liar, the personal meeting with you is off. But if he sounds legit, you'd better go through with it." Background noise at The Iguana's house indicated that he hadn't finished the business at hand. "Now go sizzle the screen with Butterflies. Make a great movie and lots of money for your poor old agent slaving for you out here in Hollywood. Who loves ya, baby?"

While The Iguana presumably resumed his nocturnal pleasures, I wandered aimlessly around my house. Even before this disturbing phone call about Dino, I'd been having second thoughts about him. It had all begun when I returned home yesterday and found him terribly excited. At first I thought it was at the prospect of seeing me. It wasn't.

The day before I had asked David to mail Dino a platinum American Express card, since I didn't want him to feel like a toy boy going around borrowing money from me all the time. Dino had put the card to work at once. He called and bought tickets for rock concerts, one involving an air fare and a two-day departure to Chicago. With the card, he'd lined up a number of youthful pursuits for himself.

I appeared delighted at Dino's heavy entertainment agenda. What he didn't seem to realize and what I knew instantly was that none of those pursuits of pleasure involved me. Money as represented by the card had given him a freedom he was eager to taste.

"Why not?" I asked myself, not realizing at first that I was speaking to an empty room. Why shouldn't he be free to go and do what he wanted? After all, he was just a kid, and that's what kids are supposed to do. Maybe right now was the only time this teen-ager would ever be free in his life.

For the first time since I'd foolishly entered this relationship, I felt a pang about sleeping with Dino. It was not right, and it made me feel dirty. I was too old, and he was too young. It was not a relationship I was proud of; if anything, I was ashamed that my loneliness had led me to this. Screen goddesses can be a lonely lot, in spite of thousands of letters I got every week from men around the world claiming I hadn't really been fucked until I'd been plowed by them.

The tickets to the rock concerts had dramatized just how fragile my relationship was with Dino. It didn't matter what had happened in the past. We had other interests to pursue now, and we also faced the problem of this mysterious Navarro creature. "Desiderio," I said out loud. It had such a romantic ring, perhaps not the butch stud-ism of Dino.

I am not a cruel person, and I certainly didn't intend to dump Dino at one of his rock concerts. Even though I planned to ease him on down the road, I would see to it that there were a few gold bricks along that road, enough to get him by in style. I'm no Merv Griffin or Liberace, or even a Rock Hudson. For having warmed my bedsheets during one awful, desperate period of my life, Dino would be rewarded. Not all at once. I'd have David parcel out the largesse, so he wouldn't spend everything at once. I'd like to see him get out of this modeling, Hollywood business. Get into something solid, with a future to it.

I'd choose the right time to tell the news to Dino, and I suspected it wouldn't break his heart at all. If anything, I think both he and I would be relieved at no longer having to pretend a love relationship neither of us felt.

The vast living room seemed too confining, and I felt I had to get out and breathe the night air. Opening the doors to my garden, I went outside.

The day with its news about Mia had left me confused and filled with anxiety. I wanted to blame Mommie for all the mess I had actually made for myself. I kept feeling that if she hadn't cut me off, I wouldn't have gone crazy. I'd done a lot of stupid things. Involving myself in Hollywood was one of them. I felt I'd been cut loose from a vital connection, and I followed some strange byways after leaving Mommie. Taking up with Dino was one of the dumber stunts I'd pulled.

I not only wanted my Mommie back, I wanted to get myself back. My old self. The days when I was more confident and secure, the way I was when I was twenty.

The wooden bench I sat on was cold and wet with dew which soaked through my flimsy gown. As if in a trance, I sat here anyway. The breezes in my garden were soothing. I shut my eyes and held my face up to the moonlight, as if its beams would keep me young and eternally desirable.

Suddenly, I bolted up, filled with fear. It wasn't anything like a rustle in the bushes or someone stepping on a dried twig. If anything, the garden was deadly silent.

In the distance my gardener had planted a thick clump of bushes. I'd ordered it done for more privacy. It could also conceal from the other side, as I thought those bushes were doing right now.

Someone out there was watching, spying on me and the house. Jumping up from the bench, I raced toward the house, bolting the door behind me.

Hysterically I pressed the intercom to alert the night guard that I thought there was a prowler on the grounds, hiding in those bushes.

Shortly after one o'clock, the night guard came into my office. "There was someone," he said.

"Did you catch him?"

"He got away."

"Did you see him?"

"No, but we found this crushed cigar butt out there. Recently smoked. An obvious amateur. No pro would smoke in the night while staking out a house."

I examined the cigar butt. It was a genuine Cuban cigar, the kind Castro smoked. I knew the smoke well. Daddy Kelly smoked them day and night. "Be more alert the next time. I could have been killed."

As I turned to go upstairs to bed, I decided to head for one of my guest rooms. I didn't want to return to Dino's arms. Or was it Desiderio's arms? Let him sleep the rest of the night in peace. The next day would be time enough for him to learn about the change in our relationship.

For me, I knew it would be a restless night. On top of everything else, I now had to face the question of why someone – a Cuban killer, no doubt – would be stalking me.

CHAPTER TWO

"When my mama calls, I come!" Dino said. "Oops, I just realized that could be taken another way. After all, English isn't my first language."

I smiled faintly, the way an overtaxed parent might do with a bright but tiresome child. The morning sun was streaming into the library. He was fresh-faced and eager looking, his bright teeth so white they appeared artificial, as in a toothpaste ad. He was dressed simply this morning: a pair of ripped jeans with the knees sticking through. There was also a five-inch rip near the crotch. He wore a simple red undershirt which outlined perfectly developed arms.

"Dino," I said softly, looking him straight in the eye. "Or would you like me to call you Desiderio."

He looked astonished, a look I know so well. I'd last seen it when I accidentally walked in on my latest lover in bed making love. With another man. Dino had a very expressive face, which told me he was already figuring his way out of this latest trap.

He settled back into the seat and closed his eyes for one brief moment. "Dino, Desiderio, is it really important what we label people in life."

"A philosophical point I could go into. Yes, I think we go through life wearing labels people put on us. I know I have."

He opened his wide eyes even wider and looked into mine. "Shouldn't we make our own labels? Be what we want to be? Not something the world wants us to be?"

"Perhaps." I settled back in my wing chair.

"Damn it! If I want to be a chic Italian model named Dino, the toast of Rome, sought after by Valentino and everybody else, why shouldn't I? This is America where you can be whatever you god damn want to be."

"Correction. America where you can try to be whatever you want to be."

"I want to be Dino and not some poor and starving Cuban refugee."

"I know that." I finally reached for his hand and held it, not like a lover, but like a kinder, older person offering comfort to someone young and confused. Again, I looked into his eyes. "I'll help you be what you want to be."

"You will, mama, you promise?" In his excitement, he squeezed my hand, really hard.

"I promise."

He sat back in his chair and closed his eyes, his face filled with relief. A sudden thought brought his head rearing up again. "You won't be angry because I lied to you about who I was?"

"No," I said softly.

"Where do we go from here, mama? Things aren't the same between us. They haven't been for the past twelve hours. I'm beginning to think you've changed. I've lost my mama and I'm not going to get her back again. Tell me I'm wrong. Tell me."

"You may have lost that old mama who was just about as crazy and confused as you are." I ran my fingers along his arm in a ripple of reassurance. "You may have gained a friend, and in the long run that's what you'll need more than anything else."

"You mean that? You're not going to kick me out?"

"There will be some changes in the living arrangements, but you'll be fine."

"Can I stay here with you?"

"Maybe you'd rather stay with your father."

"Rafael?"

"Yes, and you're going to see him today. You watch TV a lot, and I know that you know he fled Havana and is here in Miami."

His eyes lit up. "I love my father. I've missed him so."

"Dino...Desi. Let me call you Desi, that is, if you don't call me Lucy. Is your father going to make trouble for me? I mean, because of my involvement with you? I need to know. He's demanding a meeting with me."

"I doubt it. He's a warm and generous man. A good heart. No trouble."

"I don't understand something. If he didn't want trouble, or wasn't going to demand money, why didn't he contact you directly if he wanted to see his long-lost son?"

"He did, mama. Several times. I didn't return his calls when he first landed in Miami. The police put him through to this number. I knew he'd blow my cover as Dino. Just when I was getting into the part real well. I couldn't let him ruin it for me."

"I will meet with your father and so should you. He's a hero to the Cubans in Miami."

"You'll like him, mama. He looks just like me, except he's all grown up."

. . .

Installed in the relative safety of the Star Island villa, where high walls and verdant gardens sheltered memories of Mommie and Daddy Kelly, I felt lonely and cut off from the world as I awaited the arrival of Rafael Navarro. Dino/Desi preferred not to be here for the meeting.

"I'll be back later tonight. You meet with Rafael and see what he wants. He probably wants to take me with him, but I want to stay with you, mama. You may have to decide that for us. Talk with him first. Then I'll come in. After all, it's my life."

After Dino/Desi left, I pondered the bizarre circumstances of this meeting. I was to come face-to-face with the father, who was about my age, of my lover who was decidedly younger. It was not a role I would have written for Sherry Kelly.

It was getting late. Perhaps they were held up in traffic. Frustrated, not wanting to think about the meeting, I turned on the TV news. To my surprise, newsreel footage of Rafael Navarro flashed on. Dino/Desi was right. It was like seeing a vision of Dino/Desi himself twenty years from now. The same olive skin--or was it mahogany?--the same jet-black hair, although he didn't have quite as much of it, and the same brown eyes with long lashes. Those were state-of-the-art father-son beauties, looking more like classic movie stars than Cuban refugees.

"I was dead in my life there," Rafael told a newswoman in an obvious reference to Castro's Havana. He spoke perfect English.

As the story unfolded, it seemed that Rafael had become a pawn in the international cat-and-mouse game between Cuba and the United States. The Justice Department was cooperating with Castro in bringing international air piracy charges against Rafael.

"It was either flee or die," Rafael said to TV cameras. "Can I be blamed for saving my life?" The question was directed at the American people.

Cameras switched to the other archive footage showing the landing of a commercial jet at the Miami airport, with 58 passengers on board. The announcer explained that Rafael--aided by three friends on board--overpowered some crew members, then flew the plane to Miami. Once at Miami, most of the passengers asked for political asylum, others preferring to return to Havana.

Mesmerized, I stayed glued to the TV screen. Outside the Federal Justice Building in Miami, Cuban Americans protested in favor of Rafael. The camera focused on one bitter young Cuban male who held up a sign: AMERICA – WHAT KIND OF JUSTICE IS THIS?

At the sound of limousines pulling into the driveway, I flicked off the TV and went to my window where I gazed down. My dark-suited lawyers, led by my old flame, David Miller, were going to charge a hefty fee for this afternoon's session.

In contrast to the well-dressed lawyers, Rafael emerged from the rear seat of one of the limousines. He was wearing a pair of tight-fitting jeans and an old army shirt which was virtually unbuttoned. I suppose if a man possessed a chest like he did, it was no use keeping it a secret.

In about ten minutes, the maid knocked on my door and told me David wanted to confer with me privately.

. . .

The dress I'd chosen for the meeting seemed entirely appropriate; elegantly tailored, but straight-laced and business-like, a kind of "lesbian chic," which I imagined would be suitable for a youthful cosmetics mogul in any of the romance novels of Judith Krantz.

Even though we conferred constantly on the phone, it had been many months since I'd come face to face with David. Today, he was my attorney. Three men ago, he'd been my lover.

At the ripe age of fifty-five, David Miller remained the

quintessential star-fucker. The mother-daughter act of Mia and Sherry Kelly was just part of a parade of conquests said to have ranged from Lana Turner to Nancy Davis, from Ava Gardner to Marilyn Monroe, from Joan Crawford to Joan Collins, from Grace Kelly to Doris Duke. He didn't mind if some of those beauties were ten, twenty, and, in one case, thirty years older than himself. The only qualification was that they had to be a star. Not just a movie star; a star in any field. The story that he had once seduced Margaret Thatcher was never proven, and he personally denies persistent reports that he was the former paramour of Jackie Onassis. Zsa Zsa Gabor, perhaps, but not Jackie O.

When David wasn't fucking stars, he often represented them in court. Cleverly recognizing that Hollywood was crawling with too many attorneys and that Miami at least had the potential of becoming the second film capital of America, David had moved to Dade County where he'd joined a prestigious all-Hispanic law firm. "I was their token nigger," he'd confided to me. As a blond-haired WASP with connections that ranged from Henry Kissinger to William Buckley, from intimate associations with everybody from Gerald Ford to Ethel Kennedy, David was a formidable man to have on your side. At least Mommie thought so, as she'd retained David as our attorney for the past fifteen years, ever since Daddy died and left us to cope for ourselves against the horde of money-grubbers who wanted to share in our vast fortune. Those types emerged from under the rocks daily.

David regularly serviced Mommie, and back in the days when she was speaking to me, she often referred to his prowess as a lover. Mommie was quite frank on the subject. "David has a perpetual erection," she'd confided. "I think the technical word is priapic. But I prefer the French, toujours pret."

"You mean not exactly hard, but not soft either?" I asked, truly wanting to know.

"He seems to lose all feeling in his penis – and can go on using it for hours. It gives a woman such pleasure." Along with certain kinds of tax shelters, David invented multiple orgasms, making him a sought-after entity at many a dinner party. My nickname for him is 'Rubber Hosa.'"

Had Mommie not been so graphic, and had her errant daughter not been so curious, I might never have sampled David's technique. But like one of those demanding readers of the National Enquirer, I wanted to know.

The opportunity came when David flew to Paris to represent me in a legal dispute I was having with a handsome French count who did not want to leave my bed and board peacefully, and was demanding money, a great deal of money. David represented me brilliantly in the case, and got rid of the Frenchman tout de suite. We finally bought the bastard off for a mere fifty-thousand dollars. The count's name translated from French into English as "dead mountain." Need I say more?

Romantic dinners at Lasserre and Le Grand Vefour eventually led to long, lingering nights at the Hotel Bristol which eventually led to long, lingering continental breakfasts in bed at the same hotel.

I might have discreetly gotten away with my affair with David, and Mommie might never have found out about it, had not this dreadful, overpriced Hotel Bristol upset me so. What a pretentious, money-grubbing cockroach pit it was.

I was furious that I was having to pay extortionist prices at that crummy hotel when I should have been ensconced in my own 18th-century town house in the Seventh Arrondissement. Daddy Kelly, at least according to the way I read his will, had not only left the town house to me, but all of our other mansions as well.

Without even consulting me, Mommie had ordered a radical renovation of the Paris manse in a style I found hideous. When I arrived in Paris, I'd found electrical wires dangling, plaster ceilings collapsing around me, and hammering around the clock. Those are the events which forced me to check into a hotel, and which probably provoked at least some of my rage against the Bristol.

I was so furious that I'd demanded that David sue Mommie, hoping that a court of law (and a team of very expensive lawyers) would determine once and for all that I, not Mommie, owned the estates Daddy had left me.

Although David pleaded with me for hours not to pursue the case, I was determined. I issued David a firm and unyielding ultimatum. If he didn't file the case by tomorrow morning, not only were he and I through, but I'd have a new law firm representing me within 48 hours.

This ultimatum had thrown the Hispanic law firm in Miami into chaos. They had prided themselves on representing both Mommie and me. Now I was forcing them to take sides. After a careful review of all the documents pertaining to Daddy's death, the firm decided to go with me, not only because they felt I had the better case, but because I was younger and was likely to stick around for another thirty years to give them business, long after Mommie had gone to her heavenly rewards.

It was a painful choice for David, but in the end he sided with me. That meant he was persona non grata in Mommie's commodious bed. She'd issued orders that both of us were to be barred from her estate in Key West. I think what hurt Mommie more than the law suit was the eventual realization that I, a younger and prettier woman, had stolen David from her. I don't think Mommie really loved him, and would have, within a few months, probably have deserted him anyway. But once Mommie discovered that David and I were an item, he suddenly became the "love of her life" and I – "ungrateful and errant daughter" – the interloper. Mommie filed counter lawsuits against me, news of the affair got into the press, and the case was on. It will probably drag on for years. Lawyers love these kinds of cases.

My decision to abandon David and flee to Hollywood to accept a movie offer, and even my decision to bare all in Playboy, were ostensibly the reasons my "shocked" Mommie had disinherited me. But I knew the reason was really the lawsuits and the "theft" of David.

Just then I heard his gentle rap upon my door. I checked my make-up for one last reassuring look. I don't know why it is, but a woman wants to look her best when facing yesterday's flame, even if she was the one who walked out of the relationship.

The mirror gave me the assurance I needed.

. . .

David might be fifty-five years old, but as he stood before me he appeared twenty years younger, my own age. I suspected he'd had a facelift. He looked amazingly like Robert Redford in his better days, except that David was a far larger man than Redford--in all departments--and didn't have that actor's unfortunate tendency for premature aging.

He just stood looking at me. Then he moved toward me and took me in his arms. Before I could control him, old Rubber Hosa had me close to him, his long tongue exploring my tonsils.

Breaking away gently, not harshly, I quickly rechecked my appearance in the mirror to see if he had ruined my makeup.

"Hello. Glad to see me or is that a big gun in your pocket?"

"I think of you every night. I've never gotten over you. I don't think I'll ever get over you."

"I saw you photographed with Madonna," I said, a bit too petulantly.

"I saw you photographed with Madonna," he said, "lip-locked."

He had me on that one. Those attorneys always have a comeback for everything. I guess that's why we hire them. "I'm a little edgy today."

"Don't be. Rafael Navarro doesn't want money from you. There is no question of extortion. Through the police he tried to get in touch with his son but Dino wouldn't take the calls. Rafael only wants a reunion with his son, and he's not even demanding that if Desiderio refuses."

"That's the first good news I've had all day."

"I don't think he'll cause you any problems about Desiderio. If anything, he seemed a little proud that the fruit of his loins had bedded Hollywood's most glamorous star, not to mention one of the world's richest women."

I smiled. Suspecting that he had eaten away too much of my lipstick, I sat down in front of my vanity mirror and reapplied more warpaint.

"The father might be proud of the conquest--but not the rejected suitor," he said.

"I didn't go directly from you to Dino or Desi, or whatever his name is. There were two other men in between."

"I heard they were both gay, so I didn't get too jealous."

"Gay or not, those guys had their very appealing moments."

"I'm sure."

"How's the law suit coming?" This conversation with him was getting too personal.

"I think your father was deliberately obscure in his will, as if he wanted you and Mia to take on each other in court. Of the fourteen estates, only the Key West mansion clearly belongs to Mia. A judge will have to rule on the others."

"You're my attorney. What do you think?"

"I think your father meant for you to have the properties." He paused. "Ultimately. Mia, at least the way I read it, has the right of occupancy for all the estates, including the one we're in, during her lifetime. The two of you, of course, will have to arrange your schedules so you don't show up at the same house at the same time."

This was not what I wanted to hear. I wanted a clear title to the properties.

"Fighting Mia is not going to be easy. Like you, she has a formidable arsenal of weapons. By taking her to court, you have foolishly removed yourself as heir to one of the world's most fabled fortunes."

"Don't you think I know that?" Anger came into my voice. It wasn't anger directed at him, but at myself for being so foolish.

"Would you at least consider dropping the law suits?"

"Of course, I'd consider it. I've made a mess of everything. But isn't it too late? Hasn't she adopted Anishi Mishimi and made her if not the sole heir, at least a major heir?"

"She has indeed. But that can be undone. You need to go back to your mother. Beg to her on bent nylon if that's necessary. You'd better get back in her good graces or you'll kiss her fortune good-bye."

"That means I'll have to get rid of Anishi, sooner rather than later. You are having her investigated?"

"Give us a bit of time. We've got twelve people on three continents working on it right now. Whatever she did before she arrived as a servant in Mia's household, she didn't exactly advertise it in the papers. Even Nazi war criminals were less successful in covering their pasts than this Anishi Mishima."

"Hell, I bet you guys haven't even found out her age, much less her biography."

"She claims she's thirty-six, your age. But now we have documents that indicate she grew up in Tokyo during the war. The woman doesn't look it, but we suspect she's nearly sixty years old."

"My God, she may be closer in age to Mia than I ever thought. What's her secret? A Fountain of Youth? The one Mia is always searching for?"

"I don't know. We did learn that Anishi takes injections, and she's giving those injections to Mia too. We don't know what the serum is yet."

"Maybe you and I had better start shooting up."

"Maybe. If Anishi is nearly sixty, she's a timeless wonder. Our report to you will include a lot of photos snapped of the woman, usually when she wasn't aware she was being photographed. She's amazingly youthful for her age."

Somehow the subject of how young looking Anishi was upset me. "We've got to go to this meeting downstairs," I said, showing my impatience.

All business-like when called upon, he turned to go. At the door, he paused, looking back at me as if troubled by something.

"Has Mia every shown any lesbian tendencies?" he asked abruptly.

"What a question! That's like asking if General Eisenhower were a closet homosexual. Although I doubt it, it may one day be revealed that Senators Nunn and Thurmond, even Colin Powell, were all closet homosexuals, but Eisenhower, never. Maybe General MacArthur. Mia is a straight arrow. Look at the prizes she's bagged during her lifetime--all male."

"I don't know. We're getting reports that Mia and Anishi carry on in front of their staff like lovers."

"I find that astonishing. On the other hand, I don't know why anything would shock me any more." That brought to mind a little item I'd read in a gossip column. "David." I said his name more like it was an accusation. "You're not hustling your memoirs to Random House, are you? Memoirs in which Mia and I are featured?"

"Definitely not!"

"You wouldn't lie to me, would you?"

"Once or twice I've lied to you. After all, I'm your attorney.

I do have memoirs, but they're not being peddled to Random House or any other publishing house. You and Mia are heavily featured."

"What do you plan to do with them?"

"They're like an insurance policy for my old age."

"You don't see Jackie hustling her memoirs. Or even Sinatra. That man's memoirs could outsell yours. Even Mommie's bedded that one. I turned him down. As a star fucker, he's probably the only man in America who's got you beat. His repertoire takes in everyone from Patti Duke to Gloria Vanderbilt."

"He's got twenty-five years on me, and a cast of stars who were a lot more interesting in their day than the handful of hopefuls running around today. Maybe I'll overtake him one day."

"Not in this day of AIDS," I cautioned.

"I'd give them up, all of them, for you. If only you'll take me back."

"I'll think about it," I said with an enigmatic smile, ushering him to the door. I told David to bring the meeting to order in my library, and that I'd be right down.

For reasons I wasn't completely aware of, I shut the door behind him and went to gaze upon my figure in the full-length mirror. I didn't think that my present "lesbian chic" outfit would impress Rafael at all.

Instinctively, I felt what he wanted was Marilyn Monroe in high heels, a white dress, and a flaming red mouth resting under tantalizing blonde hair. Aware that the legal meter was ticking, I deliberately delayed the meeting for another thirty minutes as I changed my outfit and surveyed the result. It was as if the cameras were about to roll on The Seven-Year Itch. If Mr. Rafael Navarro could display his chest in that army shirt, I would show him a thing or two--definitely two. Mr. Flash-It wasn't the only one with a chest.

After my makeover, I breathed in deeply and looked at myself in the mirror for one final moment for reassurance. Then I made my way carefully down the steps in the too-high heels. Again, I sucked in the air at the entrance to the library door, enjoying the scent of my perfume. I opened the door and made an arresting entrance. I could feel all the paid-for-by-the-hour attorney eyes collectively staring at me. But mostly I felt the eyes of Rafael. He was practically undressing me.

"It's true, it's true," he announced in near perfect English to the suits. "America is a land of sweet dreams."

. . .

My appearance in front of a battery of attorneys evoked many similar gatherings that Mommie had taken me to ever since I was eight years old. "Some day my fortune will belong to you," Mommie had said after Daddy died. "You've got to learn how to take care of it." False promises. I'd been disinherited.

At the head of the table, I was seated two chairs from Rafael. Two Miami lawyers separated us, one wearing a cheap after-shave lotion. I'd have to contact the firm later with a new mandate: No attorney representing me was to attend a meeting wearing after shave lotion. With my sensitive nostrils, attuned to enjoying only the world's most expensive scents, the odor offended me.

Even though I'm sure Rafael was wearing nothing but his own natural body odors, and he appeared to be freshly showered, I could still smell him. It was the intoxicating smell of the male animal in heat. Deliberately, I refused to make eye contact with him. When Brown Eyes met Baby Blues, I knew it would be the eye contact of the decade, surely rivaling that day when Marc Anthony first gazed upon Cleopatra.

"So, Ms. Kelly, do you agree?"

I jerked to attention, the way I used to do in my private school with my own tutors. In his most formal voice, David was addressing me.

"Yes," I said, not wanting to reveal to him that my mind had drifted. Regaining my composure, I sucked in the air and breathed deeply. Unfortunately, I practically overdosed on that cheap after-shave lotion from the lawyer next to me, who had leaned toward me to make a whispered point. I quickly demanded that this attorney go and fetch me a pot of espresso, freshly made. Rebuffed, he got up and left.

In my most imperial manner, a direct imitation of my Mommie, I turned to gaze into the alluring eyes of Rafael. I could see his meltdown begin. "I think I could accommodate Mr. Navarro." I could feel my thighs begin to part involuntarily, and I feared my pronouncement would be misunderstood.

Rafael gazed lovingly into my eyes, making me wonder what sort of an accommodation he too had in mind.

"Good," David said. "Then you agree?"

"Desi – I know him as Dino – will return here later tonight." I turned to look at Rafael again. Although I'm not exactly sure, I think he had unbuttoned yet another button on his army shirt. For all I knew, the next thing he'd be doing was unbuckling his jeans and unzipping his fly. How brazen! But suddenly, images of my crossing my legs and flashing for all the word in Kinky came drifting through my head, and I decided I had been too harsh in my initial judgment of him.

"If I may ask one small favor," he said.

Here it comes, I thought.

He jumped up and in seconds occupied the seat of the after-shave attorney. My security guard moved toward him, but I motioned him away. For some reason, I didn't feel in harm's way.

"I want you to help me arrange a meeting with a Cuban refugee I knew in Havana," he said. "He's in a Dade County prison."

I cast David a puzzled look. "The only Cuban refugee I know is Dino."

"He has news of my wife," Rafael said. "Tricia. Desi's mother. She disappeared thirteen years ago after organizing a rally against Castro. I can find out nothing about what happened to her. I live every day not knowing if she's dead or alive."

A sense of desperation and sincerity in him appealed to me. "Did you love her very much?"

"I did back then," he said with what I thought was complete honesty. "We were very young. I'm not the same man I used to be. I know that if she's still alive, she'd be a completely different woman after what she's gone through all these years. I don't know if we'd love each other today. But I need to know if my wife's alive or dead."

"Exactly how can Ms. Kelly help you in that?" David asked.

Rafael got up from the chair and with a kind of controlled energy walked around the table in desperation. He looked over at me, with eyes pleading. "I'm no fool. I know you people have great power. You could probably arrange a meeting with President Clinton if you wanted one. Surely, Senor Miller, you can arrange a meeting with a mere Cuban prisoner. This man Martinez knows whether my Tricia is alive or dead."

"David?" I asked, making his name a question mark. "If this is his only request, it seems reasonable enough. Do it!"

"I'm sure we can set something up," David promised.

"This afternoon?" Rafael implored, eager almost like a child about to receive a treasured present.

"This afternoon," David said, signaling one of the junior attorneys.

Just as the after-shave guy returned with the espresso, the other junior attorney raced from the room. If I know David, the young man was already at work arranging the meeting.

Getting up, I surveyed the table of lawyers. "Mr. Navarro is free to stay here at the villa until his son returns." I looked first at Rafael, then at David. "That is, if you gentlemen think he's safe. That he won't attack me."

"You needn't fear," David said, even though I detected a slight apprehension in his voice.

"I do not have to attack women," Rafael said defensively, "They usually attack me."

At that remark, the room remained silent for a little too long, just enough to make everybody uncomfortable. When David stood up, the other attorneys rose too. The meeting was obviously over. I kissed David on the cheek after he promised to get back to me with the time of the meeting with this Martinez creature. "I'm here for you...always," David whispered in my ear.

"Send your bill," I said, and walked away. Turning my back to both Rafael and David, I wandered out to my poolhouse.

Ted was nowhere to be seen, but Maxie spotted me and rushed to make me a martini. I needed one.

"Holy Mary, Jesus, and Joseph," Maxie said. "Did you see him?"

"See who?" I asked vaguely.

"Dino's father. Or should I say the world's sexiest man? He's the perfect male animal. God's finest work. Forget that thong I designed for Dino...Desi. I have found myself a new model to wear it."

"How you carry on. Considering all the bodies I've seen in my life, I hardly pay attention to the arrival of the newest one."

"You mean, if you've seen one male body, you've seen them all? Sugar, you sweet lying thing you. You've been salivating ever since this Cuban stud arrived on your doorstep. This guy is one in a million. He's what happens when a faggot like me dies and goes to heaven."

"Oh, Maxie, please go away and give me some time alone. You carry on so over these hunks. After having sampled fifty thousand of them in one lifetime, I think you'd be rather blase about the whole thing."

"Mother Maxi? Never." After mixing my drink, he retreated to the main house.

Impulsively I called after him. "I saw him first, bitch!"

. . .

Lounging by the pool, I thumbed through my phone messages. From the frequency of calls ranging from my director and producer, Jerry Wheeler, to The Iguana, I knew there was serious trouble raging about my upcoming movie, Butterflies in Heat. It was typical: Just as shooting was about to begin, there were always those last-minute catastrophes.

Since Jerry had agreed not only to produce but to direct the movie, I decided to return his call first. He was already in Key West scouting locations.

When his voice came on the wire, it was a little too shrill and high-pitched, a sure sign of trouble. "The shit's hit the fan. Mel Benson's out as your co-star. He refused to sign our fat deal."

"He never wanted to play a male hustler anyway," I said. "Afraid it would ruin his image. It was only that fabulous amount of money we offered that caused him to give the role serious consideration."

"You and he, at least I thought so, would have heated up the screen."

"I don't think I'm Benson's type of woman. Too much for him to handle."

"It wasn't you that caused the catastrophe."

"Don't tell me it was The Iguana butting in and screwing things up, like he usually does."

"The Iguana was involved all right--God, I hate that sleaze-- but he wasn't the real culprit. It was the bikini scene at the beginning."

"I've read the script. Benson is supposed to climb out of the pool wearing revealing swimwear. I lovingly appraise every inch of his body as the camera moves in for a close-up of the crotch. How I love starting a film on a tasteful note."

"The close-up of the crotch in 'Longtime Companion' – that's where I stole the idea – was effective. I saw Benson in the revealing bikini. There it was for all the world to see: A thin stubble of okra."

"Poor Mel. You mean, the world would laugh him off the screen playing a well-endowed male hustler?"

"The Iguana proposed a solution. Get your friend Maxie to design a bikini for Benson that's padded. Maxie's been stuffing Hollywood crotches since the Thirties. When the idea was proposed to Benson, he hit the ceiling. No faggot was going to get his hands inside the Benson crotch – to pad or do anything else. Since the final contract hadn't yet been signed, Benson walked."

"You've got eight or nine other actors lined up, all panting for the role. It probably won't matter who you eventually hire since my name alone will carry the movie."

"What would you say to Brad Cruz?"

"I'd say he could put his shoes under my bed any day or night of the year. Now we're talking the second sexiest man in the world."

"Who's first?"

"You'll meet him, I assure you. At least with Cruz, you won't have to pad his crotch for the bikini scene. The Cruz missile should be ample enough. Unfortunately, it's not his kind of part."

"Since this is a short shoot, we just might get Cruz before he begins his next picture. That is, if you'll personally put up another three million for his salary. Hell, if we add that to the fifteen million we've already offered, plus points, he can't say no."

"Do it! I'll guarantee it. Don't even let The Iguana know about it. If you can get Cruz, get that boy at any price. I've always wanted to do a film with Cruz. Just keep The Iguana away from him. Those two don't get along."

The sun emerged from behind two palm trees, temporarily blinding me. When I looked up again, I saw a dreamlike Adonis standing before me wearing an extremely revealing thong.

"I have a better idea yet," I told Jerry, suddenly inspired. "The actor you get for the part doesn't have to fill the bikini. The close-up shot of the crotch can be someone we hire just for that scene. I'm looking at him right now."

"The world's sexiest man, right?"

"Standing before me."

"This I've got to see."

"You will. All in good time, cunty. All in good time. Mother Nature did not create all men equally."

"I've got to get off the phone and get hot on that Cruz offer. Even if we haven't signed an actor for the part, shooting has to begin on schedule. Naturally, you're practically in every scene. There are a lot of scenes we can shoot without the hustler."

"I'll be there, my dear, ready, willing, and able. I'm the ultimate professional."

"The best and most surprising news for last. Your Mommie Dearest has agreed to let her mansion be used for the background filming for Sacre-Coeur."

"You're out of your mind. Mommie would never let a film crew onto her property. She despises film crews, and most movie people too. She's only fucked five movie stars in her life. She reserves that legendary box for kings, presidents, senators, and Supreme Court justices, with perhaps a governor thrown in on a bad night."

"It wasn't your Mommie that actually agreed to it. Anishi Mishima signed the contract. She seems in control down there."

Even though it was hard to concentrate on this tantalizing business with Rafael standing in front of me virtually nude, a thrilling thought crossed my mind. With such a deal, I could gain entrance to Mommie's estate once again, from which I'd been barred. I felt that if allowed to speak to Mommie alone, I could convince her to take me back. After all, I was her only child. "The deal sounds great. Go for it."

"I'll see you soon," he promised, although it sounded more like a threat. "Keep those breast exercises going. Remember after the crotch scene, the next scene is when you remove your top – showing not altogether fallen breasts – and jackknife from the diveboard into the pool to impress the hustler that his latest client isn't as old as he might have feared."

"Can't wait!" I said sarcastically, slamming down the phone. Almost twelve inches from my eyesight, and standing over my prone position on the chaise longue, was The Thong, a basket of goodies that seemed to require my immediate attention.

. . .

"Do you mind if I join you?" Rafael asked. "Wait here until Desi returns?"

I stared up at him from my prone position. If anything, he had virtually thrust the contents of that thong in my face. "Please." I motioned to the chaise longue next to mine. As he settled in comfortably, I appraised his body. He was probably thirty-seven, although he looked twenty-six. He amply filled Maxie's specially designed thong. "I see you've met Maxie."

"Charming fellow," he said, settling into a more comfortable position.

"Did he have much trouble convincing you to wear his latest creation? He did a special bra for me. Seems he specializes in clothing designs for the body parts of both men and women."

"Maxie and I got along just fine--just fine. Mariposas hold no fear for me. I'm completely relaxed around them. They've pursued me all my life. Far from being insulted, I'm flattered. I know they go after only the best specimens. I don't mind them looking--that's harmless, but exhibiting is as far as I go."

"I like a man who's that self-confident. If only we had more men like you in the U.S. Congress. From what I've seen on TV and read, more than two-thirds of the men in Congress are afraid to take a shower in front of another man. Personally, I think Sam Nunn and Jesse Helms could shower anywhere without fear of molestation. From anyone, male or female."

"When I become president of Cuba, I'll allow gays in the military. I stand for personal freedom. That's why I hate Castro so much. What an ass!"

Did he really say he was going to become president of Cuba? At first, I didn't know but what he might be joking. As I looked into his eyes more intently, I was convinced that was his ambition. Those eyes revealed a lot. "Do you think you have a chance to be president?"

"I do. I'm very popular in Cuba, at least with some of the people. I'm even a hero to the Miami Cubans, although many real Cubans don't trust their Miami cousins. They fear that when Castro is overthrown, these Cubans will return to Havana to take over everything."

"That's a real possibility."

"I used to be one of Fidel's most ardent supporters. My wife was a freedom fighter on the opposite side of Castro. I know that's why she disappeared. Fidel ordered it. After that, he never trusted me, even though I continued to believe in Communism for many years. As a pilot, I was still allowed to fly, but all my routes were domestic. That is, until I hijacked that plane to Miami. My first international flight in thirteen years."

"You knew it was time to get out."

"I did and that's why I slipped aboard that plane. I learned that Fidel had issued orders to have me killed. Too many people were talking. Saying that I could run the country better than Fidel. Trust me, I'm really well known in Cuba. People know I'm for them and their best interests. We're suffering. Our country is going, how do you say it in English, down the tubes?"

"Going down the tubes," I repeated. "You speak English like a native."

"I'm not just a pilot. I also taught English, often to my fellow pilots. When I was really young, I flew many places for Castro. Places where the only language we could communicate in was English. Shakespeare is my favorite writer."

"I've never made a film based on one of his plays."

"I hear you're a marvelous actress. I'm really excited about seeing one of your films."

"I'll have Ted or Maxie screen a copy of Kinky for you. It displays some of my best assets."

He looked over at me with the sharp eye of an appraiser. I

suspected Kinky's reputation had preceded it, although I knew we weren't shipping the film to Cuba.

"Dino...Desi likes the film a lot," I said.

"From what I hear, he's fallen in love with its star."

"I can explain that, and you've been very kind not to rage in here like some maniac father stealing his son from the clutches of Michael Jackson."

"I understand. In fact, I was very flattered when I heard about you and Desi. A chip off the old block, as you say in English. I'm very, very proud of my son, and I want to be with him again. He's grown up without me."

"It was a foolish adventure on my part--one that I'm not particularly proud of. I was at loose ends at the time."

"We've all been there. You don't judge what I used to do, and I don't judge you." He held out his hand for mine, and I freely offered it. Observing that, he held it for an extra long time.

"In the days before Castro, it was an old tradition to take our sons to the bordellos when they turned fourteen. The fathers would wait downstairs, drinking rum or whatever with the girls while an older and more experienced puta upstairs introduced our young men to the ways of mature love."

"What a quaint tradition. But I hope not an apt comparison."

"If it had been the old days, I would have done the same for Desi. But you've done the job for me, and I'm grateful."

"Thank you," I said, slightly embarrassed. Me, of all people, embarrassed. "Dino...Desi and I have ended our brief and somewhat embarrassing interlude. He's free to go. With you, if you want him. Of course, I'll continue to help him. I'm speaking financially. Get him launched in life. Doing something. He wants to continue to model, but I don't think there's much future there for him."

"Desi's future is already set. In a year or two, maybe even months, I will find a position for him in my new government in Cuba. There will be much work for him there. We've got to rebuild our country."

"What a big job!"

At this point, Ted rushed onto the patio with a cellular phone. "It's David."

True to his efficient nature, David had quickly arranged the meeting with Geraldo Martinez. For some reason, Rafael insisted that I go with him, and for yet another reason, I found myself saying yes. I didn't know why, but all of a sudden, it had become vitally important for me to find out if Tricia Navarro were dead or alive.

CHAPTER THREE

Long before I became a movie star, I was a master of disguises. Many places I visited in my youth would have landed me on the front pages if I'd been photographed entering or leaving their premises. Early in life, around the age of ten, I decided I didn't want to be restricted by my fame. As time went by, I developed, with the help of friends such as Ted and Maxie, many closets of clothes which I continually update, mixing and matching from my vast collections of garments, to provide the essentials of my many disguises. I have at least five major disguises, the most successful of which is that of a sexy Italian-inspired Gina Lollabrigida.

Rafael was amazed at my transformation, although he thought I looked more like Sophia Loren than Ms. Lollabrigida.

En route to the meeting with Martinez, in the back of my limousine, I felt cozy and snug in the presence of Rafael. I knew the question of Dino/Desi loomed for me, but right now, I wasn't thinking about him. I'd told my staff to have him wait at the house until our return.

With all my personal problems whirling around me, I somehow couldn't believe that I was off to see a Cuban refugee. Surely I had about a million other problems that also demanded my time. But despite all that, I wanted to be with Rafael now more than I wanted anything else in the world, except being restored to my Mommie's will and getting rid of that adopted daughter.

Rafael sensed my anxiety about this meeting. He seemed like the kind of man who was immediately intuitive of a woman's needs. He didn't say anything, although he occasionally looked into my eyes. A lot of men had looked into my eyes before, but never like this. Forgive this awful comparison, but he used his eyes like a vacuum cleaner, pulling the object, or person, he viewed inside his soul. If only the camera could pick up on that, what a film star he would make. Forget Mel Gibson, Tom Cruise, Kevin Costner, and such oldies but goodies as Clint Eastwood and Harrison Ford. Rafael Navarro had all of them beat.

A tightening of the grip on my hand brought me out of my detached musings into the main business of the day, the meeting with Geraldo Martinez. Suddenly, I didn't want to hear what Martinez had to say. If he revealed that Tricia were dead, that meant the loss of a wife for Rafael and a mother for Dino/Desi. Even after the passage of so much time, both men would suffer. Somehow, I cared about these men and I would feel the deepest sympathy for them. On the other hand, if I learned that Tricia were still alive, my role in these men's lives would be severely diminished, and I didn't want that either.

. . .

Inside the prison, the formalities went quickly enough. I was not surprised that the security guard mistook me for a brunette puta girlfriend of Rafael. After an interview and as the guard was showing us to the door, his hand brushed across one of my most famous assets, my much-photographed rear end. I was not offended. To be mistaken for a cheap slut amused me. What an actress I am.

After we were ushered into a waiting room, Rafael was summoned about fifteen minutes later for the interview. I asked him if he wanted me to join him – after all, I was not a bad interrogator – but he didn't think so.

In this bleak, forlorn waiting room, I waited and waited for what seemed like hours. Just as I thought he had forgotten me, or had been detained himself, he reappeared in a sweaty, irritable rage.

"Nothing," he said. "He will tell me nothing."

"Are you sure he knows anything?"

"He knows plenty. He was one of the chief henchmen for Castro, one of his leading assassins."

"If he were so important to Castro, why did he flee to the United States?"

"Good question, and I don't know. Maybe they clashed over something. Maybe Castro wanted to slip him into the States to commit a major act of sabotage. Kill a president, blow up an atomic generator, something like that. But the dumb ass brought his drug habit with him. It eventually landed him in jail."

"Does he speak English?"

"I taught him. Castro insisted that his top henchmen speak English. That language was needed when they traveled outside of Cuba on propaganda missions. Often we had to talk to some of the Russians or East Germans in English."

He took hold of my hand again, and with a certain desperation, said, "I'm going in for one last chance, but if he doesn't confess, I might kill him right here and now. He's got to tell me about Tricia."

"Let me," I quickly interjected. "Let me speak with Martinez alone. I think I can find out what happened."

"You? How could you possibly...?"

I smiled kindly but enigmatically. "You wait here."

Minutes later, as I came face to face with Martinez, I knew I was staring at a hardened killer. Rafael might look like a movie star, but Martinez looked as if he'd lived an entire lifetime in the lowest bowels of a prison ship. With skin the color of soured olives, and wearing a sweat-stained, sleeveless shirt, he was lean, mean, and cruel, with something of the aura of a frequently beaten animal. At first, he appraised me with all the hatred he probably reserved for a victim whose throat he was about to cut.

I smiled, and tried to be as tantalizing as possible. Minutes into the interview, I realized that my puta role was paying off. I was Martinez' dream girl.

Small talk would be a waste on this killer. It was time to get to the point. "I have power and influence beyond your wildest imagination," I said. "I know you're a man who knows how to deal. If you give Rafael the information he wants, I'll see that you're vastly rewarded."

"I don't need your help, you crummy puta."

That came as a complete surprise to me. I thought he'd be desperate for help from any source. "I don't think you understand me. Money. Lots of it."

He smiled grimly. "Information isn't cheap."

I scooted my chair back. In the distance, a security guard observed us, somewhat nonchalantly. He looked hardly awake, as if he'd had a bad night.

In a scene from Kinky right that minute that was being shown on screens around the world, I crossed my legs.

Cleverly, I'd forgotten to wear panties. Following the same voluptuous, languorous rhythms I had already made famous around the world, I flashed in front of Martinez, winning his complete and immediate attention. In his entire rotten life, he'd never seen state-of-the-art female plumbing like what he was staring at now.

"I want that information, and I'm willing to pay for it. How does one-hundred thousand dollars sound?"

Martinez, it was clear to me, thought he had died and gone to heaven. Not only was he being offered one-hundred thousand dollars, but he was getting the view of a lifetime. "I'm sure Castro didn't pay you that kind of money," I said. For me, this meeting with Martinez would be an easy triumph. When you have money, I long ago learned, you don't even have to be beautiful or clever. You can get almost anything you want any time of the day or night, any year or any decade.

The inevitable questions ensued from a bulging eyed Martinez. Never once during the financial negotiations that followed did he take his eyes off the honeypot. Naturally, he was chiefly concerned with my honesty, my integrity, and whether I actually had the money at all. How did he know he'd ever really get the money after he turned over his information?

Slowly, very slowly, I removed my wig, letting my blonde hair fall loosely about my shoulders. The guard noticed the transformation, but did not leave his post. "I'm not a cheap puta. I'm Sherry Kelly. Yes, the one with the gold bars. When I talk money, I mean it. I've got millions that I haven't even counted yet, and real estate I've never seen."

Martinez was startled at my revelation. A strange look crossed his face.

It took another fifteen minutes before he and I struck a deal. For the bribe, I'd get a full report on everything that happened to Tricia. David and his Hispanic team would conduct the interview, and would have the money, all in small bills, waiting for Martinez in his office after he was released from prison in a few days. The refugee would only get the money if he gave David and his interrogators the full, unedited story.

Martinez, still staring straight at the honeypot, told me, "You're one hot pussy, and you're making an offer no man can refuse. I'll take your deal but I should have held out for one more demand:

"A taste, just a little lick, of the creampuff you've been showing me."

"That's not part of the deal."

"You mean that bastard traitor Rafael has got it all for himself?"

"Any time he wants it."

"I see he's had no trouble at all getting over the loss of his bitch wife. She was a liar and a spy, and deserved a worse death than even she got."

"Loss? Was?" I uncrossed my legs and moved menacingly toward Martinez, scooting my chair up as close as I could. I made eye contact with him and I stared him down. "Loss? At least you've answered one big question. She's dead. You killed her. I know you did."

"A deal's a deal, cunt."

"A deal's a deal. You'll give us a full report. My men will have to interview you here. Even before your release. Don't give them your usual lies. Don't spare any details. It'll be the easiest money you ever earned, you slimy little bastard."

I got up and walked out of the room. Some time later in a setting less bleak than this one, I would tell Rafael that Tricia was dead.

Passing by the security guard, who seemed impressed with me, I asked, "How long has Martinez been in here?"

"Only since last night. Drug charge. A user--not a dealer. He'll be out in a few days. Maybe even hours. If we kept drug users in prison, we'd arrest half of Miami."

I thanked him and went on my way. Maybe I was paranoid, but I had a lingering suspicion that Martinez might have been the man stalking me in my garden, the one who had so successfully eluded my security guards. I'd have to find out if he smoked Cuban cigars.

. . .

Back once again in the relative safety and security of my limousine, I reached for Rafael's hand. Gently, I encased it in mine, then held it up to press my lips against it. With his other hand, he caressed my cheek. "This is your way of telling me that Tricia's dead, isn't it?"

"She's gone, but in your heart you've known that for a long time."

He settled back on the seat and closed his eyes, like a man who has completed a long and dangerous journey. "I've known for a very long time."

"Martinez confirmed she was killed, almost certainly on Castro's orders. I'll know more details – probably the full story, and whether it was actually Martinez who did the deed, in about a week."

"Bastards, both of them." He sat up in the seat, clenching his fists. "They'll get their reward, those two. I once saw a newsreel of Mussolini hanging upside down in a square in Milan, being beaten by a mob. That fate would be too good for Castro."

"Do you think Desi knows his mother is gone?"

"I'm sure he does, but I'll tell him anyway. There's always that doubt until you know for sure. This is for sure, isn't it?"

"I can't be absolutely certain, but it appears very likely. I got as full a confession from him as I could."

"Do you mind if I ask how you got this information?"

"It's not important," I said enigmatically.

Like the gentleman he was, he did not press me further on the matter. He leaned back against the plush upholstery of the limousine. One lone tear ran down his cheek. "Until I knew my wife was dead, I felt I couldn't invest myself into a new life. Oh, sure, I've been with several women since she disappeared. I'm no saint. But I selected women where there was never any chance of a long-term commitment. At any moment, even when making love to another woman, I expected Tricia to rush in the door to reclaim me."

"I think Tricia was a very lucky woman."

"That's very flattering, and thank you. Now I wish we'd spent more time making love and less time arguing about politics. She was a dedicated advocate of capitalism, and I was the firebrand communist. I believed Castro was correcting so many of the ills of the Batista government that I was willing to overlook a lot of things. Like throwing his political enemies into prison, and torturing and killing whomever stood in his way. I was so young, so dedicated to his ideology and to the idea of a proud and independent Cuba. What a fool I was! Tricia was right all along. I should have listened harder and heard what she was telling me. She gave up the greatest gift of all--an unfinished life-- for what she believed in."

"She sounds like a remarkable woman." The more we talked of her, the more I felt jealous of this idealistic, dedicated woman. I found myself making unfavorable comparisons between ourselves. What good had I ever done for anybody, except contribute to charities without any real knowledge that the money I was giving ever reached the people they promised to help? I looked at him, and I was surprised at how much I cared for this man, who was, after all, a virtual stranger to me, from a wildly different culture, and who I had met under stressful circumstances only hours before. Yet I felt a closeness to him far greater than that which I felt for people I'd known all my life. There was never this kind of intimacy with David. Even in the height of our passion, I never fully trusted David. I was never certain if he were making love to me, to my money, or to (god forbid), a younger and more appealing version of my Mommie. As the limousine neared Star Island, I wondered what role to play in the lives of Rafael and Dino/Desi. How did I fit in? Was I to go from being Dino/Desi's lover to becoming his mother? How confusing. If it were confusing to me, I could just imagine what it would do to the poor kid.

Now that I had served my purpose – coercing Martinez into confessing to Tricia's death and reuniting Rafael with his son – would both men just walk out the door?

Less than a half-mile away from the villa, a sense of impending loss overcame me. I reached to touch Rafael's arm, a little too possessively, I feared. "What are you going to do?" I asked. "I just realized I know nothing of your living arrangements in Miami. I know you're a local hero and all that. But I don't know if you have any money or what."

"The answer is simple. I'm broke, I'm homeless, and after the Miami Cubans came out to greet me and cheer me on my way, they went home. No offers of help, nothing. After the hero's welcome ended, a fellow I knew long ago in Cuba said he knew of an opening as a dishwasher at a cafe on South Beach. Another guy said he might get me a job working at

Madonna's house – as a gardener. He said he thought I was her type."

"It's amazing, isn't it? After the parade is over, you're left alone holding a deflated balloon." I moved closer to him, as if I expected to draw warmth and comfort. "You don't have to be out there alone. You could join my outfit. As my private bodyguard."

Even as I said that, I felt embarrassed. Would it be viewed as too obvious a come-on? I was also painfully aware that it sounded like a bad rewrite of a recent Kevin Costner/Whitney Houston movie.

"Protecting you?" he said, looking deeply into my eyes. "I think other than becoming president of Cuba, there is nothing I would like to do better in this world. I might ask why you think you need protection? Because of all your money? Kidnappers?"

"That is always the case. Only the other night, someone was in my garden stalking me."

"If you're with me, no harm will come to you."

"Then you'll protect me?" I feared that I sounded like a too-eager schoolgirl about to get laid by the high school football captain.

"I'll do it. I'll protect you day and night. Never let you out of my sight. That was my intention all along, you know."

"I don't understand."

"From the moment I first laid eyes on you in front of those lawyers, I never intended to let you get away from me ever again."

"That sounds very romantic. I like that."

"I want you. I'm ready to wait a respectable time before getting what I want. But I don't want to wait too long. On the other hand, you're a very sophisticated woman, and I'm sure you've said adios to bourgeois values that call for a drawn-out period of courtship. This isn't Cuba in 1902."

"I've never been strong on bourgeois values."

"I knew you weren't," he said, the sound from him coming out almost like a sigh.

The limousine pulled into the driveway of the Star Island villa. A transformed young man with a short haircut and a dark blue suit and conservative tie was waiting under the portico. It was Dino/Desi, looking remarkably five years older than he usually did. Almost like a yuppie from Wall Street with a briefcase. I glanced apprehensively at Rafael, who hadn't seen his son since he was a little boy. If anything, Rafael in his blue jeans and casual open-necked shirt, looked like the son, not the father.

I sensed the tension rising in him.

"Are you okay?" I asked.

"A little nervous. A thought has just come to me. Before I can get on with my life, I've got to not only get to know my son again, but get rid of him as my romantic competition. What a job!"

. . .

The long-lost father and son came together in a passionate embrace that seemed to last forever. They were hugging and kissing more like long-departed lovers than as co-participants in a father-and-son reunion. I turned away in embarrassment. In my WASP world, men carried on like this only if they had the hots for each other. After a respectable time had gone by, I turned to look at Dino/Desi and Rafael. Each man was crying, but these were tears of joy. In some way, both men reminded me of children. Daddy Kelly always claimed men should not cry, regardless of the circumstances. Seeing me standing under the portico like a wallflower at a high school dance, both Dino/Desi and Rafael reached out their arms to me and brought me into their circle. We seemed to dance around the terrace like a cuddly trio, a scene evocative of one in the film, Cabaret, starring Liza Minnelli.

When the reunion dance came to an end, I invited both men inside my home, although the courts had not ruled yet on just whose home this was. In my gigantic parlor, that was more like a greenhouse than a living room, the men ordered Cuba libres from a member of my staff. Since I found this a putrid drink, I asked for a dry martini instead.

The hugging and kissing, the passionate embraces quickly became a faded memory, as a sudden sense of formality descended over the men. It was as if each man had realized the awkwardness of the occasion. Regardless of the embarrassment felt by either of them, nothing equaled my own apprehension. Throughout my life, I have been used to entertaining more than one suitor at a time. During one particularly hectic chapter in my romantic life, I had five lovers under my roof at the same time. The occasion was a party.

This time it was different. The father-son aspect had to be considered, naturally. I was not the first woman who'd ever faced this dilemma. It was as if Dino/Desi was but a rehearsal for the real thing, although he must never find that out.

Over drinks the men relaxed a bit. On the other hand, I continued to feel a high degree of tension. I knew how to relate to each man individually, but not when they were together. It was then I realized the depth of the silent communication that existed between a father and son. Maybe we didn't have to spell everything out in great detail, like the fine print in one of those contracts that David was always insisting that I sign. Rafael looked at me with great intensity and a kind of possessiveness. It was a look of love and prideful ownership, and that gaze was not lost on me and certainly not lost on Dino/Desi.

At one point, Dino/Desi rose from his chair and came to join me on the sofa. The sofa was one of the largest on Star Island but he managed to squeeze himself onto the same cushion where I sat. This did not please Rafael who turned to look away, glancing idly into my garden. Or was it Mia's garden? Dino/Desi took my hand and held onto it a little too hard. Long an expert in retrieving my hand, I slipped through his grip and walked to the mantle of my fireplace. It was a graceful action, one sent as a signal to Dino/Desi, who quickly received it. I suspected that deep in his heart he was relieved that he didn't have to pretend to be my lover any more. It was a relationship that had embarrassed both of us and received unwanted media attention.

To Dino/Desi, I was still a prize, and in his hustler-hungry world, world-class prizes like Sherry Kelly were not released gracefully and without careful consideration.

Dino/Desi stood up awkwardly as if ready to leave the room. Suddenly realizing he had no place to go, he idly put his hands in his suit pockets. "My greatest dream, papa, was to have the pleasure of introducing you to my Sherry. Now I see you two already know each other. It seemed to happen rather quickly. I wasn't out of the house that long."

"Son, you'll know many women in your day." Then, smiling kindly, he said, playfully, "Of course, you're not as good looking as I was at your age, but you'll do just fine. Standards today aren't as high as they used to be."

Dino/Desi became immediately defensive. "I'm every bit the man you were, maybe more. I've got the credentials to prove it. Sherry Kelly is only one of my trophies."

This last statement did not upset me as much as it might have some women. I have long ago grown accustomed to suitors viewing me as a trophy. One former lover once told his friends that he had "bagged" Sherry Kelly, as if I were some big game he'd shot in the green hills of Africa like a macho bully pig such as Ernest Hemingway would have done.

I looked first at Dino/Desi, then at Rafael. Both men seemed more like fighting roosters. Gone were the hugs and passionate kisses under the portico. If anything, this father and son seemed ready to do battle. Over me, I feared.

I stood between them. "Sherry Kelly is no trophy to hang on any wall. I belong to no one, never have. I am my own woman."

"I didn't mean it that way, mama."

"I'm not anybody's mama, and have no intention of becoming one."

"I'm sorry," Dino/Desi said, looking as if he had been scolded.

During this interchange between Dino/Desi and me, Rafael had remained silently on the sidelines. Now I witnessed a new look coming across his face. No longer the brave Cuban pilot hero, he looked, if anything, petulant. "Did you tell Sherry how you escaped from Cuba? The year, and I remember it well, was 1988. You were only twelve! You left without saying good-bye."

"I had to get out," Dino/Desi said. "You were trying to make a communist out of me and all the time I knew I was a capitalist. Just like my mama."

"It was very painful when I learned that my twelve-year-old son, the only thing real I had left in my life, had run off to Grenada with a Russian general."

The room grew suddenly silent. Dino/Desi glanced apprehensively at me, as if Rafael had diminished his manhood in my eyes.

Like the consummate actress I was, I refused to show my reaction to such enticing news. I also wanted to make it perfectly clear that I was not judgmental about such things. "I'm sure the Russian military brass has its share of child molesters, just like the U.S. military."

"I had to do it," Dino/Desi said. "It was my only way out and I took it."

"What happened then?" Rafael asked.

"A long and not very interesting story. I dumped the general. A dedicated capitalist like me can't stand Russia anyway. When the U.S. invaded the island, I quickly switched bed partners. Like Sherry said, the U.S. military brass has many child molesters, maybe not as many as the Catholic church, but a lot."

"How did you get off the island?" Rafael said. "Years have gone by and I know nothing of your life."

"I'm too young to publish memoirs. I eventually made it to New York. Not much time went by before I was a successful model. That's how I first came to the attention of Sherry here. When you look as gorgeous as I do, you don't have to knock on doors to gain admittance. All you have to do is sit by the phone. Pick it up, of course, and listen to the offers."

Rafael turned his back to us and faced the garden. "What you're saying is that my son is a puta? A boy puta?"

"Call it what you like but I'm doing just fine." He turned and left the room going toward the library.

Rafael moved to follow him.

I gently touched his arm. "Be kind to him. He was just a baby, and he had to make it in the world the best way he could. It was probably hell for him."

"The whole thing makes my stomach turn. My own son."

"It's over now. All of us have done many things in life we are not proud of. God knows, I have. So have you. I know it."

He looked tenderly into my eyes. "So have I," he said softly. "So have I."

I kissed him gently on the lips. "Please go into the library. Be with him. You must tell him about Tricia. You should be very kind to him after you tell him."

"Yes." He brushed my cheek lightly with his lips. "We must talk to each other. We must become father and son again."

I stood alone in the living room. It was as if I had suspended my own life temporarily to get involved in this drama between father and son.

. . .

While Rafael and Dino/Desi talked in my library, I retreated upstairs to my study. Ted was already here in full mud pack. He wanted to look his youthful best for the bars of Key West, although I feared that even bulldozers shoving loads of dirt couldn't fill the crevices in his poor, tired face that had already seen more than its share of bars, not to mention bathhouses and latrines.

It's Jerry," he whispered to me in a tone of conspiracy, holding the phone at arm's length for me.

"Good news!" Jerry shouted into the phone. "That extra three million worked. Cruz went for the deal. Eighteen-million dollars up front...and points."

"And points," I said, uttering a little sigh, even though I considered the signing of Cruz very good news. "Eighteen-million dollars. I wonder if any man is worth it."

"The most I ever paid anyone was five hundred, but he was very special."

"Five hundred – that's more like it."

"Of course, Cruz has lots of other commitments. We'll have to adjust the schedule. All scenes with Cruz will have to be shot first."

"I can handle that."

"The crucial scene, the last scene in the movie, where you shoot Cruz as you're slowly descending that giant stairway in a negligee, will have to be shot first. I know that sounds crazy, shooting the final scene on the first day, but because of the logistics and everyone's schedules, that's how it's gotta be."

"Better that I should spend the first day shooting at him instead of making love to him. At least I'll get to know him better before we film our love scenes later. I'm looking forward to those."

"I'll volunteer to stand in for you during rehearsals."

"No thanks, I'll do my own rehearsals with Cruz."

"Sherry, when his lips meet yours, the most experienced smackers that poor boy has ever known, you'll heat him up. Singe the wings off any butterfly."

"Thanks for the vote of confidence."

After his call, the ever-efficient Ted reminded me that I had to prepare myself for dinner. He had already run my bubble bath. I was expected to host a father-son reunion dinner in an hour or two, and I wanted to look my best.

After immersing myself in my bath, I emerged feeling like the Queen of the Nile. I wrapped a turban around my head and slipped into a white terrycloth robe.

"I want tonight to be very special," I said to Ted. "We'll display the Mona Lisa at the far end of the dining room. Please adjust the spotlights accordingly."

"Hot damn!" he said. "I've never actually seen the Mona Lisa."

Mia and I are art collectors, world class. Much of our trove consists, rather inconveniently, of stolen art. Mommie's idea, not mine. Our most valued possession is the Mona Lisa. The one in the Louvre is a 16th-century copy. We own the original La Giaconda. At this point, I'm not sure if I own it or if Mia owns it, but one of us certainly possesses this fabled treasure. I only bring it out of storage on rare occasions. It's not something you leave hanging unguarded on a wall while you jet off to the Riviera. Over the years there has been occasional press speculation that Mia owns the world's most famous portrait. Art historians usually dismiss such speculation, and so-called "experts" almost always deny that a second Mona Lisa even exists. For once, the sleazy tabloids are right. Not only does such a work of art exist, it is the da Vinci original. Pity that it can't be displayed more often, but for obvious reasons, that's not possible."

Trailing a member of the staff along with Ted, I followed both men down a long, windowless corridor to a walk-in vault that is so secure that silly Colin Powell and all his armies couldn't blast it open. Only Daddy Kelly, Mia, and I had ever entered it.

I, who knew the combination from memory, opened the safe

and walked inside, leaving Ted and the Cuban butler standing outside. In moments, I was out of the safe and screaming.

The Mona Lisa, which had always hung on the main wall of the vault against a black-velvet backdrop, had been removed.

I turned to Ted. Almost as if I couldn't believe my words, I found myself saying, "The Mona Lisa is gone. Get David on the phone. My entire household staff is about to be placed under arrest." I turned to look at the Cuban, a young and handsome man in his twenties. "Ted," I shouted, "make a citizen's arrest of this one right now."

"Senora, I can explain. No one stole your treasure. Your mama came for a visit last week, but left a few days before you got here. She knows the combination to the safe. No one saw her enter it, but she must have taken the painting."

"That bitch!" I shouted. It occurred to me that the Cuban was right. When the trouble between Mia and me began, I should have flown here immediately and removed all valuables from the safe. Since we both shared the house, though at different times, and the combination to the safe, why didn't I realize she'd eventually come here and empty it?

I know why I didn't think of it. I didn't think of it because in my heart, I still trusted my Mommie, and had failed to realize just how sneaky she had become. There was no honor left in her. God knows where the Mona Lisa was hanging. Getting back the painting had suddenly become my new primary concern.

"I don't care what I'll have to do to achieve this, but La Giaconda is coming home to mama," I said to Ted. "A commando raid on the Key West mansion is just one of the possibilities I'm considering. No one is going to deny me the right to my inheritance. No one."

When the men had left the corridor, dispatched onto their various tasks, I returned to the safe where I searched desperately for a little black box. It contained a possession more valuable to me than the lost painting. It held my childhood diary. I had foolishly left it on Star Island in the safe, hoping to return it to California when I had the first chance.

The black box was missing, and I knew Mia had taken it. For years when I was growing up, I kept the black box beside my bed, carefully locking it up after I recorded the events and feelings of each day. There were literally thousands of chances when Mia could have read the contents of the box if she'd wanted to. But the Mommie I'd known always respected other people's privacy, perhaps because her own privacy had always been invaded by others ever since she'd been a small child. She'd never raided my private closets or secret drawers, and her tendency to respect such secrets had lulled me into a false sense of security about the supposed safety of the now-missing painting.

It never occurred to me that she'd take this most valued possession of mine. She must have changed, and she was no longer the Mommie I had known, respected, and loved.

After satisfying myself that the black box was gone, I closed the safe and went upstairs to dress for dinner. While still in my robe, I stood on the balcony. The night air was warm but it made me shudder anyway. If she'd read my diary, she'd know my darkest secret, a secret so horrible that no living person knew it except me. Even I didn't want to admit to this horrible truth.

. . .

Mourning the loss of my treasured diary and painting, I bravely presided over a long dinner table attended by Rafael and Dino/Desi. The tension between the two men had eased. I didn't know what Rafael and Dino/Desi said to each other during their long talk in the library. Before I came down to dinner, Maxie reported to me that he'd heard shouting in Spanish coming from the library. Whatever their disagreements, whatever their problems, they seemed to have resolved most of them, at least temporarily.

As if to dramatize the shifting alliances, each man greeted me differently, and it was in the subtleties of their approaches that I realized how my feelings toward each one had changed. Dino/Desi approached me more like a nephew paying homage to a wealthy aunt. He gave me a light peck on the cheek and complimented my outfit, a gold strapless evening dress cut low. It was designed to show off my shoulders and breasts. Rafael, still in his blue jeans and open shirt, stood before me, almost like a Cuban field worker paying homage to a great queen. Yet he didn't seem intimidated by my regal presence. If anything, he appeared perfectly natural and completely sure of himself. His eyes began at my feet and traveled upward, lingering a long time at my cleavage before continuing his journey upward until he met my eyes. He gazed at me with an intensity that turned to hunger. With his eyes he was telling me he had needs and desires that only I could satisfy. In a sudden move before taking his place at the opposite end of the table, he gave me a quick kiss on the mouth. Did I detect a quick flicker of the tongue? Instinctively my tongue darted out to savor the lingering taste of him. All of this action wasn't wasted on Dino/Desi, who took his place at a chair placed between us at the long end of the table.

In honor of my Cuban guests, the chef had prepared black bean soup followed by paella. I'm not a great lover of Latino foods, but I ate heartily, enjoying the chunks of lobster and the shrimp, although I would have preferred a plain boiled lobster with drawn butter. Since Dino/Desi and Rafael seemed to have nothing to report on their reunion in the library, I spent most of the dinner discussing my recent troubles. I figured that it was important to Dino/Desi's growth and education that he learn about some real problems in the world and not concentrate entirely upon his own stunning image. I explained about my Mommie and her strange new companion who'd appeared menacingly like some rising sun out of the East. They also learned I'd been disinherited.

Then I told them the good news. Brad Cruz had signed to play opposite me. Dino/Desi had a puzzling reaction. He seemed very jealous that Cruz had been cast in the film. In his heart, I think Dino/Desi had hoped that I would ask him to star opposite me. He hadn't been threatened when Mel Benson appeared ready to make the film, because he considered Benson "an old man." He more readily identified with Cruz and seemed to resent his success and achievements.

"Desi," I said, as if reading his thoughts. "You're too innocent-looking, too young to play a hustler. With that angelic face of yours, only choir boy parts are suitable for you."

Dino/Desi looked at me strangely. Suddenly, he slammed down his fork, as anger flashed through his eyes. "How do I fit into all this cozy new arrangement? What part am I supposed to play?"

"You're our son," Rafael said quietly. "Sherry is the mother; I'm the father; and you're the son. We're a new kind of American family, just the three of us."

No one said anything, and my own reactions were too confused to sort out. These changing roles were coming upon all of us without much preparation. Rafael was acting as if he and I had an iron-clad love commitment to each other, and I'm not sure we had gone that far in our relationship yet.

"I mourn the death of Tricia," Rafael said, "But since I've known in my heart that she's been dead for years, I am not mourning her tonight. If anything, I feel at peace tonight. I'm ready to get on with my life. Ready, willing, and able."

Dino/Desi jumped up from the table. "This is all well and good for you to say. But you're going just a little too fast for me. All of a sudden I've lost my girl friend. I have a papa I haven't seen in years. Sherry suddenly emerges as my mother on the same day I learned for sure I've lost my real mother. You both will forgive me if I need some time alone to sort out these matters. I'm going to head for the clubs of South Beach. I need loud music and even louder companions. I need some distraction." Tossing his napkin on the table, he turned and left.

I sat here stunned, not knowing what was going to happen next. For a brief moment, I wanted to call out to Dino/Desi and ask him to come back, but decided against it.

"The boy's right," I said to Rafael. "Maybe we'd better slow things down a bit. I'm getting a little confused myself."

He appeared little concerned with all my thoughts and feelings, and not at all perturbed by Dino/Desi's outburst and desertion from our table. Closing his eyes, he seemed lost in some dreamy trance.

"Is there a graceful way to handle this?"

"Perhaps. I'm a daydreamer and an optimist. Tonight for the first time in my life, I know I am going to translate my daydreams into reality."

"I don't understand."

"You will. I'm thinking that when we get married, when I become president of Cuba, you're going to make the most stunning first lady in Latin America. Vamanos, Evita!"

. . .

After Dino/Desi had long gone and after dinner ended, Rafael and I retreated to my living room. I expected only awkwardness and sexual tension between us, but there was none of that. After his flirtatious way with me, I anticipated that he'd attack me when we sat together on the sofa. But commando tactics like that weren't part of his agenda. He actually wanted to talk, and so did I.

After several cups of strong, aromatic black Cuban coffee, I began to get to know him. Before our evening ended, I felt I knew him better than I did many of the so-called friends I'd seen for years. He was open and honest about his life, or so it appeared, telling me revealing details that a less honest man would have skipped over or even lied about. Nearly every person I meet in the world tries to impress me. He didn't at all. I felt I was getting a "warts and all" portrait.

The irony of sitting in a favorite living room of Daddy Kelly did not escape me. I recalled many a night when he endlessly lectured Mia and me about the evils of Communism, always ending with the prediction that the system would take over the world, that Castro's Cuba was only the beginning of the gradual infiltration and corruption of the Western Hemisphere. Here I was sitting and sipping with a former dedicated Communist who had at one time passionately believed in Castro's ideology, and had often enthusiastically followed many of his orders.

If Daddy were alive, I know he'd order Rafael from his house and grounds, even if Rafael had renounced his former loyalties. That would not have mattered with Daddy.

Rafael was a skilled interviewer as well as confessor, and he asked very pointed questions about my life. He'd never known anyone rich before, and almost anything I had to tell him came as a surprising revelation and a glimpse into a world and life that had been both forbidden and unknown to him.

I fear I wasn't as candid about my life as he had been with me. I'd discussed my schooling, my business affairs to a degree, various places I'd lived, even my rather foolish decision to work in Hollywood.

What I left out, of course, were my romantic involvements. I left the impression that he was talking to a girl who would almost qualify as a candidate for the convent. Most pages of my life I kept deliberately blank. I feared that he might become insanely jealous if he heard of my former involvements. I never discussed my former relationships with anybody. I long ago learned that whatever confidences I trusted people with always ended up on the front page of the *National Enquirer*. As a result, I no longer confided in anyone, especially Mia, who seemed to want to know more about my private involvements than anyone else in the world, with the possible exception of my "unauthorized biographers."

When it was time to go to bed – the mantlepiece clock said three a.m. – a feeling of fright came over me. I wasn't sure if he planned to follow me to my bedroom, and if he did I didn't know whether I was going to let him in or else suggest he cool his ardor for another day. He made it easy for me. At the top of the stairs, he entered my bedroom, searching it thoroughly. At first, I wasn't certain just what he was doing until I remembered I'd hired him as my personal bodyguard. He bolted the French doors leading to my balcony, then opened the mahogany door which connected my suite with a slightly smaller room. When he saw that it was empty of anyone's clothing and personal belongings, he announced to me, "This will be my room. I'll be right next door. At the slightest suggestion of anything wrong, you call out for me."

He approached me, his eyes locking into mine. His mouth came down hard on mine, commanding and possessing, then invading with his tongue. I gave myself completely to him and waited for him to lower me gently onto my satiny, fluffy bed. But that was not to happen. Just at the moment I felt I could be embraced by him forever, he whispered into my ear. "Good night." Those soft words were followed by an invasion of that same ear with his tongue, then a gentle nibble, then a final farewell. He turned and left, shutting the French doors behind him as he disappeared into the other bedroom.

I stood alone and somewhat dejected in my boudoir, as if I'd lost something. The loss was even greater considering that it was something I'd never possessed. I turned to my bathroom where I did all those special things a woman does when she knows she's preparing herself for her lover in bed. But after my toilette, I returned to my bedroom and the emptiness that lay here in store for me.

I might be the love goddess of the world, but I had an awful confession to make. Although pursued by some of the world's leading lovers – everybody from rock stars to movie stars, from princes from the House of Windsor (what a forgettable experience) to the young son of a fallen American leader (a sincere although strangely passionless form of lovemaking), I was disappointed in love.

Many men, once they got me into bed, simply could not perform. My reputation had preceded me. Perhaps they wanted a woman weak and vulnerable, and I represented power and money. All too often they became impotent. Apologies filled the air, but a lingering embarrassment hovered over both of us after such an unrewarding experience.

Impotency wasn't always the case, and I had known some of the world's great lovers, who viewed my money and power as an aphrodisiac. Strangely, many of my most satisfying encounters were with homosexual men. This often surprised me, since I felt these lovers would be happier in the arms of another man. Totally confused one day, I asked one of these men, Tracy Walker, why he wanted to bed me instead of his usual boyfriends.

"The answer is simple. You're a very appealing gay male in a woman's body."

Perhaps I never fully understood the implications of that, but it was the best god damn explanation anybody had come up with so far.

I tried to read some magazines, hoping they would put me to sleep. But they didn't. Invariably, I came to references to me, or, even worse, unflattering pictures of myself, and instead of putting me to sleep, the unfair media attacks made me more awake and alive than ever. Opening the French doors to my balcony, I breathed in the night air before returning to bed, leaving the doors open.

Finally, around four a.m., I drifted off to sleep. Surely I didn't sleep long. The first sound was faint, but it was enough to awaken me. The second sound would have awakened drugged armies. Shattering glass filled the night air.

I woke up screaming. I knew in my heart that this was an assassination attempt, and I had only moments to live. The first word out of my mouth was RAFAEL. It was more than a scream. It was a call for help unlike any I'd ever uttered--a piercing, shrieking rage for this man to come and rescue me from a long dark night.

. . .

Yanked from my bed, I was thrown onto the floor as a body covered my nudity. That body I realized was also nude. A rape. I struggled against my attacker until the masculine scent of Rafael eased my fear. In the distance I heard shouts coming from the patio. It sounded like Dino/Desi.

"Stay here!" Rafael commanded. He rushed to the balcony to see what was happening below on the patio. I still lay on the floor, not really knowing what was going on.

Rafael was yelling down at Desi in Spanish. Even though I didn't understand the exact meaning, I knew he wasn't being kind.

Getting up from the floor, I reached for my robe. Slipping into it quickly, I joined a completely nude Rafael on my balcony. Lights were being turned on around the house. The noise had awakened Ted and Maxie. Maxie appeared in full turban drag, and Ted wore his usual nighttime mud pack.

"Dino," I shouted, "are you okay?"

It was obvious he was drunk. His shirt looked half ripped from his body. He glanced up at Rafael and me standing on the balcony above him. I suddenly realized that seeing me in my sheer nightgown adjacent to a nude Rafael made it clear that we'd been aroused from a bed of passion.

The patio lights revealed lots of broken glass, and it was obvious to me what Dino/Desi had done. Stumbling around in the dim light, no doubt in search of a drink, he had found the liquor cabinet. It was a faux-Roman column from the movie set of Cleopatra, starring Elizabeth Taylor. Mia always purchased props from Taylor movies whenever she could. The column was hollow, lined with glass shelves, and filled with bottles and crystal decanters. Apparently, when Dino/Desi had reached for a bottle, the pins which supported the glass shelves had collapsed, sending liquor bottles crashing onto the tile floors of the patio.

"You're a pretty sight," Rafael said to Dino/Desi, in English this time. "Could you mariposas help my boy get to bed, or do I have to come down there to clean him up myself?"

Ted took charge. "Putting men to bed is my specialty," he called up to us with a smile. Ted took one arm, Maxie latching onto the other like he'd ensnared a tasty morsel. Together, the two men led a staggering Dino/Desi to a shower room which adjoined the swimming pool.

Feeling that Dino/Desi was in experienced hands for the remainder of the night, I turned to go back to my bedroom. I went to the fireplace and on the mantlepiece found some cigarettes and a lighter.

In a scene straight from a Bette Davis movie, I turned to gaze upon Rafael. He stood at the foot of my bed, buck naked and not ashamed of it. Unlike Mel Benson, the man didn't have anything of which to be ashamed. Since he wasn't the first nude man I'd encountered in my life, I inhaled deeply and appeared calm, cool, and collected, three words Mia always used in her etiquette instructions of what I was to do when faced with such a situation. I tried hard to maintain eye contact with him, although I must admit that I did find my eyes straying below the belt – except in this case there was no belt.

When a rare specimen like this wanders into my eyesight, the world's sharpest appraiser of male flesh – that is, moi – I had to give my professional opinion. On a scale of one to ten, I'd have rated him a definite twelve.

He didn't say anything at first. There seemed a narcissistic streak of the exhibitionist in him. He didn't move toward me; he actually didn't move at all. He just stood there. Not even one of those rippling muscles rippled. A naturally muscular man, he didn't need to pump iron in front of me.

"What are we supposed to do now?" I asked, somewhat bewildered.

"I know what to do," he said with great self-assurance. "I've always known what to do from the first moment I set eyes on you. That was like an eternity ago, only I know it's been a question of hours. I'm just waiting for you to do your part."

"Give me the script: I'll play the part."

"This is not a movie. This is real life. You know what I want.

We both know what you want. But you've got to take the first step. You walk toward me." There was a somewhat embarrassing pause. "Okay, god damn it, if you want me to direct, I will. Your director is telling you to walk toward me and take what you want."

By now accustomed to following the advice of directors--at least sometimes--I moved gracefully toward him, dropping my sheer nightgown as I did. The sudden sight of my complete nudity was having a powerful effect on him. I feared I wouldn't be able to reach him after all, as a fully erect timber pole had come between us.

I need not have feared. No choreographer could have blocked out our movements any better. Without rehearsal, we knew how to move from an upright position to a prone position on the bed. At least I was the prone and passive member of this duet; he was definitely the aggressor.

I closed my eyes, preferring to feel his movements upon my body instead of witnessing them. His lips grazed my ankles, journeying upward. His talented tongue traced little half moons along my calves until he came to my knees. Bending each leg at its midpoint, he kissed, nibbled, tasted, and sucked the skin of the back of my thighs, exploring each shadow, nubble, and indentation. He was definitely a knee man. He kept finding what seemed to be taste treats completely to his liking. I could tell that it required an effort on his part to abandon that choice territory in favor of other pursuits.

He applied his greatest skill on those tender areas of my inner thighs, heading inevitably for the honeypot that millions of men around the world – not to mention what else – had dreamed of tasting. Taste it he did, in mouthful after mouthful, covering the lips of my labia in tongue-lapping cascades of luxuriant licks and kisses. He was so forceful and so aggressive that it brought out the aggressor in me. Releasing my tensions and whatever inhibitions I had left, I wrapped my legs around him and pulled his hair in great, rich handfuls moaning at a volume I hoped would not reawaken the rest of the house. He was driving me crazy, and I screamed out from the pleasure which his actions caused me. Though I could have shuddered my way into ecstacy at that very moment, I didn't want the session to end so quickly. I wanted him to go on and explore other fields, yet at the same time I knew that even if he told me he suffered from the problems facing Hemingway's hero in The Sun Also Rises that we'd have a perfect and fulfilling marriage even if our sex was limited to doing exactly what we were doing just now.

It was obvious, however, that he had other plans for me. He finally abandoned the present object of his desire to conquer new territories, including the belly, the navel, and what one of my less delicate lovers, a Texan, had called "hog heaven," my much-publicized breasts. The nipples were not made love to: they were assaulted. But it was such a delicious and tantalizing assault that it coaxed them to full-budding bloom.

I wanted this man to dwell here forever, and was almost unaware of his movements until his lips were on mine, full and hard. His tongue had found another opening to explore, and once I had entrapped it in my mouth, I gave it the sucking it deserved. In reciting my life story earlier in the evening, I had given, as mentioned, the impression that I'd spent a lot of time in convents. But after tonight, he could only be convinced that I had omitted details from my biography.

My mouth, my nose, my cheeks, my ears, even my hairline, received their happy baths. His breath still smelled of the Cuban coffee and brandy we'd consumed earlier. It was an intoxicating smell. Earthy and rich.

He kissed each eyelid gently before rising over me to offer me a taste of himself just as he'd known a taste of me. I ran my fingers along his chest. He was not a hairy man, but I found some swirls of dark chest hair which I gently tugged. I reached for those low hangers which I gently massaged as I prepared to take the swelling length of him. From his position over me, he was a mighty warrior wanting a full penetration of the weak defenses of my city.

Fearing he was going too far too fast, he paused, allowing me to get used to this foreign invader. Then he resumed his campaign, his breath growing so rapid that I almost feared that I had aroused a deep passion in a beast that was out of control, one I couldn't completely satisfy. Before the final invasion, he reached down and gently massaged my throat, and when it was ready, he pushed himself at first gently, then deeper and deeper, going down into places where no man had ever gone before, gagging me with the fullness of his manhood.

Droplets of his salty sweat were falling like raindrops on me, and I welcomed them. They added to my excitement. Instinctively, we both knew that we couldn't go on too much longer like this if we had other experiments and other plans. He pulled his hard-veined, spit-lubed length out of my throat and rubbed it across my lips and face, even caressing my closed eyelids, before rising up slightly to allow me to lap the pendulous globes of his velvet-textured testicles.

His mouth was on mine again, and it was as if he not only wanted to taste me, but to also taste that part of himself he'd left in my mouth.

His long, thick fingers were busy preparing me for entry. Desperately, I reached for my nightstand and unpeeled a condom. Then he did something no other man had ever done. He put the condom in his mouth and wet it before inserting it in my own mouth. Thank heavens it was without flavor. I accepted it gladly. Both of our tongues lubricated it before he fitted it onto himself expertly.

He was in me now, pushing gently. He found a willing participant on the other end. I was literally sucking him inside me, wanting the full length of him, enjoying the rich fullness of the male animal in a deep and needy place. My legs were over his shoulders, my inner calves massaging either side of his neck as he leaned into me, giving me what I so desperately wanted. He was a master of the stroke, of various strokes. At times, he was almost brutal, at other times, gentle and caressing. At no point did the tempo ever stop building. We were both going to the same place, moving toward it with an increasingly urgent rhythm. Whenever I felt that I was rushing toward the inevitable release, he tantalizingly held back. In a style more fulfilling than anything I had ever known, he was in complete charge of the action, and made it clear that he'd determine when the rhythm would end.

His sudden expansion and a sound that began deep in his throat were signals all too obvious about where matters were headed. The whimper grew strong and more menacing. It wasn't the sound of a man; more the sound of an animal. Then it came: That which we'd both wanted for so long. I could hear my own thundering heartbeat as I gave myself completely in wave after watery wave to this wonderful man.

Unlike dear, sweet Teddy Kennedy, or dear Eddie Fisher, he was not in and out and thank you ma'am. He collapsed on top of me, here to linger for a while. He was welcome to stay forever. "It has found its home, and it won't be leaving any time soon," he said. "Give me five minutes, just five minutes, before the curtain goes up on Act II. It will have some surprises."

He was a man of his word. Act II was followed by Act III, and by then it was nine a.m., and both of us were in urgent need of sleep.

Act III, in fact, was such a show-stopper that I might have seriously injured his earlobe had he not gently slapped me back to reality. Extreme pleasure and pain, I realized, have a lot in common: The intensity can be so great you can't stand too much of either.

Completely fulfilled, completely satisfied, I fell into careless, dreamy sleep, snuggling comfortably into his arms. Even as I did, I was smart enough to know that it was probably going to be the last carefree sleep I'd have for a long time.

CHAPTER FOUR

Hoping to be inconspicuous, I had Ted rent three of Miami's longest stretch limousines to take us down the Florida Keys to Key West. Actually, I owned the limousine company, or perhaps Mia and I owned it jointly. No one was sure any more who owned what.

Dino/Desi at first decided he wasn't going to accompany us, obviously preferring the fleshpots of South Beach. When Rafael prevailed, Dino/Desi reluctantly agreed.

The next morning, after he'd recovered from a world-class hangover, Dino/Desi made no mention of "Kristallnacht" and his drunken condition on the patio the night before. No one else seemed to want to talk about it either, especially me. He seemed relieved that he was no longer burdened by a relationship with me, and frankly, I was too. There was the awkwardness of having him afoot all the time, but if he and Rafael could live with this, so could I. Rafael was convinced that in a matter of weeks, Dino/Desi would be launched upon some new affair, "Perhaps with your mother," Rafael said both threateningly and jokingly. "You know my son."

As we left Star Island and headed for Key West, Rafael directed the two of us into the limousine in the middle, feeling that it would better protect me in case of a possible car-jack, which seemed to be an imminent possibility these days in the Miami area. Rafael was armed. One of my staff members had secured an automatic weapon for him. Ted, Maxie, and Dino/Desi rode in the rear limousine, and key staff members filled the limousine in the front.

Brad Cruz was flying in that afternoon, and I was to meet him for drinks sometime before dinner. He had declined my dinner invitation, saying he was tired and needed rest.

Ever alert and on the job, Rafael gazed through dark windows at the sunflooded Keys landscape, which seemed to consist almost entirely of restaurants, bars, motels, scrubland, and views over the sea.

After our stay on Star Island, I'd gotten to know him very well. I could honestly state that there was no external part of him I wasn't intimately familiar with, and, as for the internal man, that would have to wait. It would take a lot of time to get to know him, and I planned for the two of us to be together for a very long while. I was especially pleased to be passionately involved in a relationship that had not yet been trumpeted by those sleazy tabloids, those voracious unauthorized biographers, and those impossible paparazzi.

Before I left Star Island, a courier from David's office had delivered a confidential report on Anishi Mishima. All my life I'd made it important to know as much as possible about my enemies.

In the well-upholstered comfort of the back seat of my limousine, I began to peruse the documents which David had assembled on Anishi. The major problem facing a biographer of her life was that she had moved rapidly from one part of the world to another, changing her name, her references, and often her appearance until it was almost impossible for her life story to be documented. David admitted that entire years of her life were not accounted for, and she could have been anywhere doing anything or anybody.

Though in her latest incarnation, she claimed that she was "under forty," the evidence indicated that she was born sometime between the late 1930s on the eve of World War II and the early spring of 1942, following the Japanese attack on Pearl Harbor. She'd always been able to deduct at least 20 years off her stated age because, her face appeared timeless, devoid of wrinkles and, according to some witnesses, devoid of expression. One of her more exotic claims involved the discovery of a Fountain of Youth, an elixir so powerful that it slowly reversed the natural aging process.

David's investigators felt that the hopes associated with this elixir--more than anything else--had attracted Mia to Anishi. If there was anyone on earth who wanted access to a Fountain of Youth, it was my Mommie. A former servant at her mansion in Key West testified that not only was Anishi taking daily injections of this elixir in her breasts, she was also administering them directly to Mia, also in her breasts.

David's best conclusion was that the elixir was really nothing more than a rather unimaginative "Dr. Feelgood" formula similar to the one administered to John Kennedy during the early 60s. At least temporarily, it made the receiver of the shot feel energized and more youthful, but the effects were short-lived and addictive. Through means he didn't want to reveal to me, David was going to arrange for the acquisition of a vial of this elixir so that its contents could be analyzed in a laboratory.

Anishi's father once earned a living catering to the unusual sexual tastes of the clients of a Tokyo-based bordello. He catered to proclivities that were hard to satisfy anywhere else. One sexual pastime featured the entrails and warm blood of a chicken. A young Anishi and her even younger brother were forced to perform sexual acts with each other for the amusement of audiences who showed extreme pleasure at witnessing a brother and sister engaged in various forms of intercourse. Anishi's own specialty involved stimulating a renewed sexual vitality in the elderly--make that rich elderly--who'd thought that any kind of sexual escapade was strictly a memory from their past. One especially noteworthy technique involved the risque but rhythmical use of a feather.

After Tokyo, her trail grew thin. The mystery years had begun.

In the late 1960s, after an unsuccessful attempt to become an avant-garde artist in Greenwich Village, she went "spiritual," remaking herself into an urban guru.

That didn't last long and she returned to Tokyo and settled down, marrying a rather nondescript factory worker, with no money, no charm, and apparently not much of a body either. The reason for this marriage had never been satisfactorily explained. It was as if having led a completely jaded and debauched life, she yearned to return to the world of the ordinary and the mundane.

Long past the child-bearing age of most women, Anishi in 1980 and again in 1981 bore her husband two sons. Apparently, they lived a quiet and uneventful life until 1985, when her husband was trapped in a suspicious fire that destroyed his wood and paper workshop in just minutes. On that day Anishi had taken her two sons "John" and "Henry" on a trip outside the city.

Two weeks after her husband's death, she had abandoned her children, taking them to live with her husband's relatives in the countryside near Kobe. The relatives had vigorously objected to the use of the names "John" and "Henry," but that is what she insisted they be called.

No other recorded documentation existed of Anishi until 1992, when she showed up as a servant at Mia's estate in Key West. She always hired Japanese to staff her house and Anishi had become intimate with one of her butlers. This eventually led to Anishi's placement within Mia's household as a maid.

The butler was eventually fired, through the intervention of Anishi, but not before she had been promoted from maid to the virtual mistress of the house. With her facile charm, her magic formulas, and her soothing philosophies, she'd moved quickly into Mia's orbit. After assuming command of the household in Key West, and obtaining a limited power of attorney over some of Mia's business affairs, Anishi had sent to Kobe for her two sons, who began living under Mia's gilded roof. That surprised me, considering Mia's intense dislike of children, even her own.

As the limousine rolled on, I stopped reading David's report and sighed. When my caravan of limousines roared past Sugarloaf Key, I knew Key West lay ahead. What faced me there I didn't want to know – not right now.

. . .

Since Mia had made me virtually homeless in Key West, I was forced to rent accommodations for three months. I couldn't find a house as spacious as Mia's, as she occupied the largest and showiest mansion in town. I settled for the second-largest mansion in town, which was rather prominently located at the southernmost point in the United States.

Just as Mia had created a new family, adopting Anishi, so I arrived at this southernmost house with my own rapidly growing clan of Rafael and Dino/Desi, Maxie and Ted, two Cuban refugees, and a pair of lackeys who usually referred to themselves as "The Dolly Sisters." Women like me always have to hire men like Ted and Maxie. What straight married man, with a family of five, would spend most of his day selecting brassieres for me and buying every tube of lipstick at a boutique until I became convinced that I'd found the right shade?

I walked through the corridors of this rambling old house,

whose outside was painted in garish but strangely appropriate shades of lime green and coral pink. The owners had been reluctant to leave. However, when I offered them twenty-five thousand dollars a month, two first-class tickets to Nice, and the use of my mansion at Cap-Ferrat, they came around. Money talks.

Maxie had been on the phone with half the boutiques in Palm Beach, compiling what he referred to as my Key West wardrobe. Thank God I'd brought him along, since Jerry had been too cheap to hire me a stylist. Maxie had assembled two wardrobes for me--one when I was just being myself, Sherry Kelly, moving about Key West, and a more lavish and exaggerated wardrobe for my film scenes as Leonora de la Mer in "Butterflies in Heat." Dino/Desi and Rafael had decided to wear nothing but thongs around the premises, and the sight of all that exposed male flesh was so distracting that I almost ordered them to put on more clothes. They were certainly driving Maxie and Ted crazy. After his "night of broken glass," Dino/Desi had assumed a kind of male dominance over Ted and Maxie that was remarkable. Even though I was the star, the financier, and the rich bitch of the menage, Ted and Maxie spent more time catering to Dino/Desi than they did to me. There was even talk that both men were eventually going to work as Dino/Desi's "agents," whatever that meant.

I didn't challenge any of these agendas. My worst nightmare would be that Dino/Desi would turn to The Iguana and ask *it* to be his agent.

Just as I was arranging for afternoon tea with the thong-wearers, a hysterical Ted rushed in. "Come up to the tower with me...quick!"

Knowing I wasn't in any danger of getting raped up in that tower with Ted, I climbed up the endless flights of stairs after him. It seemed as if we were ascending to the top of the Statue of Liberty, but we finally made it to the top.

I entered a tower room, high above Key West, with a stunning view over the town and the southern seas. The owner had installed four pairs of powerful binoculars in this room, each mounted on a tripod, each with different powers of magnification, perhaps to spy down onto the daytime and nocturnal activities on the beach below. Ted directed me to a set of binoculars carefully trained next door on Belle Reve, Mia's estate. "There," he said with all the pride of a young child who'd just made a beautiful pottie for his mama. "You can see them!"

Training the binoculars on the grounds of Mia's beloved Belle Reve, I focused on two exceptionally exotic creatures: Mia and Anishi. Dressed as royal princesses from some mythical kingdom in Indonesia, each woman rode a Mongolian humpback camel circling Mia's award-winning gardens.

I zoomed my skilled binocular-aided eyes in on Mia. It was like a cameraman moving in for the close-up. I fully anticipated seeing a woman held virtual captive, her once-beautiful face now ravaged and showing every sign of an enforced confinement.

What greeted me instead was one of the world's fabled beauties, who in her maturity had never looked finer. She was clad in her favorite colors, cerise and chartreuse, which in many cases were the only colors she ever wore. Perhaps the Fountain of Youth elixir really worked. If anything, my Mommie looked more like Elizabeth Taylor than did Dame Taylor herself. In spite of her years, Mia's face evoked regal images of the original Taylor when she filmed "Cleopatra." Far from being a prisoner of Anishi, she appeared happy. I didn't know when she'd ever been happy. Even after reading the contents of my childhood diary, which I suspected she'd done, she still looked glorious. Her makeup, her hair, her lipstick – all were perfect.

I was suddenly struck by how well suited my own Mommie would be in my role of Leonora de la Mer. She looked the part more than I did. Despite my years, I still photographed like a fresh-faced virgin just out of the convent. I know that a few of my critics do not agree with my assessment.

Mia's Taylor-like face was so tantalizing as she rode her humpback that I hadn't even focused on Anishi. Finally, I did, there to encounter a serene face of the Orient who'd known more than a thousand nights in the bordellos of the East with their hidden lusts. My God, it seemed, my thoughts sounded like paperback book jacket copy. I knew exactly what David's report meant about her being timeless. She was attired in red and purple Indonesian silks shot through with golden threads, clothes eminently suited to her role as princess-in-waiting to my

Mommie as queen.

Hers was not a pretty face, not at all. She'd win no Miss Japan contests. But it was an interesting, multi-faceted, and rather mysterious face. Whereas Mia looked like an alert and alive woman of the 90s, albeit with a definite style of those 1940s glamour queens, the face of Anishi looked as if it could have felt at home in any century. Although she might have come from peasant stock, her face was serenely aristocratic. If anything, she looked like she could be the Empress of Japan.

She was a serious enemy of mine, and I would treat her with the respect that so formidable an opponent deserved. Regaining control of my Mommie and her estate from this woman would be a far greater challenge than I'd ever envisioned. She was not some slanty-eyed yellow pussy that could be shoved aside the moment I walked in the door of Belle Reve.

Staring at that inscrutable face, I felt for the first time the possibility of defeat. Up to now, I thought I would take Joan Crawford's old approach. That is, I'd tell Anishi that I'd dealt with bigger shits than her, before physically and emotionally demolishing her and throwing her out the door of Belle Reve. It wouldn't be that easy, and it'd take all my cleverness to get rid of that one.

I couldn't look any more at the women having fun with their humpback camels. I felt I should be there riding on the camel alongside my Mommie, having fun with her, being her daughter. A usurper had taken my place, and both Mia and I had allowed it to happen.

I felt on the verge of tears, and wanted to make things right with my Mommie again, but I feared that every possible obstacle stood in my way. If she had read my childhood diary, she might never take me back into her good graces.

Rafael and Dino/Desi joined me in the tower room. They, too, wanted to see what all the excitement was next door. Both men wanted binoculars to gaze upon the forbidden grounds of Belle Reve.

Unlike me, Rafael didn't know what a humpback Mongolian camel was. Of all the parties present, his reaction was the sanest. "What are those two crazies doing riding camels?"

Up until he asked that question, it had never occurred to me that the women's actions might be considered odd. I was too concerned with seeing Mia and her new daughter.

"It's a bit strange, isn't it?" I said. "Two grown women out there riding camels in the sun. God knows where they had these camels flown in from, or why."

"Maybe they get off on it," Dino/Desi chimed in. "Like Michael Jackson in Neverland."

For one brief moment, I wondered how intimately Dino/Desi knew Michael Jackson, and how much he knew about Jackson's playground. "Maybe," I said. I knew that shipping in camels was definitely Anishi's idea, not Mia's. Maybe Anishi had bought the camels as gifts for her two sons, John and Henry. Now that she had access to unlimited resources, the bitch could do whatever she wanted. Maybe she'd turn the entire grounds of Belle Reve into a zoo.

Taking his eyes from his binoculars, Rafael moved toward me and put his arms around me. Normally, I don't like to embrace sweaty men, but I found his body intoxicating. I leaned into him for protection. He had already sensed my despair, and as a very sympathetic man, knew I was hurting. He seemed to realize that although I was thirty-six years old, there was also a little girl in me, a little girl who wanted to go home. I knew that he also wanted to go back home, and that we both felt awash.

Immune to both of us, Dino/Desi kept his eyes glued to the binoculars until Mia, Anishi, and their camels disappeared from our sight. "Hot damn!" he said, breaking from his view and looking over at us. "They took those camels right inside the house. Hot damn! They don't even seem to care if the camels drop turds on their carpets! HOT DAMN! I've never seen anything like this in my whole life."

"That's my Mommie and her new daughter," I said matter-of-factly, hiding my feelings. "Mia Kelly and Anishi Mishima. Sorry I can't introduce either of you in person."

"So, that's Mia Kelly," Dino/Desi said. "She's the most beautiful woman I've ever seen in my whole life."

It was only when the three of us were descending the long, winding steps from the tower that Dino/Desi's words struck pangs of jealousy and regret in me. He'd pronounced Mia the most beautiful woman in the world. How could he say that to moi, Sherry Kelly, her daughter, his former lover, and the fleshpot – until now – of his dreams? Before laying eyes on Mia, he'd always said that I was the world's most beautiful woman.

Bubbling with enthusiasm, Dino/Desi ran ahead to the patio to join his new "agents," Ted and Maxie. At first I thought Rafael hadn't paid any attention to his son's rather cavalier remarks, but as we entered the living room, he turned to me. "My son is a young and foolish man, and he's got a lot of growing up to do. Your mother is very beautiful...for a mama. But you, my sweet, are the most beautiful woman on earth."

"Thank you, my pet." I kissed his sweat-drenched throat. "Any woman about to face the cameras on a new picture tomorrow needs to hear that."

"Now, my little hibiscus blossom, we have to go to our bedroom. In an hour or so, we're about to have Brad Cruz over for tea. I'm very jealous, and I want you to be completely exhausted sexually, every cell in your body thoroughly satisfied, *before* you meet him."

. . .

Ted and Maxie were eager to meet Cruz, but I didn't think today would be the most ideal occasion. Later, perhaps, after the shooting of "Butterflies" had begun.

I felt lucky that Cruz had agreed to play the role of the hustler in my film. The Iguana had told me that the Cruz advisers had urged him not to accept the role, despite the excellent pay. The money eventually won over, despite fears of soiling the actor's wholesome image. Cruz came from a home whose hardworking mother had often waited in line for food stamps. As a young boy, he knew what it meant to have a Christmas without presents, and he was relishing his new-found life as a Hollywood multi-millionaire.

Wanting to talk business with Cruz with as few distractions as possible, I overcame Ted and Maxie's reluctance to leave the house by offering them five-thousand dollars to go shopping. An offer like that couldn't be turned down. It also occurred to me that a meeting between Cruz and Dino/Desi would not be entirely desirable. To lure him away from the house, I called a local car dealer and quickly reviewed his inventory of expensive models. I told him that Dino/Desi would be over soon for some car shopping. However, my efforts were sabotaged when Dino/Desi got on the phone and also reviewed the dealer's best stock. Dino/Desi quickly decided that there was nothing on the lot he wanted, and, if we remained in Florida, he knew a special and very exotic car in Beverly Hills he wanted. It would have to be shipped to Key West, he announced, and he would definitely remain for tea with Cruz.

Following an intense love-making session with Rafael, I was kindly disposed to the Navarro family, and decided to let Dino/Desi stay after all, even though something told me that he and Cruz would not participate in male bonding. Rafael posed no problem, as he actually knew how to meet people and treat them intelligently, something I couldn't always say for other members of my adopted family.

I led Dino/Desi and Rafael to the southernmost terrace in the continental United States and assembled myself on the patio for my rendezvous with Cruz. I wore a simple white dress, cut low. My only affectation was to don a pair of 1945-style Joan Crawford fuck-me-shoes with heels so preposterously high that I didn't know if it would be safe to walk around in them. For Cruz, I selected my most flaming red lipstick, accentuating the mouth he was destined to kiss. I'd studied Cruz's lips closely and decided he would be only an adequate kisser. After experiencing Rafael's succulent mouth, I was convinced that no other man would ever satisfy me.

Rafael appeared in a simple T-shirt and jeans, and Dino/Desi had attired himself in his finest Valentino sportswear drag. He'd so carefully groomed himself that he looked camera-ready for a fashion shoot at a resort. I had to admit that compared with the understated wardrobes of Rafael and me, Dino/Desi was a sensation. Regardless of how Cruz dressed, it would be hard to compete.

The Cuban butler came onto the patio to announce the arrival of Cruz. "May I present Bradford Eugene Dimhart III," the butler said to everyone's amazement, including that of Cruz himself. Before Maxie's departure, I'm sure he'd written that line for the butler.

"Dimhart III?" Dino/Desi said, even before I could introduce him and Rafael to Cruz. "I like that. Why on earth did you change it to Brad Cruz?"

Cruz looked dumbfounded at first, a look I found totally in keeping with a man whom I'd been told never really learned how to read or write. Apparently, he'd had someone read his contract to him, especially the part about our offer of eighteen-million dollars...plus points. "I'm Brad Cruz." He was wearing a pair of jeans and a simple sports shirt. "Cruz sounds better on a marquee than Dimhart."

I stepped between Dino/Desi and Cruz. "This is Desi..."

Desi interrupted me, extending his hand to Cruz. "Dino Paglia," he said. "I'm a professional model."

"If you're going to model," Cruz said, "why not be a pro?"

That seemed to shut down Dino for a long moment. I decided to go back to calling him Dino. He retreated to a chaise longue where he managed to position himself as a lounge lizard in a moderately provocative sprawl, his tight pants revealing all.

As Rafael stepped forward, I introduced him to Cruz too. I'm sure that Cruz was familiar with Dino, that is, if he read the sleazy tabloids at all. I doubted very seriously if he knew who Rafael was. But I was wrong.

"Your name sounds familiar," Cruz said. "I've seen you interviewed on CNN. You're the pilot who hijacked the airplane from Cuba. Wow!"

"That's me," Rafael said. "Actually, that's bad grammar. I used to teach English to Cuban pilots. I should know better."

"Maybe Rafael might help you with the script," I volunteered. "I understand you've suffered from learning disabilities." Even as I said that, I realized it sounded more blunt and crude than I'd meant. I was just too damn nervous today, saying all the wrong things.

Seating himself on a beach chair, Cruz leaned back. "You don't believe all that crap about how I can't read and write, do you?"

"I vaguely recall something," I said, trying to recover from my blunder. "Everybody gossips so much about superstars like us." Then I smiled, "If the worst thing they ever said about me was that I couldn't read or write, my reputation would be better off."

"I've suffered from dyslexia, and I've fought hard to overcome it. My mother had the same problem. So did all three of my sisters. It ran in the family."

"I'm so sorry," Rafael said.

"Me too." I chimed in.

"But I assure you that I can read and understand scripts," Cruz said. Then with what I detected was a slightly ominous tone to his voice, he added, "And contracts."

There was an awkward silence on the patio, as a uniformed maid, also Cuban, arrived with tea. After more preliminaries, and again following a prolonged silence, Dino popped up again. "You mentioned your sisters. I ate dinner at a Mexican restaurant somewhere in New York last year. It was run by one of your sisters. I even met her. She looks like a shorter version of you in drag. The food tasted real good, but two hours later I barfed. I was sick for three days with the trots."

That autobiographical tidbit was followed by the longest and most awkward silence yet.

It was all too obvious that Cruz felt he'd stumbled into the wrong party and, even worse, the wrong film. I knew a role as a male hustler wasn't his typical macho part. It was also embarrassingly apparent that there was no sexual tension of any kind between us. We weren't going to become another Gable and Harlow, heating up the screen for future generations to sigh over. We were worlds apart, this good-looking but rather ordinary young man born into a dreary house in upstate New York. But we had signed up for this deal, and as the complete professionals we were, we were going to bully it through, even the love scenes.

I could feel Cruz checking me out, and I was used to that. Most men found me devastating. But as far as my allure for Cruz, I suspected that his impression of me was that of a talking RoboSlut. Making love to me, it was obvious, was about the last item on his agenda. I decided to zero in.

"I understand you've had some reservations about interpreting the role of Numie," I said, in my best honey-blonde purr.

"I have--quite a few. I'm trying to find this character's humanity. He's got to have a soul in there somewhere. I want to transform him into something sympathetic to audiences, even though he sells his body for money."

"Don't worry about it, my dear boy," Rafael said, sounding

almost British. "All of us sell something."

"Rafael is right,". I said. "The character, Numie, I found extremely sympathetic. He's vulnerable, and he's a loser. Nothing really worked out for him. He tried many times and at many things. But nothing ever worked. It's a lot like the Tennessee Williams character, Chance Wayne (or some such name, I forget...) in 'Sweet Bird of Youth.' Numie understands completely how fast the clock is ticking. Youth and beauty are fading away."

Cruz bristled at that remark. It occurred to me that the actor had never seriously considered that he might not always remain youthful and gorgeous.

"Numie is actually in search of love," I continued, diplomatically changing tack. "He's been looking in all the wrong places, and as the film progresses, the audience grows to love him, even view him as a modern-day tragic hero, struggling valiantly against society's restrictive values."

Suddenly smiling, Cruz relented. "That makes it sound like something I could get into. I'll give it my best shot."

"I know you will, and I also know that you'll be terrific. You always are."

He seemed taken in by my obvious flattering. However, from the look on Dino's face, I knew that the Young Professional Model wasn't impressed at all with Cruz or with anything he said. Could dear, sweet Dino, blessed with all the manly gifts of the gods, be jealous of Cruz?

"We never got to see many of your films in Cuba," Rafael said. "I did get to see one, though. Where you played a pilot. I'm a pilot myself. That was one terrific picture."

In his sweet and charming way, Rafael saved the meeting, the day, and the film. Cruz didn't really want to talk about "Butterflies," or the interpretation of his role within it, any longer. He was uncomfortable around me, and I'm sure he regarded Dino as one of the thousands of young parvenus who would have done anything to replace him tomorrow. In Hollywood, I'd heard a thousand beach boys tell me, "I'm better-looking than Brad Cruz." The actor must have long ago grown accustomed to that, if one ever could.

The mention of the pilot film sent Cruz and Rafael into a long and animated discussion about aircraft. I realized that they had more to say to each other than Cruz and me and certainly Cruz and Dino. I feared that Dino and I were just too exotic for Cruz. After all, he seemed like a simple New York State boy, whereas Dino and I were meant to sail the oceans of the world on the most expensive yachts.

As Rafael and Cruz remained deep in their own dialogue, Dino and I drifted to the far edge of the patio. Struggling to assert my new role as an older female mentor to a younger ex-lover, I turned to look into his face.

"Mama, he's not the man for the part. I can play Numie."

"You?" I said in astonishment. "You couldn't play a beauty who's past his prime. Rafael is old enough for the part, not you."

"The script could be rewritten. Why does the man have to be past his prime? Why can't he be at the peak of his male beauty and sexual prowess? To compensate, the script could say that *your* character is past her prime. The contrast between the two will be all the more powerful."

"Thanks a lot, you little twerp," I said a bit too angrily. "Remind me never to hire you as my scriptwriter."

"I'm serious, mama. I know what I'm doing. We could make movie history together."

"We could make movie history all right," I said sarcastically. "I'd probably belt you in the mouth right in front of the camera."

"Talk to Jerry about it. I want to do that part. We certainly know how to keep the sheets warm, don't we, mama?"

"I think you're out of your mind," I said, stepping back from him. "Cruz has already signed for the role. The stairway scene between Cruz and me is being shot tomorrow."

"You've got to introduce me to Jerry. I'll convince him I can do the part."

"Haven't you ever heard of box office? Cruz is a superstar. I'm bigger, of course, but together, we have a guaranteed box office draw. You're beautiful, but you're completely unknown."

"Bullshit! A lot of people fell in love with me when I posed for that Banana Republic ad. A lot of people, including, very specifically, Sherry Kelly. You should read my fan mail."

"I don't want to read your fan mail. My own fan mail is disgusting enough."

The butler came and whispered a message in my ear. I excused myself from Dino and waved to Rafael and Cruz, both of whom seemed hardly to notice me. In the privacy of the downstairs sunroom, I picked up the receiver to accept a call from Sean Nielson. I had always found this Norwegian actor hot, but I'd never actually met him, and I wondered what it was that he wanted with me. No doubt Mr. Nielson had "convinced" The Iguana that he needed my confidential number. My confidential phone number was so confidential that I think everybody in America had it. I suspected that The Iguana was selling it.

After several flirtatious sallies, with many compliments about my film role in "Kinky," big bad Sean came to the point. He'd heard a rumor that Cruz might refuse to play the hustler role of Numie. He informed me that he was standing by, ready to fly to Key West at any moment to accept the role, at a figure much lower than that required by Cruz, and minus the points. It was a provocative offer, and one I thought Jerry should have considered after Mel Benson bowed out.

"I don't like to admit it, but there are those who say I'm already past my prime," Sean said. "but I'm just the right age for this part. I've got the looks, and certainly the body, and I understand the flavor of Numie's character. By the way, did you see my workout video?"

I told him I hadn't seen the video, lying through my teeth, but I did say that I was familiar with the nuances of his body and its parts because of other of his films I'd seen.

"I'm reluctant to bring this up, but my former girlfriend did tell one of those trashy magazines that I was the biggest man she'd ever known. And she's from Jamaica."

"I'm sure you're impressive in all departments," I warbled. "Frankly, I think you'd be perfect for the role. Cruz is under contract, but if something happens, I'll go to bat for you. I really mean that."

"Thanks," he said, somewhat gleefully, although I didn't know why since Cruz had already signed. At this late hour, it was doubtful that anything would happen to Cruz.

"If this deal doesn't work out, I'd definitely consider you for another picture a few months from now," I said. "I think a blond Viking god and a goddess like me could heat up the screen together."

"You can bet on that. I'll fly anywhere, at any time, for a private audition. After all, that's how my former girlfriend and I got together for the first time. Except that she didn't send the airfare, and I didn't have much money at the time."

"In my case, I'd charter the whole god damn plane!"

"That sounds good!"

"Where were you last year when I needed you? You men always call a girl at the most inconvenient time. Usually after she's made other arrangements."

"Are you kidding? I'm your biggest fan. I think about you all the time, but I was too afraid to call. I didn't think you'd take my call."

Now he tells me. "Darling, I've got to go. I'm hosting a tea party on my patio, and I have to return to my guests."

"You've not seen the last of Sean Nielson, baby. And you've certainly never seen all he has to offer."

After a tantalizing goodbye, loaded with innuendoes about our eventual meeting, I headed back to my patio to face the awesome lineup of my guests. They included my former lover, my present (and I hoped) future lover, and my superstar box office co-star and soon-to-be on-screen lover.

As I approached the group on the patio, a wind blew menacingly up from the state of Cuba, sending the palm trees fluttering. Even though it was a picture postcard beautiful setting, with the sun going down, there was something ominous in the air. Like Cruz himself, I began to regret that I'd agreed to film "Butterflies in Heat" in the first place. A woman like me could get burned in the flame.

. . .

After Cruz disappeared to do whatever it is that handsome male superstars do in the evening, I joined Rafael and Dino on the southernmost terrace. The hysterical screams of Ted and Maxie drifted down to the patio from an open window. They were delighted with the results of their five-thousand dollars worth of just-completed shopping.

Rafael came over to me, giving me a long, lingering kiss right in front of Dino, asserting his ownership. To my surprise, Dino no longer appeared resentful. He seemed to have abandoned me as a lost cause, preferring to pursue a new and original agenda of his own creation. Whatever that was.

Although Rafael and I were supposed to play parental roles, it was Dino who directed the mood of our gathering after drinks were served. He demanded that the butler bring him a vodka and tonic, and when his father didn't object, I didn't either. Considering that he'd taken his share of recreational drugs during his short lifetime, a vodka with tonic seemed relatively harmless. Besides, I understood that Latino families start pouring wine down their children's throats before they're three.

"I have decided to give up modeling," Dino announced, with all the seriousness of the BBC announcing the surrender of Nazi Germany in 1945. "I have also decided to continue to use the name Dino Paglia. Please don't introduce me any more as 'Desi,' because I will no longer answer--ever again--to that name. From now on, and forever more, it's Dino Paglia. You'd better remember it, because one day in the not too distant future it's going to be in lights. Dino Paglia is going to become the number one box office attraction in the world."

A sudden silence came over the patio. I obviously assumed that since I was a movie star, Desi, now Dino once again, was simply using me and my life as a role model. Regardless of his ambitions, I didn't particularly care one way or the other what the child decided to call himself.

Rafael, however, had another reaction. "Your mama christened you with the name Desiderio, a name we chose because we wanted you so very badly. We were so very proud of you when you arrived, so overjoyed. You were our son!"

"I always hated the name. Besides, I can't use the name Desi in this country. Everyone will think I copied it from Desi Arnaz. You might have been proud of your little *chico* back in Cuba, but Dino Paglia is no little boy any more. Just ask your girlfriend here."

"Cut the shit," I said, tossing my badly mixed drink into the ocean. "You're getting too grand, even for me, and I've had to deal with the grandest of them all, especially Mia. No one just becomes a movie star any more. Since there are so few movie stars left, that's like saying, 'I'm going to be president of the

United States.'"

"I wasn't expecting you to bankroll me to stardom. I plan to get there all on my own, using my looks, brains, charm, and ambition, even if you *don't* hire me instead of Cruz for the part of Numie."

"To become a movie star, you'll need the sponsorship and assistance of a lot of people. With all my power and money, I also had a lot of help and a lot of luck. Even The Iguana helped me, as reluctant as I am to admit it."

"Iguana?" Rafael asked, confused. "In the islands, we eat iguanas for dinner."

"Don't be too sure about this one," I cautioned him. "If you met The Iguana, you might be the one eaten."

"The Iguana is a very powerful man in Hollywood," Dino warned me. "You shouldn't always go around putting him down."

"I'm not afraid of him at all."

Rafael got up and sat down next to Dino. He looked deeply into his eyes. "Son, I had other plans for you. When I take over Cuba, I'll need you in my government. We'll have to rebuild Cuba."

The butler appeared with another drink for me, and I hoped this time he'd gotten it right. I was amused, thinking what possible government post Rafael could ever devise that would be suitable for Dino. Director of *pubic* relations, or some such post.

Dino rose to his feet immediately, freeing himself from the bond that Rafael was trying to reinforce between them. "Cuba is not my country. Dino Paglia belongs to the world. Even America is too small to contain me. I plan to become an international star."

For one crazed moment, I felt he might succeed. It took complete narcissism and bottomless ambition to become a star. He had plenty of both.

I started to say something, but as I did the butler announced the arrival on my patio of Jerry. Since Cruz had turned down my offer of dinner, I'd decided to introduce Jerry to Rafael and Dino.

Jerry stood in the flattering lights of the patio looking somewhat like a faded star himself. He'd wanted to be an actor, too, but he always claimed that his amazing resemblance to Troy Donohue denied him a screen career. He still had that pretty-boy movie star look of the 50s, in the tradition of Tab Hunter and all those others whose names I so quickly forget. Regardless of the temperature, the setting, or the venue, Jerry always dressed in his trademark black turtleneck sweater and black slacks with white sneakers and red socks.

"Gentlemen," I said, turning to Rafael and Dino, "This is Jerry Wheeler, producer of my newest film, 'Butterflies in Heat.'"

"Producer/Director, darling," he interjected. "You always leave out the director part."

"That's because I direct myself, cuntie," I said a little too firmly, perhaps as a warning to him not to give me any trouble tomorrow on the set. I had more money invested in this film than he did, and he was the producer. "Dino Paglia and Rafael Navarro," I said.

Jerry appraised both men as if he hadn't had lunch in twenty weeks. "It's hard to tell which one is the greater beauty. I think they both belong in front of the cameras with their clothes off. I used to do those films, too." He turned to me. "Are they both actors?"

"We speak English," Rafael said, extending his firm hand to Jerry, a social mistake, perhaps, as Rafael had some difficulty retrieving it.

"I'm a pilot. Or at least I *was* a pilot. But in a few months, I'll be the first democratically elected president of Cuba."

"Aim high, I always say, you handsome hunk." After this, Jerry finally released Rafael's hand.

With great assurance, Dino extended his hand to Jerry, but only after moving penetratingly close to the producer, which in Dino's case was still some distance away.

"I've heard a lot about you, and I want you to get to know me better. A lot better," Dino said provocatively.

Jerry took the bait. "There's nothing I'd like more. Dino Paglia. You must be Italian."

"I am."

Rafael with his fierce national pride started to object, but I signaled him to keep quiet. Let Dino have his illusions, I thought. I'm sure in time he'd make the Italian people proud.

"Sherry, you wicked bitch," Jerry said when he finally managed to take his eyes off Dino. "These are two of the finest specimens of male flesh I've ever laid eyes on. Prime Grade A beef a la mode. I haven't met a man in months who measured up to my standards. In fact, not since my daddy quit fucking me have I known a really good man. I used to write on toilet walls, 'My daddy's got a ten-inch dick and a queer son.'"

I was used to such talk, having grown up with Mia and having been associated with men like Ted and Maxie all my life. I didn't know about Rafael. I carefully studied his reaction to Jerry's flamboyant humor.

"Incest?" Rafael asked, a bit taken aback. "I'm a very tolerant person, but I draw the line at incest."

"Whatever makes you happy, and whatever makes you feel good," Jerry said defensively. "At least *I've* always believed that. Just like you, Sherry, my little Jezebel."

"Oh, Jerry," I said dismissively. "Please do me a big favor and never write my biography. I'd never authorize it. Who knows what you'd make up?"

"I make no promises."

Rather aggressively, Dino took the drink offered from the butler's tray and presented it to Jerry himself. I noticed that Dino's fingers caressed Jerry's hand as he handed him his Cuba libre. "Maybe you've been looking for the right man in all the wrong places," Dino said.

Jerry looked deeply into his eyes. "Maybe I have."

Instinctively, I turned up the lights a little brighter on the patio. The present ambience was just too romantic and soothing. "I want to talk about tomorrow's shoot," I said, trying to get this conversation back to business.

"Have I got a story for you," Jerry said. "I've just been to Mia's house. What fireworks there were. Mia had just discovered that Anishi had signed a contract to allow us to film there. Mia exploded at Anishi. But Anishi fought back, to everyone's surprise, matching every swear word and dirty reference that Mia threw at her with a fuck you. Those two might have a great relationship, but it's now on public record that it's also a highly explosive one. I haven't heard such language since Cary Grant and Randolph Scott got into a lovers' quarrel in the bar of the Beverly Hills Hotel."

"My god, tell me more," I said, happy to steer the dialogue, however briefly, away from the subject of Dino.

Jerry continued, "After reading the contract, Mia is rather resentfully going through with it. I threatened to sue her if she didn't. Right now, thanks to her daughter, that pretentious dragon is coping with enough lawsuits. She eventually acquiesced to the terms of the contract, but she insists on one stipulation. If we don't concede one point, she'll turn the whole affair over to her lawyers and we'll be in court."

"What is it?" I asked.

"Scenes involving you within the house are to be strictly limited. When you're on the premises, Mia will order extra security forces. You're to be given access only to the set, and to none of the other areas of the building. You'll not be allowed to wander freely around the house. During the time you're there, Mia will lock herself in her suite. Anishi, however, has insisted that she be present on the set during each and every one of your takes. In addition, because of the strict limitations on the number of days we're allowed access to the house, we've got to shoot the scenes at Belle Reve first. We're not welcome there, and Mia's hysterical protests have suddenly become a big deal in our production schedule. We'll shoot the film's dramatic high point first instead of last, confusing as that will be."

"I know, the stairwell scene. Me shooting Cruz, my rebellious lover, as he's walking out on me for a younger woman. Listen, cuntie, don't you think that scene is just a little bit evocative of 'Sunset Boulevard?'"

"So what? You know me. I never film a scene unless it was a hit in a previous movie. Even if I retain some of the visuals, I change all the words. That way, no one ever sues."

"I can't believe Mia is going through with this," I said. "She's a smart woman. Don't be surprised if she's got a restraining order issued before tomorrow morning." I sighed, sitting back on the chaise longue, trying to look both gorgeous and businesslike at the same time in front of all three men. "At least I've found a way to get back into Belle Reve. You made it so easy for me."

"I'm always here to help."

I sat up abruptly. "I have to warn you about something. Daddy Kelly never taught me how to shoot straight. He and

Mia were always out somewhere at target practice, or killing things on safaris. Not me. I was a complete guns and ammo failure."

"During our brief but intense time together, Mia told me what a crackerjack shot she was, probably as a warning," Jerry said. "She also ordered me, at risk of bodily harm, not to film anyone flashing crotch within her house unless their nether regions were covered. She's so old-fashioned."

"I haven't been rehearsing any target shooting," I said, "because I assume that the character of Leonora isn't any gun expert either, preferring to hire other people to do her killings for her."

"That's right, and you're perfect for the role. It's practically a fucking documentary. But in this one instance, I got the perfect gun for you. It belongs to Mia."

"Mia lent you that revolver she keeps beside her bed?"

"That very one. How did you know? Of course, she lent it to me with the strict provision that I'd do everything in my power to get you off her grounds as soon after the filming as possible."

"I know that revolver well. It's one of the most ornate revolvers ever made – encrusted with gold filigree, rubies, and diamonds. Throughout her life, Mia has kept it beside the bed of whatever house she occupied in case a rapist breaks in."

"She told me that pistol may have belonged to Alexander the Great," Jerry said, "but even I know gunpowder wasn't invented in those days."

"I think you misunderstood her," I said. "She probably said that the gems along its barrel belonged to Alexander the Great. She's a world-class gem collector."

"That's right. But everyone was surprised that Mia wore relatively modest jewelry yesterday. She said that she'd had exact replicas made of the jewelry Elizabeth Taylor was photographed in recently, and La Taylor seems to have abandoned many of her more ostentatious gems, at least during the daytime."

Dino went to the bar, picked up an ice cube, licked it gently, then dropped it in Jerry's glass.

"A most curious thing happened," Jerry said, looking up at Dino. He lapped the ice cube. "When I went up to Mia's bedroom to inspect the revolver, there was a copy of the Mona Lisa placed against a black-velvet curtain beneath a spotlight over her bed. I'd heard that Mia would never display a copy of anything, so just to piss her off, I asked her, 'What's a copy of the Mona Lisa doing above your bed?' That seemed to annoy the hell out of her, and she said 'That's no copy, you idiot, it's the original. The copy's in the Louvre.' Imagine that, Mia must be getting senile."

"She's not senile. She's telling the truth."

"With the Kelly women, I never know what to believe."

"I've got a great idea," Dino said brightly, trying desperately to get the focus of attention back to himself again. "Sherry, you've got to be on the set early tomorrow morning, and Rafael, I know you'll want to accompany our star here to bed. Why don't I take Jerry out for dinner? I've got an American Express platinum card, and I know there's lobster and caviar somewhere in Key West."

A little too eagerly, Jerry agreed. "He's right. We want you looking your billion-dollar best tomorrow morning, don't we?" He turned to Rafael. "Don't wear her out tonight, you brute."

"Don't you worry about that," Rafael said, rising to his feet. He didn't bother to extend his hand to Jerry this time. "When 'Butterflies in Heat' is translated into Spanish, the title, unfortunately, will mean something else. I mean, in Cuba, a mariposa is..."

Jerry interrupted him. "I know exactly what a mariposa is. I even know what a mariposa in heat is."

"I bet you do," Dino said, grabbing him by the arm as they hurriedly moved from the patio to one of my rented limousines in the driveway.

I took Rafael's hand and watched as Jerry and Dino disappeared into the depths of the limousine.

"I feel I've lost a son," Rafael sighed.

"I feel you never had one."

He turned and kissed me. "Maybe someday you'll bear me a son."

"Maybe someday." I turned to him and held him close. "I'm afraid."

"About the scene tomorrow?"

"Having to shoot Brad Cruz – all that. Going back to Belle

Reve. Meeting Anishi. Being so close yet so far from Mommie. It's all been too much."

"I'll be with you."

As we headed back into the house, I wanted to believe him but didn't dare. Life doesn't give you that kind of protection or that kind of assurance. Ted had noted only the most urgent calls on a pad beside the phone on the desk in my bedroom, but I ignored all of them, at least for tonight. I wanted to lie in Rafael's arms and think of nothing but him.

CHAPTER FIVE

My homecoming to Belle Reve didn't follow the biblical script of the prodigal daughter returning to the welcoming arms of a forgiving family. Moi, the errant child, had come back to Mia's mansion, the house where I had spent most of my childhood, not with a welcome, but with a snub. Everyone made it abundantly clear that I was allowed to use the memory-filled building for only a brief, legally predetermined time, and not as a home, but as a stiffly formal backdrop for a movie.

As my limousine arrived in front of the mansion, I gripped Rafael's hand. Dino had insisted upon coming with us, even though I'd tried to persuade him not to. Over breakfast, and throughout part of the ride to the movie set for the first day's shooting, he continued to argue that he and not Cruz should be cast in the role of Numie, the male hustler. I dared not ask him how his dinner went the night before with Jerry.

A small crowd had gathered at the gates to Belle Reve. They weren't hostile at all, and in fact, seemed to be members of my fan club. To judge from their rather provocative outfits, they were mainly from the gay branch of my fan club. As Rafael ushered me through the waving, shouting crowd of adoring fans to the gates of Belle Reve, I was struck by a face that stood out among the leather queens, the muscle men, and the early-morning (or in some cases, very late night) drag queens, one of whom was made up as Sherry in "Kinky."

It was the face of an old woman. She and I locked eyeball to eyeball, and behind her thick glasses I sensed a hatred I'd never known before. It was only after locking into the depths of those tired and bitter eyes that I glanced upward to read her placard. JEZEBEL! SLUT! WHORE!

Gently but firmly, Rafael took my arm and guided me inside the gates, where I had known happy but also painful times.

Jerry rushed up to greet us, turning his most appreciative attention to Dino before even acknowledging me as the star and chief financial backer of his upcoming film. Forcing Jerry to take his eyes off Dino, I said to him, "Listen to me, cuntie, the star is over here." He got the message and rushed over to kiss my hand. He curtly acknowledged Rafael, treating him almost like my trick instead of as the future president of Cuba.

"My fabled beauty," Jerry gushed, "Helen of Troy at her peak never looked as devastating as you do today. Today, on that stairwell, I want you to make screen history."

"Gloria Swanson's Norma Desmond is a tough act to follow, but I'll give it my best."

Jerry took me by the arm and gently ushered me into Mia's gigantic living room lined with its collection of Old Masters, many stolen. I quickly scanned the room for the Mona Lisa until I remembered that Jerry said he'd seen the purloined painting in Mia's bedroom. I only hoped that she kept the draperies tightly drawn so as not to bleach out the colors in the Key West sun.

"There's someone I want you to meet," Jerry said. "Anishi Mishima."

I whirled around to cover my rear flank. Here, I encountered the camelback rider who looked like an Asian princess. In the early morning light, her regal splendor was gone. She was dressed without artifice with a red headband, very little makeup, and a simple batik dress, no doubt left over from her flower-child wardrobe of 1967. She was smoking a marijuana cigarette whose roach she held up to her mouth with a diamond-encrusted cigarette holder, one which I recognized as part of Mia's extensive collection.

"Welcome to Belle Reve," Anishi said in perfect English. "It's modest, but Mia and I call it home. I keep urging her to sell this place and buy something better suited to our needs, but she has some sentimental attachment to it. For reasons I don't truly understand."

"I understand," I said, a little too triumphantly. "You are so kind to have us here. I noticed you wanted Jerry to deliver the rent money up front. All in small, unmarked bills."

"Please," she said, as if I'd tested the boundaries of good taste and her patience. "Commerce so early in the morning bores me."

"It was commerce that built this house," I added. "Commerce that propelled me to get up at this ghastly hour and endure the insult of being directed by Wheeler here."

"Now, now," he said. "Be kind and not too nasty."

"Ms. Mishima," I said graciously. "This is Rafael Navarro." I didn't bother to explain who he was.

"I know who you are from TV news," she said enigmatically. "The representative of an oppressed people."

"I will set them free," he promised.

"Perhaps," she said with absolutely no conviction.

"Time is money, and we must get on with our first scene," I said. "Is there any place I can use as a dressing room? Perhaps my old bedroom suite?"

"That's out of the question," she said with all the imperial authority of an Oriental despot. "All the upper floors are off-limits to you. I will agree to allow you access to the cabana beside the swimming pool."

"I know it well," I said, wanting to give this interloper a bare knuckle-blow across her kisser.

"You will, of course, be done with your silly little film and be out of here as soon as possible."

"We have no intention of lingering longer than is necessary."

"Good. Mr. Wheeler here was kind enough to provide me with a copy of the script. When I heard you were playing the lead, I had to make sure it wasn't porno before I agreed to let it be filmed here."

With that catty remark, she came just a little closer to feeling the famous Kelly double-punch, but I restrained myself for the good of Jerry's film. "We'll try to keep it clean. I know you're a woman of high moral standards, and we wouldn't want to offend."

She flashed a look at me that was filled with daggers. In that often inscrutable face, she registered a horrified understanding that I might know more about her background than she wanted to have publicized.

Enjoying this one moment of early-morning vengeance, I stared down the face of a woman who'd spent more than a thousand nights in the bordellos of the East.

She never once lost eye contact with me as she sucked in the drugged smoke of her marijuana cigarette. She turned her back to me to face Jerry. "If your clumsy film crew breaks anything, the deal is off," she threatened. "Don't make more noise than you have to. Mia can't stand loud noises."

"We'll be just as good as children in Sunday school," he promised cheerfully.

"Naturally, I hired extra security guards today. *You* must obey them. This is, after all, our home and you must abide by our rules."

I started to say something about having to excuse myself to prepare for my first scene, but was awestruck by her next move. She moved to the main sofa in the living room and sat down, removing the upper part of her dress to reveal her breasts. Modesty was obviously not one of her characteristics. I stared at her breasts, which were nothing compared to mine, but formidable nevertheless. Then she reached for a leather container placed on a coffee table. She removed a long syringe and proceeded to inject the contents directly into her left breast. As she pulled the needle out with a certain fury, she glared at me. "I suffer from heart disease. I have to do this six times a day."

"Oh." I stepped back in the direction of the cabana. "I see."

Out on the patio in the early-morning glare, the camels were grazing happily on Mia's flowerbeds, no doubt thinking they had stumbled into an abundantly stocked desert oasis. Mia's pack of Dobermans ran over to greet me. Immediately, Rafael moved in to protect me, thinking perhaps the dogs were about to attack. But they smelled me and seemed to remember me, welcoming me back to Belle Reve. There was something wrong with the dogs. They weren't barking like they usually did.

Her breasts covered once more, Anishi stood beside me looking at the dogs with a kind of contempt as if she hated each one of them.

"The dogs look listless somehow," I said. "Are they well? They've lost weight."

"They're fine. They're going through a purge and a period of adjustment. I plan to transform them into vegetarians. Before I arrived at Belle Reve, Mia was actually giving them a diet of all this disgusting meat, cooked rare, practically oozing with blood. I found the idea nauseating and put a stop to it."

I turned from her and the deprived dogs and went to the cabana dressing room with Rafael at my side.

Dino was already here checking out his looks in my brightly lit mirror. It seemed that he was preparing to go before the cameras and not me. Seeing me come in with Rafael, he glanced up. "Jerry thinks I could play the part better than Cruz," Dino said, "but Cruz had the gall to show up today anyway. He's ready to roll." An ominous look came over his face. "Last night Jerry promised me that if something happened to Cruz, I'd get the part."

"Nothing's going to happen to Cruz. Besides, if he bows out for some reason after a week or two of shooting, I'm going to recommend Sean Nielson for the role."

He shot me a look of anger and bitterness. It wasn't quite the look of the eighty-year-old hatemonger outside the gates of Belle Reve, and it didn't have quite the same jealous contempt of Anishi's, but it was still a look that could kill. Not only Cruz stood in his way this morning, but now I seemed to be a road block to his movie stardom. Without saying any more, he stormed out of my dressing room.

"I'm sorry, my pet," Rafael said. "The boy was away from his papa for too long. He learned too many bad habits from too many bad people."

"I know." I wanted to shift the attention away from Dino. "I want you to do me a big favor. Get on the phone and order me twenty-one of the best prime sirloins in town."

"You must be very hungry."

"Right now, I couldn't eat a thing, but I know seven dogs that can."

. . .

The atmosphere was tense and uncomfortable as cast and crew gathered for the first day of the shooting. Shooting in this sense had a double meaning. We were not only shooting a film, but I was also supposed to evoke a realistic sense of shooting Cruz with a gun as the dramatic highlight of the film. My character, Leonora de la Mer, could not tolerate his abandoning her for a younger woman. I never liked the script, and even now as I began to shoot the film's climatic scene on the first day, I wondered why I'd ever accepted the part. What movie audience in any theater in the world could ever believe that a man would walk out on Sherry Kelly for another woman, regardless of how young?

Cruz was polite, courteous, and professional in all regards, although not particularly effusive as he and I chatted briefly before the scene began. Once again, I extended an invitation to dinner at my rented villa, and once again, ever so graciously, he declined. Cruz had a nervous energy about himself this morning, as if he'd been trapped with the wrong co-star in the wrong film and wanted to escape from both of them.

In the distance, Anishi kept a hawkeye on the proceedings, although she didn't approach us. At any minute, I expected her to shout "CUT" and intervene over some real or imagined infraction of the terms of the contract she'd negotiated with Jerry. She certainly didn't try to interact in any way with Cruz, and it occurred to me that she might not even know who he was. She didn't look like a woman who attended movies, or paid much attention to movie stars or to the ins and outs of the film industry.

While waiting for the film crew to set up, I wandered alone into the patio. Rafael was chatting with two cameramen, inspecting their photographic equipment. Dino had mysteriously disappeared. Anishi rose from her divan, where she had arranged herself like an empress, and moved menacingly as if she were about to challenge my presence upon the patio. But when Jerry approached her with a problem he was having with the lighting, it momentarily distracted her.

Pretending to inspect the world-class sculpture in the garden, including works by Rodin and Barbara Hepworth, I ever so slowly moved into position closer to the second-floor balcony that opened off Mia's suite. She always preferred to be cooled by ceiling fans and sea breezes instead of air conditioning.

Concealed behind hibiscus, I gazed up at the balcony as a vision of cerise and chartreuse suddenly appeared in her nightgown. It was a scene I'd witnessed often during my childhood. She wore sunglasses whose frames were encased with pearls, something Joan Collins might have acquired to pose for a magazine cover. Although the sun cast a glare, I could clearly see her, even though she stood quite a distance away. She was more radiant than any movie star, even more radiant than me, although it was I who in just a few minutes would be facing those cruel cameras. I never knew if my Mommie were truly as beautiful as she appeared, or if part of her radiance was because of her money and power.

A manservant appeared on the balcony, handing a telephone receiver to her. "Your call to Ms. Taylor is going through, madam."

Rather obsessively, Mommie always tried to place calls to Ms. Taylor whenever she could. Sometimes the star would take her calls; at other times Ms. Taylor was too busy, or too involved, to deal with a fan who disconcertingly seemed to mimic the star's frequent physical changes.

"Elizabeth, darling," I heard Mia say. "It's still early morning here in lil 'ole Key West, but I know it's still late at night out there where you are. How glad I am you're up and about." After some preliminary chitchat, some of which I couldn't hear very well, Mia, in her clearest tone, said, "By the way, I have decided to grant your request. I'm sending you two-million dollars for AIDS research, although I don't know how AIDS particularly affects me. I make it a point never go to bed with anyone who is HIV positive. In fact, I'm not going to bed with anyone these days, my schedule being what it is, although I'm very lusty, very horny, and just about ready for another love affair."

Apparently, Ms. Taylor had a rather lengthy response to that, and it was a few minutes before Mommie said anything else. "In the old days, before AIDS, people wanted money from me for about a thousand different causes. Civil rights, civil liberties, civil service, things like that. And believe me, I did my bit on a very personal level for the Civil Rights movement. I even fucked Martin Luther King Jr."

At this moment, Jerry, master of the inappropriate, hysterically waved his arms for me to return to the living room to shoot the stairwell scene. When he spotted me in the garden, Maxie began rushing toward me to check my costume and makeup. Fearing all this commotion would alert Mia to my presence below her window, I retreated quietly from my stake-out and walked rapidly toward the living room.

A technician was waiting with Mommie's jewel-encrusted revolver, the one allegedly owned by Alexander the Great. He had not rehearsed the scene with me before, because Jerry wanted to capture my hesitancy, not only in shooting Cruz, but also my reluctance to use the weapon I now fingered so gingerly. Any instrument of death, even a kitchen knife, always held great terror for me. I don't think Mia had ever used the revolver either, although it had remained beside her bed as a lethal ornament ever since Daddy Kelly had given it to her in 1953. That rapist for whom it was intended never materialized.

Just to get the feel of the revolver, I held the gun and pointed it toward the stairwell that I would soon be descending with dramatic flair. "I trust this gun is loaded only with blanks?" I said, turning to the technician.

"It is, I assure you."

At this point, Anishi appeared in front of me. She reached for the revolver, firmly removing it from my hand. I reluctantly surrendered it.

"Mia has demanded to see the revolver before shooting begins," she said. "She plans to count every gem on the barrel. If one gem is removed, damaged, or tampered with, there will be very big trouble." Grandly, she walked away, mounting the stairs toward Mia's suite.

I looked at the technician. "What a bitch! That one has the nerve! Imagine? Implying that I might be a jewel thief. If I wanted any god damn jewelry, I'd go out and buy it." The technician looked at me strangely, almost as if he didn't believe me. "I'm very rich, you know," I said, a little too loudly and a little too defensively.

"Yes, ma'am, I've heard that."

I welcomed the attention of Maxie running over to check my makeup again. It seemed I must be coming unglued if I felt compelled in any way to explain to a technician that I wasn't poor. That's what Anishi and Mia had done to me, not to mention that damn Jerry. Of all the houses he could have used for Sacre-Coeur, he didn't have to rent Belle Reve. How could I concentrate on playing my character, when I was surrounded by all this other crap?

After Maxie had finished with me, Rafael came over and started to kiss me to wish me luck. But Maxie quickly intervened, warning him not to mess up my makeup. "If you need to kiss someone, make it me," he said, puckering up.

"Some other time." Rafael smiled, guiding me to the stairwell. At the top of the stairs, Anishi appeared and returned Mia's revolver to the technician. Apparently, Mia had examined and counted every gem along the gun's barrel, and carefully appraised the gold filigree work as well. Cruz appeared behind me wearing a tank top and a pair of blue jeans, one part of which was artfully ripped to expose his kneecap. It was an outfit Dino might have worn, perhaps even more successfully.

"Good luck!" was all he said to me before turning for some last-minute pointers from Jerry.

With a mounting dread and an awful sense of apprehension, I ascended the stairs, the same steps I'd used thousands of times as a child, to take possession of the revolver.

. . .

Jerry rushed up the stairs with some last-minute directions, but I wasn't really paying attention. I'd already decided how I was going to play the scene, and his directives annoyed me. Last night, Rafael had removed the bullets from his revolver, and we had enacted the scene several times in my rented villa. He was such a good and convincing actor that I realized he could play the part as well or even better than Cruz. Fortunately, Dino was away entertaining Jerry all night, so I didn't have to get him involved in the rehearsal, thereby falsely raising his expectations.

Cruz came to the landing of the staircase and was checked by a female makeup artist. Maxie had been rejected as the makeup artist, as he wasn't Cruz's kind of guy, although Maxwell LaLanne knew more about makeup than anyone else in Hollywood, with the possible exception of the late Joan Crawford. There were those among his admirers who claimed that Maxie had invented makeup.

Cruz gave me a little "Hi" sign before turning his back to me. Out of the shadows on the stairwell appeared Maxie, who made one final adjustment to my eye shadow. According to the script, it was dawn at Sacre-Coeur, and I was to appear in my nightgown, having been aroused from my sleep by my butler who'd informed me that Cruz, playing the role of Numie, was leaving me. The white nightgown I wore was low-cut, filmy, and very revealing, as were most of my film costumes. I didn't specialize in nun parts. Maxie retrieved Mia's revolver for me. Just handling the weapon caused me to shake visibly, as I have always had a terror of firearms. I fondled the revolver, giving it the respect I always afforded a lethal weapon. I held it firmly in my hand and signaled Jerry I was ready.

From below, the cameras moved toward me menacingly, as I appeared before them in full voluptuous figure. Everything from my gold high heels to my carefully coiffed, soft hair was perfect. Cruz had been filmed going down the stairs from my bedroom carrying a small suitcase, representing all the possessions he owned, having abandoned forever the jewelry and the well-tailored wardrobe I'd purchased for him. He was leaving Sacre-Coeur much as he'd arrived here, with only the clothes on his back.

"Don't leave me," I shrilled hysterically down to him.

He turned and looked up at me, not seeing the revolver I'd concealed behind my back. "It's too late, Leonora," he said. "I should never have come here in the first place."

"If you leave me, I'll kill myself."

The camera caught the skepticism and contempt permeating his face. "A thousand men have walked out on you. What's one more? Of all the men you've bedded, I'm the least important." With that, he spun on his heel and walked down the steps.

I slowly aimed the revolver at him. As the camera moved in for my close-up, I appeared demented, hysterical, and crazed with vengeance and passion. The next closeup focused entirely on the revolver, whose elaborate tooling and glittering gemstones winked seductively under the intense lights. Despite the fact that everyone outside the camera's view was concealed in relative darkness, I seemed to feel the presence of Anishi, who stood about twenty feet away in the vast second-floor hallway of Mia's mansion. I hated having that woman witness my every action.

As the script called for, I aimed the revolver at him and fired. He let out a shriek not called for in the script, and then a sudden exhalation of breath. Blood suddenly appeared on the bare skin of his shoulder. At first, I thought it was stage blood. He turned around and glared up at me with genuine pain and fury, yet another scene not contained within the script. It was a look I would carry with me for the rest of my life. Within seconds that look changed to that of a deer gazing imploringly into the face of an armed hunter about to end its too-short life. Within a heartbeat, his eyes grew heavy-lidded and he stumbled back before tumbling limply down the long staircase.

I dropped the revolver in shock, exactly as the script called for, but I would have let it go anyway. Sensing that there was something unlucky about it, I could no longer hold it in my hand. When I saw him falling backward down those steps, and two members of the film crew rushing to his aid, I knew that we'd gone from the script into real life. In this cinematic world of make-believe, the bullet had been real.

Appearing from the back hallway, Rafael braced me, or otherwise I, too, would have fallen down the long staircase. The technician reached to retrieve the revolver on the floor, although I knew at once he shouldn't have. It had now become a murder weapon, and he seemed to be deliberately tampering with the evidence.

From the bottom of the stairwell where Cruz lay on the cold marble floor, I heard Jerry screaming hysterically.

Anishi suddenly approached me from behind, and I whirled to defend myself as she came menacingly close. "Look what you've done now!" she said before rushing down the stairs.

From the bottom of the landing reverberated the words I so dreaded hearing: "HE'S DEAD!"

A gofer on the set raced to grab the hall phone. He no longer felt compelled to conceal his identity, that of a media spy. Once he'd reached his contact, he bluntly stated the story. "In Key West this morning, Sherry Kelly, on the set of 'Butterflies in Heat,' fatally shot actor Brad Cruz in a series of not fully explained events." Showing all the talent of a skilled professional journalist, he then started to spin out the background to the incredible story, but my mind could no longer absorb details. I clung to Rafael for support, but I knew I was sinking into a dark abyss. He seemed to sense that too, and picked me up to carry me to an empty bedroom as Maxie rushed ahead of him, opening doors, trying to find a suitable place for me to lie down.

With all the force left in my body, I gripped Rafael's arm. "I didn't do it. Tell me it never happened."

He said nothing but gripped me tighter.

Dimly, I looked around the bedroom where they had taken

me. It was my childhood room. I felt comfortable here, as if I'd returned to familiar ground after having completed a perilous journey.

I suddenly jerked up in bed. A technician monitoring a CNN broadcast had amplified the sound so that the news blasted all over Belle Reve. Everyone in this vast mansion, including Mia herself, could hear the first of what would, I'm sure, become thousands of news reports.

"We interrupt this program to bring you a bulletin from Key West, Florida."

A different voice, that of another announcer, came on the air, "Reports are sketchy and as yet unconfirmed," the announcer said, his voice booming all over the house. "While filming a movie, Sherry Kelly accidentally but fatally shot Brad Cruz. The world's richest actress, in front of dozens of witnesses, shot the world's most popular actor during the filming of a movie they were making, 'Butterflies in Heat.' Our sources tell us this happened as part of the movie's predetermined plot. But in a scene that tragically strayed from the script, the gun Ms. Kelly was holding fired real bullets instead of blanks. Complicating this bizarre story even further, these events took place in the historic mansion owned and occupied by Sherry Kelly's estranged mother, Mia Kelly. Key West police have surrounded the murder house, letting none of the building's dozens of occupants out pending further questioning. Thousands of curiosity seekers, both locals and tourists, are rushing to the scene of the shooting."

The sound suddenly died. Someone had obviously pulled the plug.

A sudden commotion near the open door to my bedroom alerted me to the cold fury of Mia. To my amazement, she was supported on the arm of Dino. Even though she still wore those pearl-encrusted sunglasses, I could feel her accusatory eyes boring in on me. "You killed him. Right in my own home. In front of witnesses. How could you do this to me?"

My pent-up nerves and overtaxed brain mercifully intervened to give my mind the rest it needed. I fainted.

. . .

"HE'S ALIVE!"

The voice I recognized was that of Rafael, and the news was the best I could have heard. I came to full consciousness and looked into his reassuring eyes. Hovering beside my bed, he held onto my hand, giving me the courage I so desperately needed. In a neutral, non-emotional voice, he gave me the details. "The bullet entered his left shoulder. He was rushed to Florida Keys Memorial Hospital, then moved to the orthopedic ward of a better-equipped hospital in Coral Gables after Ted chartered a plane in your name. Specialists were waiting there to examine the wound. At last reports, he was conscious and talking to his lawyers."

My old bedroom was dark, and at first, I thought he'd pulled the heavy black draperies I always insisted on having installed in each of my bedrooms so that I could make the day black whenever I wanted. But when I saw that the draperies were open, I realized that it was night. "The last thing I remembered," I said feebly, "it was early morning. What happened to the day?"

"Ted was a genius. I think this mariposa has been around movie-star scandals before. A few moments after you fainted, he administered some kind of injection. I've been here with you all day. You were breathing regularly but never woke up."

"Then I've spoken to no one until now?"

"Apparently, that was part of Ted's plan. Belle Reve has been swimming with the sheriff, his staff, and all sorts of law enforcement people. But you had passed into a coma and couldn't be questioned by anyone."

Thank God for Ted and thank God that Cruz is alive."

Because you've remained in a coma all day, David had time to fly to Key West on a chartered plane, along with his damage-control crew. He's issued several official bulletins from Belle Reve. At first, Mia refused to allow him to even enter the premises. He forced his way in. Everyone heard them. Their dialogue really got nasty."

"Mia must be hysterical with this invasion of her sacred house."

"She is. So is Anishi. If Mia is hysterical, Anishi is positively shrieking. She blames you for planning this whole thing just so you could sneak back into Belle Reve."

"What brilliant logic. I'd shoot Cruz to get back into Belle Reve?"

"So far, the sheriff hasn't let anybody leave. All the film crew are still here, even though Mia and Anishi are violently objecting. Mia's own lawyers are flying in, and I expect when they clash with David's blue-suited boys, there will be fireworks."

"This is a nightmare. I can't believe it's happening."

"It's happening, all right, and the question everybody is asking is who put the real bullet in that revolver. It was a 35 caliber, the same bullets I use in my own weapons."

"Am I a suspect?"

"Everybody is. It turns out that many people had access to that revolver when no one was looking. Even me. I'm a suspect too. As if I wasn't already in enough trouble with the government with the case pending against me for air piracy."

"It's insane that I would put a real bullet into that gun. Why would I want to kill Cruz? This is going to cost me millions. Think of the lawsuits alone."

"There will be plenty of those. But no one seriously thinks you're the culprit. Some people think I might have done it. But the list of suspects is long. Me, of course, Mia herself. Certainly Anishi. Ted, Maxie, and a dozen other film crew members. Even Dino."

"Dino?" I sat up in bed. "He was alone with that revolver?"

"Yes, when Anishi brought the gun to Mia's bedroom, your mama was talking to my son."

"He insinuated himself into Mommie's bedroom? How was that possible? What does Mommie have to do with him?"

"I haven't spoken to him alone yet. I'm going to grill him. When Anishi brought the revolver to Mia's bedroom, she was in the bathroom adjusting her makeup."

"That I could believe. She always does that when confronted with a handsome young man, regardless of his age. She has never insisted that a man be of any particular age. Only past puberty."

"He was alone in the bedroom for at least four minutes before Mia came out."

"He wanted Cruz out of the way so he could play the part of Numie himself, but I hardly think he's stupid enough to put a real bullet in the gun. I don't think he wanted the part bad enough to kill for it."

"I don't think he did it either, but I'll conduct my own investigation. Frankly, I think Anishi put the real bullet in. She's capable of anything--that one."

I caressed his cheek. It gave me comfort to think Dino wasn't involved. "I'm in such a coma I can't think straight." I wrapped my arms around him, stifling a sob. "I need you so. Don't ever leave me."

"I'll be here for you."

"I hate to break up this enchanting love scene, but it's not the final reel yet." The voice was deep-throated and stiffly formal, yet somehow familiar, like the sound of a long-ago lover.

I opened my clouded eyes to stare into the stern face of David.

. . .

Jolting up in bed, and breaking from Rafael, I had a momentary pang of guilt, as if David were my husband who had caught me in the arms of another man. In my still-dazed glow, I'd forgotten that he was now my attorney and no longer my attorney/lover. "David," I said sharply, quickly regaining a grip on my emotions. "Doors were made to be knocked on!"

"Forgive me, my pet, but I wanted to get to you before anybody else. A lot of people are scheming to talk to you, but I'm first."

"I already beat you to it," Rafael said, standing stiffly and looking jealous and suddenly threatened. I didn't know what, if anything, he knew about my past dalliance with David. "Do you want me to leave?" Rafael asked.

"No, stay," I said, possessively linking my hand with his.

"I'd prefer to talk to my client alone," David said to Rafael, "but if she insists..."

"I insist."

"This place is a madhouse," David said. "There are a thousand plots and subplots unraveling here. Everybody has an agenda, it seems. Blackmail. Fraud. Chicanery. Robbery. Extortion. Art theft. And not the least of all, attempted murder in front of witnesses. These are just some of the things my legal eye has seen since arriving back at Belle Reve, where I used to expect a bigger welcome."

Rafael looked confused.

"He was Mia's companion," I told Rafael, hoping to cover up the suspicion of any former romance between David and me.

"This man and your mama?" he said, as if he sensed there was a lot more going on here than he'd at first suspected.

"My job at the moment is not to figure out what everybody is doing," David said, "including your own son, Mr. Navarro. Incidentally, he's back to calling himself Dino Paglia."

"We know that," Rafael said.

"My job is to protect Sherry, and I've done that to the best of my ability. We've kept the press at bay. You'll still have to meet with some stiffs from Monroe County. They'll have a few questions, but I've managed to put their minds at ease. The story is you were just a victim. Of all the suspects, you have the perfect alibi. At no point were you ever alone with the weapon. Every time you held it, you were seen by somebody. There's no way you could have inserted real bullets into that damn revolver. Besides, as I'm sure you're going to figure out, this incident will cost you millions. Despite that, there's just no motive you'd ever have to shoot Cruz."

"Is he going to sue?"

"His lawyers are flying to Miami to meet with ours tomorrow. Cruz doesn't blame you for the shooting, and has told police he knows of no one connected with the film who might want him killed."

"I know who's behind it," I said. "Anishi Mishima."

"That's what I think too, although I haven't said that to the police," David said. "I have given them a lot of clues. Pointed their noses in that direction, you might say."

"Jerry must be in a rage," I said.

"What is going to happen to this movie is not an immediate concern," David said, "but my advice is to bail out of the project completely and cut your financial losses. Of course, we'll have to cope with a screaming, hysterical Jerry." His face grew stern. "I know you're in a lot of trouble yourself, Mr. Navarro. With the air piracy case and all."

"I want you to represent Rafael," I quickly interjected. "Take his case and bill my account for your labors."

David looked reluctant.

"For my sake," I added quickly.

"For your sake, I will," he said, "although our firm doesn't usually handle air piracy cases."

"It wasn't piracy," Rafael said. "I was fleeing for my life."

"I know," David said impatiently. "But charges are not being brought against you right this minute. We'll deal with your case another day. Let's get on to more immediate problems. Your son is one of the suspects. I don't know if you've told Sherry yet, but Dino was alone with the revolver in Mia's bedroom for at least four minutes while she was in her dressing room. The question of what Dino was doing in Mia's bedroom can wait for an answer on another day. He was there. Mia admits it. Dino admits it too."

"You're not suggesting a sexual liaison between Mia and my son?" Rafael asked, his face turning red. "Why, she's old enough to be his mama!"

David looked at me.

"No, I'm old enough to be his mother," I said, perhaps a bit too defensively. "Mia is old enough to be his grandmother."

"That's the world's most glamorous granny," David said.

"And you should know," Rafael said, as if he were accusing David.

"If Dino is a suspect," I said, "I want you to represent him. The boy, I just know in my heart, is innocent."

"I'll represent him too. Again, as a favor to you. With all the work you've given me, I'm not exactly chasing ambulances in Miami for cases these days."

"We did ask you to interrogate Martinez," Rafael said. "Any news...about my Tricia?"

"We have a full report. I regret very much to tell you this, Mr. Navarro, but your wife was abducted, imprisoned, tortured, and murdered in a Havana jail cell in 1978. It's a gruesome story, the kind I hate having to bring to light, but in three days we'll have most of the evidence. Video-taped confessions, things like that. Our agents are checking out the loose ends of Martinez's story right now. But the evidence is rather clear at this point. Oddly, Martinez is probably telling the truth for the first time in his life, and no one can really figure out why."

"Tricia," Rafael sobbed. "I could rip Martinez into pieces with my bare hands. Wait till I get my hands on that rotten piece of slime."

"Don't touch him," he said. "Don't ever touch him. If you and Sherry wish, our firm will find a way to deal with Martinez. But it will be legal. We'll at least get him deported back to Cuba. We haven't answered another important question yet. If Martinez were still viewed as a cohort of Castro, why did he come over to Florida in the first place? We suspect it was to cause a major act of sabotage. Perhaps an assassination. But we can't prove that yet. We'll have to watch him closely."

"I'm amazed that he talked to you," Rafael said to me. "Confided so much to you about my Tricia."

"So am I," David said. He looked over at me. "I'm sure Sherry must be surprised too."

Rafael caught David's expression and my own conspiratorial look, but he never asked any other questions.

"Mr. Navarro, I must ask that you excuse us now," David said. "Sherry is about to be asked some questions by the learned minds of law-enforcement in Monroe County. It has always been my policy to have a private meeting with one of my clients before any police interrogation begins. In this case, please view her as an actress and me as her director. Unfortunately, during such a briefing, I always insist on no witnesses."

"I understand and respect that," he said. He kissed me on the forehead and left the room, promising to return as soon as my briefing from David and the police interrogation were over.

"Sweetheart," he said after Rafael had left the room. "I've sized up these rednecks. They're awed at the prospect of meeting you. This is a moment they'll tell their grandchildren about. While you get dressed, I'll give you some pointers."

"What part do you want me to play?" The demure librarian?"

"No, my darling. I want you to dress exactly as you did during your now-infamous scene in 'Kinky.'"

. . .

As David looked on, perhaps enjoying a "remembrance of things past," I stood before a full-length mirror in the dressing room which adjoined my former bedroom. Fortunately, Mommie had not changed a thing. My wardrobe was intact, even jewelry I'd left behind.

I did notice a minor Renoir which Daddy Kelly had given me for my sixteenth birthday still on the wall. He'd wanted to place it over my bed, but for some reason, I've never been able to sleep in bedrooms containing Renoirs, and always insist that they be removed before I get a proper night's rest.

The dress I actually wore in "Kinky" had been placed in a safety vault in Trenton, New Jersey. No doubt it will be worth millions a century from now, and will be more famous than the white dress Marilyn Monroe wore in "The Seven Year Itch." I often stash objects of value in vaults in Trenton. What thief would ever think of going to Trenton to rob me?

From my old wardrobe, I managed to extract a low-cut white billowy dress that approximated the style of the dress worn in the film in which I flashed before the eager eyes of a stunned world. Only dear, sweet Maxie would have known the difference, but that hawkeye can tell if you've moved a false beauty mole one millimeter.

After applying heavy-duty war paint – all flaming lipstick red – I stood back to survey the results in the mirror.

"Skip the interrogation," he said. "I want to throw you on the floor and fuck you until the rooster crows tomorrow morning."

"You've done that before. Really, I love you these days for your legal skills, not your boudoir talents."

"You're charming... you always help me remember why I like you so much. Now be especially kinky, and get us out of this mess with the police."

After giving me instructions on what to say and do, he led me into a sunroom, now lit with lamps, which lay off the second floor of Mia's manse.

Here, I encountered Johnny Yellowwood, who represented the top law-enforcement authority in Monroe County. Mommie had summoned him here many times over the years to eject various servants she'd accused, often falsely, of stealing. I'd never met the gentleman before.

He bore an amazing resemblance to Andy Griffith – that is, an Andy Griffith from hell. On seeing me, he practically salivated. He was backed up by a chorus line of policemen in full uniform with guns, who obviously weren't needed for the interrogation, but who had come along for the show. I was the premier attraction.

David introduced us. As he'd instructed, I personally shook each cop's hand, although in at least three cases I had a hard time retrieving my paw.

"Ms. Kelly, although I've met that fine filly of a woman, your mama, I've never had the pleasure of gazing upon your eminence until tonight. 'Course, I've got videos of 'Kinky,' and in the men's room down at headquarters, we've got that nude centerfold of you. Might have to take it down, though, 'cause whenever some guys go into the can to take a crap, they're usually gone for half an hour or so."

"Mr. Yellowwood, you flatter me."

"Call me Snake. I don't know you well enough to tell you how I got the name Snake."

"Please leave that to my imagination."

"You don't have to imagine it, if you get my drift."

"I get it." I smiled demurely. "You don't dress like a cop at all."

"No, ma'am, I find that it puts folks at ease if I don't show up in my full ball-clanking cop drag."

"I especially like men wearing white shoes, a Panama hat, white pants, and a flowered Hawaiian shirt just like what you're wearing now. That's just what that old ball-clanking President Truman used to wear when he visited the Little White House in Key West."

"I remember him, and the shirts he wore. Of course, I was just a kid when Truman came here. The years have passed, but I'm still as good as ever. No woman ever complains about meeting Snake and especially Snake Junior."

"I'm sure they don't."

David ushered me to a chair discreetly placed, no doubt by himself, ten feet in front of the men for my interrogation. I deliberately didn't cross my legs, although I knew they were waiting in anticipation. David stood beside my chair, like a Prince Consort in attendance to a reigning female monarch, waiting to answer any question or to object to any line of questioning he felt might be incriminating.

Snake was a virtual hound dog panting in an August heat wave. "I must say it's shore hot in here."

I moved my legs as if to cross them but rested them in my second most tantalizing way, as if at any minute they would take off with a life of their own and wrap themselves around a man's neck. The staff of cops was mesmerized.

"About this shooting," Snake said, taking off his Panama hat and wiping his brow. "I must say, you are one hell of a good-looking woman. I start slobbering when I get around a woman like you. Not that there are any women like you." He yelled to his assistant. "Slim, bring me some god damn Kleenex in here!"

Slim rushed to the bathroom obeying the command, as Snake turned back to me. "We should call him Fart since that's all he ever does. He's also got the smallest dick in Monroe County, where the competition is keen. Not that I was ever a candidate in *that* particular contest. Not on your life."

David interrupted. "This is all very interesting, but Ms. Kelly has had a bad day and needs her rest. You must proceed with the questioning."

Slim came back with the Kleenex and Snake wiped his face. "Your attorney tells me that at no time were you alone with your mama's revolver. Is that true?"

"That's right," I said.

"And certainly I think everyone in the room can agree that since this shooting is gonna cost you millions, you were about the last person who wanted Cruz dead."

"That is an obvious conclusion," David said.

"I also understand that this Cuban bodyguard of yours also wasn't alone with the gun," Snake said. "That right?"

"Rafael Navarro was with me at all times. Never once did he touch the revolver."

"What about this wop kid, Dino Paglia?" Snake asked. "I hear he was alone with the gun for four or five minutes in your mama's boudoir. I also heard that you and this hot little stud...how shall I say this.. *know* each other. That's know as in David *knew* Bathsheba."

"Dino Paglia and I were lovers." At this point I crossed my

legs, but discreetly. The men leaned forward and Snake's sweat became a running river. But I let them only see as far as San Diego--not all the way to Honolulu.

"What motive would this kid have to want Cruz killed?" Snake asked, becoming almost visibly aroused at my presence.

"None whatsoever," I said, although David had started to object that it was unnecessary for me to answer such a question. "He literally worshipped Cruz. He had a large picture of the famous frontal nude of Cruz in that film...oh I forget its name. Dino insisted on putting the Cruz picture over our bed when he made love to me."

David looked astonished.

Snake, however, seemed to accept that. "We certainly have enough men like that in Key West, so I understand your predicament. Too bad you of all people couldn't find a real man."

"They're so hard to find."

"I know...I know," he said. "Just like they are in Key West." He laughed hysterically. "That's why old Snake here is kept so busy. I say, 'send down more fags.' That way, I'll have more women to myself."

"I see the advantages for you."

"That rules Dino Paglia out as a suspect, and I hardly consider your mama a suspect. She had no motive, other than to get this god damn film crew out of her house."

"That would be a relief for her, I'm sure."

"It seems these two swishes who work for you--Ted and Maxie." He turned a smirking face to Slim beside him. "Don't you love it?" Then he looked back at me, or rather at my legs. "It seems they too had brief moments alone with the weapon."

"Those two! The only guns they've ever handled were behind the zippers of a man's trousers."

Snake laughed at that. "I guess you're right. I can rule those two queenies out as suspects. Now about those film technicians..."

Before Snake could formulate his question, David interrupted. "Ms. Kelly does not know any of the film crew and had never met any of them before today. She knows only the producer and director of the film, Jerry Wheeler, and you've already established that he never even handled the revolver."

"I met that swish too," Snake said. "Is he hysterical! Like you, he's about the last person who would want Cruz dead. His movie is being flushed down the toilet."

"There is one suspect you haven't mentioned," I said. I felt the pressure of David's hand on my shoulder, a long-established signal between us for me to keep quiet. I ignored it. "Anishi Mishima. She not only took the gun from the technician, but she disappeared down the hallway with it. I personally saw her go into a powder room with the revolver. She was in that room for five minutes during which time she could have reloaded the gun with real bullets. Her motive? She wants to make more trouble for me. She wants me in deep shit. She's trying to grab my Mommie's fortune. Check it out."

"Wow!" Snake said, sitting up. "She did admit to taking the gun from the film technician. Her story is that she was carrying it to your mama's bedroom so that she and Mia could inspect it in case someone had removed one of them jewels. No one ever said anything about her going into that powder room alone!"

"I saw it with my own eyes," I said. "I think that in the confusion and hysteria, no one noticed it but me. But I keep an eye on that one since I don't trust her for a minute, even *in* my sight, much less out of my sight."

"Makes sense to me," Snake said. He turned to look at his crew, none of whom seemed to be paying attention to the interrogation. "I think Ms. Kelly here has led us to our first real suspect."

"Is Ms. Kelly free to go?" David asked.

"Yeah, I guess so," Snake said. "How about a little supper with me later tonight?"

"Sounds fine with me, but I've made other plans. That Snake Junior sounds like a mighty interesting fellow."

"He is, ma'am, he is indeed." The sweat was once again pouring from Snake.

"I'll take a raincheck," I said coyly.

"That's a promise I'm gonna hold you to, ma'am." He demanded that Slim hand him a piece of paper and a pencil. He scribbled a phone number and handed it to me. "Here's my private number. You call me here any time of the day or night. In this county, you have nothing to fear. I'll take care of everything for you in more ways than one."

"I'm honored."

"Is my client and her bodyguard free to leave the grounds?" David asked.

"They are indeed, but no one else is. At least not for the moment."

"Snake," I said in my most enticing, come-eat-my-pussy voice. "Will you do me one teeny tiny little favor?"

"You name it, though in my case, 'teeny tiny' seems hardly appropriate."

"How nice! But please, don't tell Mia or anyone else--just your guards at the gate--that Rafael and I are free to leave. Since I made 'Kinky' and posed for that nude centerfold..." I paused and crossed my legs a bit more. The airplane had definitely departed from San Diego and was heading for Honolulu. "Mommie forbade me to come back to Belle Reve. But I want to stay here long enough to persuade her to take me back and get rid of that Anishi."

"That sounds like a reasonable request to me," he said.

David looked at me in total astonishment, not comprehending why I wanted to remain at Belle Reve when I was free to go.

"Thank you, Snake. I'll owe you one." The plane was about to land in Honolulu. I raised my right leg a little higher. Honolulu had come into view.

. . .

Later that night, Belle Reve – now under press and police siege – was supposed to be settling down for a long tropical nap before the excitement of another morning. I sat with Rafael on the balcony of my childhood overlooking the sea. He held my hand firmly to offer me comfort and security. This former Communist was encased in one of America's hotbeds of capitalism, as represented by Mia and me, and at times I wondered if the poor man knew what had happened to him. It had all been too fast. Although only hours before he'd been a stranger to me, he had become virtually overnight the most important person in my life.

"America is a fantasy," he whispered softly, as if speaking

to the night breezes instead of to me. "The fancy limousines, the glittering mansions, the fabled art, miles of precious gold and diamonds...and the women. Your mama and you. You don't look like real women at all, but female fantasies, the kind fourteen-year-old boys have wet dreams about."

"Mommie and I are just your typical mother and daughter."

"I doubt that, but you're the only family I want." He lifted my hand to his lips and slowly and ever so seductively began to gently devour finger after finger. By the time he'd reached the pinkie, a noise from the courtyard below shattered the quietness of the Key West night.

Dino and Mia had entered the patio. In the soft, forgiving pink lights which illuminated the garden's many fountains, they looked like a fantasy indeed, almost as if posing for some perfume ad or perhaps the cover of a romantic novel. Even though we couldn't see her face very well, she appeared radiant, her gown billowing in the night breeze. Dino's tight-fitting white pants and white long-sleeved shirt matched his perfect white teeth. His next modeling assignment should be a toothpaste commercial.

With Rafael at my side, I stood back, concealed in the shadows of my balcony, but still within full view of the events transpiring below. Rafael and I were voyeurs, and I felt guilty invading the privacy of others. Still, the scene was too compelling to avoid watching.

In the silhouette of night, Mia and Dino could have been young lovers. Age and the changes decades bring didn't seem to matter at all to these two partners right now. He was at least a foot and a half taller than her, and he seemed to tower over her as he pulled her close. Here they lingered, as if glued to each other with no possibility of ever coming apart.

A harsher, less forgiving set of lights was suddenly switched on, evocative of a row of police spotlights. In a long, slinky red silk gown, split high up the thigh, Anishi stormed onto the patio, destroying both the romance and the illusion.

"Why are you cheapening yourself with this scumbag Mexican hustler?" Her voice pierced the night.

"I'm not a god-damn Mexican. I'm Italian. The Italian stallion."

Mia braced herself against a nude, larger-than-life copy of

Michelangelo's David. "Who I entertain in the privacy of my home is my own affair. Need I remind you who it was who brought this crummy film crew into Belle Reve? But like the ill wind, it did blow some good. It brought me this devastatingly handsome young man. My daughter's trick. When Sherry discovers he prefers me to her, she'll die. She'll just die. Now get the fuck off this patio, turn off those lights, and leave us alone to continue our unfinished business."

"He's just a kid, and a filthy one at that," Anishi charged.

He seemed two feet taller than Anishi. Just as he'd towered romantically over Mia, now he towered menacingly over Anishi, blocking her view and access to Mia. "Kid! You said kid? KID? How old do I have to be? Just because I wasn't sucking off Jap soldiers before they got into their planes to bomb Pearl Harbor doesn't mean a god-damn thing. I'm here now. I'm alive. Mia and I have found each other. She's just what I've been looking for all my *short* life."

"You're out for a meal ticket and nothing else." Anishi tried to peer around Dino to stare at Mia, but he blocked her approach.

"Meal ticket!" he blurted out with a rage and fury which Sherry had never heard in his voice before. "Like, America's highest paid male model needs a meal ticket. You're one to talk about meal tickets. You broken down yellow whore. I know all about you. You're a bloodsucker. A vampire of death who descends like a giant bat onto the rich. You take and take like a parasite until your host is ready to have you arrested, and then you flee into the night with your stolen goods. Let's face it, Ms. Teriyaki, you're yesterday. I'm today."

"I know more about life than a punk like you will ever know. I have wisdom. I have experience. I will bring Mia her youth again. My elixir."

"To hell with your fucking elixir. What is in those injections anyway? Speed? You're shooting speed into Mia's veins? Making her think that will make her young again?" He reached for Mia and possessively held her. "I'll make her young again. By loving her. I'll give. Not take like you."

"You dirty rotten little bastard," Anishi said. "You'll pay for this." She seemed on the verge of tears. It was like a real emotion, not one faked for Mia's benefit. Anishi spoke directly to Mia as if he had disappeared from the picture. Her voice was suddenly soft, but compelling, luring one into a web.

I still stood on my balcony, squeezing Rafael's hand.

"Tomorrow when you come to your senses," Anishi told Mia, "tomorrow and only tomorrow, I will be here waiting for you. When this miserable crew is out of Belle Reve, we'll go back to the way we were."

"We'll see about that tomorrow," Mia said, in a harsh and strident voice that sounded amazingly like that of Martha in the Taylor/Burton film, "Who's Afraid of Virginia Woolf?" Mia had two voices, the more graceful of which evoked Dina Merrill, the aristocratic American actress and a woman of good manners, culture, and breeding. The second voice was that of Martha, an embittered shrew on a drunken night. Both voices could be summoned on command, and both were equally effective. "Right now," Mia shouted in her Martha voice, as if making an announcement to the world. "This delectable young man and I are retiring for the night to my beach cottage, at the far end of this property. The one with the picture windows opening onto a romantic view of the god damn sea. There, if my suspicions are correct – and I'm never wrong in such matters – I'm going to get one of the most memorable fuckings of my well-fucked life."

Rafael and I stood speechless as we watched Dino and Mia disappear into the night to launch their sexual escapade. Even before they'd faded from view, a plan had already taken shape in my mind.

"My darling, darling man," I said, gently brushing my tongue against his perfect lips, which tasted of wine. "You and I have a rendezvous tonight with a woman even more famous than Mommie."

. . .

Ted could not only get anybody in the world on the phone, living or dead – he had the unlisted number of God – but he could arrange anything. This included the private jet to Europe he was about to charter for me now.

After issuing instructions to him, I turned with a smile to face Rafael.

"Who is this famous woman we're going to meet? You've really got me intrigued."

"Her enigmatic smile, reproduced countless times around the world, has made her the enchantress of the ages. Next to Cleopatra, of course."

His eyes lit up. "You mean, La Giaconda? I fell in love with her when I was a six-year-old boy."

"Tonight you're going to meet the real lady herself--not the imitation."

"I can feel a stirring in my cajones."

"Put them on ice until later," I said in my most commanding voice. "We've got to move fast."

Although he was a man who liked to lead--a future president, no doubt – tonight he trailed me as we quietly slipped into the dimly lit second-floor hallway of Belle Reve. At that far end of the monumental corridor, a security guard slept in a chair. With all the action centering on the poolhouse which sheltered the thrashing passions of that mighty duo, Mia and Dino, not much appeared to be happening within the main house. Mercifully, the ever-watchful Anishi lived in the south wing of the house.

Tiptoeing across the hallway, I slowly opened the door to Mia's room. Again, luck was beside me. In her haste to sample the erotic charms of Dino, she'd forgotten to lock her door. Maybe with the security guard in place, she didn't think it necessary. Earlier that evening, I had made it my business to find out who would be on night duty, and had instructed Ted to learn the name of the Cuban guard's favorite wine. By the time he reported for night duty at Belle Reve, at least two bottles had been consumed with what the guard had declared as the best three lobsters he'd ever eaten.

Gently, Rafael shut the door behind us, as I entered Mia's room. Only the intense white light from a single spotlight illuminated a carefully delineated part of Mommie's bedroom. It seemed to form a halo over the portrait of Mona Lisa placed above the headboard.

Up close to him, I whispered in his ear. "That's my painting. Daddy Kelly gave it to me, and I've come to retrieve it. With your help."

"Sure you're not stealing? I don't want art theft added to my air-piracy charges."

"I'm sure. As I said, it's my painting."

"It may be wired." Shoes and all, he walked across Mia's satiny bed, as I gave a brief shudder, hoping that this would be the last time he ever got near her fabled bed which had provided hospitality to so many of the world's most famous men. Since she collected presidents, and since he was likely to be a future president, I had to be careful I didn't lose him to her.

After carefully checking the painting for an alarm, he didn't seem to think it was wired, and placed a calculated bet that no bell would go off if the painting was removed. This surprised me, as Mia knew perfectly well she couldn't report the loss of the painting even if it were ever stolen.

He took down the Mona Lisa, and for a brief moment seemed to cuddle the relatively small painting in his arms, as if reuniting with a long-lost love, perhaps even his Tricia.

Overcoming my momentary jealousy, I touched the painting. There were three small bumps in the upper right-hand corner, which I'd always searched for as a child. Daddy Kelly used to have me trace my fingers over these now-familiar bumps so I'd be able to recognize the painting by merely feeling it. The three little bumps were here. I was convinced that this was my stolen painting, and not some fake Mia had substituted at the last minute.

"Now, Smart Lady, how do you propose we escape from this heavily guarded house with La Giaconda?"

"Easy as pie." In the far corner of the room, I pressed a concealed button and a large armoire mysteriously rolled forward. Stepping behind it, I parted red-velvet draperies to reveal a hidden door. I pressed the combination and the door swung open, offering access to a cement stairway and a long, narrow tunnel.

"What the hell!" he said. "Just like something in the movies."

"Our avenue of escape. Follow me."

Without question, he trailed me through the musty tunnel which was automatically illuminated the moment we entered it.

After what seemed like a nearly endless journey, we finally reached the end of the tunnel and arrived at a simple but very thick steel door. Here, I pressed another combination which caused the door to open onto a view of a deserted beach. I walked out onto the sands in my high heels, something Marlene Dietrich could have done in one of her more maudlin movies. Not a person in sight, although I expected visitors at any minute.

"A tunnel?" he said. "I don't believe it. Why a tunnel? The way I figure it, Mia doesn't need to escape from bill collectors."

"Years ago, Mia was having a torrid affair with that raunchy old billionaire, J. Paul Getty. He told her he would never live at the edge of the sea the way she did in Key West. Kidnappers could appear out of the ocean, sweeping in well-organized commando raids from virtually anywhere to attack the house. As other famous people were kidnapped throughout the 60s and 70s, Mommie began to realize Getty was right. She'd been the victim of kidnapping attempts before, so she had this tunnel built at enormous expense. There's also an entrance that leads directly to my bedroom, as you'll discover later this morning. At least, I hope you will."

"I get it. At the first sign of an attack, you and Mia could run to safety."

"Exactly, the same way we're doing tonight." As he gently cradled the Mona Lisa, I stroked it too, as if that would somehow mysteriously protect her from harm. In the distance, the lights of a car blinked on and off three times, and then began moving closer and closer to us.

"Get down," he said as if issuing a military order to one of his former commando units. "They'll see us."

"Easy with our lady there," I cautioned him, still fearful for the safety of the Mona Lisa. "This limousine is reserved for us."

In minutes, Ted, accompanied by a uniformed driver, was ushering Rafael and me into the back seat of the cavernous limousine. Ted immediately took over the care and safeguarding of our precious cargo, as the handsome driver of the limousine – hopefully from a company I owned – drove immediately toward the Key West airport.

At the airport, a helicopter waited. As we got airborne, Ted settled into the back seat with La Gioconda and me. Rafael, reliving his former occupation as an aviator, preferred to sit up front with the pilot.

"I never know what to expect from you," Ted said to me. "First, trying to kill Cruz. Second, stealing the Mona Lisa. All in a day's work, but god, my nerves do suffer."

"My darling little cuntie," I said to Ted. "I'm going to triple your salary, but before the month is over, what you did tonight may be the smallest of the many favors I'll ask of you."

He kissed me on the cheek, even though I wished he wouldn't do that. I was never sure from moment to moment where his mouth had been. Judging from the satisfied smile on the face of that limo driver, I had a pretty good idea what he'd done en route to pick me up. I held his hand gently. I owed him a lot, and was grateful he'd come along to help me get through this dreadful time of my life. "About the other thing," I said to him in a soft voice.

He knew at once what I meant. "I checked your bedroom in that rented house. I looked right where you said. The bullets to Rafael's revolver are missing."

"You looked in the upper right-hand drawer?"

"I looked in every drawer. The bullets are gone. And you're right. That detective you asked me to hire confirmed that the same bullets used in Rafael's revolver could also be fired from Mia's revolver. I might know a lot about *guns*, but I don't know one bullet from another."

"Neither do I, but at least you've confirmed that someone could have taken one of Rafael's bullets and inserted the bullet into Mia's revolver."

"That's what our private dick says."

"That means Dino could have done it," I said. "Who else had access to our bedroom?"

"Dino, as you said. Rafael. Me. Maxie. The maid. The plumber. The air-conditioning man. The guy who came to sanitize the carpet. The people from the fabric place who strung up all those black-velvet draperies that you--like Elvis--always insist upon. Practically anybody at the house. I think we hired ten servants there, not counting the maintenance people who come and go. Are you going to tell Rafael?"

"Not yet. But I'm sure going to let David know what's happening. He must know in case that bullet is traced back to us. Dino is a crazy kid but I can't believe he would try to kill

Cruz so he could replace him for a hustler part in some stupid movie."

"Don't kid yourself. You know that lots of people have committed murder – well, almost –to get a part in a film. A few years ago when I still had my youth and beauty, I would have murdered for a good part. Today, people would even have someone killed to get a spot on a cheerleading squad, much less an important role in a film with you. These are competitive times, sugar."

"I refuse to believe that Dino had anything to do with this. It had to be somebody else. But who?"

"As I said, it could be anybody." I squeezed his hand again. "I can't trust anybody anymore." I gave him a reassuring smile. "Excluding present company."

"You can always trust me."

As I settled back in the rear seat of the helicopter, which was beginning its approach to the Miami airport, I wondered if I could trust even my dear friend Ted. Both Mia and I knew how easy it was to buy loyalty. But the moment an adversary topped your offer, the loyalty vanished.

"You hang around," I said to him.

"Even when you and Rafael are governing Cuba?" he asked.

"Even then. I'm sure I'll need you in Havana even more than I need you here."

As the helicopter landed at the Miami airport, Ted in his usual efficient way had arranged everything. By then, the Mona Lisa had been draped in black velvet, carefully padded, and placed into a hermetically-sealed crate. Ted had even arranged for a squadron of airport security guards to accompany us from the just-landed helicopter to the waiting 727. God knows what he had paid for all this, but when Ted traveled with me, I always saw that he had access to unlimited funds for bribes. It's just the way Sherry Kelly travels the world, and a girl can never be too careful.

Rafael looked at the transatlantic aircraft looming above us in astonishment. "We're flying out of Miami tonight?"

"No, darling, we're staying. She's going." I pointed to the Mona Lisa.

"Are there any other passengers?"

"She's the only passenger. The whole plane just to herself.

Mona deserves to fly in style."

I stood by Rafael's side as Ted rushed aboard the plane to make last-minute arrangements.

The next few minutes went by too slowly for my tastes, although everyone was operating at peak efficiency. I waved goodbye as the painting was taken aboard. Once Ted was satisfied that it was properly secured, he got off the plane and trotted over to join us.

"It's okay," he said to reassure me. "Everything's going to be fine. Her escorts will be waiting at the other end. Everybody, and I mean *everybody*, has been paid off. Your bankers over there must have bribed a hundred people. In response to my phone calls, they said that any request from Sherry Kelly gets their most serious consideration."

"Where's our lady going?" Rafael wanted to know.

"To the land of Strauss and strudel. To Austria. After the plane lands in Vienna, she'll be taken by private limousine to a salt cave in Land Salzburg, a technique I learned from the Nazis, who knew more than anybody about stashing paintings out of sight during times of stress." I turned to him and smiled. "Perhaps we'll go and visit her some day."

"I'd sure like that," he said, as a pink dawn was breaking across Miami's skyline. Standing with Rafael and Ted, no one said anything as the 727 carrying the world's most famous painting disappeared into the morning sky, heading back to the south of Europe from whence La Giaconda had been so rudely taken so long ago.

I rubbed the stubble of Rafael's bearded cheek. "And that, my darling man, is what you can do in the middle of the night on sudden notice if you possess unlimited funds. Now let's hustle ourselves back to Belle Reve and Key West on that helicopter before we're missed. Tunnel time again."

CHAPTER SIX

Bursting into my bedroom, Mommie dearest, Mia herself, looked radiant, as if every lusty cell in her oversexed body had been appeased by Dino. Although brimming with anger, a virtual Maggie the Cat in a rage, she looked as if she'd spent six weeks at a spa and had been worked over by at least three leading beauty clinic specialists.

"WHERE IS LA GIACONDA?" she screeched at me. Not even a good morning hello to her long-lost daughter.

At my side, after an almost sleepless night, Rafael stirred in bed.

Sitting up, hardly awake, I asked, "Do you mean the one at the Louvre? Or the real one?"

She glared at me. "Don't get smart-ass with me, cunt. You know exactly the one I'm talking about. The one you stole."

"If I'm not mistaken, you stole my painting from Star Island." "It was *my* painting. Always has been."

"I doubt that, unless Da Vinci personally gave it to you. I've been in bed here all night, and if you gaze upon this creature beside me, I'm sure you can see why."

Mia had spent her entire life playing out her most intimate moments in front of servants, waiters, chauffeurs, and boyfriends who came and went, and I do mean that literally. She viewed such people as mere background props. It was only when her attention was diverted to Rafael that she seemed to notice him at all. Sleepy-eyed, he sat up in bed, exposing more of his golden chest. A thick lock of hair dangled over his left eye in an especially tantalizing way.

She looked at him with rising interest. "Maybe it's these new contact lenses I'm wearing, but I could almost swear that this is an older clone of *my* new boyfriend, Dino."

I was certain that during the heavy love-making of the night before, Dino hadn't told her that his father was on the grounds sleeping with her daughter.

"Good morning, Ms. Kelly," he said in a slightly blurry voice. "It's a pleasure to meet you, although I would probably have chosen another occasion. Forgive me for not rising to greet you, but I'm naked."

"I know," she said, eying him with intense interest. "It looks like you've already risen to the occasion. We're talking tent city!"

He turned over in embarrassment.

"No need to pull back the sheets and reveal all," she said primly. "If you're in my daughter's bed, I can just imagine what's below those sheets. Sherry here, you see, is a size queen. I, on the other hand, have always pursued presidents, ambassadors, statesmen, great scientists and such artists as Picasso, regardless of penile dimensions."

"Yes, Mommie," I said, resenting and embarrassed at her reference to me. "We know what enlightened intellectual sessions you've had. Like on bent, nylon-covered knees giving Hubert Humphrey a blow-job at the Democratic Convention in Chicago."

She turned her violet-tinted eyes in rage at me. "So very like you. Reminding me of one of my more embarrassing indiscretions."

"Mommie, you've got to leave the room and let us get dressed."

"As soon as the sheriff okays it, I want you out of Belle Reve," she ranted. "Of course, you can leave this Latino god behind if that's your desire. Sloppy seconds, they so ungraciously call it, but in his case, I'll make an exception."

"I understand you also made an exception last night," I said in my most accusatory voice.

"Yes, daughter dearest, I did. I must say you do know how to pick men. But you've gone and ruined my moment of triumph--that of taking your young boyfriend away from you--by finding one who is obviously more experienced and even better-looking, if that's possible." She turned to him again. "Are you South American? For God's sake, don't tell me you're Mexican. You're not some wetback Sherry picked up after you'd crossed the Rio Grande in the nude? A lot of women are doing that these days. Mexicans are coming across the border without a stitch of clothing!"

"I'm a Cuban pilot who flew to my freedom in Miami."

"I thought I recognized you. You were on TV. Looking like a movie star. If only they'd remake 'Test Pilot.'"

"Some day in the very near future, I'm going to be president of Cuba. I'll invite you down for the inauguration. It's just a short flight from here. Maybe you'll make some investments in the newly democratic and capitalistic Cuba. Get our people working again. I'm Rafael Navarro."

Her reaction to the name was similar to my own. "Sounds like the silent screen star, Ramon Navarro. He was gay and Mexican too, if I remember. I get all you south-of-the-border types mixed up." She paused and then her eyes darted around the room as if expecting to see the Mona Lisa hanging on one of the walls. "I suppose since I'm the reluctant host, I should invite you for breakfast. I don't know if my Japanese chef knows how to prepare eggs ranchero, but I'll find some salsa in the kitchen and drip it on everything."

"That won't be necessary," he said politely.

"Hey," I said, sitting up rigidly and exposing my breasts. "I would love to have breakfast with you. After all, it's our mother-daughter reunion. It's been a long time, and I understand you have another daughter now. An adopted one."

"Another of my many embarrassments which I'm going to have to correct. My whole god damn life has been nothing but one embarrassing incident after another."

"We all feel that way at times," he said.

The sight of my exposed breasts seemed to remind Mia of my film career. "By the way, I didn't see 'Kinky,' but I heard it was beyond disgusting."

"I looked beautiful. Everyone told me that."

"Your beauty came from me, bitch. Don't ever forget that."

"While on the subject of your adopted daughter, and while on the subject of my purloined Mona Lisa, I have something to report. Just as I entered the corridor last night to go to bed, I spotted Anishi going into your bedroom. I assumed she was going to tuck you in and give you a Fountain of Youth injection."

"I wasn't in my bedroom last night. I was at the poolhouse auditioning. The young man must have enjoyed himself immensely. This morning, he proposed marriage."

"Marriage?" Rafael asked, dumbfounded. "You and Dino? Marriage?"

"I didn't say I accepted his proposal."

"We'll discuss your marriage proposals later," I said. "In

the meantime, I think you'd better consider Anishi your Mona Lisa prime suspect."

"I know the painting cannot have left Belle Reve," she said. 'The place is heavily guarded. Everybody is searched going in and out. I'm also having the entire house searched today, including the attics, the cellars, the crawl spaces, and especially this suite."

"Search all you want. I don't have the Mona Lisa." My last words stabbed the morning air.

She glared at me again and almost blurted out a response. Seeming to think better of it, she remained silent. After a moment's hesitancy, she said, "I'll see you two at breakfast. We do have some matters to go over." She turned and looked at me with a ferocity that was a bit frightening. "Like getting your much-photographed and overexposed ass out of Belle Reve just as fast as you hauled it in here." She softened both her features and her voice as she turned to say good-bye to Rafael. "Come casual to breakfast. I'll have one of my staff bring you a bikini. Remember, the sight of a male body does not offend me. Later, you can go for a swim. John F. Kennedy himself swam in my pool. Nude, of course. Robert Kennedy himself swam in the same pool. Nude, of course. Even darling Teddy Kennedy swam here. Nude, of course."

"None of those three was an impressive sight, believe me," I chimed in. "But when my date, John F. Kennedy Jr., came for a visit, he too swam nude. And you were much more impressed. Admit it!"

"Perhaps I was," she said enigmatically. "But then his endowment probably was part of the gene pool of his adorable grandfather, Black Jack Bouvier, through the legacy of my dear friend, Jacqueline. Junior, thankfully, managed to escape the curse of those other Kennedy men."

He didn't seem to know what we were talking about, although this was typical banter between Mia and me. It was also the signal that in spite of her protests, we were resuming our long-interrupted mother-daughter dialogue.

At the door, a vision in cerise, she paused once more in front of us. "We will discuss the whereabouts of Mona Lisa later. She's mine. But I do have something of yours. A diary. That little black book with all its disgusting secrets is definitely yours. Later, and we must be completely alone at the time, we'll go over some of the things you wrote." She turned and left.

. ° .

For the power breakfast, I wore a white cotton dress and a pair of white high-heel shoes, something Sharon Stone might pose in for a magazine layout – nothing too flashy, everything graceful and simple. Instead of the full haute couture drag a less appealing woman might have chosen, I decided to dress down, calling attention to my own natural beauty instead of to my wardrobe.

Mia, as promised, did have a bikini delivered to Rafael. It was sheer white, and I was sure that once he emerged from the water, it would be virtually transparent. Not wanting to expose that much of himself, he slipped a pair of white shorts on over the bikini, at least for breakfast. He was not a prudish man, and had nothing to hide, but as future president of Cuba, he wanted to maintain a certain decorum. He did appear without his shirt, however. I walked onto the patio with him on my arm.

Mia, minus her newly acquired possession, Dino, was already seated on the artfully arranged patio that resembled in an eerie way a stage set from "Suddenly Last Summer." When she'd begun to move into her 50s, she no longer appeared in clothing too revealing, except for plunging decolletage, of which she was justifiably proud. This morning, instead of calling attention to her body, she seemed to want to dress for power and money. Her tailored red dress and elegant shoes were something Nancy Reagan might have worn when she was running the Free World in the 1980s. In the pre-White House days, Mia and the actress, Nancy Davis, were never friends, and always made a point of avoiding each other if they encountered one another at cocktail parties. Mia had never made a play for Reagan, so that was not the cause of their feud.

Could it have been some silly thing like fighting over Peter Lawford long ago? Surely not Peter Lawford. That otherwise charming man claimed that Mia gave better blow-jobs than Nancy, and perhaps that had made Nancy jealous. Who knows? At any rate, during the Reagan administration, Mia didn't receive her customary invitations to the White House.

At the sight of Rafael and me, she rose to her feet and extended her hand to him, making too obvious a point in ignoring me. As I seated myself deliberately between Rafael and her, I gave my usual order to a Japanese servant, perhaps a spy working for Anishi for all I knew. Rafael ordered scrambled eggs and ham, like any red-blooded American boy, no doubt destroying Mia's preconceived idea of what Cubans ate for breakfast.

My breakfast arrived, and I ate heartily, barely listening as Mia and Rafael talked about his grandiose plans to unseat Castro. From the poolhouse, a sleepy Dino emerged completely nude and plunged into the pool, oblivious to our gathering on the patio.

"About that marriage proposal," I said to her. "Give us the Las Vegas odds about whether you'll accept."

She held up what looked like opera glasses to observe Dino's fine form in her swimming pool. The boy was a natural athlete. "Dino's a bit young but as you both can clearly see he's a real man."

The prospect of her marrying Dino was a bit much for me. Kissing Rafael after we'd eaten, I excused myself and headed back upstairs to my bedroom where I had some serious phone calls to make.

In the corridor, I encountered Anishi. She pulled me into one of the dozens of rarely used rooms within Mia's mansion, where drawn curtains blocked most of the streaming daylight. "I need to speak with you. It's very urgent."

Reluctantly, Mia's real daughter trailed the fake one into the too-dark room.

. . .

In a jade-green floor-length dress, Anishi stood in front of me wearing sunglasses so large that they nearly concealed her already-inscrutable face. My feelings about her were very mixed. On the one hand, I was prepared to treat her like the enemy and interloper I perceived her to be; yet another part of me responded to a vulnerability I never knew existed in her. In spite of her carefully conceived facade, she seemed just as afraid as the rest of us. Trust her? Forget it. My guard was up. In fact, I'd decided only that very morning that I couldn't trust anybody. Even now, my own Mommie could be moving in on Rafael the way she had on Dino.

"Ms. Mishima," I said, using my "Executive Suite" Barbara Stanwyck voice, "I don't think you and I have much to talk about. I want you out of Belle Reve sooner than later, and you are also determined to see me out the door. May the best woman win! We both know who that is!"

"Please," she said in a voice so soft and soothing it sounded dangerously hypnotic. A clever trick on her part. "A month ago, we might have had a certain confrontation, with me saying bitchy remarks to you, and you responding with even bitchier remarks to me. Let's face it: You're a bigger bitch than I ever was or ever could be!"

"You've got that right. So don't fuck with me. I've got a full day's agenda. You're wasting valuable time. Mine."

She flicked on a light switch, which illuminated the bulbs around an old-fashioned dressing mirror salvaged from the 1940s, the kind Broadway stage stars used to stare in while applying their before-curtain makeup. I stared at her face as reflected in the mirror. In spite of the sunglasses and heavy makeup, she appeared older than I'd thought at first.

Through dark glasses, she must have caught me eying her a little too intently. "It's true," she said, turning to face me, "I bear the telltale signs of having lived a not altogether perfect life."

"Notorious, from what I hear."

"Perhaps, but then, Mia and you aren't free from that charge either. Let's dispense with our personal histories. No one wants to look back. It was all too painful."

Growing impatient, I demanded to know, "What do you want with me?"

By the look on her face, I knew her answer to that question wouldn't be direct. "Every suspicion you've had about me--and we don't need to list them – is probably true. I did insinuate myself into this household. I needed a place for John and Henry, my sons. A place of luxury and comfort. All other doors had been closed to me. Mia was our meal ticket. She believed everything I told her about my injections."

"What are you shooting into her veins?"

"Nothing harmful. Some vitamins, a little energy boost...stuff like that. No Fountain of Youth elixir."

"Then you admit the injections are a fraud?"

"A harmless fraud, but they are effective in that they convince her that she's looking and feeling younger. Regrettable proof of that is her taking up with this young hustler, Dino Paglia. She really feels that she has the allure of a sixteen-year-old, and I think Dino convinced her of that, too."

"You're after her money, of course, money that rightly belongs to me."

"Not all her money--just enough to provide for John and Henry."

"You're too honest with me. That means you're lying."

"I've spent my life telling lies to people. Telling them what they wanted to hear. Telling the impotent they were virile. Telling the ugly they were beautiful. But unlike many regular liars, I can also speak the truth. I rarely do, but I can speak it on certain occasions. Like right now."

"I feel this is some god damn verbal duel we're having. We're mouthing words, but we're not saying much."

"I'll give you red meat. I was planted in this house by someone. Someone really important. I don't know who is really behind my being here. My only clue is that it's someone very important."

"I'm not exactly sure who you mean. Spiro Agnew? Marilyn Quayle? Tricia Nixon?"

"Don't make fun. It isn't funny, believe me. I came here to hustle money and to make off with some objects of great value. Not the Mona Lisa. That was a dirty trick you pulled on me this morning, making Mia think that it was me who stole the painting."

"You admit you're a thief. Why not an art thief?"

"Call me whatever you like. True, I've taken a few things in my life, but only if I thought I deserved a reward. Forget that, for the moment. I came here, as I told you, to hustle. That's still true. But that's only part of a larger picture. There's some enormous conspiracy going on, and I don't even know what it is. It's a large and well-financed scheme. It's like..." She paused, hesitant to go further. "It's like some force is at work to overthrow the government of the United States. By very violent means."

"You're just assuming a lot, aren't you? You have no real proof. As you said yourself, you don't even know who you're working for, and Mia hardly represents the U.S. government, even though she's fucked presidents."

"I don't know who's really behind what. I didn't elect to come to Mia's house. I was invited here by someone. The doors were suddenly open to me. It was known that Mia always employs a Japanese staff. Not only that. I was known for my elixir. Being Japanese and having the elixir got Mia's doors thrown wide open to me. Of course, once inside, the rest was up to me. I had to ingratiate myself with Mia, and no one could do that for me."

"You don't even have a suspicion as to who's behind your being here?"

"I speak to someone about once a week. Maybe more often. He has a deep voice. He speaks English but with a certain Spanish accent. It could be Cuban but I don't know for sure."

"Why would some powerful Cuban want you in Mia's household?"

"It's obvious to me. It's about Mia. It's about getting her money. But, you stand in the way of that. That's why your life may be in danger too."

"Why are you telling me all this? Are you trying to frighten me? Like I need any more upset after this Cruz thing."

"There's something going on. It could destroy you. I have every reason to believe you're on their hit list. They could destroy me and my sons, too. That's why I'm appealing to you for help. You have the wealth to hire armies if necessary. Whether you know it or not, you have a great deal of power. As for me, I have nothing. Only my cunning which doesn't seem to have done me any good at this point."

"There's a plot afoot to destroy me?" Her warning had sent a chill through me.

"You stand in the way of these people. They want you eliminated. They want you isolated from Mia. I did too for a long while. But as I learned more about them, I grew afraid. I began to view you, your power, and your legal arsenal as an ally for me. That's why I signed that stupid deal with Jerry Wheeler to let the film crew work here. You don't think it was because Mia wanted or needed the money, do you? It was chicken feed to her. I planned this. At first I would pretend to be hostile to you so no one would suspect. Then secretly I planned to meet with you. Like we're doing right now."

"You brought the film crew in here and put that real bullet in Mia's revolver. You wanted me to kill Cruz. You were behind it. I was set-up."

"Maybe that would have been true a little while ago. I'm sure that I'd have been the one they'd have ordered to switch those bullets. But I didn't. They don't trust me any more. I'm no longer doing everything they want. They've gotten to someone else. It's someone I think is very close to you. I mean, very close. Right within your inner circle."

"You mean someone as close as Rafael Navarro?"

"Don't rule that out as a possibility. Maybe the hijacking of that Cuban plane was deliberate. Maybe he was a plant. For all I know Castro ordered him to hijack that plane. I don't know. But think about it. For the sake of our lives, *think about it*. I know you can never trust me. We both admit that, but can you trust him? And who could ever trust that cheap little hustler, Dino? He may be cheap but he's extremely effective. He's bedded two of the most famous and wealthiest women on earth in a matter of weeks. And how loyal is Ted Hooker to you? That one could be bought, I assure you."

She was starting to make sense to me, and I didn't like that at all.

"These people may be plotting to have you killed. From what I've heard, you came very close to dying one night at your home in Star Island. Quite recently – right before you arrived in Key West. You were being stalked in your own garden. The stalker could have killed you then."

The memory of that awful, eerie night in my garden came back to haunt me. The intruder spying on me. Perhaps an assassin. There had been someone there. He'd left a Cuban cigar butt. All of a sudden I was starting to believe her, something I never would have thought possible. If she knew about that intruder, then she knew about a lot of other things too.

"What do you want from me?" I grabbed hold of her arm and shook her. "You're not feeding me data to protect my health. You want something. Tell me and make it quick."

"I'll be blunt. I want you to provide for and take care of my sons, John and Henry. For the rest of their lives. Don't make them suffer as I have. I've tried to protect them from the real world. I thought I was doing them a favor, and I did it with love. But even though they're seventeen and eighteen years old, they are amazingly simple and innocent, without any of the guile I developed to help me survive when I was their age. Despite their naivete – and god knows they're going to seem especially naive to you – they're good boys, and smart, too. Because of my own horrible childhood, I guarded and protected them so much that sometimes I fear that their emotional development has been stunted. It's probably that of an eight and nine-year-old adolescents. They're not tough, they're not cunning, and they're not trained in any of the survival skills which you and I have used so well. Other than me, they've had only each other to relate to over the years. I'm sure my obsession about protecting them from the world was neurotic, but I kept everyone else away from them. I've even done most of their tutoring. Without me, they'll be devoured by the world, particularly the world I'm leaving behind for them."

"You sound like you expect to blast off to the moon."

"No, I can't run out of here now even if I wanted to. *They* – whoever in the hell they are – would track me down and have me killed for sure. I have to stay here even though I don't want to be part of their schemes. I did at first. But now I'm convinced. Whenever I do exactly what it is I am supposed to do here, I'll be killed. That's for sure. I truly believe that with all my heart. My time is very limited. I'll be called upon to perform certain tasks. Then they'll kill me whether I'm Mia's adopted daughter or not."

"On the contrary, they might be planning to have Mia killed. You'll inherit her money, and then they'll extort that money from you."

"I know that. I lie awake at night thinking up all these horrors."

"It seems like being with Mia has been very lucrative for you so far. My God, you got her to adopt you as her daughter. She must have grown senile in the last few months."

"So far, it has been very profitable. I'll admit that. The cheap hustling side of me thought it was a pretty good deal at first. Then the survivor side of me – the former porno performer in the child bordellos – started talking to me and making a lot more sense. I already know too much. It's like I told you. When these assholes are through with me, they'll have me killed. That could be a lot sooner than you or I think. They want me gone. They'll use me until they no longer need me, and then they'll have me killed. I wouldn't be standing here telling you all this if I didn't think it was true."

"This could be some clever trick you're pulling. The same way your air force tricked us that Sunday morning at Pearl Harbor. One part of me actually believes you. The other part isn't sure."

"Let me start by offering you proof." She went over to a closet and removed a key held by a gold chain concealed between her breasts. She unlocked the door, then she turned the combination to a safe. Reaching in, she handed me a vial of something. "This is what they want me to start injecting into Mia. I don't know what's in it."

"You haven't injected any of this into my mother yet, have you?"

"No, although they think I've been doing it regularly. I want you to have the contents of this vial analyzed in a laboratory. I don't even know what it is, I swear it."

"Give it to me." I took the vial from her, handling it gingerly. I respected such things in life, almost as if it carried a curse.

"You must do something, and I don't know what to do or even what to tell you to do. Mia knows little of these matters and tends to dismiss any concerns which people bring up. In my position, there is very little I can tell her."

"I'll think about everything you said. I'm not making promises or anything. About you. About your sons. No promises about anything."

"Will you at least meet John and Henry? Later today? Please. I know you have urgent business now. But later today?"

"Okay."

"As final proof of my sincerity, I have something I want to

return to you. One thing that is very definitely yours and should never have been taken by me. I'm deeply ashamed." She reached back into the safe and removed my diary. After a millisecond of a pause, she handed it to me. "I'm so very sorry. They wanted me to steal it. They were looking for evidence against you. But the evidence in this diary won't be used against you. It makes you a victim."

I trembled. "Does Mia know what's in this diary?"

"She does. It's dreadful, but that woman has faced a lot. Now this painful memory from the past."

I took the diary, feeling my privacy had been invaded as never before. That was saying a lot, considering just how deeply and how frequently my privacy had always been invaded.

For a long moment, I stood looking at her. As clever as I thought I was, I could not have predicted this conversation or these transactions. As experienced as I was in dealing with all kinds of sordid and despicable people, this encounter with her was a first for me.

"You'll talk with me again?" she asked. "Very, very privately?"

"I certainly will," I said without the slightest hesitancy. "We'll talk. But we'll do more than that. We'd better start protecting some asses around here. Our own."

. . .

It was only when I returned to my bedroom to discover Ted and Maxie listening to the TV news that I realized I was the hottest story in America. It was the Cruz shooting. Media were giving this news more coverage than they did the invasion of Normandy in 1944. All kinds of the most lurid speculations were being broadcast, even the suggestion that Cruz and I were lovers and that my shooting of him was done in a jealous fury.

"Turn it off," I called to Maxie, who did as he was told before rushing over to check my make-up. I signaled to Ted. "I'd better call Cruz with my sympathy at the hospital. I dread making the call, but I guess I have to."

In minutes, Ted had the Miami hospital on the phone. Although perfectly conscious according to reports, Cruz chose not to receive my call. A "spokesperson" for the actor said that his attorneys would be in touch with David Miller.

"You can bet on that," I said.

According to Ted, Jerry would soon have a major heart attack, a big one, if I didn't meet with him at once about the future of "Butterflies." The big question was, what was going to happen to our film now that Cruz was out? Jerry's entire life depended on this, and I owed him that meeting as soon as possible. I also learned that twenty calls had come in from The Iguana, something about Sean Nielson, among other urgent messages. I decided to put even hunky Sean and certainly that reptilian agent on indefinite hold.

Maxie wanted to stay in the room with us, but I told him to go into town and buy me some black lingerie. Lingerie was the last item I needed in my wardrobe, as usually I didn't wear any, but I just wanted Maxie out of the room as Ted made some crucial phone calls. The fewer people who knew the exact details of my business affairs, the better.

An hour earlier, a mysterious call had come in from the sheriff. "Snake wants to meet with you...very privately," Ted said.

"He wants to fuck me," I said with disgust.

"I'm sure he does. But Snake claims it's vital business. He possesses some information you need to know."

"Information?" I asked, somewhat baffled. "Maybe he does know something. Maybe who shot Cruz. Maybe he wants a bribe if it's someone close to me. Maybe."

"That's one maybe you'd better get the answer to. He may know something really important. Of course, he'll want money for his information."

"I've always paid for information. You set up a private meeting."

I did not speak to Snake personally, but Ted arranged for us to meet in two hours at Palm Island, where the Kelly family had always maintained a sprawling, Spanish-style tropical retreat which we had escaped to during my childhood whenever the fast-paced life of Key West became too much for us. As Ted rushed off to make twenty-five other urgent phone calls in my behalf, Rafael came into the room, walking over and planting a wet kiss on my lips. He wore a towel around his waist, and was dripping wet from the pool.

"I hope you put on an impressive show for Mia," I said sarcastically with rising jealousy.

"She was very impressed. I even managed to upstage Dino and he was completely nude."

"How nice to see the both of you keeping her amused."

"Now, now, you are still my lady love and always will be."

"That's reassuring."

"Desi...Dino tells me that Jerry has offered him the role of Numie in 'Butterflies.' Opposite you."

"No way! I have my own actor in mind. At this point, I don't think I'll ever make the film."

"You look troubled. I mean...really troubled."

"I am. It's been a little much." I went for a towel and as I dried off Rafael's splendid physique, I said I'd have to meet privately with the sheriff.

"I'll come with you."

"He wants to meet with me alone. He knows something. Maybe who put the real bullets in Mia's revolver. I'll tell you everything when I get back."

"I really want to come with you."

"He doesn't want witnesses. I'll have to do it alone."

At the doorway, he turned and looked at me with a sad smile. "It's already been an exciting day, my love. Kidnapping La Giaconda. Now a strange meeting with a crooked sheriff. Don't you rich American women ever do anything legal?"

I smiled back at him before retreating to my dressing room. Right now I had to make myself gorgeous for my most important meeting with that Snake.

Maxie returned with the lingerie and wanted to review every item with me in painstaking detail. I had to put that project on hold.

I told him to make me up like my character in "Kinky" instead. Ted came into the dressing room carrying a velvet box. It contained the Capetown Diamond, the third largest such stone in the world. Again, I wasn't sure who really owned it: Mia or me. But I was wearing it. Better me than Anishi. In front of Ted and Maxie, I opened the velvet box. Both men screamed with glee. The stone was a bit overwhelming to these zircon sisters.

When it came time for Ted to appraise the diamond (and Ted could usually guess the price of any diamond to within a thousand dollars, more or less) he held it up to the light and seemed to weigh it. "What a rock," he said, enthusiastically. "Speaking of Rock, this baby is bigger than one of the balls of the late Rock Hudson, and that's saying a lot."

Maxie cradled the stone with loving care and affection. A man who used to think four pounds a week was a good salary back in London in the old days had never come into such close contact with an item as precious as the Capetown Diamond.

"Please," he said, with a certain pleading in his eyes, "just once in my wasted life, can I try it on? Just this once? I'll remember this moment forever."

"Okay, but in fairness to you, I must warn you: This diamond carries a curse."

"Hell with the curse! It's worth it, just to tell people in bars for the rest of my life that the Capetown Diamond once adorned my finger. No one will ever believe me, but I'll tell them anyway."

He placed the ring on his finger and waved the diamond in the air. Later, I had some difficulty getting it off his finger, as he seemed perfectly content to let it rest there forever.

Although he wanted to go with us to the island, he was given instructions to stay at Belle Reve and report back to us on anything or anyone conspiring against us during my absence. He didn't understand why it was so urgent that I meet with Snake, but thought it might be part of that ongoing investigation into the Cruz shooting.

Snake had arranged for Ted and me to sneak out the back entrance to avoid the press and the thousands of curiosity-seekers. Under sheriff's escort, we piled into the back seat of a limousine to drive north up the Keys to a marina where a boat would be waiting to take us on our journey to the luxurious but isolated family compound I hadn't visited in years.

Ted and I had some urgent business to discuss--none more urgent than the vial given to me by Anishi. I removed it from my purse and handed it to him.

Without even knowing what it was, he was suspicious. He held it away from his body in disgust. "I think someone could catch something from what's in that bottle."

"That's what we want to confirm. Get it to David. Tell him not to continue with the plan to steal a sample of Anishi's elixir. We've already had it handed over to us. Much more importantly, we want to know what horror is lurking in this tube."

"Okay, but you give me the most awful jobs. Me, who several times barely avoided contracting AIDS myself, although God only knows how or why I haven't already caught it. Now this awful thing in the vial."

"Just put it away for the moment, and tell me about only the most urgent phone calls of the day, plus one or two just for fun's sake. You know how I like those best of all."

"Okay," he said, settling back into his seat. "O.J. Simpson called. He wants to date you. He likes honey blondes."

"Name sounds familiar. Some sort of sports figure?"

"A washed-up football player. Does commercials for Hertz."

"I don't watch commercials and I certainly don't keep up with football players. If I wanted to date a football player, I wouldn't date someone over the hill. How old is this guy?"

"Over fifty, I think. He's married to some blonde. I forget her name."

"The way you talk makes me think he's black."

"Black as Othello. That's not all. My private club, Pecker-Checkers of America, gives him five and one-half inches. We've got plenty of witnesses who agree."

"Don't bother me with such silly calls. A washed-up black football player with a five-and-a-half-inch dick who does car commercials. Darling, when my offers dwindle down to that, I'll retire."

"There's more. You got a call from the White House."

"Mia and I are always getting calls from the White House. Does Clinton want another contribution? You'd think I'd given enough."

"It's something else. It was from Vince Foster."

"Who in hell is that?"

"A Clinton cronie from Arkansas. He's a big shit at the White House now. I hear he's actually running the joint."

"Clinton wants me to come to a gala? He'll let me sleep in the Lincoln bed? Hell, Mia's already been fucked in the Lincoln bed by one president. Maybe more."

"I don't know what it is. Foster certainly wasn't telling me the juicy details. He insists on speaking to you personally."

"Okay, I'll think about it. What's your hunch?"

"I think I know what it's about. It was already leaked to the press that Clinton has seen 'Kinky' three times. I think he wants a date, sugar."

"A date. Are you sure?"

"Who knows? It could become another John Kennedy and Marilyn Monroe thing."

"I doubt that!"

"Don't rule out the possibilities. Maybe he wants a quiet and intimate dinner. Maybe it'll be at Camp David while Hillary is out in California promoting her health care agenda. I think prexy has the hots for you."

"I'm not interested. After reading that Gennifer Flowers interview in *Penthouse*, I'm definitely not interested. Poor Hillary. A few months ago, I might have considered Al Gore, but only if the lights were turned out, and only if I could jolly him up a bit. Until further notice, turn down all offers for dates with the president."

"I don't know. That Foster is going to keep calling. I hear when Clinton gets the hots for someone, he doesn't give up the chase easily. After all, he is the president. Even if he summoned me, I'd have to go and you know he's not my type."

Before we knew it, the limousine had arrived at the boat dock to take us to Palm Island. I held his hand tightly once we boarded.

"Something wrong?" he asked.

"I'm suddenly afraid. I think there's a lot going on around here. A lot that concerns us, and we don't know what's happening."

"I think after meeting with Snake you'll know a lot more."

"Perhaps," I said. "Shit that I don't want to hear."

. . .

Brimming with his usual magnetic charm, Snake waited impatiently for me in the gigantic living room of the Kelly family's Palm Island retreat. He was wearing the familiar

Panama hat which he graciously removed when I came into the room alone. Still in the same yellow-stained white pants from our first interview, he wore a different shirt, a florid mass of pink and red flowers on a black background.

"You're looking good enough to eat," he said.

"How kind," I noted, extending my hand to him. "Have a seat. Make yourself comfortable. Ever been here before?"

"Not as an invited guest like today. But I've been here many times, especially when Mia used to throw big parties. She didn't exactly encourage me to socialize with her guests, but I provided security and male charm, compliments of the Monroe County sheriff's department."

"I was surprised you wanted to see me so suddenly. I know how busy you must be with the Cruz shooting thing."

"Busy ain't the word for it. Every newspaper and magazine in the world is trying to get Ole Snake on the phone. Actually, I was taking a much-needed break when I decided to call your fairyboy to tell him I wanted to meet with you."

"A little siesta in this hot sun is good for anyone."

"Wasn't exactly a siesta, ma'am, if you know what I mean."

"Love in the afternoon?"

"You got it. Me and this fifteen-year-old Cuban hooker I'd picked up on a drug charge, me and her were getting it on hot and heavy. She was screaming, 'Take it out. It's splitting me wide open. I've known macho hombres but never a man like you.' It was at that very moment I got the inspiration to call you."

"I see," I said softly, still sitting demurely on the sofa.

"When I got the inspiration to call you, I pulled out right away. Well, not right away. Too tight. Took two of my men to get me lifted off the launch pad and unglued. I'm afraid I bloodied up that bitch a bit."

"I see," I said, repeating my earlier observation.

"Decided to save it for you. The full load, baby."

"You're very kind, and that is such an enticing invitation. But I want to put Snake Junior on hold. At least for now." I lit a cigarette and blew smoke his way.

"I reckon I understand," he said. "We are here for business, not sex – I can assure you. You struck me as the kind of super-rich billionaire pussy that a man like me can do business with."

"You can indeed do business with super-rich billionaire pussies like me."

"Hot dog! I knew I could. I got some things to talk over with you. But, first, let's clear the air with this Cruz shooting now that me and you are alone."

"I'm not exactly sure what clearing the air means in the case."

"I am a man of the world, and I do know that money talks. You can unburden that famous chest of yours. Get real confidential. You meant to shoot Cruz after all but wanted it to look like an accident." He relaxed a bit on the sofa, as if under very different circumstances he'd played out this scene before. "Don't you worry about a thing," he finally said in his most comforting voice, after he'd mulled over several ideas in his soggy brain. "I'll retrieve whatever evidence there is, and we can get rid of it. Whatever you want in Monroe County, I can take care of. I've got the shit on everybody in these parts."

"I didn't mean to shoot Cruz. Someone planted the real bullet. I don't know who, but I'd certainly like to know. Please keep looking for the suspect."

"That's a relief." He didn't look relieved at all. He looked like a fat deal was going down the drain.

"Just because we can't make a deal about the Cruz thing doesn't mean the end for us. I'm sure there's more going on here than the Cruz shooting."

"How right you are! In fact, I'm ready to move on to other fish to fry."

"Fine. "Let's throw some of the little fuckers on the grill." I smiled and leaned forward so that he could better enjoy the cleavage between my breasts in my too-tight white dress. He didn't miss his golden opportunity. "What goodies do you want to share with me?"

"Right up front, I've got to be real blunt with you. I have to tell you that even though I'm an important man in this county-- hell, let's face it: the most important--sheriffs don't get a lot of pay. Not when they have expensive habits like I do. I want to live the good life too. Just like you."

"How can I help you lead the good life? I don't give away free lunches."

"I'm not a stupid man, your rich ladyship. I know all about

singing for my supper."

"God damn it, get down to it. What in fuck do you want other than my honeypot?"

"I want to be on your payroll."

"Exactly what are you prepared to do to earn that?"

"I'm prepared to give you information. Plenty of information. Information that might even save your ass. This Cruz shooting. This Anishi Jap woman. This and that. I know everything going on in Monroe County. And what I don't know I can find out. All for Pretty Woman sitting across from me with her juicy cunt and her big tits leading men to lust and thoughts they shouldn't have."

"Okay, I can afford it. You're on the fucking payroll. How would ten thousand a week sound?"

"Wha..." He looked like he had shit in his pants, which I think he might have done. I detected definite movement in his pants of some sort.

"When you make up a payroll, you ain't one of those cheap twats. Now, Mia...that's another story. I remember once when she hired me..."

"Cut to the chase, sheriff."

He looked at me with a leer. "You're one hot pussy who likes the red meat poked to her."

"You got it, big boy."

"Okay, for openers. Did you know why I chose this place to meet with you?"

It's secluded. It's private. It's where you can talk business away from the paparazzi of Key West."

"Amen to all of the above. There's another reason. I admit I don't know all the answers yet. But I want to feed you a little bit of information. Did you know that Secret Servicemen--no doubt ordered by Bill Clinton himself--have been checking out this house?"

"Hell, no," I said, sitting up to an upright position. A note of alarm swept across me. "Wait. "I think I know. After the bashing he took about that gays in the military thing, Clinton needs a retreat. A call did come in from the White House today. I bet Clinton wants to hide out here for a few days – perhaps with Hillary and Chelsea."

"Perhaps with you, hot mama."

"Surely not!"

"Don't kid yourself. Everyone knows about that 'Kinky'-loving bastard. I'm a Republican myself. He doesn't just want to watch your pussy on the screen. He wants to eat it just like he ate Gennifer Flowers."

"You really think that."

"I know so. Clinton has this guy up in Washington. His name is Dick Knight. Secret service all the way. He's flying in tomorrow. He's checking out this place. Knight always flies to check out the lay of the land before the president arrives. Clinton is definitely planning something in this house, and I think with you. He'll get some cronie to pop the question to you."

"The question. What question?"

"It'll be put diplomatically. But it'll boil down to this? Will Sherry Kelly, who flashed her pussy before all the world, give Clinton a private screening?"

"I haven't been asked that yet."

"It's coming up in more ways than one. What's your answer going to be?"

"I don't know. It's not something I'm into. But since he's the president I'll have to think about it. If that's the offer, and I decide to go along with it, I don't want Rafael to know. You'll see to that. Right? You might begin earning those ten-thousand big ones every week."

"I'll see to it," he said with total confidence.

"You have certainly started earning your paycheck, ole boy."

"You've haven't heard anything yet. I didn't know you were going to cough up ten grand a week. Just you wait and see. For those kinda bucks, I'm prepared to tell you a lot more. Almost on a daily basis."

"What else? There's more?"

"A lot more. Since you don't want to try Snake Junior on for size right now, sample this little tidbit. There are some people— and I admit I don't know who yet – who seem to know that the president is considering asking you for a date. Right here at Palm Island. It seems these people are planning to get in on the act."

"You mean assassinate the president?"

"I don't know. At this point, I don't really know. But I do

know this. They have rented a home right near here, and they are filling it up with medical supplies. Like they're getting ready for some sort of operation."

"You don't think the president is seriously ill. Keeping it from the public and planning a secret operation here where he hopes to hide out until he recovers?"

"I don't think that at all. I think the president doesn't know a god damn about these people. I think he's being set up in some way. Maybe an operation is going to be performed on him."

"What would that be? A castration? What?"

"I don't know, bitch. Don't seem so fucking impatient. Ain't I telling you enough already? Some of it you've got to find out for yourself."

"How can I?"

"Through David Miller. Don't he do your dirty work anyway?"

"He works for me, yes."

He reached into his shirt pocket and handed me an address. "I at least found out where the medical equipment is coming from."

I looked at the address. It was from a Dr. Euler from a clinic outside Gstaad. "I know this place. I have a winter chalet there."

"Then why don't you find out exactly what kind of operations Dr. Euler performs? When you do that, you'll know what kind of operation he's planning to perform on the president."

"Shouldn't we warn the White House and let them look into this?"

"They would think you're insane at this point. Why don't you get the evidence first? Then let those boys know what you know."

"I think you're right. I think I need a better case than this before approaching the White House."

"You've got the money. You can afford a plane ticket to Switzerland. Why don't you find out who this Dr. Euler is? When you know what kind of doctor he is, we'll know a lot more how to handle this."

"All right, I'll find out. I can do this." I got up and reached to shake his hand. "You and I are partners. From now on."

"I'm glad to be welcomed aboard. And so well paid."

"This is going to be the beginning of a beautiful friendship."

"I feel that, too, ma'am."

As I turned to leave, I blew him a good-bye kiss. He deserved at least that.

. . .

After lunch the next day at Belle Reve, Rafael and I disappeared. He was demanding an immediate blow-job which I was only too glad to deliver. After that, I took a shower and enjoyed the breezes blowing across my shady terrace overlooking the sea.

He wanted a long afternoon siesta. Before turning in, he said, "You Americans never seem to get enough sleep. But you do deliver state-of-the-art fellatio."

As agreed with Anishi, I kept my promise to meet her sons, John and Henry. Of all the urgent matters facing me now, meeting her two sons seemed the least important item on the docket. But it was important to her.

For the occasion, Maxie had seen to it that I was dressed as an Oriental princess. As I appraised his creation in a full-length mirror, I agreed with his assessment. I was indeed more Oriental-looking, more regal, and more stunning than any real Oriental who'd ever appeared on the screen. Forget Jennifer Jones in that awful movie whose title I mercifully can't remember. It's best to assign such a film to oblivion, unlike a movie such as "Kinky" which will be shown centuries from now.

Maxie even re-arranged the place where I'd be seated on the terrace. Here, surrounded by pillows, he assured me that it was time for the cameras to roll. I don't know why, but I felt compelled to dress alluringly on any occasion I'm going to meet men for the first time, even though in this case those men were only seventeen and eighteen years old. Who knew their actual ages or where they were born? Like Anishi herself, births and deaths seemed to have been blotted out of her ledger. I couldn't be sure that John and Henry were even her own children. Perhaps she'd kidnapped them from someone. With Anishi, nothing was as it appeared.

I sent Maxie to fetch John and Henry for our interview. If Maxie had been sent to fetch a stud like Dino, there would have been a certain risk. But I was familiar with Maxie's opinions of Japanese men or boys, meaning he didn't find them alluring at all. I knew John and Henry wouldn't be molested during their brief time with Maxie en route to their meeting with me.

Within minutes, hardly time for a molestation, Maxie had ushered the boys onto my terrace and had gently shut the door behind him to leave us alone. A brief flicker of a drapery at one point made me feel that Maxie might be eavesdropping on our dialogue, but it could have been the breeze. With Maxie, though, you never knew. He used to spend hours secretly feeding some of his best gossipy stories to Louella Parsons or Hedda Hopper.

"You're beautiful," the one who introduced himself as John said. "I wish my own mother were as beautiful as you are. You're like some goddess."

"Anishi has her own kind of beauty," I said with as much conviction as I could muster for the occasion. "Few women on earth look like me. I know that. But you must make do with what you have in life."

John had a certain winning way about him. Whether I liked him or not--and that would be determined later – I had to admire his judgment and taste in appraising me.

Not a word from Henry. He looked like John's twin, perhaps a year older. Both boys appeared to be of high school age, but with the Japanese you could never be sure. They might be college graduates, for all I knew.

"I'm Henry," he finally said. "Is it true you have more money than Mia?"

This one I definitely knew was Anishi's son. I smiled as enigmatically as the Mona Lisa. "When both Mia and I finish counting our money – which in this one lifetime we haven't been able to do – I'll give you the net results."

"Wow!" Henry said. "That sounds like a lot of money."

"It is." With my kind of dough, you didn't need to offer explanations. I looked the boys over very carefully, as they no doubt were appraising me. The way their eyes kept returning to my partially exposed breasts and to my shapely legs convinced me they were, quite possibly, heterosexual, as so few men are these days, with the glorious exception of Rafael. Both John and Henry spoke with appallingly perfect American accents. In fact, everything about the two boys, except for their appearances, suggested they were born in some small town in Kansas, not in some suburb of Tokyo, or some other ungodly place. Their clothing looked as if it'd been ordered from a J. Crew catalogue.

"We've met your friend, Dino," John said. "He was swimming nude in the pool. I mean like real naked. I haven't seen many naked men in my life. That Dino. I didn't know that men ever grew *that* big. Much less boys. Dino is our same age. Do you know what I'm talking about?"

"I know exactly," I said, trying to conceal the fact that I happened to be the world's leading authority on the subject.

"Dino tried to get us to take off our swimsuits and go into the pool with him," Henry said. "But we were too ashamed."

"And what do you have to be ashamed about?" I asked with perfect cruelty, resenting the question even as it escaped from my tongue.

"I didn't want Dino to see me without my suit," Henry said. "You see..." He hesitated. "John and I aren't...well, we aren't as fortunate as Dino."

"Few men are. Trust me on this. Don't concern yourself with that too much. It'll make you too insecure. There's not a god damn thing you can do about it."

"But we saw this ad in a magazine," John piped in.

"Forget it!" I commanded. I looked both John and Henry squarely in the eyes. "Do you like girls? Have any girl friends?"

"We like girls a lot," John said. "We don't have any girl friends, but we find the subject very exciting. We've seen 'Kinky' four times."

"Dino said girls won't be attracted to us," Henry said. "'Cause we're not built like him. He said he could get any girl he wanted. Any woman, too."

"He also said any boy or any man," John added.

"He's telling the truth for once in his life."

"What about us?" Henry asked. "Will I ever be able to get a girl? Or John here?"

"Indeed you will. All you want one day. Perhaps not the size queens attracted to Dino. But there are other types out there. Japan is full of women who would be attracted to you. If you don't find anything there, you could always find someone in Thailand. Hell, you could even buy someone in Thailand. You're fairly good-looking. Frankly, you guys aren't my type, but you'll do just fine. That is, if you're not going to spend the rest of your lives imprisoned behind the walls of Belle Reve."

"Anishi doesn't let us go out and be with kids our own age," John said. "She's afraid someone will kidnap us."

"Mama knows best."

"You're very reassuring," John said, "about the girls."

"Don't worry about it. Of course, don't go for any girl that Dino's already had. He will have ruined that poor woman for life, falsely raising her expectations to dizzying heights. Go after a virgin. That way, she'll have no means with which to compare your performance or endowment with that of other men. Back in the old days, men all over the world got away with that clever trick until we women got wise to their game. You do know what a virgin is, don't you?"

"Sure do," Henry piped in. "That's a girl who hasn't been porked."

As attuned to American culture as these boys might be, I didn't expect either of them to understand the word pork. "Where did you learn that expression?"

"From Anishi's redneck southern boyfriend," John said. "Our mother slips off to see him every Friday night at the Mangrove Mama night club up the Keys. She uses Mia's limousine after she has gone to sleep. Once, when Mia was away, Anishi even brought her boyfriend here. He was a little drunk, but he told us he was here to feed our mother the pork."

Henry turned to John. "You stupid little kid you. John at the time thought he was going to offer her some ham."

"We spied on them that night," John confessed. "That's where we learned about porking."

"We didn't learn all that much about porking," Henry said. "We learned more about that from watching your movie 'Kinky.' A lot more."

"Mother's boyfriend isn't much." John said. "He's often

impotent. He's also built very small like us. Not like Dino. Anishi claims she is helping him recover from a sexual problem. She says he's sexually dysfunctional."

"Doesn't sound like much of a boyfriend," I said.

John and Henry didn't say anything for a long time, but kept looking me over. I guess I appeared to them like some screen goddess suddenly turned into flesh.

"Boys!" I said, in a perfect imitation of Mae West in the 1930s. "I don't have much time today. Got a lot on my mind. Let's meet again as soon as possible. Maybe we'll have dinner one night and get to know each other better. I think your mother would like that. You seem like nice boys to me, with a lot more to learn. Quite frankly, both of you seem a bit too obsessed with sex, but that's understandable. First, you aren't getting any, so you have to talk about it all the time. Also, men or even boys meeting Sherry Kelly for the first time rarely can talk about anything but sex. However, at our next meeting, I'll direct the conversation. We'll talk about how school is going. What you want to do with your life, shit like that. I'll also try to wear a pair of blue jeans and a loose-fitting blouse, perhaps my hair tied up with an Hermes scarf like QE Segundo wears, something horsey and traditional like that. That way, I won't distract you too much."

"It was sure nice meeting you, Ms. Kelly," John said.

"After all the subjects we've covered today," I said, "I think you know me intimately enough to call me Sherry."

"Sherry." John repeated the word as if he'd discovered a new friend or at least a new playmate.

"May I call you Sherry too?" Henry asked.

"Sherry it is to you, too."

"I know it's time for us to go," John said. "We never like to stay around longer than we should. We get on Mia's nerves if we do. But can I ask one last favor?"

"Fire away," I said, trusting they know American slang well enough to know what I meant and wouldn't take that as an invitation to launch new bombs on Pearl Harbor.

"I'd like to kiss you goodbye," John said.

"Okay," I said, "but only on the cheek – no tongue."

"It's a deal," John said. He bent over and kissed me gingerly on the cheek.

Without asking, Henry bent over and kissed me on the other cheek.

As John and Henry turned to leave, I called to them. By then, I had risen from my artfully arranged position on the pillowy sofa and was standing like Claudette Colbert used to do in any of those sentimental World War II movies like "Since You Went Away."

Without saying a word, both John and Henry turned and came running back to me for a long and final hug. They needed it, and they seemed to know I needed their embraces as well. Maybe all of us were a little afraid.

As I watched the boys leave my terrace, I felt a pang of regret. For the first time in my life, I was sorry I didn't have children of my own.

"Sherry Kelly, baby," I said out loud, just to the sea breezes. "Get a grip on yourself. You're coming unglued thinking thoughts about child-rearing."

This time it was Ted, not Maxie, who interrupted my reverie. "Your next guests," he announced cheerfully.

"God damn it," I said. "Don't I have time to even powder my twat?"

Before Ted could answer, a frantic Jerry appeared on the terrace. He was followed by the increasingly notorious Dino.

. . .

"I'm ruined," Jerry screeched at me. "The film is ruined. We're ruined!"

"Look at all the publicity this film has gotten," I reminded him. "Millions and millions of dollars worth of free publicity aimed at movie audiences around the world."

"My God," he said, "in all the hysteria, I never even thought of that."

So far, Dino hadn't said anything. He appeared in total control. In a white shirt and white pants, he also looked gorgeous. Apparently, Mia working him over, or perhaps Jerry, probably both, hadn't taken any great physical toll on him. "I know I can save the day here. I'll play Numie opposite you. I can see it now. A smash hit worldwide. Introducing Dino Paglia in 'Butterflies in Heat,' a film by Jerry Wheeler with

Sherry Kelly appearing as Leonora."

"Dream on, little boy," I said harshly to him. "Your billing sucks. Sherry Kelly always appears alone above the title. Get it? *I always do a solo dance above the title.*"

"We can work out the billing," Jerry said as if to soothe an errant child.

"Listen, cuntie," I said, speaking to him as harshly as I ever had before. "I'm not doing this film. I'm out. I certainly am not doing the film opposite Dino, regardless of what he did to convince you he should have Cruz's part."

"Without you, we'll lose millions at the box office," he protested. "My lawyers will sue."

"Never fear when Dino is near," said the arrogant little prick or, in his case, the arrogant big prick.

"What does that mean?" I asked, regretting that I was going for his bait.

"If you're out of the film, we can get an even bigger name and millions of dollars worth of additional publicity."

"Who's bigger than I am?" I demanded to know.

He paused for a long moment, enjoying the spotlight. What a ham. With a slight smirk, he announced. "Mia Kelly."

I sank back into the sofa, taking a deep breath. "She'd never do it."

"Like hell, she won't," Dino said, his voice rising. "I've already gotten her okay."

"Dino," Jerry said, his voice petulant. "You've been holding out on me."

"I'm sure he has in more ways than one," I said. "First, I don't believe Mommie has ever made such an agreement."

"Ask her!" Dino commanded. "Just ask her. Anyway, you're too young for the part. It calls for a much older woman. Older and gorgeous as is the case with Mia."

"Introducing two unknowns in the film." Jerry said. "Except that one of those unknowns is a name known all over the world."

"Sounds like you've got yourself a picture," I said. "I hope you make millions."

"You've already signed to put up a lot of your own money," he reminded me.

"So I have. A deal's a deal."

"What if I need extra financing?" he asked.

"Go to your star," I told him. "She's got half the money in the world, the half that I don't have. I'm sure if she wants to star in a film, she'll provide the extra financing."

"What a break," he said. "I'm liking this idea more every minute. I've got to get to work right away. Get the script to Mia. We'll get a body double for the nude scenes." He paused. "You wouldn't consider..."

"Forget it, cuntie, find yourself another body." Before he turned to go, I added, "And if you still plan on using that stairway shooting scene, you'd better check Mia's revolver real carefully. She might end up pumping real bullets into your cute boyfriend here after about another week."

"Thanks for the advice," he said. "We'll check it out real good. I think we'll go down in film history with this one."

After he rushed away to new adventures, Dino remained on the terrace. "This interview is officially over," I said. "Be off with you, my lad." My voice deliberately mimicked Bette Davis playing Elizabeth I.

"Not so fast," he protested. "Mama..."

"I'm not your mama," I interrupted him. "Perhaps one day, but not today."

"Be reasonable. I'm offering you one last chance."

"Chance at what?" I asked, as if I didn't already know.

"*Me*. You and I could get back together again. The way we were."

"Sounds like the name of a song," I said sarcastically.

"We could start over again. I'm willing. You, of all people, know I'm able."

"I'm with Rafael."

He grew angry, although he tried to conceal it. "Rafael is thirty-six years old. In just four years, he'll be an old man. Is that what you want? An old man? I'll be young for years and years to come. Maybe I'll never grow old. Even when you're fifty, you'll still be enjoying a young and virile Dino."

"In the unlikely event I ever make it to the golden age of fifty, I'm sure I'll be interested in things more memorable than the stud services of one Dino Paglia."

"Don't put me down. You forget that your mother, the richest woman in the world, is in love with me."

"Cut the bullshit, kid. Mia is in love with only one person. That's Mia herself. Beach bums and half-assed actor-model types around the world have thrown themselves at her, offering all kinds of services. If she accepted any of them, I doubt if she even remembered their highly forgettable names the following morning. Her only motive for giving you a tumble was to get back at me. You're nothing to her. Never will be. You're trying to play in the big league, and you're only a minor player."

"I'll remember every fucking word you said to me this day," he claimed. "Every fucking word. I'm going to become the biggest male star of all time. You'll eat those words just the way you used to eat me. I made you choke back then, and I'll make you choke on your words as well. Just wait and see. I'll be bigger than Brad Cruz ever was."

"Speaking of now-alienated Cruz, are you the one who put the real bullets in Mia's revolver? You're one of the prime suspects. You stole the bullets from Rafael, didn't you?"

"No, I didn't, bitch. I don't have to kill Cruz or anybody else to get ahead in films. In my case, I can depend exclusively on talent and beauty."

"I think you may be right about becoming a movie star."

"You really think so?"

"You already have the inner personality of a major star. All you need now is to get launched. You certainly appeal to both sexes. I think you just might become one of the biggest *Italian* stars of all time. What Valentino was in the '20s, you'll be at the millennium."

"If you're telling the truth, I'll let up on you."

"I actually meant what I said. Although I didn't see it when I first met you, I think you're enough of a bastard to make it big. I can just imagine what you'll be like at twenty-four--and what you will have learned by then."

"With your blessing, I'll go on my way."

"And after today, the darkness will hide you."

"That's only a stupid song! No darkness will ever hide Dino Paglia!"

"You're not even Eve Harrington. You're Norma Desmond!"

"I don't give a fuck about those old broads, and never heard of them, anyway. I've already had to cope with enough old broads in my young life."

"My child, let's keep in touch. I feel our story isn't over yet. We still might be able to use each other, although at the moment, I don't imagine that happening anytime soon."

"It's a deal. But I've given you your last chance to bag me. You blew it, in more ways than one."

"Thank you for the towering opportunity."

"In a way, I'm glad you turned me down."

"Why's that? You don't strike me as the type who takes well to rejection."

"I don't have to handle rejection at all. How would I know? I've never been rejected before. Until now. Until you. For that, I'll owe you one. And here it comes: It made me sick at my stomach to go to bed with you. I laughed at you as the 'old cow' to my friends. And the only way I could get it up with you was to think about someone younger whenever we were between the sheets."

Far from reacting in anger to this vicious assault, I controlled myself. When a woman such as myself gets involved with a cheap hustler like Dino, what else can she expect? In some way, his attack on me assuaged some of my guilt for involving myself with anyone so young. I wasn't proud of it at the time, and thinking about it right now actually disgusted me. I rose from the sofa. "I'll show you to the door."

He kept staring nervously at me, as if expecting me to strike him, perhaps to shoot him in the heart with Mia's now-famous revolver.

I did none of those things, not that he didn't deserve them. "I'm glad you told me what you did. Now that we're parting, I'll also reveal some deep dark secrets to you. You're the worst lay in Hollywood, kid! Or New York. Certainly in Florida, for that matter. I faked it every time. I've had better fucks from waiters I picked up at the Cannes Film Festival. Rafael's got you beat in every department. I always knew you were thinking about someone else during our unmemorable rolls in the hay together. I think I even know who it was you were thinking about. You see, one day I opened a desk drawer only to discover that Banana Republic ad, the same ad that brought us fatefully together in the first place. My initial contact with you wasn't particularly unusual. Many people liked that ad. I understand it's pinned up on dormitory walls around America.

But in the particular copy which I found in that drawer, you had cut out the girl, leaving only the other cutie--the male--in the picture with you. I entirely agree. He is mighty cute. A hell of a lot cuter than you. And probably a better lay, too." I slammed the door behind a stunned Dino.

Noting that it was nearly four o'clock, I move briskly back to the sitting room off my bedroom, where Rafael was still sleeping with a smile on his face, no doubt put there by me.

CHAPTER SEVEN

Evening was descending over Key West and no news had come in from the lab where David had sent the contents of that vial. I needed to know at once what these mysterious people wanted to inject into Mia's veins. I also had to warn her what was up. She was a suspicious person and wouldn't trust me, but it might save her life. Before approaching her, I needed some good, strong evidence which I hoped the lab would provide. Still, no word. I'd asked Ted five times in the last hour if any news had come in from Miami. But nothing. Someone on the staff there kept promising me some information, and I'm a woman who doesn't like to wait. One advantage of having unlimited money is that you are rarely kept on hold. It was something I wasn't used to.

I didn't want to see anyone, even Rafael, until I got news from Miami. I was also waiting for a call from David about Dr. Euler. Increasingly a private detective, instead of a lawyer, David was to find out just what kind of doctor Euler was. I didn't think that should be too hard. After all, Gstaad's virtually a village. Everybody there knows everybody else's business. The gossips even found out that night I ran off with Julie Andrews for a little fun and games. I thought I'd learn about Dr. Euler in an hour, but so far centuries seemed to have gone by.

Just as I was thinking about placing another call to David, Mia--a vision in cerise and lavender--suddenly appeared in my dressing room looking amazingly like Elizabeth Taylor in "Raintree County."

"You God damn slut!" she shouted in lieu of a more formal greeting. "Apparently, you didn't get my command. I told everybody that if the Mona Lisa wasn't returned by six o'clock tonight, all of you were to leave Belle Reve at once. I'm calling the sheriff to have you arrested."

"On what charge?" I asked defiantly. "Stealing the Mona Lisa? Wouldn't the press outside your gate love to get that one on the wire services?"

"You bitch! I can't win with you. Never could."

"I will not stay here as an unwanted guest. I have many

other mansions to live in."

"Mansions I own, you big-tit cow."

"Mommie, you really shouldn't call me names. It's not kind."

"Would you shut that cocksucking mouth of yours? I'm tired of you and your lies. I now know you stole the painting. I want it back...and now. It's mine!"

"Mommie," I said like that so-called "tough little slut" Shirley Temple might have sounded. "I had nothing to do with the theft of your painting. I am telling the absolute truth."

"The first sentence you ever uttered was a lie."

"What was that?"

She was near tears. "That you loved your mother."

I moved to embrace her for recalling that long-ago time, but she backed away from me on unsteady heels.

"I don't think you're safe here," I said. "I feel your life is in danger. You've got to come with me. Flee from Anishi."

"You god damn flasher!"

I don't think I'd ever seen her this furious at me.

"Thanks to you, my home, my person, my life, my precious privacy. Everything on tonight's news. Paparazzi are staked out right now trying to get a shot of something going on here. I feel I'm in a prison."

"I'm sorry. I really am. I never knew any of this was going to happen."

"That centerfold. 'Kinky,' that awful movie. Those were just the appetizers. Sherry Kelly was saving the main dish – slimy afterbirth it was, too – to feed to me later."

"Mommie, I want only love and happiness for you. It's all I've ever wanted."

"When you're not pursuing the largest thing trucking to shove up that gaping hole of yours, you're thinking about only one thing. That's Sherry Kelly. Let's face it: You're self-enchanted."

"And you're not?" My words stabbed the air with a ferocity I'd meant to conceal.

"Let's say, my darling daughter, that I at least have something to be self-enchanted about."

"You're very cruel. I should never have let you see that movie about Joan Crawford, 'Mommie Dearest.'"

"Joan Crawford was a wonderful woman. I knew Joan. I loved her."

"I thought you were more of a Bette Davis fan."

"I was. But I loved Crawford in a different way. Crawford's adopted daughter – that's one vicious little..."

She shuddered, obviously equating Crawford's daughter with me. The only difference was I didn't have to write a memoir to hustle a buck.

"Why are we discussing the dead at a time like this?" she asked. "They're dead. I'm alive. Their problems are behind them. You are creating daily ones for me."

"*You* are indeed alive. "But you must simmer down." I looked around the room fearing for a moment it might be bugged. Something told me it was definitely bugged. I couldn't discuss my suspicions with her now. I'd have to contact her later. Maybe by then I'd have some concrete proof. If she wouldn't believe me, she might believe David, although I doubted that. If she decided something was true, the biggest lie became the truth, at least to her. I feared when confronted with unassailable proof of her danger, she would still think I was maneuvering somehow.

"About your starring opposite Dino in 'Butterflies in Heat,'" I asked, deliberately changing the subject. "I'm talking about your being offered the lead. As my replacement. You've replaced me in his affections. Why not replace me in the film? Jerry did offer you the part, didn't he?"

"I've been offered the lead." She appeared defiant.

"Will you do it?"

"I'm considering it."

"For God's sake, why? In the old days, you'd never have considered such a thing."

"I'll tell you why," she said, almost spitting out her words. "Dino has convinced me that I'm at the peak of my beauty. He said he doesn't know how long it will last--I owe that little brat one for reminding me--but right now, right at this moment, I look the most spectacular I've ever looked in my entire life. What's wrong with my wanting to share that beauty with the world? Immortalize myself. After our film is released, no one will ever mention 'Kinky' again."

"Are you going to show all?"

"Hell, no, I don't have to. Did Elizabeth Taylor ever show all? No, because she is a great actress, and because she can act. With you, my ungrateful and untalented daughter, the only way you could capture attention on the screen is by flashing. I'm no flasher. Never was. Never will be."

"Regardless of how much you show, good luck in your movie debut."

"Right now I've got more important problems than the movies. Like getting your gang out of Belle Reve."

"But Snake forced us to stay here. We're all suspects. We can't leave."

At the door to my dressing room, she paused. "Even that is a lie. Everything that comes out of that overworked suction pump of a mouth of yours is a lie. I happened to know that you and Rafael are free to go. There's no one to detain you. You and your two fairies and Mr. Stud Service, Senor Navarro, can move your asses across the street to that rented house. Not that I haven't enjoyed your visit. It's topped MGM's 'That's Entertainment.'"

Suddenly, she was gone. Her kicking me out made me wonder what I was going to do for a second act. I hadn't written one yet.

Ted rushed into the room. A phone call had come in from Marathon. It was Snake.

"I can't talk now," Snake said when I picked up the phone. "But I just wanted you to know I'm on the job."

"That's good. Keep crawling around, Snake."

"No, no, don't hang up! I've got news. That Secret Service guy. That Dick Knight I told you about."

"What about him?"

"He got here early. Right this very minute he's checking out your pad at Palm Island."

"That's trespassing. Have him arrested at once."

"Now, now, sweet pussy. Do you think the sheriff of Monroe County should barge into your home and arrest a member of Clinton's elite squad. Do you really think that, especially with every slimy news hound in the world looking for scandal. The cameras would be rushing from Belle Reve up to Palm Island."

"On second thought, I don't think that would be a good

idea. Scratch the command."

"Now, you're talking sense, Pretty Woman. I've got to go." He abruptly hung up.

Rafael came into the room. I rushed to embrace him, losing myself for a protected moment in his strong arms. But I backed away slightly, fearing he, too, might be a saboteur or an agent. Oh, God, he didn't plant that bullet in Mia's revolver! I had to get a grip on myself. I was starting to fantasize, seeing conspiracy around every corner.

"Are you okay?" he asked, steadying me.

"I'm a little shaky. Mia has just ordered us out of Belle Reve under threat of arrest."

"Then let's get the fuck out of here! It's not that we don't have any other place to live."

. . .

Before I'd settled with Rafael in the mansion across the street from Mia, a call came in from David. His private plane--no doubt financed with money he'd made representing me--would land at the Key West airport in just ten minutes. He had to return to Miami immediately, but wanted to meet privately with me at the airport. He didn't trust the security at the mansion I'd rented, and he, like myself, had reason to suspect that Mia's house was bugged. I blamed Anishi, but he wasn't sure.

I agreed to meet him at once at the airport. Rafael was getting a little suspicious of my comings and goings but I assured him I had to meet privately with my attorney and would return shortly to the manse he and I had rented. I also told him I'd be perfectly safe while gone, although not really believing that.

Later, as I stepped out of my limousine near the darkening runway, I recognized David's plane as it bounced along, coming to a halt. A breeze from the Gulf of Mexico blew extra hot at that time, like a wind from the Sahara. The setting sun seemed to have left so much heat in the air it could burn skin.

After hoisting me into the cockpit and assuring the pilot he could get a fast blow-job if he headed for the men's room of the airport, David pulled me inside.

"A lot is happening," he said. "We've found out about this

Dr. Euler. He's a specialist in lobotomy. He also experiments with the AIDS virus, presumably to find a cure for it."

"Oh, my God!" I screamed until he muffled my mouth with his broad hand. "It's Mia," I shouted, darting away. "They're setting up that way station to perform some sort of operation on her brain. At first I thought Clinton. But now I think it's Mia."

"We don't know that for sure."

"Then just who in the fuck do you think they're going to perform a lobotomy on?"

"It appears Mia is the target. At this point no one knows Clinton will show up. You haven't even invited him. It has to be Mia. Some force seems to be at work to pilfer her money, and now that I don't work for her, my options about helping her are relatively limited--at least until the affair becomes more public. Anishi is very suspicious, but she's not really behind this. It's much too well organized for that one. Some bigger brain and a lot more money are at work here."

"We've got to go to Mia at once."

"You know she wouldn't listen."

"Then how are we going to warn her?"

"I have contacted her legal firm. I have given them what evidence I possess. I mean, she hired those pussies as her lawyers. They're rotten. They're on the take. But she might listen to them instead of us. At least she pays enough for the shitty advice they give."

"What if I tried to call Mia right now?"

"Go ahead."

I grabbed his phone. "How do you work this god damn thing? I'm an old-fashioned girl used to having things done for her."

He quickly dialed Mia's number. "This is David Miller," he said to what was probably a Japanese servant. Mia didn't answer phones. Neither did Anishi. "I'm here with Sherry Kelly. We have to get a message to Mia at once. Put her on."

"Just a minute," came the reply.

The servant was gone for a long time. When he came back, he said to David, "Ms. Kelly told me to tell Mr. Miller and Sherry Kelly to fuck off!" He abruptly hung up.

"We'll deal through her attorneys," I said. "We definitely

will. She thinks I'm plotting to kick Anishi out of her life. Earlier today she wanted to talk to me about my diary. Now she won't take my call. Typical Mia."

"There's more," he said.

"What now?"

"That vial you sent up."

"Your lab certainly took long enough with it."

"That's because they're not really sure what it is. It's definitely the AIDS virus but some weird mutation. No doubt from the laboratory of Dr. Euler."

"He's a world specialist, you say. I don't know a hell of a lot about AIDS, but we've been talking stupidly about shooting the virus into somebody. Isn't this just shit talk? Doesn't the virus die when exposed to temperatures lower than body temperature?

"That's what I always thought," he said. "But the lab claims this virus is alive. It must be a mutated breed a lot stronger than its daddy. The virus will reactivate itself, or so it seems, after an injection into a human bloodstream."

I sank back into my seat. It'd been a long day. This was a little much even for the crazy world Mia and I inhabited. "Why would anyone want to even try to give Mia AIDS?"

"Maybe the same people who would like to perform the lobotomy on her. Or Clinton. Maybe even you."

"How can we put a stop to this?"

"No crime has been committed yet. We can hardly call your friend Snake and have somebody arrested. In fact, we don't even know who to arrest. What a case this would make!"

"Snake might help us after all."

"He sells out to the highest bidder. You can't trust that fart."

"Right now he's on my payroll. Until he meets someone better bankrolled than me, if that's possible. He can do something for us."

"What on earth?"

"I can arrange for him to have spies day and night in Mia's house. For a fee, of course. I'm sure Snake can arrange that."

"But she already has a house full of servants."

"Tomorrow she'll lose some of those servants."

"Like how?"

"How in the hell do I know? That's Snake's job. Maybe they

don't have green cards. I don't know. All I know is that he can find some reason to either throw them in jail or else get them deported, even if they do have green cards."

"How could he possibly get them thrown in jail?"

"Try this on for size. What if he finds lots of cocaine stashed in their bedrooms? What if they are using Mia's house as a cover? They're not servants at all. They're drug-dealers pretending to be servants."

"Sounds to me you couldn't get away with that."

"We're not talking my getting away with it. We're talking Snake getting away with it. He's been burying bodies for people all over Monroe County for decades. This is simple for him. After all, his men are already all over Mia's house right now. That's how the discovery will be made. They're already there investigating the Cruz shooting. It's perfect."

"I'm an attorney. I can't advise about this other than it sounds like you're out of your mind, as always."

"In other words, I'll get into the jams and you'll bail me out."

"That's the way we've always done it."

"True, I've got to protect Mia at all costs. Right this very moment, right now as we speak, I'm contemplating a Swiss vacation."

"You wouldn't even think what I think you're thinking."

"Wanna bet? I could be airborne by three o'clock this morning? After all, I have a chalet in Gstaad."

"It's too risky. You could get killed. You could end up getting the fucking lobotomy performed on you or the contents of some mysterious vial shot into you."

"You know I'm street-smart."

"You are god damn smart. But all you have to do is make one mistake. It could be the end for you. I can get you out of legal trouble. I can't always be on hand to save your life. I don't know how you could expect to learn anything about Dr. Euler by going to visit him."

"I'm a great interrogator."

"C'mon, honey, don't even think it."

An urgent message came in. He picked up his phone, and a frown crossed his brow. "I've got to fly out of here. We've got to return to Miami at once."

The pilot was nearing the plane. David opened the door and helped me down.

"You're right, Dave," the pilot said. "The kid I met in there was a real sword-swallower. Drained every bit of me and wanted more. But I knew I had to get back. Good evening, Miss Kelly." He tipped his cap to me and boarded the plane.

David kissed me on the mouth rather passionately. "For old time's sake."

"Take care."

"It's you I want to warn to take care. But it wouldn't do any good, would it?"

"Not when I'm determined."

"Then keep me abreast of all your plans as soon as they're filtered through that overtaxed brain of yours. At least we'll have a fighting chance if I know where you are at all times and I know what in the fuck you're up to. Remember, I can have commandos at any site in the world within minutes if you ever need rescuing."

"I know that love, and knowing that makes me feel a bit safer every night."

"It's going to be Switzerland. Right?"

"Right."

"Okay, then, I'll call you when we learn the location of Dr. Euler. He sounds like a ghoul from hell."

"Probably. When I decide what name and disguise I'll use, I'll have Ted call in the details. You set up the appointment. I'll be some rich bitch from California with a troubled kid." I paused. "I love you." He kissed me again.

I hated prolonged good-byes so I turned my back to him and proceeded at once to my waiting limousine. I had to get Ted on the phone. Not only did we have to provide instructions to Snake about the servants, but he had some travel arrangements to make at once.

In the back seat of the limousine, I settled in comfortably, wanting these few moments alone. The driver reached back and handed me a message from Ted, just as I was planning to get him on the phone. The Mona Lisa had safely been hidden in Land Salzburg.

I suddenly was coming up with another problem. I needed Ted to track down Dino, and I'd thought it might be some time before that young man and I had need of each other. But like a speeded-up movie, events were breaking fast. A plan was spinning in my head, and Dino was just the actor I needed to play the part. All that remained was for the fee to be negotiated. I was certain he could be bought.

When I returned to my rented house with Rafael, I learned the move from Mia's had been successfully completed. My diary was now locked up in a safety deposit vault, where I should have put it long ago. Our happy little menage, minus Dino, could resume its domestic agenda for an hour or two before I plunged it into even more chaos than that which had existed before my attempt on the life of Cruz.

I'd already spoken to Dino before I arrived in the limousine, and I expected a visit from him before midnight – if for no other reason than to fulfill a certain acting assignment I'd hired him for. No, not the lead in "Butterflies." More "living theater" than that. For the brief role I sketched out for him, he'd demanded and I'd agreed to a payment of one-hundred thousand dollars, all in cash, small bills only, plus free transit to and from Switzerland.

Everyone in the world, or so it seemed, had been trying to reach me on the phone. Apparently, all the telephone circuits in Key West were blinking on overload. Even the press in Croatia wanted me, although I've always had a strict policy of never granting interviews to countries east of Rome. Rome with its paparazzi was bad enough. Why take a chance by going farther east?

In his incredibly intuitive way, Ted had sorted my calls into various categories. I decided since I had only a little time, I would take only the most "hysterically urgent."

"Mia called," he said.

"Mommie?" I asked in astonishment. "She just refused to take a call from David and me. *That* one!"

"Mia hadn't expected you to leave Belle Reve so suddenly. She claimed no one follows her orders any more. She certainly didn't expect you to disappear so quickly with your brood. She said she wants to have a private 'fairy-free and stud-free' – meeting with you to talk about the contents of your diary. She claims that there are some things you must know about yourself."

"Set it up. As soon as possible. On the other hand, it must wait until I get back. It would be pointless now."

"Another call has come in twice," he said provocatively. "From the White House."

I waited to hear the punch line, but he was strangely silent. "The star is standing here waiting to be informed. The White House is a pretty big place. Just ask Mia, who's spent a lot of nights there. Get her to tell you what happened one night when she wandered into the wrong bedroom."

"Vince Foster again."

"Did I get an invitation to the White House? To attend some boring dinner with vile food? A stupid cultural entertainment evening? Crap like that?"

"Forgive me for being coy, but this is strictly hush-hush. If word got out, it'd be the scandal of the century. Forget Gennifer Flowers."

"You're still not making sense."

"It was put ever so subtly. You're not invited to the White House. It seems the president of the United States would like to receive an invitation from you. For a private meeting. Perhaps at your Palm Island retreat."

I leaned back. "I can't believe this."

"Honey, don't you get it? I was right. Bill Clinton--at least the way I hear it – wants a date with you. A date. Like what hookers call it when they're meeting a john. Except Clinton doesn't want you to charge him."

"Sort of doing it out of patriotism." I was stunned, mostly because of the indiscretion of it all, the potential for scandal. Bill Clinton, president of the United States, and Sherry Kelly, the world's richest woman and reigning sex queen of Hollywood, caught together in a boudoir.

This potential rendezvous required some thought. I considered the options, even though Rafael was the love of my life. Clinton certainly wasn't my type, but he was the president of the United States. I think any invitation which was extended from that office deserved at least to be considered. I had known men far more famous, richer, and important than Bill Clinton, thanks to my Mommie and my own steam. But right at this moment, the spotlights of the world were being trained on Clinton. Or at least those spotlights which weren't otherwise occupied with me.

Clinton and Kelly. The more I thought about it, the more I moved to dismiss the idea. But it was something to think about. I mean, we're talking the president of the United States here. Leader of the free world. Unlike presidents of yore, Clinton apparently hadn't been bedded by Mia. At least to my knowledge. In her case, I could never be sure. "Tell Foster I'll get back to him."

"You've got to respond in some way," he said. "If you don't Foster will keep calling."

"If I remember, you've threatened me with this before. Tell that damn mole of yours at the White House that Clinton will hear from me in a few days."

"I'll call Foster at once."

When he came back, I said, "Pack some furs for me, including the world's most expensive ermine coat. And pack a few for yourself too, cuntie. We're going to visit the high alpine peaks of Europe." I paused. "And get me the Capetown Diamond. I'm going somewhere where I'll want to wear it."

"Who knows where you'll take us next. The Alps? Sounds better than fag-hating Colorado." Trained in show business all his life, he had a technique of saving one final tidbit of any interchange as a curtain call. "There was one final and exceptionally hysterical call."

"Here it comes," I thought to myself. Always expect the unexpected. With a sense of mild to moderate irritation, I learned that The Iguana had arrived in Key West. He had screamed at Ted that since I never returned his calls, he had decided to show up in person. Ted informed me that The Iguana had "a surprise" for me. Little wonder. That Iguana was always full of surprises.

The Iguana had checked into a suite at the Pier House. I decided that, however distasteful, I had to finally confront my agent before my flight to Switzerland. I owed him at least one face-to-face, as horrible an experience I knew that would be, considering his looks. After all, he had flown all this distance. The movie he'd agented ("Butterflies") was rapidly collapsing. Perhaps, he'd already met with Jerry and learned of the billing for the new cast, Dino Paglia and Mia Kelly, not necessarily in that order.

For reasons unknown to me, The Iguana hated Key West and had vowed never to set foot here again. Snake knew all the dirty secrets about this, and perhaps had threatened The Iguana with arrest (or blackmail?) should he ever again cross the Monroe County line. Because of the consequences of those past scandals, I knew The Iguana would lay low while in Key West, not be his usual hyper-embarrassing self, and probably cause less than his usual share of trouble.

I discussed the unfolding situation with the man in my life, Rafael, and it was agreed that we should go to the Pier House right away for my meeting with my agent. I didn't want The Iguana to start salivating and slapping his long lizard tail at the sight of Rafael. I asked my bodyguard and lover, the future president of Cuba, to wait in the limousine, or better yet, adjourn to an al fresco bar and order himself a Cuba libre while I negotiated this interview alone. He warned me to be careful. Not that I needed to be warned when facing a reptile like The Iguana. During my increasingly infrequent personal encounters with him, I always wore a breast plate of armor.

. . .

At the hotel desk, I put through a call to The Iguana's suite, no doubt the most expensive one in town, and no doubt paid for by moi.

"Who loves ya, baby?"

When the sickeningly syrupy voice of The Iguana came onto the phone, I knew the reptile had been fed a diet of too many hibiscus blossoms since his arrival in Key West. No chastisement, nothing, not even a mention of my having failed to return his thousands of urgent phone calls. That meant only one thing: The Iguana had arrived on this coral rock with contracts. He obviously wanted to wing out of here as fast as possible, but only after he'd secured my autograph on every one of those pieces of paper. After all, mine was the world's most sought-after autograph. My signature guaranteed heavy cash around the world. I realized that if I ever ran out of money – not bloody likely – I could spend the rest of my life sitting on a street corner peddling my autograph to the masses.

The Iguana had already told me he'd be out on his terrace

talking to the "biggest names in Hollywood" about lucrative deals for me. Although the sun had already set, I was to join him there for a sundowner. With a sigh, I agreed.

I was slightly suspicious, however. Considering all the illicit activities which had occurred in bedrooms occupied throughout the years by The Iguana – no doubt, unspeakable acts of sexual atrocity – he was the type of guy who demanded and got high-security doors with industrial-sized bolts whenever he checked into a hotel. Perhaps the mighty Snake himself might try to barge in at any minute to serve The Iguana with a search warrant for any of my agent's past indiscretions.

Bracing myself for trouble, I rode the elevator to the second floor, reaching the suite whose number I'd been given. I was surprised to find the door slightly ajar. Somewhat intimidated, I opened the door to the suite and entered an area that was very dark except for the faint glow of a night light. As my eyes adjusted to the dark, I noticed that the draperies were shut tight – typical for any room occupied by a reptile, I thought. The Iguana always liked heavy draperies concealing whatever activities were occurring within bedrooms occupied by his well-fucked body. He claimed he'd had the "biggest and best" of Hollywood's golden era, and continued to have "the biggest" stars today. After intensive auditioning, he did launch the careers of a few male stars with improbable names during the 1950s. However, in the spring of 1993, with all those attractive wannabees buried in the past, Sherry Kelly was his hot meal ticket.

The room had a slight smell of incense to it. For one brief second, I was tempted to turn and leave. If The Iguana wanted this urgent meeting with me, he could join me in the bar downstairs. Perhaps Rafael would decide to join the party. Safety in numbers, I'd always been told. Not wishing a repeat of that long-ago, touchy-feely interview he'd had with Cruz, I would place myself between the two.

The more I thought about leaving, the more I liked the idea. A world-class star like Sherry Kelly didn't do quickie gigs in hotel rooms.

I reached for the door handle to open it and return to the hotel lobby, where I planned to call The Iguana. As I did, a strong hand blocked my exit. I whirled around to confront what

I assumed would be either a rapist or an assassin. I was crushed into the arms of what appeared to be a nude man. A powerful, extremely well-built nude man.

As my mouth opened to scream, it was quickly rewarded with the longest, smoothest, and most velvety tongue that has ever been recorded in the saga of human sexuality.

. . .

As far as I was concerned, this Viking god could go on with this kissing scene all night and into the next morning if that was his desire. It's not that I'm a girl who can't say no. I've said no plenty of times in my life, more than you'd ever think. But when God Himself (Herself?) sends a towering and muscled giant from the halls of Valhalla to give me a greeting such as I was getting, I figured it would be foolish to spurn the gift.

While the heavy kissing and tonguing were going on, my hands, taking off on a voyage of their own and without conscious direction, were doing some intensive exploring. There was a lot of territory to explore. This guy couldn't be real. He was like some fantasy that Tom of Finland would create rock-hard nude for gay readership. Forget Stallone. Forget that Arnold, whatever his last name was. You know the one? Not my type at all. Surely, there was only one man in Hollywood with a body like this.

Sean Nielson!

Using all the strength and willpower in my body, and summoning a steely reserve I never knew I possessed, I broke away from my attacker. Like a blind person, my hands went to his face, gently circling his features.

"Sean?" I asked, not really needing confirmation. "It's really you!" I knew it was no imposter, since there is no other Sean Nielson.

"It's really me, baby. You don't have to identify yourself. I'd know you anywhere. After that kissing scene we just had, I should say I could taste you anywhere. That's a kiss I'll remember for the rest of my life."

His use of the word "scene" brought a quick understanding to me of the situation. This wasn't real. It was a scene from the script of "Butterflies." Leonora slips into Numie's room one night to seduce him. Knowing what she's up to, Numie hears her coming and hides behind the door. He agrees to the seduction, but only on his own terms. Hiding behind the door, he lunges for her and attacks her, knowing that what she really wants more than anything in the world is to be raped. At least in the script, many of her neuroses are based on her perception that she's constantly being "violated" by the world.

"This is a scene from the movie," I said, not really making it a question. "The Iguana is behind this. It has his touch. He's flown you here to replace Cruz in 'Butterflies.'"

"How about it?" he asked, smiling. "Do I get the part? You already know from our phone conversation how much I want to do it."

Not answering at first, I moved through the darkened room until I found a light switch on a lamp. It cast a soft yellow glow over the room. After all, I didn't have a chance to check my make-up. There could be no lipstick left. Soft yellow or forgiving pink were The Iguana's favorite lights. Because of his looks, he could never appear in harsh lights anywhere in the world out of fear of offending someone. Neon was especially cruel. To my disappointment, he wasn't nude at all, although he might as well have been. My hands hadn't explored that far south yet. Just like the script called for, he was clad in a pair of Calvin Klein briefs. What was that silly bigoted singer's name? Marky Mark or some such crap? Forget him. Sean Nielson was the model to pose for Calvin Klein underwear. Unless his picture would cause a backlash, setting off millions after millions of cases of penis envy in the American male. No need for Maxie to stuff any crotches around here.

I continued to eye him provocatively. He was obviously waiting for me to make the next move. "If I recall the script," I said, "the next scene calls for Numie to glide Leonora to the bed, where he mounts the attack. Of course, that means the briefs have to go. If I further recall, Jerry, that pervert, planned to see a humpy male ass rising up and down on that bed for the camera's benefit. I think I interrupted you before the scene had reached its inevitable finale."

"You did indeed, my pretty one. Just give the word, and the briefs disappear. I'll give them to you as a souvenir." He enticingly fingered the elastic band of his underwear.

"Hold it. Don't tempt me more than I'm already tempted. I'm only flesh, you know. Weak female flesh at that."

"Whatever. It looks great to me."

"Where in hell were you only a few weeks ago? Before everything changed in my life. Why didn't you call? Why didn't you show up at my doorstep instead of that Dino Paglia?"

"It never occurred to me that the very beautiful and very, very rich Sherry Kelly would be interested in me. In my mind, you were booked solid every night. Even if you were spending the night alone, I assumed your time would be devoted to either counting your billions or perhaps polishing your gems."

"If you only knew how untrue that was."

"I hate myself for not working harder to learn you had this thing for me. God knows, I'd have come running at any time of the day or night you needed me."

"I would have liked that."

"I gather I don't have the part. There have been many changes in your life since Hollywood."

"Many changes."

"Too bad. During my seduction of Leonora, your agent suggested that I actually penetrate you. It would make the film realistic, and add millions to the worldwide box office gross. Up that close to you, and with me pounding away, I surely would have gotten a hard-on. Where would I have put it?"

I'm sure I'm missing out on the biggest thrill of my life."

"Not only the biggest, the best."

I flashed a genuine smile at him. I liked a man with so much confidence. In his case, and unlike Snake, I felt Sean had a right to be confident. He had half the women--not to mention men-- from around the globe propositioning him.

Noticing a terrycloth robe on The Iguana's queen-size bed, I tossed it over to him. "Better slip that over you before you're attacked."

I opened the doors leading to The Iguana's terrace. Here I stood as the soothing breezes from the Gulf of Mexico bathed my body. I felt like a woman in love. But with whom? Was Sean Nielson still my dream fantasy? Or had the fantasies been replaced by a real man, Rafael? I always had this thing for blond men until Rafael – not Dino – had converted me to the allure of a brunet.

In a minute, he joined me on the terrace. He didn't say anything at first, just took my hand and held it without pressure.

"Oh, that film," I said. "The latest word is that it will star Dino Paglia and Mia Kelly, not necessarily in that billing order. I had to bow out. After that Cruz shooting, there have just been too many problems. In the unlikely event that Jerry dumps Dino tomorrow, or at the least, the following day, the part is yours. You're right for it. I'm sure Mia would love to appear opposite you, as I would myself. I'm the major backer of the film, and I've got a lot to say about who plays Numie."

"Thanks, I think I could really play the role. I need something new and different in my career. A challenge."

I reached up and gently kissed him on the cheek. God, this Viking smelled good. "This is Sherry Kelly you're talking to. By that, I mean you're not going to leave Key West empty-handed. I'll see to that. Imagine flying back to Hollywood with that dreaded Iguana in the next seat, without having obtained either me or the role of Numie. I hope the bastard at least flew you here first class."

"He did. But a guy has to be careful around that one. He's got roving hands and no sense of shame."

"I know."

"So do most people, men and women, around the world. I've had--how do you say it in English--my basket felt up so many times I should charge admission."

"Indeed you should." I stopped for a moment, listening to the laughter drifting up from a nearby open-air bar. I wondered if Rafael were having more than one Cuba libre. "Three weeks before I left Hollywood, I received the screen treatment of a novel I'd optioned. I really like the book. It's called 'Declining Fortunes,' hardly the story of my life. Unfortunately, the screen treatment made the man's part far better than my own, and I had seen it as my first really serious picture. But it's a great role for a man. Sexy, powerful, strong--all the things you are. Hollywood hasn't given you a chance. It's not some dumb action movie. It's a real part, with real human drama. With you as the lead, I'll consider putting up the money for the film. Are you interested?"

"Sounds terrific. I trust your judgment. I'd love to do it."

"I'll have the script sent to you. Unfortunately, we'll have to let The Iguana broker the deal. I have a contract with him, and that one sues."

"You've been more than generous. As you said, I've yet to get my really big chance. This could be it."

"And let's get on with it before we're too old for Hollywood or for anyone else."

"I'm for that and I totally agree with you." He edged closer to me, and I didn't budge, not one inch. "You'll never be too old for me."

"Or you for me. As Gore Vidal once said about that oldtime actor, James Craig, Craig could put his shoes under Vidal's bed even today, regardless of how old, gray, and decrepit Craig looks. I feel that way about you. You'll be just as alluring to some hot woman when you're sixty as you are to me today."

"I feel the same way about you." He put his arms around me. "I like an expression you have in English. 'What might have been.' Let's seal 'what might have been' with a good-bye kiss."

Once again I found myself pressing tightly against his body and sucking on that supremely talented tongue.

Suddenly, the draperies concealing the bedroom from the terrace were yanked violently back. Here, in steaming Hispanic rage, stood one defiant Rafael.

"PUTA!" He yelled at me. "YOU GRINGA PUTA! I can't trust you out of my sight for one minute!" He turned and headed rapidly for the door.

"Rafael!" I called to him, breaking free of Sean. "I can explain everything. It'll take a little time, though."

I turned to Sean. He blew me a kiss. I whirled around and rushed to the door. "We'll be in touch," I called back to him. "I promise, we'll work out a deal."

"Good-bye, my Sherry. I've been in your same trap before. Go after him. Good luck."

Slamming the door to The Iguana's suite, I raced down the corridor after Rafael. I couldn't let that Cubano walk out on me because of one little tongue kiss, regardless of how enticing it might have been.

Like Scarlett O'Hara in "Gone with the Wind," I was determined to get my Rhett Butler back.

Not when tomorrow became another day.

Tonight.

. . .

When I finally located Rafael at one of the hotel bars, he was having more than his share of Cuba libres. On the way there, four fans stopped me and asked me if I were *the* Sherry Kelly. Thanking them, I politely informed each of them that I was a female impersonator and begged them to catch my late show at the Copa.

Rafael was alone at the bar. As I approached him and gently touched his arm, he pulled away. "Go back to your blond," he said. "He'll take better care of you than some lowlife Spik commie like me."

"That's not true, and you know it. I'll explain everything. Come back with me to the car."

"Why should I?" He glared at me. This was the first time I'd ever known rage in him. Jealous rage.

He raised his voice, and at first I was slightly embarrassed at attracting such attention. Like Mia Kelly, many of the moments of high drama in my personal life had been played out in front of audiences. Fortunately, Key West bars were used to such outbursts and didn't pay much attention to them.

"Come back to you to act like one of your mariposas?" he snarled. "Be your bodyguard? Light your cigarettes? Get someone on the phone for you? Fuck you when you get horny?"

"I never meant to treat you like that – and you know it. It's just that things have been happening so quickly that I haven't really had time to concentrate on us. Give me a break. Since we came together, things haven't been ideal for romance."

"I'll grant you that much. It's all been too much."

"Soon we'll go away on a long honeymoon. You and me on some forgotten island somewhere. If I recall, I own quite a few."

"Is that a marriage proposal?" He stared at me long and hard.

Dumbfounded, I stepped back. "I guess it was. I just proposed marriage to you."

"In my country, it's usually the man who proposes the

marriage."

"I knew you'd never ask me. So I had to ask you."

"I would have asked you, but I feared you'd say no." He turned back to the bar and downed the rest of his drink in one gulp. I signaled for the waiter to bring him another, and then even ordered a gin and tonic for myself. Whisky is more for social drinking. For the serious negotiations of life, I have always followed the example of QE Segundo and asked for a gin and tonic. "I want to marry you. I think I fell in love with you the first day I saw you."

"You didn't fall in love with me and you know it. You had the hots for me. I had the hots for you. We got together. It will take years for us to fall in love. Some day, in the future, when I'm president of Cuba and you're my first lady, we'll be sitting in some Havana living room of Cuban wicker, everything painted white. Maybe a few potted palms and a view over a garden and the sea. You'll look over at me and take my hand. With your other hand you'll gently run your fingers through the graying of my temples. When you look into my eyes with a certain kind of tenderness, that's when you will have fallen in love with me. And me with you."

"Maybe you're right. I sure like the sound of that. I look forward to that day. In fact, I could play that part. I see myself as a new Evita Peron rising out of Latin America."

He grabbed hold of my arm, almost hurting me. "Cut the shit! You don't believe a word you're saying. It's just a role to you. It isn't real. Everything is a role for you and your mother, especially men. To women like you and Mia Kelly, men are just supporting players. They come and go. You hire and fire. Have you ever loved just one man in your whole life the way I loved Tricia?"

I slowly sipped my gin and tonic, not wanting to answer right away. It was as if I were QE Segundo at Buckingham Palace, slowly drinking by myself and trying to recall the last time in some almost-forgotten decade I'd gone to bed with Prince Philip. I decided to be honest with him, as he didn't like liars. "I've never loved anyone. Once or twice I thought I was in love, but everybody I've ever loved turned out to be a hustler."

"Like my son?"

"Like your son. Whatever he and I had is so unimportant that it doesn't deserve a mention."

"Unimportant to you, perhaps. Not to Desi. It seems to have been his launching pad into a rich life. Like I suspect the blond giant was doing back in that hotel room. Using you like a launching pad."

The scene with Sean, I explained, was a set-up, artfully arranged by my agent, The Iguana. The lizard hadn't known of my involvement with Rafael, and thought I would be interested in the blond giant, as foolish an idea as that was. "You've got to admit," I said, "that very few people know of our relationship. Certainly not the sleazy tabloids. It was just an attempt on Sean's part to get the role by staging one of the scenes from the film script. Nothing more serious than that."

"But you kissed him. I walk in on my woman kissing a man wearing a bathrobe. An unbuttoned bathrobe at that. Wearing nothing but a pair of underwear briefs. And with a very obvious hard-on. My God, he looked almost as big as me."

"Don't be an idiot, darling. No one's as big as you."

"Do you mean that?"

"Of course I do. What woman could settle for any other man, even Sean Nielson, after having spent a night with Rafael Navarro? You're the best."

For the first time since this sordid drama caused by The Iguana began, he smiled. "You've got a point there."

"Let's forget this stupid night ever happened. *Please.*"

"Perhaps I will. Perhaps I won't. I'm not giving in to the great Sherry Kelly as easily as that."

"You mean you plan to make me suffer a little bit more?"

"That, and other things."

"I'll pay you more attention. I won't treat you like a servant. I'll treat you like a man worthy of respect. The future president of Cuba."

At that remark, he slammed down his drink and turned on me with renewed anger. I reacted in surprise because in wanting to please him, I had tried to say the right thing.

"You think my presidential ambitions are a joke, don't you?"

"Not at all."

"You seem to mock them and me. I bet right this minute you're thinking that after you've dumped me for the blond, I'll end up washing dishes in some Cuban fast food-joint in Miami."

"I don't believe that."

"Then prove it."

"How can I?"

"By helping me campaign for president. By being at my side. Maybe even as my wife."

"We can't campaign in the streets of Havana. Castro will have us killed."

"We'll start my campaign in the Cuban ghettos of Miami. Even if I can't draw the crowds at first, you'll attract them. They'll come just to get a look at the star of 'Kinky,' and maybe stay around to listen to my message."

"I see." I thought for a long moment, trying to search out a role model I could identify with. Elizabeth Taylor did campaign for her husband at the time, that dreadful uncircumcised senator from Virginia, the homophobe John Warner. Imagine Elizabeth Taylor – of all people – campaigning for a notorious homophobe. If she did that, what would be so strange about my campaigning for a man who wanted to be president of Cuba?

"We want to overthrow Castro. Launch the revolution. We'll begin the revolution in the streets of Miami. Half of Cuba is there already. I'll invite my people to return to their motherland and to vote for me in a free and democratic Cuba after Castro is gone."

"Oh, what the hell? Why not be a dishwasher instead and save yourself all the trouble?"

He turned and flashed anger at me again, as if I had insulted his male pride. Then he realized I was joking, and somehow, my flippant remark broke the awful tension between us.

He grabbed me, right in front of God knows who, and jabbed his tongue down my throat in a kiss designed to make me forget that Sean ever existed, if such a thing were truly possible. It was his way of taking possession of his woman again, and I was only too willing to be possessed.

"Get us a suite at this hotel right now," he demanded when he finally withdrew from my throat.

"Why? We have a great big rented house here."

"I've got to have you. *Now*. I can't wait."

"If you're that eager, I guess I can afford the price of another suite." As thoughts of The Iguana came back to me, I was certain that I was already paying for the most expensive suite at the Pier House, and soon would be paying for another.

On the way to the lobby to register, he whispered into my ear. "I'm going to do something to you I haven't done before. I'm going to fuck you up the ass. It's going to hurt. Maybe a lot. But it's your punishment for kissing that blond giant."

Punishment like that, I could take. After registering without luggage, a quaint Key West hotbed custom, I literally rushed to the suite with him at my side. If anything, I led the way.

Once in the room, with hardly enough time to remove clothing, I took the pounding of a lifetime. The next time I went on the Howard Stern show, I could truly admit to being butt-fucked. I would be walking crooked for a month, but I'd have a lot of memories.

As I lay gasping for breath on the bed, a smug and satisfied Rafael retreated to the shower. The persistent ringing of the phone made me eventually decide to answer it. After all, how many people in the world could possibly know where I was?

It was from The Iguana. "Who loves ya, baby?" he said. The beast had tracked me down. I was to meet him in the bar downstairs. Emergency was written on everything he said. After gaining his assurance that he'd be seated in the most dimly lit corner of the bar, without any illumination of any kind on his face, I agreed to the rendezvous. But this time I not only planned to obtain Rafael's permission, but requested that he station himself nearby within the same bar in case I needed him.

With The Iguana, one had to anticipate surprises.

. . .

"Who loves ya, baby?" The sound of his voice reverberated through the bar.

In a far and darkened corner of the bar, The Iguana sat downing his vodka. The agent drank vodka by the quart and still continued to negotiate deals worth millions of dollars. He'd certainly made millions for me, even though I hardly needed the loot. Only The Iguana knew how many millions he'd forgotten to turn over to me. You didn't hold a slimy lizard like him to a strict accounting, but after all, I hadn't gone into films to make money anyway.

"You adore me," I finally answered his trademark question. I took a position in a bar chair near him, but left a wide space between us. I never liked to get too close to him, because The Iguana covered his corpulent body with Chanel no. 5, a perfume I find offensive.

I assumed The Iguana was flashing his famous smile at me, although in the dim light it was hard to tell. Armies had marched through that gaping mouth. Most of that smile was toothless. The Iguana could have afforded to buy a dental clinic, yet he preferred to keep his original rotting teeth, even though some were missing. He had a sentimental attachment to the teeth that had enjoyed so many feasts of prime meat over the years.

"I trust you enjoyed the big surprise I planned for you. An octoroon dick on a Viking God. Even thinking about that pole starts me salivating. I didn't touch an inch of it except to feel it and check it out. Saved all of it just for you."

"Sean and I didn't make it."

"Don't kid an old pussy like me, baby. You probably ripped off those Calvin Kleiners two seconds after entering my suite. Just like I wanted to had my heart not been filled with generosity for you. You and I are two of a kind. Two brightly rouged and garishly painted pussies hustling our moneymakers from coast to coast."

"I've never sold it. As for you, who would ever buy?" That came out a little more harshly than I'd meant. I didn't want this to turn into a Joan Crawford versus Bette Davis type of meeting. But his remark angered me. "You know only the Old Sherry. I'm the New Sherry. Born again."

"Oh, my God, you've converted to Jesus. It's a remake of 'Sadie Thompson.'"

"I've not converted to anything. I'm just a faithful woman for a change. True to only one man."

"Not that Dino Paglia fag?"

"Not that one. His daddy!"

At that revelation, The Iguana almost spat out his vodka. I think he lost one of those decaying teeth in the process. As he choked on that body part, I said, "And I owe it all to you, you sweet hibiscus-eating reptile. You set up the meeting where I fell madly in love with Rafael Navarro."

"Now, now, baby, don't get carried away. Spik cock ain't your thing. Didn't Gore Vidal compare it to a piece of tiny okra?"

"He did, and he was right in some cases. However, the Latino male comes in many shapes and sizes."

"He's using you, baby. A hustler if I ever saw one. That shit's in legal trouble. He's fucking you to pay the bills. Wise up. With Rafael, you're paying for it by the inch."

"A fair exchange."

"That guy must be terrific, but let's cut this lovesick crap and get down to business. I didn't haul my delectable big ass all the way to Key West to sell a romance novel. A town I hate, incidentally. What with that god damn sheriff, Snake, trying to get me on a child molestation offense."

That was suspicion confirmed for me. I never really knew what Snake had on The Iguana. "Snake and I are real close."

"You mean he's on the payroll?"

"Sorta. I'll see that he doesn't interfere with you any more."

"Thanks."

As The Iguana ranted on about various deals--each guaranteed to "make millions" for me--I occasionally eyed Rafael sitting at the bar. He'd already brushed away two hookers and one handsome young blond sailor who'd obviously propositioned him, even trying to cop a feel. Rafael had switched from those lethal Cuba libres to club soda with a twist of Key lime. That Rafael. He was some pain in the ass, and I mean that literally.

Apparently, The Iguana had been talking about "Butterflies" and how he wanted Sean to play Numie.

"I'm out of the film," I abruptly announced.

"Don't joke with this slimy pussy sitting across the table from you," he said. "You've got millions riding on the deal. You need to retrieve some of your loot. It seems that we can get out of this Cruz mess by giving him the full eighteen million that would have been his salary. There will be no lawsuit. No press conferences. A cool eighteen million. And that's that."

"Not bad for one minute's work. The most expensive minute an actor's ever been paid in the history of show business."

"Babydoll, he did get shot for his trouble, which leads to my next question. My vaginal cavity is just itching to ask it. Why did you shoot Cruz? He wouldn't let you go down on him, some shit like that? I mean, he wouldn't even make it with me, and I've had lots of stars bigger than Cruz. Rock. Robert. Ty. Errol. Even horsedick Forrest Tucker, not to mention the even bigger John Ireland. Errol was a waste of my time. Too drunk to get it up. Ty wasn't memorable at all. Liked to take it up the ass. And I could do that better than he could."

"I'm not interested in your sordid back lot affairs with long-dead stars. I didn't put that bullet in Mia's revolver. I don't know who did it. But I sure would like to find out. I don't trust Snake to carry out the investigation either."

"Don't mention that fucking Snakeshit again. He set me up with that jailbait. I thought the boy was of age, or at least close to it. He certainly looked it, anyway. Turned out that he was only fourteen. Snake is a blackmailer, as if you didn't already know. He's like a copperhead, water moccasin, and rattlesnake all rolled into one horrible poisonous viper. I hear, though, he's got a fourteen-inch dick."

"No, more like Gore Vidal's description of the tiny piece of okra, I'm sure."

"Too bad. At least I thought I was being roughed up by a real man. Another illusion shattered."

"Why do you get into such messes with these guys?"

"If you've got the name, why not play the game?"

It was hard to keep The Iguana talking business. Invariably, he steered the conversation back to sex. "The film, remember?" I asked.

"What about it?" With you out, the picture's dead."

"Mia may want to play my role. I'm perfectly serious about that."

"Mia Kelly in a film? Either you're nuts or she is. Why would Mia lower herself to become a show gal?"

"Because I've made 'Kinky' and was adored around the world, and she wants some of the same adulation. Or maybe just to show the world she can do it. She also thinks she'll photograph better than me, if you could imagine such a thing."

Right away, The Iguana's lizard brain went into overdrive. I'm sure he envisioned the millions of dollars of free publicity that "Butterflies" would receive with Mia playing the lead. "There is a possibility here," he said finally. "At least in the third world. In the third world where nobody can read or write, they know images. Since Mia looks exactly like Elizabeth Taylor, everybody in the third world will think Taylor's in the film. Her big comeback. You don't make a comeback getting cast in 'Flintstones.' My God, Taylor might come back without even coming back. How sensational! We'll make up your mother to look like Taylor as she appeared opposite Newman in 'Cat on a Hot Tin Roof.'"

"What fun!"

"Could Sean appear opposite Mia? I promised him a big part."

"Jerry wants Dino, I announced."

"Baby, you're drunk. What did Dino do to convince that faggot Wheeler he could co-star in a legit movie?"

"When Dino drops trou, he's convincing.

"But it's still ridiculous. Mia Kelly playing opposite that punk. I'm going to make myself the agent on the deal. You owe me one for setting up that meeting with the love of your life, the Navarro Spik. I want to collect on your debt to me right now. I wanna be Mia's agent. And I'll insist on hiring Sean for the male role, with your approval, of course."

"Go for it. You have my blessing. Mia doesn't have a theatrical agent anyway. You'd be perfect for her. She'd love you. Any woman who'd stoop to going to bed with Clarence Thomas would at least find you less than repulsive. Handsome, even."

"Handsome? I used to be the prettiest boy in Hollywood. No contest."

At some point in every one of our interviews, that "prettiest boy in Hollywood" line came up. There was no way that the grotesquely deformed Iguana could have been the prettiest boy in Hollywood, or any other town, village, or hamlet in the world. I always chose, however, not to challenge his claim.

"I was hotter and better-looking than Dino in my prime. And, although I didn't tell you at the time, that Dino is the hottest stud I've seen coming down the turnpike, and your mother sitting here has had them all."

"You should meet his daddy."

"Can't wait," he said, already starting to salivate and drip.

"Forget it!"

"I've got my work cut out for me. I've got to save 'Butterflies.' It's your loot I'm saving. Remember that. You'll owe me another one."

"I know. You're a man who likes to collect debts. Do what you can. I don't want to do the film. In fact, I'm considering retiring from films."

"Retiring? Bullshit! You've only begun. You're the hottest box-office star in the world. I plan to make millions off you." Realizing what he'd said, The Iguana stopped short. "I mean, I plan to make millions for you. Millions, my sweet pussy galore. Millions. Sweet millions." Even more than male genitalia, this old lizard, whose ancestors must have existed at the dawn of time, salivated over millions.

"Millions, hell! I'm a billion-dollar-baby and don't you forget it, you black hole of Calcutta."

"Baby, let's don't go into name-calling. It's vulgar and I hate vulgarity. You know that in business dealings I'm always the gentleman. An alleycat at night but a gentleman negotiator during the day. I never mix business with pleasure."

"Right. Like the time you tried to go down on that executive at Paramount while negotiating a contract for me. I had to bail you out of that mess, and that happened at ten o'clock in the cold bloody light of morning."

"I couldn't resist what he had dangling in the men's room. You of all people know about temptation."

"Don't ever pull that stunt again."

"Baby, you're a new Sherry, and I'm a new pussy." Darting out his lizard tongue, he leaned closer to me, the stench of his breath similar to the poison gas sprayed into the trenches of World War I. "What about that script I gave you? 'Virgin Bush'? It's the hottest property in Hollywood."

"One look at the title and I tossed it."

"You didn't read it? The hottest script in Hollywood? Can't you hear? I made up the 'Virgin Bush' title at the last minute before giving it to you. The writer came up with some dumb title that wasn't commercial. We can retitle the fucker. If you agree to take the role, you can make at least twenty-five million dollars, perhaps a hell of a lot more than that. At the rate you're spending money these days, that's a lot of loot. It'll pay the bills of a lot of hustlers. You'll never have to touch those beautiful gold bars you've entrusted to those icky gnomes in Zurich."

"It's a great part?" I asked, wishing I hadn't. The actress side of me had taken the bait. I wondered if it were indeed the hottest script in Hollywood. David could find that out soon enough for me.

"Do it, baby, go for it. It'll outgross 'Kinky,' and we're still counting your money on that one. You don't even have to show tits and ass. It also calls for the part of a handsome blond Nazi lieutenant who befriends you and ultimately rescues you from occupied Belgium. Let Sean have that one."

"Perhaps I will. I promised Sean the lead in 'Declining Fortunes.'"

"Hate the title. Later for that piece of shit. First, Sean has to get established in a major role. You and Sean will make all previous Hollywood couples look like dying brats in an AIDS ward. Gable and Lombard. Bogart and Bacall. Tracy and Hepburn. They're history. You and Sean will be the couple to end the 20th century in Hollywood. I've already arranged for a dual centerfold in *Penthouse*, both of you nude together. Trust me. Have I ever given you bad advice?"

His question caused me to pause and glance briefly at Rafael. He was still at the bar, still eying our table intently, as if he'd have to assault The Iguana at any minute.

"See that stud at the bar?" he asked. "He's been looking over here at me all night. I can spot them in a minute. I'll have to excuse myself pretty soon. It seems I've found my date for tonight."

I smiled. "Back to business first, cuntie. It's true. All the advice you've ever given me has been good. *Kinky* turned to gold. That's why I hired you. You may no longer be the prettiest boy in Hollywood, but you've got one effective twat. I'll read the damn script. It'd better be good or I'll cut off your nuts if I can find them. If that script is as good as you say, I'll definitely consider Sean."

"Thanks, baby. You won't regret this. I'll send the first twenty-five million over to your house – whatever house you're in at the time. In small bills so it'll take longer to count and so you can enjoy it more. After counting it, you can go out and buy yourself something pretty."

"I can't make the film without Rafael's permission."

"Bullshit! When has Sherry Kelly ever asked anybody's permission to do anything?"

"True of the Old Sherry. The New Sherry asks permission of her daddy. Don't worry, you wretched old hag, I know how to win him over. I'll promise to give him the money to launch his presidential campaign."

"PRESIDENTIAL CAMPAIGN! You're on drugs! We've been talking real shit up to now. He's going to run for president? He's hardly got here and may face indictment from the U.S. government."

"Overthrow Castro!" I said, growing impatient. "Don't be a silly bitch. I don't mean president of the United States."

"Baby, you may be getting into deep shit with this Spik. Take it from your mother. You've got enough troubles. You don't need to take on Cuba too."

At this point, a waiter arrived with an urgent message for The Iguana. He pulled a little flashlight out of his pocket and read it in the dim light of the bar. He crumbled the paper and smiled, preferring to translate the message for me instead of actually letting me read it. Whenever The Iguana did that, there was always something in the message he didn't want me to read. I knew his translation would never be entirely accurate.

"That message was from Dino Paglia," he said triumphantly.

"Dino? What does he want with you? I'd think with Mia and Jerry, he had enough to do."

"Can't you figure it out? He's probably heard that Sean Nielson is in town. I'm sure he knows that Sean wants to appear in 'Butterflies.' Dino is waiting in the lobby of the Pier House right now. He's here to convince me to use my influence to keep the part for him and not give it away to Sean."

"That Dino. The little devil. He's supposed to be seeing me later. On business."

"Baby, he's your discard. Wouldn't be the first time I picked up your discard."

"No, it wouldn't."

"This brings up a possible conflict of interest."

"Since when did a conflict of interest ever make you lose a

night's sleep?"

"What I mean is, in my mind, as a purely mental thing, I'd already made a commitment to that stud at the bar. The one who's been eying me all night." He nodded in the direction of Rafael. "Since you owe me one, here's what I want you to do. Go over and offer him five-hundred dollars. I'd give you the cash myself but I'm running low tonight. However, I'll credit your account. You'll get every penny back. Slip him the five-hundred dollars. Tell him there's plenty more where that came from, and that it comes from me. Let him know I'll be back here at the bar at midnight. He's to be waiting here for me. In the meantime, I'll hoist my gaping hole – which is starting to twitch in anticipation this very minute – out of this uncomfortable chair."

"Believe me," I promised him, "I'll take care of that stud at the bar."

"Thanks, baby. I know you don't want me to kiss you since you don't know where my mouth has been recently. But imagine that I've just planted a big sloppy wet one on your hot ruby-red lips."

The very idea caused me almost to vomit, but I smiled demurely and blew him a farewell kiss. He waved goodbye to me.

In front of Rafael, and for his benefit alone, The Iguana did his impression of Jack Lemmon in drag in "Some Like It Hot."

Rafael muttered something about mariposas and turned his back to The Iguana.

At the doorway to the bar, The Iguana waved his little pinkie in the air. He turned to me once again. "WHO LOVES YA, BABY!" He then flitted off into the night, pursuing as reptiles do various nocturnal adventures, this time with Dino.

. . .

With Rafael at my side, I headed for the front of the Pier House to find our waiting limousine. Understandably, I chose not to give him the five-hundred dollars, and utterly failed to set up a rendezvous between him and The Iguana. I figured The Iguana would be busy enough tonight with the son, although I also had plans for Dino.

As I headed out of the hotel, a crowd had formed. People surged toward us, and some screamed my name. A TV news camera was on the scene. Apparently, those so-called fans of mine didn't really believe my line about being a female impersonator at the Copa. One reporter almost knocked my teeth out with a microphone. Why did you try to kill your lover, Brad Cruz?" he shouted in my face.

Rafael pushed the reporter back. Using all the strength and power in his muscled body, he cleared a pathway for me to the waiting limousine. The crowd seemed almost equally divided between the pro-Sherry forces and the anti-Sherry Kelly forces. As I was hustled into the limousine by Rafael, one hastily scribbled sign caught my eye. SHERRY KELLY IS THE ONE WHO SHOULD BE SHOT!!!

Trying to wipe that endearing sentiment from my mind, I eased into the safe haven of the back seat of the limousine. Ironically, it seemed I'd spent most of my life in the back seats of limousines, and I always felt secure in most of them. Even now, the vehicle afforded much-needed protection against the unruly crowd.

As the limousine slowly eased its way through the rapidly growing mob, an old woman, perhaps in her eighties, pressed her nose against the window of the limousine which was closest to where I was sitting. Her ugly mouth formed the words HARLOT. Then she spat at the window with such fury and loathing I shuddered, cuddling closer to Rafael.

Only when the limousine pulled into the gates of our rented southernmost house, and only when those gates were locked, did I breathe a sigh of relief. That relief, it seemed, was premature.

Inside, Ted and Maxie were directing a staff whose intensity matched that of the personnel working within Eisenhower's headquarters during the third hour of the Allied attack on the beaches of Normandy.

"Oh, Sherry," Ted said. "Thank God you're here. Things have been awful. I've had to hire more staff. The whole world wants to interview you. I've been at your house in California plenty of times. We've spent Sundays there together. You used to get only three or four calls. Polite calls, from people like Onassis. Kevin Costner. Cher. Harry Winston. That was it.

Never like this..."

"Which of the calls are the most urgent?"

"Mia wants to see you just as soon as possible. She said it's about your diary. David must speak to you at once. The White House called again."

Pulling him to the side so we could confer in private, I said, "Handle that boyfriend of yours up there in the White House. Stall him. About the last thing I want right now is a date with Bill Clinton. Why would he want to date me now when so much media attention is focused on me?"

"Maybe Hillary isn't putting out any more."

"And maybe he's nuts, or drugged, or something."

"The furs arrived," he said, "including that sable which I wish I owned, and that thrillingly glamorous ermine that is possibly the most expensive coat I've ever seen anytime, anywhere, in my entire tawdry life. They've been loaded onto the plane I chartered for you at the Miami airport. By armed guard the Capetown Diamond was sent there, too, and it's also on board the plane. Why are you trying to dress like a rich woman?"

"You'll find out soon enough."

"We'll be quickly cleared for takeoff once you arrive in Miami. That's been seen to by David himself. I'm always surprised at the incredible amount of influence he has up there in Miami. I've never been to Switzerland. I'm just dying to go. Visit all those alps and see all those mountain climbers. They have such strong legs. Maxie has really been badgering me to find out why we're going. But that one blabs every word she hears to anyone who'll listen. Always has. Always will. She should have been Hedda Hopper."

"Tell Maxie he'll find out soon enough. Now get us ready for the flight." I was sounding more and more like General Eisenhower myself.

As I raced upstairs to my bedroom, I screamed for Ted to follow me. When I entered the room, I heard Rafael taking a shower, even though he'd just showered not long ago at the Pier House after our rather memorable backdoor session together. Like Ted, he'd never been to Switzerland either, and hoped to be the first of several Cuban delegations going there for discussions on trade and banking policies.

"Trading Havana cigars for cuckoo clocks," I'd thought to myself. Although I smiled, I didn't say anything, not wanting to anger him. In my dressing room, I began to take off my clothes in front of Ted, not that he was very interested. "Get that god damn Dino on the phone."

"Where's he at?"

"The Pier House in The Iguana's suite. Auditioning for the role of Numie. Tell that arrogant hustler to get his ass over here in thirty minutes. On the double. That's when we're leaving for Miami. Put the role of Numie, The Iguana's overstretched ass, Mia Kelly, Jerry Wheeler, Sean Nielson, and everyone else in the world on hold. If he wants those one-hundred-thousand dollars I promised him, he'd better show up here and quick. And look good while he's doing it. He's got to look great for the role I've planned for him."

Freshly showered and freshly made up, I left dozens of instructions to various staff and members of the household.

An urgent message had come in from David. Weren't all my messages urgent these days? He'd learned the name of the clinic in Switzerland which Dr. Euler ran. It was high in the mountains overlooking Gstaad. As my attorney, he'd arranged a meeting there for me with the doctor. I was to be in disguise, of course. They wouldn't know I was Sherry Kelly. A super rich, super-demanding bitch from California, perhaps, but hardly the world-famous Sherry Kelly.

David was amazing. He often disagreed with what I did, and many, many times had urged me not to carry through with one or another of my schemes. Admittedly, some of them weren't all that brilliant. That lawyer, through an arsenal of personal charm and legal clout, could get anybody in the world on the phone and negotiate practically anything.

So far, of all the people in my entourage, David was the only one who knew of my latest plan in its entirety. Even Rafael hadn't been told the full details. Dino, that rat, knew only his part, and in his case he never cared about anyone else's role anyway.

Since I'd decided I couldn't trust anybody, I figured I'd be safer if I didn't reveal complete details to even the most trusted members of my entourage. Using a technique Daddy Kelly had taught me long ago, I had deliberately dispensed information these past few hours in unrelated bits and pieces, parceling them out to people strictly on a "need-to-know" basis.

Ted came back with another message.

Seeing him, I asked, "Not the fucking White House again?"

He whispered in my ear, "Anishi is here. I've got her waiting in the library. Something's gone wrong. She must see you at once."

"Okay. But this isn't the most opportune time for a Japanese lotus-blossom tea."

"I think it's really urgent. Otherwise, I'd have gotten rid of her."

"I trust your instincts. You've never steered me wrong yet."

After telling Rafael who I was about to meet, I headed for the library with Ted. "Did you get that lowdown, no-good, two-timing hustler on the phone?"

"Dino's on his way here now. To judge from the noise in that suite, The Iguana had some major objections to his leaving. Something about unfinished business. That beast even got *me* on the phone and called me names I haven't heard in years. But then he had second thoughts and decided to send a thank-you instead."

"What do you mean?"

"He said 'tell Sherry thanks.' And then I don't really understand any of this, but he promised to return the five-hundred dollars you loaned him, or paid out in his name, or something..."

"Ha! That old reptile is going to be plenty disappointed when he returns to the bar, unless he gets lucky with some newly arrived stranger I had nothing to do with."

I opened the door to the library and went in, always trying to act my imperial best around Anishi. She rushed toward me in tears. I'd never seen her look so vulnerable. I assumed it must be one of her many Oriental tricks, probably a performance she learned in some unspeakable brothel somewhere.

"Something's happened to Mia, hasn't it?" She called me about the diary. But I can't face that now."

"No, no. Much worse than that. John and Henry have been kidnapped."

"Are you sure? You know those two adorable little boys and

I had a talk. I think I might have inspired them to go out and find some girls. It's only natural for boys that age to wander around at night."

"Nothing like that. I know who kidnapped them."

"The people you work for? That mysterious voice on the phone?"

"Don't you see? They felt I was out of control. How better to control me than kidnap John and Henry? This way, I'll be forced to do their bidding."

"Any ransom note?"

"I don't expect one. They're not holding them for ransom. I just know they're holding them so they can control me."

"Won't Mia get suspicious with the children mysteriously disappearing like that?"

"Not really. They were getting on her nerves. She wanted me to send them away to school. I'll tell her that's what I did. Just carrying out her orders, as I always do."

I turned to comfort her. "Let me handle this. Believe me, I can. But I'm on an urgent mission right now. Hold tight. I don't think any harm will come to your boys until I get back. There are just so many brush fires I can put out in one night."

She started to protest, but I signaled to her that it was hopeless. "I'm involved in a matter of life and death right now. And I'm not just being dramatic like the actress I am. If I thought John and Henry were in serious physical danger, I'd do anything I could to rescue them right now. I will rescue them, but at the right time. Sudden or stupid moves on our part right now could harm them. We've got to know more information. Now, I want you to go back to Mia's. The return of your boys has to be negotiated carefully and seriously. I have the cards to play that hand, but you've got to trust me."

"But they may force me to do something awful."

"Don't do it! Here's a number where I can be reached. Call me first. Call David Miller. Mia's safety must be protected."

"But what about John and Henry?"

Once again, I attempted to comfort her. "I think in a few hours I'll learn much more about what's going on. Even what you're involved in. And how Mia fits into all this."

"I don't really know myself."

"You're probably telling the truth for a change."

"I'm not lying to you. I believe you're the only person who can help me now. The only one to save John and Henry."

"I will--and that's a promise. But you've got to do something in return. If you get the go-ahead to shoot something different in Mia's veins, don't do it. Say you'll do it. But lie. Buy us some time. That vial you turned over to me. It's got something to do with a dreadful virus. Maybe even worse than AIDS but like AIDS."

"No, no." She put her hand to her mouth. "I don't understand. Why give Mia this? How would this help them?"

"I don't know that we'll ever answer that. It sounds crazy. If we knew the answer to that, we'd know the answer to a lot of other things."

"I could never shoot that poison into her veins."

"Even if John and Henry were threatened?"

"I couldn't defy them forever. But if you'll get back here soon, I could say I was shooting that virus into her but I wouldn't be. In the short term I could get away with that."

"Of course, you can. But don't trust anyone in that household."

"I'm putting myself and my children at great risk for you. Protecting John and Henry is more important to me than saving the life of your rich mother."

"I know that. That's why we're making a deal. You protect her. I'll rescue your boys. I give you my guarantee – as much as it's humanly possible."

"That's a promise I'll hold you to, and I mean that!" She reached for my hand. "You've turned out to be the best friend I've ever had."

I withdrew my hand. "I'm not your friend. Never will be. I'm a person who's made a deal with you. I want you to carry out your part of the deal, and I'll carry out mine."

"I'll carry out my part. But you must come back soon. This is an awful time to be taking a vacation."

"This is no damn vacation. I'm flying into a holiday from hell."

CHAPTER EIGHT

On our private chartered plane to Zurich, and only after a long and detailed telephone conference with David, I settled down to relax. In different compartments of the plane, Rafael and Dino were asleep, and Ted was getting a late-night beauty treatment from Maxie.

Flying to Switzerland at this very moment seemed like a crazed idea. I was completely nuts. To find out some vague information, I was not only putting my own life at risk but the lives of others on the plane with me. I felt I had no right, and was tempted for a moment to tell the pilot to turn back to the east coast of the United States. I even started to get up to head for the cockpit, but something told me to settle back and complete my mission, even though at this point I wasn't sure exactly what my mission was.

"I'll wing it," I said to myself very softly. "Just like this plane."

David always warned me that some of my schemes would backfire and cause me great harm one day. It was advice I never took, but perhaps should have.

I decided to fly the rest of the way to Switzerland in silence, lost in my thoughts. I knew sleep wouldn't come. Rafael, as always, was a tremendous help to me, but even he had his own Cuban agenda.

Frankly, I didn't know what to do. Who to turn to. Could I really trust anyone? I felt lonely and isolated and wanted a strong bond with Mia. But even she was against me. She didn't know what she was getting herself in for, and I too hadn't known how I was entrapping myself.

What I knew was that beginning now, I had to free myself from some mysterious force and rescue Mia too. There would be no clear and easy escape from this.

If only Daddy Kelly had been alive and here to help me now. He was the only man I'd trust to deal with this pack of jackals. Understanding the application of power and money, he wasn't afraid to use either when his financial security appeared threatened from any front. But Daddy had died a long time ago, and I was now forced to turn to weaker men.

I suddenly bolted upright in my seat. The perfect opportunity, the way out had emerged, and I hadn't seen it until now. My present evidence, and I planned to accumulate much more, presented a far greater challenge than could be solved by an attorney, even one as clever as David. I couldn't expect to get him on the phone and have him take care of a matter as grave as this one in the way I'd done in the past.

At least according to my one reliable source, Ted, the president of the United States wanted to arrange a date with me. He'd get it. Our white-trash president might arrive expecting one of those juicy blow-jobs he was so fond of, but there would be another surprise for him. Reportedly, he'd been mesmerized while watching me in "Kinky," and had practically foamed at the mouth. I could lure him to Palm Island after all. He could also be at risk, and in all fairness, I should warn him.

If I had some strong evidence that I was in danger, that Mia was in danger, and even that the president himself was in danger, he could help me with far greater forces than I could summon.

Of course, the president might not believe me, and, I felt, again through David's help, that I needed to prepare a formalized "white paper" filled with my limited evidence and accusations.

A seasoned attorney, Clinton might view me – other than as the obvious hot puta cocksucker – as a deranged and super-rich billionaire political hysteric. I smiled to myself as I imagined what he might say: "Drop the panties, if you're wearing any at all, and I suspect you aren't. Let's fuck, and then I'm out of here. Don't you worry your pretty little head about these dark forces. I'll take care of those bastards."

I closed my eyes as our private plane entered the air space over the European continent. My earliest childhood memories involved places in Europe far more than places within America. Daddy Kelly, Mommie, and I had always flown to Europe or else rented practically the top deck of whatever luxury liner struck our fancy. In Europe, we'd purchased art, much of it stolen; we'd bought houses, and, yes, we'd paid for bodies to satisfy our libidos in the middle of the night.

I was heading home again, or at least going back to one of

my homes. I hadn't been to it in three years, and I'd almost forgotten that the place had existed until David mentioned Gstaad to me. I remembered I owned a chalet there, although this was definitely the wrong season to visit it.

As a young girl, I had met the Shah of Iran there when he'd had his brief ski-bunny fling with Mia. It had been a glorious place for us, and it was a glorious time. I recalled getting drunk there with Roger Moore and Julie Andrews. That Julie Andrews. No "Sound of Music"-edelweiss that one. I recalled that on another night, Elizabeth Taylor had arrived with Richard Burton. If memory serves, they were accompanied by Peter Lawford, the actor Mia had captured from the "fellatio queen" herself before she'd gone on to marry a divorced future president of the United States. (I enjoy dropping subtle clues here and there.) At one point in the evening, Taylor had even called Lawford a "cocksucker," but I think she'd meant that as a term of endearment.

Snaring Peter that evening from Mia, I escaped with him into the fleshpots of Gstaad. But we never connected. Intoxicated, he'd fallen asleep. I left our hastily rented suite at the Palace Hotel, just in time to run into one of the most charming princes of Europe. No, not that one. I said charming.

Two limousines waited at the airport to drive my party to Gstaad, where my chalet would serve as our refueling stop before my upcoming interview. I think Maxie had been working out my new disguise using Ted as a mannequin. I felt nervous and not at all certain what I was letting myself in for. My fear was so great that I was even tempted as we landed in Zurich to call the whole thing off, to order the plane refueled and to direct it to Paris, where I'd begin a new life. Away from Hollywood. Away from politics and politicians. Away from everything I'd known before.

Even as I considered that, I knew it was that impossible dream. I'd have to go to that clinic. I'd also have to return to Key West, if I were lucky enough to get out of this shit alive. As much as I wanted to run and hide, I knew I couldn't. It was on to Gstaad.

. . .

Before Maxie made me up for my interview at the clinic, I wandered alone downstairs in my large, high-security art gallery, where concrete walls and a thick iron door kept the contents from prying eyes. Here, I wanted to familiarize myself once again with some of the paintings which Mia had acquired from who knows what source. Not from any legitimate gallery, that was for certain.

Instead of coming downstairs to admire my stolen art, Rafael chose instead to inspect the landing pad and my private helicopter, which I'd ordered to remain in state-of-the-art condition in case I should ever show up in Switzerland and decide to "resort hop" the way Mia's friends used to.

Actually, I'd requested that Rafael inspect the helicopter. If we followed through on my plan, I didn't trust limousine travel. My party might be hijacked along the road, and all of us kidnapped. My plan involved making a quick getaway from the clinic by helicopter, flying it to Geneva, and boarding a private plane to carry us back to Miami.

Before making an appearance at the clinic, however, I needed to find some peace with myself. Viewing art, even stolen art, tended to soothe my nerves, something I needed badly at a time like this. I could lose myself in paintings and wander back to other times and other places.

I first gazed upon Rembrandt's "The Storm on the Sea of Galilee." Stolen in 1990 in Boston, it was valued at more than fifty million dollars, although Mia had acquired it for a relatively modest eight million. The turbulent sea the ship's passengers faced in the Rembrandt seemed to parallel my own stormy emotions this morning. No peace to be found here.

Finally, I found the painting that brought me the inner serenity I needed. It was Jan Vermeer's "The Concert," valued at more than fifty million dollars and also acquired by Mia for eight million, at the same time she'd purchased the Rembrandt for the exact same amount. Painted around 1665, the scene of the concert was so soothing, so unlike what I faced here in 1993, that I wished I could wander back through time to spend the afternoon listening to sweet chamber music.

Such was not to be the case. Ted summoned me upstairs where Maxie was waiting to transform me from Sherry Kelly into a rich-looking bitch, an image inspired by Joan Crawford in "Mildred Pierce."

Forget Faye Dunaway in "Mommie Dearest." After an hour with Maxie, I emerged looking more like Joan Crawford than Crawford herself. Wearing Yoko Ono sunglasses and a white 1940s-style turban, I encased my entire body in the world's most expensive ermine coat before heading up the mountain. I looked like I could write checks for millions at about the same rate most people purchased soft drinks.

It seemed I had indeed been writing too many of those checks lately. In fact, in the past few days I think I'd spent more money than I ever had at one time in my entire life. After this crisis was over, I was determined to cut back, lead a more modest life somewhere.

The drive to the clinic was tortuous. Rafael was the driver since I couldn't trust any Swiss chauffeur. All Swiss chauffeurs can be bought. I'd spent two hours rehearsing Dino. No one, not even Rafael, knew why I needed Dino to help me. I hadn't told anybody my full plan except David. If I couldn't trust David, who could I trust? Ted and Maxie were eager for more details about what I was up to, but I hadn't told them either.

At some point, the road narrowed. Near a phone booth and a glassed-in alpine shelter station, a driver waited to take us the rest of the way to the hospital. He had a jeep or some such transport waiting for us. The only vehicles I really understand (or can even identify by name) are limousines. Ted and Maxie were to wait by the limousine for us. An armed guard – no doubt from the clinic – stood nearby. He was especially good-looking, and I felt Ted and Maxie would be amused while we were away.

Rafael was heavily armed under the fur we'd given him to wear. There might be an armed confrontation later. That is, if Ted failed to get the guard to drink from the brandy flask we'd prepared at the chalet for him. One drink of that stuff and the guard would be unconscious for hours.

The driver of the jeep or mountain-mobile, or whatever it was, didn't want Rafael to accompany me up the hill. Since the clinic had already been informed that I was bringing Dino, he already had clearance.

"I never go anywhere without my bodyguard, you stupid shit," I barked at the guard. First in English, then in my perfect

German, and later in my even more perfect French. I figured this fucker had to understand at least one of those languages. At any rate, one of those languages worked. He agreed to let Rafael accompany me, fearing the wrath of what a rich bitch like me might do to his future employment. Obviously, I was a woman not familiar with being denied anything.

In the back of the jeep, I tried to think about anything but the interview. I'd already rehearsed it too many times, and felt I would not be spontaneous if I continued to think about it. I thought about how Mia had sent me to a school in Gstaad for about nine months long ago. It seemed I'd been taught all known languages here except Spanish. At school, it had never occurred to me that I would ever need to converse with anyone who spoke only Spanish. Even as I thought that, I realized how wrong that schoolgirl impression was. If I were to have a future with Rafael, if I were to become the next Evita Peron of Latin America, I would indeed have to learn Spanish. I spoke Italian fluently, so I hoped the knowledge of that language would make learning Spanish easier for me.

As we neared the top of the hill and the end of the road, I reached into my purse and removed the Capetown Diamond. If the director of the clinic didn't realize from my outfit and appearance that I was super-rich, he'd get the idea when I flashed the Capetown Diamond. Unless, God forbid, he'd think that a stone this large might be a fake.

The clinic was surprisingly small. I'd expected a hospital of many rooms. If anything, this clinic had only six rooms. I took a deep breath, almost a sigh of relief.

The very sterile-looking clinic, both inside and out, was painted an antiseptic white, even though in some dark cellar must lurk horrible drippings from AIDS patients and parts of brains lobotomized. It seemed designed almost as a deliberate attempt to blend into the surrounding snowfields.

Checking my warpaint once again, I entered the clinic, trailed by Rafael and Dino. Except it wasn't Dino Paglia any more. He'd undergone a name change. As we'd informed a baffled Rafael, he was to be known as my son, Sebastian Del Lago.

If money speaks, it certainly did at this clinic. No waiting room for me. I was told that the director of the clinic, Dr. Karl Euler, would see me right away, as I was eagerly expected. I was ushered down a long, dimly lit corridor by a red-faced and burly nurse who looked as if she'd spent a life in a Russian bathhouse giving massages to soldiers as they emerged from their showers. This concentration-camp Sally was one tough-looking broad.

However, when it came time to knock on Dr. Euler's massively reinforced oak door, she tapped ever so gently. A red light flashed on the door. Rafael wanted to accompany me inside, but was told to wait in the anteroom with Dino/Sebastian. Presumably, Dino/Sebastian would be called in later. For his role today, Dino/Sebastian had been dressed by Maxie like a young preppie with a navy blue blazer and tight-fitting charcoal-gray slacks. It was a new image for him, that of a school kid.

Dr. Euler was seated behind a large desk placed in front of a gigantic picture window overlooking the mountains. The morning sun streamed in, and I was glad I'd worn such huge sunglasses, especially considering that I had not gotten my beauty sleep the night before. Upon seeing me, he rose to his feet and walked toward me. Only then did I realize how short this midget was. I towered over him. He looked to be a well-preserved fifty and was a noted surgeon, a brain surgeon, or so I'd learned from David's briefing. His work in Switzerland was extremely controversial, and he didn't seek or want publicity of any kind in medical journals.

"Madame Del Lago, welcome to our clinic and welcome to Switzerland. Is it your first visit to our beautiful country?"

"Yes," I said in my most imperial Joan Crawford voice. "I have all the cuckoo clocks and watches I'll ever need, and I loathe chocolate."

He looked insulted, but smiled anyway just like the Swiss always do when they are concealing how much they actually despise you.

I extended my hand only after he'd extended his. Instead of shaking it, he bowed low. In his case, that was very low indeed. He kissed my hand, no doubt coming into intimate contact with the Capetown Diamond. Through his thick glasses, he appraised the stone like a jeweler, but made no mention of it when he straightened up.

"It is a pleasure to welcome you here. I must say, I find it astonishing that a lady such as yourself has never visited Switzerland. Zurich perhaps? Surely Geneva."

"I occasionally frequent ski resorts in Europe. I'm fond of Zurs."

"I figured you must have, but that's in Austria."

"I know. Switzerland is much too democratic for me. I prefer a more imperial country like Austria. Kurt always welcomes me personally whenever I visit. I don't believe all those stupid stories about his being a Nazi killer, do you?"

"Incredible libel."

"Besides, Kurt wouldn't be the first Nazi I knew. Some of my closest and most intimate associates – both financial and social – came from such backgrounds. Who am I to concern myself with someone's past political affiliations if they get the job done for me? Actually, I detest politics, don't you?"

"I never concern myself with such stupid matters. I have devoted my entire life to science. I'm interested only in helping my patients achieve a better life. A more peaceful existence. Which, I assume, brings us to the purpose of this meeting."

"Good for you for getting to the point quick. I like that in a man." At his invitation, I seated myself in a tapestry-upholstered chair beside a brightly burning fireplace framed in chiseled granite blocks.

He preferred not to sit in the chair opposite me. Closely observing my every move, he stood with his back to the fireplace. "Like you, I don't have time for idle conversation," I said. "I came here for your help. You are my last resort. I'm desperate. It's my son, Sebastian Del Lago."

"Exactly what seems to be the problem?"

In my harshest Crawford voice, the one she'd used in "The Damned Don't Cry" or some such title, I spoke to the doctor. A mask of ferocity consumed my features. After all, he was facing a world-class actress whether he knew it or not. "I'll tell you what the god damn problem is. My son's a cocksucking faggot. He's sucked off every member of my all-male staff. The chauffeur. The butler. The gardener. The maintenance men. The repairmen. The plumber. The..."

"You don't have to continue. I know of such matters. Even in Switzerland, we have such men."

"Don't tell me to send him to any more psychiatrists. I've

sent him to the biggest and the best. He usually ends up seducing them. He's a very seductive kid. He's right outside. You'll meet him. For all I know, you'll be next on his list."

"I doubt that. I am immune to the sexual advances of young men." He eyed me, especially my shapely legs, although his gaze kept returning to the Capetown Diamond. "I'm also immune to the charms of beautiful women, too. I've never been to bed with a man or woman, and at this late date in my life, I don't intend to. I'm just not interested in sex. Never was. I'm wed to my breakthroughs in brain surgery and AIDS research, an unusual pursuit, but both fields interest me."

"I understand that. Sex isn't all that wonderful anyway. In fact, sexual desire is actually controlled by the brain, isn't it?"

"You might say that."

"I mean, it's all images and fantasies, isn't it?"

"You might say that."

"All right, god damn it. If it's there in the brain, can't that part of the brain be cut out? After that's done with, can't a boy resume a natural, normal life without the desire to suck every cock dangling?"

He paused a long time. "Such an operation might be very expensive. Very expensive indeed. I don't know how much money you're willing to spend."

"Cut the shit, doctor! Who in hell do you think you're talking to? I'm Evita Del Lago. I've bought clinics which are a thousand times bigger and better-equipped than this pissant alpine refuge hut!"

"Please." He flashed anger. "Don't demean our operation here. We've made important scientific breakthroughs." As if calling attention to his small size, he added, "You don't have to be big to make big contributions."

"Money? What kind of money are we talking about here? First, to cut that vile perverted crap from Sebastian's brain, how long would that take on the operating table?"

"An hour, maybe more. Two hours at the most."

"What do you say to two-million dollars? Deposited in your name in any currency you want in a Zurich vault? Swiss francs. German marks. Gold bullion if that is your desire. Perhaps with a Nazi swastika on it for old time's sake. One-million dollars an hour. Knowing you as well as I do, I'm sure you'll run into complications. Extend the operation at least another hour. That's two-million dollars. Sounds like your little hovel here could suddenly get a hell of a lot bigger."

Dr. Euler could hardly conceal the greedy gleam in his twisted little eyes. "Let me see the boy before I make my decision." At his desk, he barked an order through his intercom to the Bitch of Buchenwald to send Sebastian Del Lago into his office.

In less than a minute, Dino/Sebastian appeared, looking more seductive and alluring than I'd ever seen him, a child molester's fantasy. For all I knew, he was causing Dr. Euler to experience his first hard-on.

"Sit down, son," Dr. Euler said.

"Thank you." Dino/Sebastian didn't sit, but seemed to glide into the chair. With his jacket unbuttoned, his pants rode high, revealing a promising big bulge.

None of that escaped Dr. Euler's eagle eye. "A trained seducer, I see," Dr. Euler said. "What man could resist? Your son, in my opinion, could make a heterosexual man turn gay."

"He's already done that plenty of times," I added.

"I'm flattered, doctor, that you are so appreciative of my charms," Dino/Sebastian said in his most seductive voice. It even rekindled an old passion in me.

"You can't devote your entire life to sex," Dr. Euler said. "There are other things."

"Why not?" Dino/Sebastian said. "With Mommie Dearest here paying the bills, why can't I devote my life to what I most enjoy? Sucking cock?"

"The child has a point," Dr. Euler said.

"I'm no child," Dino/Sebastian said, his fingers hovering ever so lightly above his bulge.

"We'll certainly determine that later," Dr. Euler said. "My physical examinations are very thorough."

"I bet they are," Dino/Sebastian said with a smirk. "Do you do the anal probe with or without a condom on your finger?"

"Young man," Dr. Euler said, trying rapidly to regain his composure. "You will be thoroughly sedated when you're examined. You will not know the nature of my examination. The procedures and techniques of my physical examinations of patients are known only to me."

"I bet," Dino/Sebastian said, smiling at the surgeon.

"Your sarcasm won't serve you here," Dr. Euler said. "Please leave the room. I must confer in private with your kind mother."

Eying the doctor one last time, Dino/Sebastian blew him a kiss and left, shutting the door.

Dino/Sebastian had earned his one-hundred thousand dollars for his acting assignment.

"I see what you mean about the boy," Dr. Euler said. "The boy tries to seduce every man he meets. Even me, who's totally immune to his charms, or that of anyone else for that matter. If I'm not mistaken, Madame Del Lago, that child was actually propositioning me."

"You're not mistaken."

He arched his back. "I'd like to keep your son here for a while. His case is a delicate matter. It will require a lot of my time and concentration. Forgive me, for the use of the word, but it will require my genius."

"How long is long?"

"The preliminary examinations will take at least two months. Then the operation. I will present various male stimuli to him to see if he responds sexually. Only when I'm satisfied that he has been cured and that my operation is a success can I release him back to you."

"Obviously, this will cost a lot more money," I said.

"Obviously."

"No problem".

"I may even have to use myself, my own body, tiny as it is, in the post-operative stimuli of your son. You wouldn't have any objection to that, would you?"

"None whatsoever."

"We have to keep this minor surgery as a secret between the two of us. And my nurse, of course. We are a small operation. That's why I have to participate so actively. No other reason."

"I understand such things. If you can achieve my goal for Sebastian, then anything you decide to do with him, pre- or post-operative, is fine with me. I'm only interested in results. Not the means by which those results are achieved."

"I like dealing with a lady of your business sense. It makes my work all the easier."

I eased back in my chair, the morning sun catching the glint in the Capetown Diamond. With Dino installed here for a few days--at a far greater reward, of course--and with Dino seducing Dr. Euler, my plan would be perfect. Especially when Dino supplied that knock-out drink to Dr. Euler. If there was any information or evidence to be gathered at this clinic, Dino would find it, especially after the bitch nurse went home for the day, leaving Dr. Euler alone with Dino. Thank God, I could put this boy's talent to use.

The buzzer on his desk sounded. No doubt a message from the Bitch of Buchenwald. He listened intently. "I see," was all he said before putting down the receiver. "A trivial matter has come up." He eyed me with a certain growing alarm which he artfully tried to conceal. "Trivial, but it requires my immediate attention. You must excuse me." He headed rapidly for the door and went outside.

The sound of a lock or bolt on the door was heard. Surely he hadn't locked me into his office while he was out? Suspicious, I got up from the armchair and headed for the door. I could always pretend I needed to go to the women's room. That excuse always sounded true. I turned the handle to the door. It was locked.

Noises, loud noises, came from the hallway. Someone was shouting in Spanish. It was Rafael.

"Sherry!" I heard him yell. "Sherry!"

In the background, I also heard Dino shouting. A struggle was going on. I furiously tried to open the door again, pulling desperately at the handle. In frustration, I banged on the door and kicked it, as if that would magically open it for me.

"Rafael!" I screamed.

I turned and faced the brilliantly blinding sun streaming through the giant window. My scheme had backfired. Someone had alerted the clinic as to my true identity. I just knew that. Someone very close to me. At least it wasn't Rafael or Dino. Of that I could be sure. I feared for their safety.

I wanted to escape from this horrible room and get off this dreadful barren mountain, but wondered if that would ever happen now. Scheming wouldn't help us any more. Only sheer brute force would prevail here. Employing it could get us killed.

I dashed for the phone. It had gone dead.

I felt locked in a coffin.

. . .

What do you think about when you realize you're going to die? Two things come to mind. One was my front-page obituary on every major newspaper in the world. All media would chronicle a virtually wasted life. A silly one at that. I'd never stood for much of anything as I'd always been too busy pursuing my own pleasures. I'd given to charities, plenty of them, but the gift of money came easy for me. I'd never really given of myself to anybody. I felt vain and foolish as I'm sure my obituaries would document in graphic detail, episode after episode. "A lurid past," one of them had already written of me. Perhaps it didn't matter. The vilest crap had already been written about me while I was still alive. I couldn't foresee that my death could bring out much worse in journalism.

My money was my second concern. Since I'd no longer control it, who would? The answer was Mia. Regardless of all our feuding and fighting, deep down, I loved her dearly. She was my sole heir. I was always the competitive and errant daughter and in the end, she'd always been the forgiving mother. Of course, in her case, I also had a lot to forgive from time to time. I wasn't the only one being foolish or making mistakes. When she went on her way, she could be the one to dispose of the Kelly billions, favoring this or that charity.

As the sun rose higher in the sky, the room became hotter and hotter. That blazing fireplace didn't help. I could take off my ermine coat, but I felt it protected me in some way. Like a coat of armor.

Looking at my image in a large gilt mirror over a console table, I felt I did look like Crawford in "Mildred Pierce." To distract my mind from the danger, especially that faced by Rafael, I began to run that movie scene by scene through my head. I'd forgotten a lot of it. But I vaguely recall Crawford removing a revolver from her purse and shooting Zachary Scott.

How stupid of me to forget. Rafael had placed a revolver in my purse as a "last resort" protection. Unlike Mia's revolver, the one with the jewelled barrel that had shot Cruz, this mother-fucker had had a life of heavy usage. Like Crawford, Bette Davis, and Barbara Stanwyck on the late show, I would pump lead into the first attacker who invaded Dr. Euler's office to capture me. At least with the revolver I had a fighting chance.

Reaching into my purse, I pulled out the revolver and fingered it. I concealed myself behind a shelf of medical books. Whoever came into this room, probably the Bitch of Buchenwald, would no doubt be armed. I'd shoot her and she'd shoot me. If I came out of this alive, did that mean I'd join the NRA along with Charlton Heston?

The day seemed to wear on. Nothing was happening. No one was coming to either capture me or rescue me. Had Dr. Euler ordered that Rafael and Dino be killed? He probably wouldn't have them shot. No doubt lobotomized after extensive physical examinations. His clock said two o'clock in the afternoon. I couldn't believe this. Had his staff forgotten about me? Why didn't they come to kill me or else confine me to a prison?

I searched the room for avenues of escape. From the fireplace, I picked up a large wrought-iron poker and crashed it into the single giant window in the room. The poker just bounced back at me. That window didn't even seem to be made of glass.

My sensitive nostrils detected smoke. I feared the building had caught fire. I'd be burned alive in here. The smell of smoke grew stronger and stronger. Something was definitely burning. Outside the door, there were footsteps racing about and shouting in German. I spoke German fluently. No one was yelling fire.

With my ear close to the door and as best as I could interpret the hysteria, it seemed that documents were deliberately being destroyed by fire, but not the building itself. That gave me a momentary sense of relief. The idea of becoming a 1993 Joan of Arc didn't set well with me.

My stomach churned. I was surprised at myself. I knew I should be clawing at the walls, tearing my hair out, and screaming for help. Yet faced with such an emergency, I felt I was behaving in a remarkably calm way. That meant I hadn't given in completely to the idea of death. I still had hope that I could escape from this mountain.

The noises eventually died down. Even the smell of smoke drifted away into the alpine peaks.

At two-thirty, the sound of a helicopter circling overhead could be heard. Surely I was mistaken. Was the clinic going to be bombed with me in it?

Suddenly I heard footsteps racing toward Dr. Euler's office. Someone was at the door. It was being unbolted.

Rushing to conceal myself behind the library shelves, I took aim at the door with my revolver. My finger tested the trigger. Whoever set foot into this office was dead meat. I'd see to that.

As I fingered the trigger, the door burst open. In a half-second, I would have fatally shot the invader. But some impulse made me hold back. Perhaps the shooting of Cruz had inhibited me. I'll never know.

"Rafael." I dropped the revolver and raced toward his open arms.

He grabbed me, not to embrace me, but to pull me along down the corridor. "We're out of here. I don't know what's going on. Hurry."

I ran behind him toward a small mountain plateau at the back of the building. Here, ready to fly, was my helicopter from Gstaad, piloted by who knows. That unknown pilot tossed us a ladder.

"Hurry," Rafael shouted. "We've got to board. They might shoot at us." He sensed my hesitation. "Climb the fucking ladder!"

I reached for the ladder, but as I did I looked down. A big mistake. Looming before me was a giant grave, a drop of some ten thousand feet. I turned to Rafael. "I'm afraid of height."

"Don't look down," he commanded like a Cuban guerilla fighter. "Look up. Climb the ladder. I'm right behind you."

"I can't." My whole body was paralyzed with fear. Even though I knew it was my way to escape, I couldn't move.

"I'll go first," he said, pushing me aside. "Then pull you up."

He quickly climbed the ladder and reached back for me, as the helicopter continued to hover overhead.

Not looking down into that pit like he said, I reached for his hand. As I did, the huge Capetown Diamond slipped from my finger and plunged into the valley. I looked down to watch it go. The diamond glistened one fiery time as it picked up a ray of the sun before disappearing from my life forever. Someone would find it one day and become a victim of its curse. Then that awful drop came into my eye range again, and I went into panic.

He grabbed for my other arm, desperately trying to find my hand to clutch. He caught the sleeve of the coat instead. With my right hand, I held desperately onto a rung of the ladder. The ermine coat was slipping from my body. I could feel it sliding. I feared that I would plunge along with it to my death, using it as my burial shroud.

He caught my left hand and held firmly. My left arm had become free of the fur. I reached to catch the fur that was falling from my right arm. As I did, the coat slipped from my body.

"Forget the god damn coat!" he shouted.

As the ermine plunged toward the valley, I looked down again. It seemed to drift into the alpine air like some furry bird from the dawn of time before it began its descent to earth. The world's most expensive ermine was returning to the forested hills from which it had come.

He literally pulled me the rest of the way up the ladder and into the helicopter. Before he closed the door, he held me between his strong firm hands. My back faced the ten-thousand foot drop. If he were on the wrong side's payroll, I was a goner. He truly had the power to plunge me toward the earth like my former Capetown Diamond and my former ermine.

"Promise me, puta bitch," he said, "that I'll never catch you with another man ever again."

"I promise," I shouted almost into his mouth. "Let me inside, you jealous Cubano bastard."

He yanked me inside and slammed the door.

Like a giant green monster, the helicopter took wings and flew toward the safety of Gstaad. I looked down only once as the glistening white clinic faded from view. Then I turned and clutched him as I'd never held any man before in my life.

. . .

In the relative safety of my Gstaad chalet, I began to try to piece together what had happened while I was locked away in Dr. Euler's office. It quickly became obvious that no one knew the full story yet. Everybody, including Ted and Maxie, had only a self-serving fragment to report. When the dust settled, I was going to conduct my own investigation. Unless David had betrayed me, a highly unlikely possibility, there was a spy within my camp. I'd grill Maxie and Ted later. Right now, Rafael and I had urgent business to attend to.

"Where's Dino?" I asked when Rafael returned from paying off the alpine rescue pilot he'd hired in Gstaad. Could Dino be the double agent? That boy could be had for a price.

"We don't know. But we're going to find out."

"He escaped?"

"He's being held somewhere."

"I'll pay the ransom."

"I suspect this ransom won't be in the form of money."

To the Kelly family, all kidnapping ransoms were in money. He made no sense to me.

"I think Dr. Euler and two of his laboratory assistants have Dino. They're holding him somewhere under guard in a chalet about nine miles from here."

"Call the Swiss police."

"I think there's another way out of this. An easy way."

"My darling man, there is no easy way out of anything."

"I've spoken to Dr. Euler. He knows you're Sherry Kelly. Someone apparently called him during your interview there. I don't know who that someone was. In Cuba, we'd find out. We'd strip them and begin to work on their testicles. You'd be surprised how effective that is."

"In this case I suspect there aren't any balls to work over."

"You mean a woman?"

"Not exactly. I'll explain later. Dr. Euler called here?"

"Once he learned you were Sherry Kelly, he figured you were at this chalet. It seems that the entire world knows about you and this chalet. Apparently, you've been written up in magazines. He wants to meet with you."

"It could be a setup. After today, I'm not walking into another trap with Dr. Euler."

"He wants to meet you in a bar at the Palace Hotel."

I was stunned. "That's rather public. I could go there."

"The meeting must take place in an hour. He says it's very urgent. I think so too. I want Dino back."

"I'll save Dino. However, there's a number I'm going to call. Mia and I used to hire security guards when we gave parties where guests would arrive wearing a billion dollars worth of jewelry."

The mention of jewelry brought a pang of regret over the loss of the Capetown Diamond. Mia would never believe my story about how the diamond was actually lost. She'd seen "To Catch a Thief" with Cary Grant and would quickly believe the robbery story, however.

"I'll call Ted to get them on the phone."

"Don't call Ted. This time, and maybe forever, I'll make my own phone calls."

"I thought you trusted Ted with all your secrets."

"I don't trust anybody any more, except you, my darling."

After I'd arranged for five security guards – all secretly armed – to appear at the Palace posing as rich guests, I left an hour later in my limousine for the hotel I knew so well.

As we neared this 1912 landmark, with its mock-fortified corner towers and neomedieval facade, I remembered telling the manager, Ernst Scherz, that I didn't like his motto of, "Every king is a client, and every client is a king." I found this too sexist. I told him to change it to, "Every queen is a client, and every client is a queen."

"It wouldn't mean the same," Scherz had asserted rather rudely, making it very clear that he preferred to keep his own slogan.

On the way to the hotel, Rafael told me how he'd escaped. The nurse armed with a gun, and accompanied by two security guards, had suddenly appeared to arrest him. According to Rafael, Dino had disappeared, which didn't surprise me at all. That boy always had a way of entering houses or institutions and finding the one room where the action was. Proof of that was how quickly he located Mia's bedroom at Belle Reve.

"Dino had excused himself to go to the bathroom," Rafael said. "I didn't see him again."

"They got him."

"I think so. They were on me before I could pull out my own

weapons. I overpowered them, knocking all three down. I made a dash for it, hijacking the Jeep. I got to the plateau where we'd parked the limousine. Ted and Maxie were there. Maxie was still in the back seat of the limousine."

"Perhaps using this cellular phone," I said, holding it up for his inspection.

"I don't know. Ted had drugged the guard with the brandy, just like you said. And just like you said, the guard went for a warm drink on a cold day. Who wouldn't? It was a very good brandy. When the guard passed out, your ever-opportunistic mariposa decided to amuse himself while waiting for us to return. He had the guard's pants down. He was, how do you say in this country, taking sexual advantage of the guard."

At that revelation, I could only sigh.

"In another Jeep, the security guards were coming down the mountain after me," he said. "I jumped in the limousine. Ted got into the back seat with Maxie and we drove back here. With those security guards, I knew I couldn't take another vehicle up that mountain without getting shot. That's when I came up with the bright idea of rescuing you by helicopter."

"You'd decided against calling the police?"

"Cuban guerilla fighters don't call the police. A shoot-out between the clinic security forces and the police could have led to your death. Dino's too. When I flew to the clinic on the helicopter, I was fully armed. I was prepared to shoot my way to you, like Arnold Schwarzenegger in the movies. There was nobody around. No Dino. All the staff, even the security guards, had gone down from the mountain. There could have been someone left. I don't know. I saw no one alive. For all I know, you were the only one there."

"This is all very strange. But then everything about Dr. Euler is very strange."

"You know what I think? I think there was some struggle going on between Dr. Euler and his staff. I think that nurse had one plan of action she wanted to follow, and Dr. Euler was against it."

"What makes you think that?"

"There's one thing I didn't tell you. I did find someone at the clinic. It was the nurse. She was dead."

"Shot?"

"In my rush to find you, I didn't exactly examine the body. I saw no blood. No bullet wound."

"A knife, perhaps?"

"No blood at all."

I rubbed his hand gently. "A lethal injection administered during a violent struggle. The way they do it in the movies."

"Who knows what it was in that crazy lab?"

As the limousine pulled up in front of the Palace Hotel, he helped me out of the back seat, then gave some instructions to the local chauffeur he'd hired.

One of my hastily hired security guards posing as a doorman indicated to me with a wink that the security staff had been posted. Only the hotel manager, my old friend, was aware of the security force. No other members of the staff had been alerted, although they were used to security guards around this hotel.

I remembered this "doorman" from a winter a few years ago. He'd been hired as my bodyguard. I think he and I once got lost together high in the snow-clad mountains. Fortunately, there was a warm refuge nearby. He smiled at me, perhaps recalling our long-ago time together. How could he forget it? I noted that he'd aged well.

As if to remind me that the old Sherry Kelly and her rampaging ways were dead and gone, the new man in my life, Rafael, took my arm and ushered me inside the hotel. This time, he was definitely going to be present at the interview. Dr. Euler had agreed to that. I wore dark sunglasses and an Hermes scarf over my head. Even so, I wasn't worried about being recognized by the Palace staff. Surely they knew that Sherry Kelly would never appear out of season at the hotel.

"I'm ready for my second interview with the good doctor," I whispered to Rafael. "The first one was such good fun. Anything for a laugh." I held onto him for security. "I think Dr. Euler has something very interesting to tell us."

"About Dino?"

"Forgive me. I know Dino is your son and all of us are worried about him. However, I think the good doctor has something much bigger than Dino to share with us."

. . .

Wearing dark glasses and a ski jacket, not unusual in Gstaad, Dr. Euler sat in a far and darkened corner of the bar, apparently alone. No one else was in the bar except the bartender and two men talking idly in French at a table nearby. A lone man sat on a stool at the main bar. All of these "patrons," or so I assumed, were my own hastily assembled security forces, although I couldn't be sure. I hoped they were armed.

I eased into the booth across from Dr. Euler. Rafael sat down beside me. None of us spoke to each other and avoided eye contact. We were here to negotiate, not discuss ski conditions in the mountains. I quickly ordered a drink and so did Rafael. Both of us preferred Perrier water with lime. Dr. Euler was quietly sipping a beer.

After the waiter returned with the drinks and left, Dr. Euler looked suspiciously around the bar, as if an assassin were lurking here. "We can dispense with the formalities. There is little time left in this country for me." He turned and looked at me like a Nazi colonel surveying the latest arrival of a train of victims heading for the gas chamber. "I can talk raw business with tough vaginal types like you. I like that."

"Then get to it, Shorty. What do you want from me, and what do I get in return?"

"You're just like the kind of woman I guessed you to be. No foreplay, no fondling, no kissing. You're the type who likes a man to shove it all the way in, and when he's in and engaged in intercourse, you're cursing him for not having more inches to stuff into you."

"Hardly the case with Rafael here."

He eyed Rafael appreciatively. "I figured so much. The son must have inherited his from you. My physical examination would have revealed all."

"Cut the crap!" Rafael said in anger at such talk. "That's no way to talk in front of a lady. Where's my son?"

I gently touched Rafael's hand to send a signal to cool down that raging Latino blood. "Please, the good doctor is merely indulging in his own kind of foreplay before he delivers the hot load. I'll direct the fuck from here." In one gulp, I downed that glass of Perrier water. Facing Dr. Euler, I said, "You killed that nurse, didn't you, you little squirt?"

"She deserved to die. Your appearance at the clinic brought my world crashing in on me. I couldn't go through with what the nurse demanded I do to you."

"Just what did the Bitch of Buchenwald have in store for me?"

"She demanded your death when she learned you were the very rich, very famous, and very perverted international film star and world-class billionaire, Sherry Kelly."

"She was going to kill me?"

"By lethal injection, then dispose of your body by chopping it into pieces and scattering it over the glacier."

"How cute!"

"I tried to convince the cunt that you don't kill the world's most famous woman and just dispose of her body like she was some cheap slut you purchased in Thailand to chop up into little pieces and eat before morning, leaving only the carcass. Murdering you would be the crime of the century, dwarfing interest in the Kennedy assassination. It might even be bigger than the Kennedy thing. It would go down in history, like the suicide of Cleopatra."

I liked the way he compared my own fame to that of the dreaded and overpowering Cleopatra. Considering the man's grasp of world historical figures, I suddenly felt much more sympathetic to him.

"I'd be discovered," Dr. Euler went on. "But that asshole nurse didn't buy that. She was coming to my office armed. She was going to shoot air into your veins after you were subdued. Fortunately, two of my laboratory assistants agreed with me. We knocked the bitch out. I took the needle and shot air into her veins instead."

"Thank you," I said ever so graciously, as if he'd presented me with some edelweiss on a spring day. "You saved my life, and I owe you one for that."

"I know a rich bitch like you has bumped off people all over the world. People who stood in her way. I knew you wouldn't condemn me for murdering this vicious smelly cunt. Not when her murder saved your gaping vagina so you can fuck and fuck and then fuck some more."

"Cut it out!" Rafael interjected. "I warned you to clean up your talk in the presence of a lady."

"Forget it, my darling," I said to Rafael. "Dr. Euler and I are talking pussy to pussy. We understand each other."

Rafael turned up his eyes in disgust. He obviously didn't understand life as lived in America, and he'd never have any understanding of life as lived in Gstaad.

"Listen, you little prick, where's Dino?" I asked.

"He is perfectly safe. Right as we speak, he is being driven to your chalet. Unharmed. Brain intact. I had to borrow him. To use as a term of negotiation."

"I don't believe this little creep from hell," Rafael said. "I'm not sure but I think this guy is a pervert."

"Would you simmer down and let me finish this interrogation?" I asked.

Rafael looked sullen. "When I'm president of Cuba, you can't talk to me like that."

"President of Cuba?" Dr. Euler asked in utter astonishment. "You lunatics in the West. You, president of Cuba. Instead of AIDS, you must have a presidential virus over there. I thought all you did was watch cowboy and Indian movies."

"Your concept of America, dear doctor, is very limited," I said. "Okay, you saved my life from the Bitch of Buchenwald. You're delivering Dino. The tally sheet mounts. Anything else to put on the auction block before stating your price?"

"Most of the documents at the clinic have been burned," he said. "I have committed a murder there. A cow who deserved to die more than anyone, but a murder, nevertheless. I can remain safely in Switzerland for no more than an hour or so. I'll be discovered. I did not want my records examined. My life's work exposed to the media. The harsh and unfair judgments made against my surgical techniques. I would be viewed as a serial killer instead of a scientific genius on the verge of a major breakthrough."

"Cool it with the lecture," I said. "What have you got? And I don't mean in your pants. I already know the answer to that one."

"I saved one envelope for you from my files, my precious little twat."

"What's a twat?" Rafael asked. "I thought I knew English slang, but I don't know this twat thing."

"My darling man, you know all about twats. All you'll ever

need to know." I turned to Dr. Euler. "I have a gut instinct--or vaginal itch, as you might call it--that the contents of your little envelope are going to cost me plenty. Care to give me a preview of coming attractions, as we say in Hollywood?"

Dr. Euler leaned over the table and stared into my eyes. I stared back. It was like looking into the doorway to Hell.

"Right this minute, one of the conspirators, Anishi Mishima, plans to inject a deadly virus into Mia Kelly's bloodstream. I should know. I supplied the vials of the serum and it will not kill at once but grow and destroy like AIDS."

I leaned back into my seat, momentarily feeling faint. The fact he knew this much convinced me I'd found my man. At first, I said nothing, observing Rafael's reaction. He looked astonished, as if wondering why I didn't rush to do something.

"I don't know everything," Dr. Euler went on. "I don't know who my former employers are. You note I said former, because after what happened at that clinic, I'm sure I'm not working for them any more. But they definitely plan to do your mother in."

"Why? Why Mia?"

"She adopted the Oriental cunt, didn't she? Maybe Madame Butterfly is now her sole heir. With Mia Kelly dead, maybe the Mishima bitch would inherit the billions, then transfer them to this unknown force. After taking her cut, of course."

"That scheme sounds very far fetched," I said.

"The world would buy it. Considering what a known world-class slut your mother is, no tabloid on earth would be surprised to learn the whore had contacted some deadly virus."

"But I would prevent that. I would block them. I have power."

I'm sure they know that, whoever in the hell *they* are. Perhaps they'd find a way to eliminate you. They certainly were able to shut down your film in Key West. And that was only one day's adventure. This pack of lunatics is capable of a lot more."

"Do you know I just might think you're telling me the truth, for once."

"I'm telling you the truth as far as I know it. Because whether you like it or not you've just become my one hope for getting the hell out of Switzerland--and I mean sooner than later."

"Doctor, rest assured. If Dino is returned like you said--unharmed--you'll have my cooperation to go anywhere in the world you want. Trust me."

"A rich super-cunt like you has vast experience in stashing bodies around the world. I demand safe passage right this minute to one of your secret havens. The Swiss police are not the only ones who will be looking for me. I'm out of the Mia Kelly conspiracy, but they are hardly through with me. They don't say good-bye and let you off like that. My fleeing, knowing what I know, is like signing a death warrant. Only you can help save my ass now."

"So it can be fucked and fucked again, you odiferous little pipsqueak," I said.

"Pipsqueak was a small, high-velocity shell used by the Germans during World War II," Dr. Euler said. "Are you suggesting that even though small, I have high velocity?"

"Not exactly. You don't know American vernacular as well as I thought you did."

"Pipsqueak?" a baffled Rafael asked. "After today, I'll have to go back to school and learn English all over again."

Ignoring Rafael for the moment, I turned my world-class negotiating skills onto Dr. Euler. "From this day forth, you're farting and farting only for me. Get it?"

"Get me out of here, and we'll talk scat for the rest of our lives," Dr. Euler said.

"What's scat?" Rafael asked.

"Dr. Euler turned to him and said, "There will be time for that kind of fun and games later. Like when I demand that the contents of your daily stool be turned over to me for a thorough examination."

"Stool?" Rafael asked. "You mean, like a high chair? You people use English words I've never heard."

"I have a place for you in the Cayman Islands," I told Dr. Euler. "If you've delivered Dino, and if you hand over that envelope to me, I'll fly you in my private jet which is departing from Geneva exactly one hour from now. You must agree, however, to ride under the threat of a gun to your head. I too may no longer be welcome in Switzerland when the dust settles here. Certain artworks, nothing important, perhaps a

Rembrandt or two, right this minute are being loaded aboard the plane. We'll have to make an unscheduled stop in the Azores to let the art off. For safekeeping, of course, until I have time to stash it elsewhere. I'm also letting you off in the Azores. I don't plan to fly you to Miami with me. Too risky there. However, my attorney, David Miller, will contact you. You're to be picked up the following day and flown to the Cayman Islands. I want you close to Florida in case I should have need of your future services. Who knows? A guy like you might come in handy. Since you're working for me, and only for me, you'll be at my beck and call, of course."

"Of course. I follow commands very well."

"I bet you do," I said sarcastically. As I said that, I looked into his face, seeing the battle-scarred veteran of a hundred S&M parlors around the world. I took Rafael's arm. "Please call the house. See if this little mongoose here is lying. See if Dino is safe."

After Rafael had gone, Dr. Euler reached for my hand, but I avoided his. "I knew you and I could do business. Two smart pussies talking smart pussy talk to each other."

"I've dealt with bigger pussies than you." Memories of that other major pussy, The Iguana that night in Key West, raced through my brain. Key West and The Iguana seemed far removed from me now.

"I tactfully waited for your Latin stud – slash – big-dicked boy friend to depart before telling you one sweet surprise in that envelope."

"What's that?"

"Administering a virus to Mia Kelly was only one part of the scheme of this rat pack. Part of their conspiracy involves you."

"I figured that, but I don't know how I'm a part of it – other than a potential roadblock to keep them from Mia."

"Read my report on the plane. It will explain all I know. Some of my report is in German, and some is in French.

"I'm proficient in both languages."

"And proficient in a lot of other things, too."

"That is for you only to imagine and wet dream about."

"I saw 'Kinky.' I know what you have. Of course, I haven't examined the merchandise personally yet. In time, however, in time."

"I don't want to know how little you have." I sighed. "Okay, on the plane, I'll learn the big secret."

"I'll tell you before we leave the bar. But first, in exchange for all your generosity--which I assume carries enough cash for me to live and to continue my experiments--I'll give you another nugget of data. The spy on your staff is Maxie. From the back seat of your limousine, he made the call to me at the clinic and revealed your true identity."

"Tell me something I don't already know. Maxie may know how to design a great brassiere, but he's a lousy spy. Left too many clues."

"You'll have him killed, naturally?"

"Not really. I'll convert him."

"Of course, you rich pussies can always up the ante."

"Indeed we can. Come out with it. The big blast-off of hot semen waiting to be shot up into my bowels. What is it?"

"First," he said with a certain embarrassment and hesitancy, "you have to let me fondle your hand a little tiny bit."

"With or without the glove? I prefer it with the glove on. Like a condom."

"Without the glove, bitch!"

I slowly and tantalizingly removed one of my white gloves. Like he was reaching for the Capetown Diamond, he took my hand and gently stroked it, fondling the fingers. He looked as if he wanted to suck the fingers, but knew that was not part of the agreement. Reluctantly, he returned my hand.

"In the envelope is revealed my role in the conspiracy. Also how they planned to involve you. You were to be tricked into arranging a rendezvous with the president of the United States. You were to think the president of the United States wanted a date with you, which he probably does. It was to be in a house on an island you own entirely. Palm Island, Florida."

"He was to be assassinated?" I asked. "As a movie star, I see a lot of films. Hopefully, his assassination wasn't to take place while he was humping."

"During his eight hours locked away with you, far from the preying eyes of his Secret Service, he was not to be fucking you, but lobotomized. By me."

. . .

As my privately chartered jet flew from Geneva to Miami via the Azores, I reflected on the "Strange Cargo" (wasn't that the name of an old movie before my time?) I'd taken aboard. There was not only Dr. Euler from hell, but the recently rescued Dino, my darling man Rafael, Ted Hooker, and the "spy in the house of love," Maxie himself, plus the usual servants whose names I could never remember.

Dr. Euler had requested that two of his laboratory assistants be allowed to fly with him, and I'd agreed. I was also taking some art to the Azores where it would be stashed until I could transfer it to Land Salzburg. Arrangements for the art stash in the Azores presumably were being made right this very minute by David, just one of the many thousands of tasks I'd given him that morning when I'd called him from my cabin on the plane. Poor, overburdened David. I loved him so. Even during our so-called passionate period, it was more like the love a daughter has for her father instead of a man-woman kind of thing. But I certainly didn't plan to tell David that and make him lose his self-confidence in the boudoir.

In addition to the Rembrandt, the Degas, and the Vermeer, my treasure trove included "The White Duck" (1753) by Jean-Baptiste Oudry, removed for "safekeeping" from the Norfolk house of the seventh marquess of Cholmondeley, England, in 1990 and valued at six-million dollars. There was also "View of Milan" (1744) by Bernardo Bellotto, removed from a castle in Czechoslovakia in 1992. Its value: Four million dollars.

Maxie and I were due for a meeting. I asked Ted to go and find him for me.

"Who do you want to look like now?" Ted asked. "I'd suggest Margo Channing."

"No Margo today," I said. "Besides, you vicious bitch, it would be Eve Harrington for me if I ever do the remake."

"I always thought I'd be great playing the Thelma Ritter part in drag."

"Get Maxie," I barked at him.

When Maxie came into my cabin, he looked old and tired. He always wore a world-weary mask of British serenity, but not quite like this. The pure light of the heavens poured in through the airplane's windows, and it was a particularly cruel light for Maxie, revealing crevices and wrinkles I'd never seen before.

That reminded me that I'd never paid much attention to Maxie at all since he'd come to work for me. I'd treated him like part of my entourage, to be summoned or dismissed according to my bidding. I'm sure that had been the story of his life, both in London and in Hollywood, with more dismissals than calls to the powder room, fitting room, or boudoir.

Up to now, I'd viewed Ted and Maxie almost as a sister act. But with Maxie sitting across from me, I realized that only Ted was the campy queen. There was no second act with Ted. Maxie, however, only played the role of the campy queen. There was a far more sinister side to him than I'd realized. A second act, maybe even a third. I'd always known that Ted was almost completely superficial, reflecting virtually anything he thought on his face, without duplicity. I suddenly realized, however, that Maxie was far more calculating, and whatever he thought wasn't readily apparent at all. He face was a complete and total mask. He donned a series of different masks if called for, and perhaps that's why he'd survived the tough acts he'd been forced to play out on both sides of the Atlantic. His early years in London must have been far more degrading and loathsome than I could have imagined.

I didn't say anything for a long moment. I sat in a deep-seated chair studying Maxie, as he no doubt eyed me, waiting for me to make the first move. We were like two chess players sizing each other up before either of us made a play.

When I continued to remain silent, he said, "The shadow over your left eye. I need to work on that. If I redo it, I think I can make you look five years younger."

Even that remark offended me. It was as if he were deliberately calling attention to my own age and vulnerability, knowing how sensitive I was on that subject.

That old Brit, survivor of a thousand gay bashings and a thousand bathhouses, seemed to detect that I saw through that small but somewhat unpleasant ploy. He tried to camouflage his remark. "After all, we girls have got to present our best faces before the world, don't we?"

"Indeed we do, my man Maxie." I emphasized the word "man" because I wanted him to know that this was no girl-to-girl chitchat about bulges in male crotches--or lack of them--or even eyeliner. He was a man, the oldest man aboard this plane, perhaps the oldest man flying on any plane on earth at this particular moment. As a man, he was accountable for his actions, and I planned to hold him responsible for them.

"This is not about make-up," he said in a voice where his irritation was only partially disguised.

"You've got that right, you dear old thing." I was almost mocking him. His phone call from the back of that limousine had nearly led to my death. "You're a great makeup artist, not a great double agent. You've seen too many James Bond movies."

"Indeed I have," he said, putting up another mask, that of a genuine movie fan. But everything he was doing was an attempt to divert me from the real issue, which was my confrontation with him for his betrayal of me. "In my opinion, that darling Sean Connery was the best Bond of them all. Do you remember that scene, I think it was in 1960, when the camera zoomed in as he uncrossed his legs at that desk?"

"Cut the crap!"

He shot me a look of pure ferocity before softening his features.

"I'm not even sure I was born in 1960," I said. "If I were, I was certainly too young to watch movies. 1960? Do you know how long ago that was? Kennedy was in the White House fucking Marilyn Monroe and waiting for the bullet."

"I knew Marilyn."

I sighed. Here, he went off again on his diversionary tactics, even though he must know they wouldn't work on me. It was as if he wanted to postpone the inevitable for as long as possible, perhaps fearing that his meager little world, the one he'd built with me, was about to collapse, as so many other fragile worlds he'd constructed had come tumbling in on him.

"I also know who killed her," he said.

His words caused me to pause momentarily. Maybe he was more skilled at diverting me than I'd realized.

Seeing he'd caught my rapt attention, he went on. "I talked to Marilyn two days before she died. I should have warned her since I knew about the upcoming plot to murder her. I've always regretted I didn't warn her."

"Some oversight," I said sarcastically. "I hope you don't forget to tell me when my number is up." Just as I was going to nail the bastard on espionage charges, he'd tossed in that tantalizing little gem about Marilyn. I was the Marilyn Monroe of the '90s, and since in some strange way I felt he might truly know who murdered Marilyn, I took his bait. "Who iced the bimbo?"

"The Kennedys didn't kill Marilyn, that's for sure. It was J. Edgar Hoover. I was at a gay party with him only ten days before Marilyn died. I used to dress Edgar in drag. All of us got drunk that night. He confessed to me what he was going to do. When I begged him not to, he slapped my face. 'Shut up, you god damn faggot,' he told me. " 'I'll kill whoever in this country I want to.'"

"You're making this up."

He looked at me with that steely-eyed contempt that Brits sometimes hold for gauche American barbarians. "Everything I'm saying is true. I asked Edgar why he wanted to kill Marilyn. I told Edgar that Marilyn was really a very sweet girl. I lied about that. Edgar turned to me, 'Listen, you limey cocksucker, *sweet girl* is going to hold a press conference that might bring down the entire U.S. government. I can't let her do that. I love this country too much.'"

"That story is so preposterous that it just might be true," I said. "Only in America. But save it for your memoirs. I bet you'll write memoirs, and I bet I'll be in them. Please be kind."

"You know I won't be kind," he said, almost laughing with a slight mockery in his voice. "I told the truth just then about Edgar. And I'll tell the truth about you."

"Listen, fucker, you've been spying on me." My face turned harsh, a look I rarely wanted to use on anybody since I suspected that it caused wrinkles. Before he could say anything, I stared him down. "Don't lie to me. I'll have Rafael throw you from the plane and you'll be nothing but a tough piece of leather for some shark to break his teeth on." I vaguely recall seeing that crazy Jamaican, Grace Jones, taking time off from blond Dolph, do that in a movie.

He did not melt in front of me the way Ted would have done. Ted would have gone into hysteria and threatened to kill himself, anything, to prevent me from punishing him. Veteran of years of intrigue, Maxie was far too clever for that. He even paused for theatrical effect before answering me. "It's true. I was spying on you. Not only that, I stole Rafael's real bullets. I put them in Mia's revolver. It was part of a plan to drive you and that movie crew from Key West. My employers--whoever they are--wanted unrestricted access to Mia. You are in their way."

"You bastard!"

"I've been called worse names than that. I can be bought, especially by you crazed Yanks. You really should know that I can't stand America or Americans. Never could. Oh, I sucked off a lot of G.I.s stationed in London during World War II. Entire battalions buggered me. But I hated them. I wanted only their life's blood, semen in this case. When they'd deposited it in me, I wanted them out of my little flat. I couldn't stand their boring company. When I came to America I arrived with only one purpose in mind. That was to get as much out of this country as I could. Pretend to be whatever the stupid Americans wanted me to be and then be gone."

"I appreciate your honesty, despite the appalling nature of the sentiments, although I view you as a complete and total liar. Like Anishi. A lifetime spent telling people what they want to hear, and almost never what is true."

"Did you really want to know how I thought you looked in the brassiere I designed for you?"

"No," I quickly said.

A flicker of a smile crossed his face before his eyes hardened again. "You're a ruthless cutthroat. I hold no loyalty to you. I don't even like Ted. He's a moderately embarrassing little faggot I use to get jobs. I just pretend at all this girl talk. It actually bores the shit out of me." He eyed me rather brutally. "I've even heard rumors in Hollywood that you once had a director murdered. Frankly, I wouldn't put that past you."

"All rumors about me are true. Doublecross me once more, and you'll find out how true those rumors are."

"I believe you. You'll stop at nothing, you..."

"Don't hesitate," I shouted at him. "Say it. They all eventually do. Go ahead."

"RICH BITCH."

"This rich bitch paid you well. Three-thousand dollars a week and lots of fringe benefits. Wasn't that enough blood to suck out of me?"

"Perhaps," he said with a certain defiance in his voice. Even though his plot was being exposed, he maintained a rigid pride, almost as if he were Queen Victoria herself. "More money than I've ever been paid in my entire wasted life. But they offered me one-hundred thousand dollars to do some spying on you. Unlike you, I've never seen one-hundred thousand dollars in my life. I've always offered my services to the highest bidder. I need money and I don't much care how I get it. Maybe the memoirs. Expose the filthy rotted underbelly of crummy Hollywood."

"Dozens have tried that already."

"Wait till I get through with Hollywood. The day I came to your house to work for you, I was behind in my rent. A jar of pickled onions in the ice box for my gin and tonic. Nothing else. No gin. The phone bill overdue, for a phone that never rang."

"Joe Gillis arriving at the home of Norma Desmond?"

"Hardly the same plot. At least I didn't have to fuck you. I needed money desperately. I'll do anything for money. Always have. Always will. It's not that I hated you. I don't admire you, though. I didn't like 'Kinky.' I don't believe in women showing tits and ass on screen. The big stars I worked with didn't have to do shit like that. You've actually been kind to me. Sort of kind. I'm the little faggy servant who comes dancing in with your Teddy boy. I'm to make girlish talk, do your hair, then disappear, perhaps to wallow around in your silk lingerie the rest of the afternoon."

"That's how I regarded you."

"There's more to me than that. I have a real talent. Hollywood denied me a showcase for my talent. I hate everybody out there for that. Design a brassiere for a big-tit star. That's the role I was assigned in life. I was trapped in this unlikely body with this unfortunate speech pattern. I wanted to be Sarah Bernhardt."

"I understand. I've been betrayed by almost everyone I've ever known. Why not join the act?"

"That's the way I figured it too. Everybody's betraying you anyway. Everybody except Ted. He's like a little puppy dog. He doesn't even know how to betray, an ingenuous lapdog straight from the farm. I know how little time I have left to live. The conspirators' money might be all I'll need on my way to the grave."

"How perfectly morbid."

"Morbid but true."

I sat up rigidly in my seat. "Listen, you old sod, you're going to tell me everything right now."

"Just before you fire me?"

"I'm not firing you. I want you to continue to work for me. Tell me every time you're approached by these farts. Find out what they want to learn. That will tell me a lot about what they're up to."

"What about the information I'm supposed to feed them about you?"

"It will be disinformation. Just like the British agent Noel Coward, pretending to be his usual indiscreet self, spread around Tangier in 1942. I read that somewhere."

"I knew Noel. I could play that. What's in it for me? You want my services. You'll have to pay for them."

"I will. But if you fuck up this time, you're shark bait. I'll have Rafael take you up in a plane and drop you over the Florida Straits."

He looked at me long and hard. "If most other people said that to me, I'd consider it gross exaggeration. In your case, I actually believe you."

"When I'm through with you, I'll deposit three-hundred thousand dollars in your account. You can go back home to London having sucked enough blood and semen out of America."

He looked at me in astonishment, as if he'd just won the lottery.

"That's right. Should you live any longer than either of us suspect, I'll add a bonus to that. But you've got to cooperate with me completely."

"I will. I promise. I'm not proud that I had to spy on you. I'm not proud of any of the things I did to survive, not in the old Hollywood, certainly not in the new. You represent New Hollywood to me."

"And you hate that, don't you?"

"I can't stand you so-called actors today. The great ones are gone. In the golden days, I stuffed the crotches of some of

Hollywood's biggest male stars. Padded the brassieres of some of its biggest female stars. No more. Could you imagine what Kevin Costner, Stallone, and Mel Gibson would say to me? Women like Joan Crawford adored men like me. Even Bette Davis at least tolerated me. A closet dyke like Stanwyck despised me, but I got on fine with Robert Taylor. I did that pretty boy many favors. Maybe that's why Stanwyck hated me. To the new female stars of Hollywood, I look like some dying ghoul found in great-grandmother's attic. The money from these jerks in Florida was my last chance. But then, you couldn't possibly understand how desperately some people in this world need money."

"I'm offering you your last chance to make it with enough money to get you to the funeral parlor on time. You game?"

He looked at me like Bette Davis facing Miriam Hopkins in "Old Acquaintance." "You've got yourself a deal."

. . .

When Maxie had gone, Ted came back into my cabin on the plane. Ever faithful Ted was always here to attend to my needs.

"Rafael is still asleep," he told me. "I must confess I slipped into your bedroom cabin. Ever so gently, I pulled back the sheets for an inspection. You are one lucky girl, woman!"

"Forget it! That's my property!"

I'd decided not to tell Ted about Maxie's betrayal. I wanted Ted to continue to view Maxie as a friend and to work with him to get us through the next week or so. I was surprised at myself for thinking "next week or so," but I honestly believed that was all the time we had before there was some sort of conclusion, regardless of how awful, to the events of the past few days.

In Geneva, Ted had picked up copies of some of the major newspapers from around the world. My picture and that of Cruz were splashed on every front page. The shooting accident had captured the imagination of half the globe. But if I gave a press interview, which I didn't plan to do, I could provide more startling information. Maybe that the life of the president of the United States was under threat.

I had big news for the president. David had agreed to help

me prepare all the papers I could gather at present, including Dr. Euler's documents about the lobotomy. Clinton would need some strong convincing. Even when he learned what I had to tell him, I'm not sure what his course of action would be. Maybe there were other people meeting in secret conspiracies around the country, plotting race wars, assassinations, even lobotomies. Maybe my conspiracy theories and so-called "proof" would be but one of twenty-five or more he received every day.

How did I know? To me, it was a land peopled by lunatics. Their schemes sounded ridiculous and preposterous, perhaps so fantastic that one of them just might succeed. It didn't seem to me that it would be particularly hard to launch a race war or even to assassinate a president if that were your desire.

It was almost impossible to see myself sitting across from the president's desk in the Oval Office, trying to get him to buy into my conspiracy theory. I'd have to use all of my sexual allure to draw that one to the honeypot. I'd been eager to learn he'd loved "Kinky," and I was certain if he were so taken with the reproduction on the screen, that he'd definitely want to sample the in-the-flesh masterpiece. It was like the Mona Lisa. Why settle for a reproduction if you could hang the genuine painting on the wall?

My attempt to convince the president of danger was a chance I had to take, even though I might make an idiot out of myself. I was prepared to take the risk. Unlike Maxie, who allegedly didn't warn Marilyn, I was going to alert Clinton of what I knew. He might know more about this group than I did, but I doubted that.

"Ted," I said, sounding his name as if I were a female CEO issuing orders to an all-male board meeting. "I've decided to have that date with Clinton after all. At Palm Island."

"You're true blue with Rafael."

"Not quite yet. I have work to do. Get your friend Vinnie boy on the phone and tell him I'd like to meet privately with Clinton on Palm Island just as soon as possible. Tell him it's urgent and I can't wait. Make it sound romantic."

"Are you sure? The president is small and Rafael so big."

"I insist."

"I can't. It's a mistake." He sounded a bit like a whiny child fearing a potential paddle from an irate parent.

"My pet," I said with growing impatience. "You know that linebacker? Long, I think he's called. The one whose pictures you avidly collect, including the secret one snapped in the locker room at the Cotton Bowl?"

"Do I ever?" Pecker-Checkers puts him at..."

"I don't care. If I buy him for you for a week, a honeymoon of sorts, will you set up this White House thing? Picture it. All alone with that nude linebacker at my secret villa on the Cayman Islands."

Without hesitation, he said, "I'll do it."

"Clinton's Arkansas crony?" Rumored boyfriend of Hillary? What was his name again? Vinnie Foster."

"Pecker-checkers list Foster at six and one-quarter inches. Uncut."

"I don't give a fuck about his dick." I leaned back in my seat. "Vinnie is making those calls. I wonder is that his secret job on the side? To pimp for the president? Surely not. But then, who knows? Mia knew JFK's pimp, who arranged more than one secret rendezvous between the two of them. Clinton might be trying to follow in JFK's footsteps."

"I'll call Vince. But I'm going to hold you to your promise."

"Get Foster on the phone. Start the negotiations. Following in her Mommie's footsteps, Sherry Kelly wants a date with the president of the United States."

CHAPTER NINE

After temporarily depositing Dr. Euler and his assistants, along with the stolen art, in the Azores, my strange cargo – after what had seemed like endless hours in the sky – eventually entered air space over Florida. I'd ordered David to arrange the tightest security available within the entire state, as I wanted a very private reception.

Strong, reliable David. He was always here when I needed him. Considering his astronomical attorney fees, why shouldn't he be? Because of all the requests I'd presented to him recently, he'd lately started calling himself my foreman. Before the story was over, I suspected there would be even more outrageous requests.

As the plane prepared for its landing, my recent actions flashed through my mind. I regretted a number of decisions I'd made. Going to Hollywood was just one of them. If I had it to do over again, I would not have become an actress. Although a screen classic by now, "Kinky" would never have been made, at least not by me. I would not have feuded with Mia either.

As I reflected, I realized that my downward cycle began when I'd ordered The Iguana to get me the phone number of Dino after having seen him in that Banana Republic ad. That had indeed been a big mistake.

At that moment, Rafael slipped into the seat next to me and buckled up as the plane descended to earth. He took my hand – the one that once had been home to the Capetown Diamond – -and kissed my inner palm. I realized that if I had not met Dino, then I would never have met Rafael, the love of my life, Hispanic or not.

As security and customs were being handled at the airport, David, who had arranged for us to meet privately, came to rescue me. Rafael, like the jealous hot-blooded Latino he was, wanted to join us, but I assured him that David and I had some strictly personal business to discuss.

He and I did have a lot to talk about, and very little time. When I confronted him in the privacy of one of the airport's customs offices, where people were usually strip-searched, his face was ashen. He seemed overwhelmed and acutely embarrassed. Perhaps I had been working him too hard, calling him at all hours of the night with my latest demands.

"Welcome back," he said. He looked like a schoolboy caught by a teacher with his hand up a little girl's dress.

"With all the demands I've made on you lately, I believe I'm interfering with your love life."

"What love life? Those days may be behind me. I'm getting old. Definitely not the man I used to be."

I stared at him intently as this was a David I didn't recognize. Before now, he'd always bragged of his sexual escapades. To hear him tell it, he was America's leading stud. For a while he said nothing, and I kept silent too. There was an awkwardness between us I'd never known before. For one brief second, I thought he was going to tell me that Mia was dead, or had been injected with the deadly virus.

With my back to him, I turned and checked my appearance in a rather grimy mirror. After an all-night plane ride, I didn't exactly have confidence in the way I looked. "I fear I'm getting old too. This is the first time I've been alone in a room with you for more than thirty seconds when you didn't make the obligatory pass at me."

"That's not the way it is any more." He said that with such a bite it alarmed me.

"I wasn't that bad, was I?" Unlike Doris Duke, I didn't make you suck on my toes for hours, did I?"

"You were fine. You still are fine."

"Fine is hardly a description of me. Fine is not a word you use to describe the reigning sex goddess of earth. It's like Kevin Costner calling Madonna 'neat.'"

"Okay, if you must know, you're too good-looking for your own good. Whatever existed between us was a horrible mistake. I'm ashamed it ever happened."

"That's not very flattering."

"Stop it!" He'd grown angry at me and I didn't know why, or was it anger at himself.

"Out with it. You're about to let me in on a secret."

"I don't know if you should know or not. Mia didn't know if I should tell you. She met with me and decided to let me make the decision."

"I thought you and Mia weren't speaking."

"We had a long talk last night. I promised her to persuade you to drop the lawsuits against her. She wants to make peace. It's very important that you drop all lawsuits."

"I agree completely. But I'd already decided that for myself before you and Mia went into a huddle. I'm flexible on lawsuits and ready to negotiate in private. The Mona Lisa, however, is non-negotiable. But I suspect that's not what you have to tell me. It's about my diary, isn't it? She's read my diary. Completely violated my privacy."

"She's sorry about that now and wants to talk to you about what she found out. It came as a complete shock to her. Usually, she knows what's going on, but you fooled her."

"Did she tell you what was in it?"

"She did."

"God damn her. She not only violates my privacy by reading it in the first place, she practically broadcasts the contents on CNN. You may be my attorney, but you have no right to know what's in my childhood diary."

"Mia thought I did have a right. A right to know a lot of things about you, other than what I learn as your lawyer."

"Why? Give me one bloody reason."

He moved closer to me and looked deeply into my eyes. "Because I'm your father."

. . .

This was no joke, a soap opera from hell. Both Mia and I both felt that many aspects of our lives were a soap opera.

Even now, as I try to recall my emotions at his announcement, I can't. I am not altogether certain what my feelings were. Whatever I felt would be different from the reactions of the average person. I'm not average. Never have been. For one thing, I'm rich and that separates me from most of the rest of the world. Besides that, I have a steely reserve at times. I do not self-destruct easily, especially when it comes to revelations of sexual indiscretions. I have always been only too willing to forgive both myself and anybody else for virtually any sexual indiscretion imaginable, as long as that indiscretion didn't physically or emotionally damage anyone.

Over the years, I have viewed sexual indiscretion as one of the minor but inevitable embarrassments of life. Some of my critics say that makes me wanton, but I take umbrage with that. I accompanied Jack and Mia Kelly since the age of two weeks on their travels across the globe, and I've have seen true evil in this world. Death. Violence. Pestilence. Famine. Torture. Mutilation of all sorts.

I know this sounds as if I were up on a soap box, and I don't mean to be. All these thoughts raced through my mind before I confronted the central issue. He and I had committed incest. Unknowingly, I hasten to add. Most definitely, I am not a person who advocates incest in any form, but despite my best intentions, innocent me seems to have committed it anyway.

At first I didn't want to believe him. The more I looked into his eyes, the more I knew he was telling the truth. This revelation had seemed to hurt him far more than it wounded tough old me.

Any great guilt I might feel about having loved him, regardless of how temporary, would be postponed until tomorrow or even the next day. Right now I didn't feel a thing. No guilt. No pain. No embarrassment. Nothing. If anything, I felt numb.

Only in this past hour, I was fearing my own assassination. To me, that was important. What he'd just revealed shocked. It didn't have the power to make me fall on the floor screaming in rage and pain, and then to demand that I be delivered immediately to the nearest psychiatric clinic. It certainly didn't tempt me to put through a call to The Iguana and demand that he arrange for me to be booked on the Phil Donahue show for a discussion about incest in the modern American family.

When I finally spoke, I decided to be Sherry Kelly, the actress, star of "Kinky," and not some mournful long-lost daughter who'd stumbled in from the cold.

"How can you be sure?" I asked, trying to sound casual, as if inquiring if he wanted more toast for breakfast.

"I can't be. Only Mia knows for sure. But there hadn't been anything between Jack and her for more than two years before you were born. There never was much between Jack and her anyway."

"That's a very important piece of information for me. That

means Daddy Kelly always knew I wasn't his daughter. All along, he knew I wasn't his..."

"He had to. We're not talking the Immaculate Conception here."

"Let's get real. "Mia's had many lovers. You were but one in a long parade."

"I was a child myself when I fathered you. Mia's latest young stud, although our affair continued over the years until she found out about us. Back then, I truly believe she was madly in love with me, at least for a while. Mia's attention span with lovers rarely lasts more than six or eight weeks, although ours went on and off for many years. During the time you were conceived, we saw each other virtually every night. We didn't know what safe sex was back then, and we certainly didn't practice it. I think our only fear at the time involved getting the clap."

"My intuition, and everything else I know, tells me that Mia is telling the truth. In fact, I really believe her. Besides, why would she try to invent something like this?"

"She really didn't want to tell me," he said. "I don't believe for a minute that she's lying. That this revelation is all part of a scheme of hers. It could be. She's devious. But in this case, I believe her too."

"I can tell you something now I never could before. When I got involved with you, I wasn't lusting for you. I was trying to get back at Mia. For some awful wrong she'd done to me at the time. I forget what it was. God damn it, but she and I have always been competitive. We can't help it. It's a sickness, I guess. That's the main reason Mommie got involved with our little hustler, Dino. That and because he throws a great fuck. She'd read in the tabloids he was my lover. She wanted to take my lover away from me, just as I took you away from her. I think she was very disappointed to learn that Rafael, not Dino, was really my lover. Her next move, and I can predict this, is to go for Rafael. Wait and see."

"Perhaps."

"Where do you go from here, *Daddy*?"

"My feeling is that we forget it. We go on as before. What existed between us on a certain level is dead and gone. All feelings, all passion. We didn't know. You were very young and dumb and I was a little bit older and even dumber."

"Forget that. You and I were never dumb a day in our lives. We were born smart. We knew what we were doing. We didn't know we were father and daughter, but we knew plenty. We were completely responsible for our actions." I moved closer to him and gave him a light kiss on the cheek. "There," I said, stepping back. "That's how a daughter is supposed to kiss her dad. That will set the stage for our future encounters."

"Can you go on with me? I mean, retaining me as your lawyer?"

"Silly boy, if anything, I feel you'll take a fatherly interest in me and protect me all the more."

"That's a relief. In addition to being my daughter, you're also my best client. I'm making a fortune off you."

"I know that, and that does lead to a rather embarrassing complication."

"Here it comes. Now that I know you're my daughter, you'll probably want me to work for less."

"If anything, I'll raise your already exorbitant fees. Sort of keeping the money within the family, so to speak."

"I know my law firm will be delighted to hear that. If you make up with Mia, perhaps we'll get her back as a client too."

"It's not quite so simple, unfortunately. Eventually, I'll want the money back."

"I don't understand."

"You never contributed child support during all those years I was growing up. You never even bought me a present. I gave you lots of presents. Expensive ones."

He looked dumbfounded. "For one thing, I didn't know you were my daughter. For another, I was just a struggling attorney when I first got involved with Mia. My God, you guys are billionaires. You weren't exactly waiting for me to send over food stamps."

"Trivial details. You can make up for your prior lack of financial support with one simple act that can be accomplished in one hour. It won't cost you a cent. Not right away."

"What, for God's sake, are you talking about?"

"As your daughter, I want to be named your sole heir. Please have a will drawn up naming me as the only beneficiary in your will. Have the original delivered to me in Key West within forty-eight hours. You can keep a copy for your own records."

He looked at me long and hard. "I think you're serious. You really want that. Compared to yours, my assets are meager. What are we talking about here? Ten million dollars? Maybe a bit more."

"Is that all? I don't know how you can afford to live. Nevertheless, those millions should go to me. It's the least you can do for a daughter you've neglected during all these years. Besides, it will make me remember you fondly."

"As long as I have known you, I've never been able to figure you out. I simply can't predict your reactions. Who can?"

"I don't know myself sometimes. Like that demand I just made. I don't know why I said that. I meant it, however. It's like a badge of honor for me. It's like a legal link to you. An acknowledgement to the world that you and I are bound together. A father leaving his daughter all his possessions. And I especially want those porno pictures you and Crawford posed for one night in Mexico. It's important that you name me."

"I will. Actually, I don't have a sole heir, but of course, I have a will."

"Burn it."

"I was going to distribute my fortune to various undeserving persons and a few groups I don't really care a fuck about."

"How nice. You've got a daughter now, and you've got to provide. Besides, if there's anything I hate, it's a deadbeat dad."

"I'll look after you more than ever before."

"Why don't you begin by giving me a big hug? Make it fatherly. Watch those traveling hands."

"Gladly. I think I need a hug too." His eyes brightened as he looked at me. Did I detect some mist in those eyes? He embraced me and I clung to him.

"You're trembling," he said, holding me closer.

"I know. I can't help it. I'm afraid. Afraid even to walk out of this airport into the world. I fear something awful is coming."

He held me closer. As I stayed in his arms, I did something I can't recall doing since I was a little girl. I burst into uncontrollable sobbing.

In the inevitable limousine and with the ever-faithful Rafael at my side, I was driven to the much-disputed Mia/Sherry Kelly estate on Star Island, former resting place of the Mona Lisa. It held a sentimental memory for me, as it was here I'd met Rafael. Could that have been only days ago?

David had said Mia would be waiting here for me, and she wanted to see me privately in her suite, without my usual entourage. I dreaded meeting her even though I longed for a reconciliation.

I hoped Anishi wouldn't be here. She must be out of her mind over John and Henry, and I'd promised to rescue them. That depended on a very, very private meeting with Snake. I just knew that he could find them if they were stashed in Monroe County. Nothing ever happened there without Snake being aware of it.

After arriving at Star Island, Rafael headed for the shower. That man certainly kept himself very, very clean. The demands he made on my talented tongue required him to be clean at all times, since everyone knew how much body odor offended me.

I hardly had time to slip into a simple white dress before a maid summoned me to Mia's suite. I felt I was being ordered to the boudoir of an empress who held the power of life and death over me. I always felt that way in her presence, even though David told me that by now, I had just as much money and power as Mommie herself.

She and I had so many matters to review I didn't know where to begin. There were so many things I wanted to tell her and even warn her about. That would be difficult, because of her short attention span and her unshakable conviction that everything anybody told her was bullshit anyway.

My Mommie was a woman of strong opinions, and all the evidence in the world could be presented to her to no avail, as she preferred her own intuition. "Why do I rely on my instincts?" she always asked. "Because I've always been right, and the world has always been wrong." In the face of such overwhelming logic, I usually retreated.

On this balmy Miami day, she had artfully arranged herself on a white-wicker sofa against a background of what had to be the world's most dazzling array of fresh flowers. She was a vision in fuchsia. Elizabeth Taylor perfume and Elizabeth Taylor diamonds coated and covered her. Today, she looked exactly like Taylor when she'd appeared opposite Burton in "Boom!"

"You're looking lovely, Mommie. I'm glad to see you again."

"What is this simple white dress? Let me guess – your next role is that of a virgin about to enter a convent? Considering your track record, what convent would have you?"

"Don't be bitchy. You've known far more men than I have. You've had a lot more years to seduce them."

"That may be true, but you'll overtake me soon. According to my estimates, your latest conquest must be number four thousand and fourteen. Yes, in your absence, your most recent love affair has been publicized by the tabloids. And everyone in the western hemisphere now knows that Dino dropped you for me, and you've taken up with a Cuban pilot who just might be under indictment from the Federal government for air piracy. God, what a class act. And did you say a *Cuban*, my darling? Need I say more?"

"What about you and Dino?"

"At least he's Italian. But you. *With a Cuban.* Oh, my darling, my dear, dear, demented daughter. What would Jack Kelly have said?"

"You've had your loaf of Cuban bread too."

"I have not, and I don't intend to ever sail the Hispanic seas. Even Karen Stone in Tennessee's 'The Roman Spring of Mrs. Stone' only descended as low in the genetic pecking order as Italians, and look what happened to her. I admit, it's true that I have lowered myself once or twice, but only in the interest of strictly scientific investigation. And I've always admitted that there were two token blacks, but both of them were world-famous in their own right. Shall I name them for you?"

"It's already well-documented. One at least will go down in the history books for greatness. The other will become notorious for judicial mediocrity."

"Oh, there you go again with those political opinions of yours. At times, I think you get all your politics directly from *The Village Voice*. Really!" She paused a minute, as if considering something I'd previously said. "Exactly what did you mean with that crack you just made, Cuban loaf?"

"You've had Dino. But of course, who hasn't?"

"A youthful Italian model from a Valentino ad, so what?"

"I think it was Banana Republic."

"Dino is from a banana republic? Is that what you're saying. Oh God, not Costa Rica?"

"No, Mommie, it's a firm that manufactures clothing."

"I've never heard of them and I don't intend to ever buy anything there either."

She looked a little too smug. Of course, she'd heard of Banana Republic. She probably owned stock in the company. I had to deflate her balloon to bring it closer to the earth's surface. "Dino Paglia is not Dino Paglia. He's Desiderio Navarro."

"Navarro? As in Ramon? Isn't that the same name as your latest toy?"

"Exactly the same. Rafael Navarro is Dino's father."

She looked at me sternly, the way she used to when as a sixteen-year-old I didn't come home until after breakfast the following morning. "You made that up."

That was all she said, dismissing the idea from her head. What she didn't want to hear or believe, she didn't hear or believe. Convincing her of what I had to tell her remained my most formidable job of the day.

I decided that this father-son talk would get me nowhere, and it wasn't really that important. There were other matters. She looked distracted, as if she were about ready to summon a servant to get someone on the phone. One of her long, rambling monologues was about to begin, I feared.

I desperately needed her attention. "We've come across evidence that somebody out there is planning to inject you with a deadly AIDS-like virus. They've forced Anishi to become a spy and a saboteur for them. You must never allow anyone to ever again give you another injection. It could be fatal for you."

There it was, out in the open. I felt relieved for having revealed that. That was, I felt relieved until I looked into her face. She'd listened, and she'd heard me all right. Belatedly, I realized I should not have blurted out the revelation in the hurried way I did. I should have gradually led up to it, presenting more evidence as I went along.

"You've resented Anishi's injections all along, haven't you?"

She held up her hand imperiously. "Don't answer. I know why you've resented them." She rose from the sofa and, like a stage actress, moved to where one of the room's most flattering spotlights cast a forgiving glow over the flowers, no doubt imports from South Africa. "You'd do anything to destroy my relationship with Anishi, wouldn't you?"

"I want her out of your life."

"And this is your way to go about that? To make me afraid to receive any of her injections? You don't have to worry. Anishi has, on her own volition, already stopped administering her injections. Without explanation, she's completely withdrawn them. She stopped right after you left for Europe or God knows where you went. I suspect you're behind this. You're behind it because you're jealous of Anishi, but you're also jealous of the way I look. When you arrived in Key West and saw me looking younger and more beautiful than you are, you couldn't stand it. It drove you crazy. Not only did I have a more glamorous look, I took your boyfriend away from you too. To top that off, the producer of your latest trashy movie wanted to star me instead of you. I've even done a test for Jerry. And for your information, I look gorgeous up there on the screen. All in living color. Fucking gorgeous. Even Elizabeth Taylor will be jealous of me. I look more glamorous than she ever did. In fact, I am *more* glamorous than Elizabeth Taylor. I want my beauty – beauty at its mature peak – immortalized on the screen. I've agreed to do the movie, and with me in it, it will be anything but trashy. It will be a fucking masterpiece."

"You are indeed beautiful, but I'm sure Anishi's injections had nothing to do with it. Your own radiance is coming through. Your beauty is natural, from within. All from you, not from some needle."

She paused as if caught off guard. For the first time today, she liked and perhaps even accepted what I'd told her. "You do have a point there."

"I have another point, too. There's a conspiracy. Someone is out to get you. First they want your money. Then they'll get you."

"Oh, they will, will they? You forget I'm Mia Kelly. I can get them too. I surely have more money than they do. Money talks. If they're out to get me, I'll strike first. But before I do that, I have to be presented with strong hard evidence that they're out to get me. Not dark suspicions from your deranged mind. Evidence, daughter dearest. Something you don't have."

"David and I will present you with all the evidence we've got. He's sending a white paper to this house in about five hours. You've got to read every word of it. Then you will see what kind of shit you're walking into."

"You amuse me with your documentation. If I recall documentation is not your forte. You're a clever fox. You've always paid people to do your dirty work. You invariably manage to cover your much-photographed ass. Except for once in your life. Once in your tawdry, slutty life, you left a written record."

"You mean, my diary?"

"You used to leave that diary lying around your bedroom. You wanted me to read it. I finally did. When you were a girl, I never realized that your leaving that diary out and about was a desperate attempt on your part to get me to read it. You wanted me to rescue you, yet I didn't invade your privacy when I should have. I should have read the damn thing when I could have done something. I failed you then, and I fear it's too late to do anything about it now. Because of what I learned in that diary, you became the profound disappointment you are to me today."

I didn't say anything for a long moment. Although she and I had suffered a million embarrassments together, our approaching encounter was the most humiliating to date.

"It's too late to do anything about it now. But you could have told me that David was my father. You know I would never have gotten involved with him if I'd known."

"You're absolutely right about that. I failed to tell you. It was my own dirty little secret. When you took David from me, I deliberately decided not to tell either of you. My own sweet revenge."

"That's a wicked game to play. Really evil."

"How dare you judge me! It's true that I never told you about David. That was wrong and I admit it. But you could have told me that Jack Kelly was your lover."

A silence descended over the suite. In some part of the mansion, telephones were desperately ringing, but I didn't really hear them. I'm sure she didn't hear them either. Neither of us could care about phones at this moment. Before we faced anything else, we had to bring the contents of my diary out into the open.

Without excusing myself, I rose from a wicker chair and walked through the open doors to the terrace. At the pool, I saw a bikini-clad Rafael dive gracefully from the board into the refreshing waters. At this moment, I wanted to join him and to flee from Mia. But I didn't. I turned and headed back to her boudoir. I didn't want to face her. Nor did I want to face what I'd written in that diary. I should have burned the fucking thing. She'd rearranged herself on the sofa, waiting for me with all the questions. I was about to embark on an interview from hell. I feared her questions because I didn't know the answers.

. . .

A deadly stillness had settled over her boudoir. She closed her eyes and sighed, resting her beautiful head against blood-red and cherry-colored pillows. "Why did you do it?" she finally asked. "Give me one reason. Some explanation?"

"How can you lie there and suggest I did anything?" I asked, gasping for breath. "I was a twelve-year-old girl. I was molested by a man who was your husband. He was not my father, although I thought he was at the time."

"You could have said no. You were hardly a prisoner. You could have come to me."

"Come to you? You of all people? Jack Kelly's pimp?"

"How dare you make such an insinuation!" She rose up from her pillows and confronted me. "A pimp? I've been the victim of every horrible slander and libel in the world, including a notorious column by that old hound, Dorothy Kilgallen, but I've never been called a pimp."

"Let's face it, Mommie dearest, you and Jack had an arrangement. He didn't interfere in your star-fucking chases, and you didn't interfere in his pursuit of little girls or even little boys. Just so long as they were underage, right?"

"Lies were spread about Jack by his business enemies. Perhaps there was an indiscretion here and there. Nothing was ever proven."

"Don't give me that crap. Payments were made. Nothing silences a molested child's family faster than money. Miraculously, potential court cases were dropped. Jack never got into trouble because he bought his way out. Hushed up everything. You knew all about it, and participated in it."

Slowly, she got up from the sofa. "Listen, flasher, what do you know about the secrets of the human heart? You never had a heart. You never had a shred of compassion or understanding for Jack, or for me, or for anyone. All you were interested in from the day you were born was yourself."

"You've always said that. If I pursued a selfish agenda, it was because I used Jack and you as role models."

"You could have done worse. Jack had his faults. Behind the closed doors of the bedroom, he was a weak and often impotent man. If he opted for little children, and I'm not really admitting that, it was because he didn't want to be judged sexually. A mature woman with needs and desires would have judged him harshly. Instead of that, he preferred the innocence of youth. A virgin who had never known a man before him and therefore was in no position to judge and condemn. That is not understandable to a woman like you, a sexual athlete of Olympian proportions. You could probably satisfy any man with your boudoir techniques, no doubt learned in some Arabian brothel, if I know you. You don't know what it was like to live in Jack's skin and be a sexual failure, yet to have unbridled sexual desires. Throughout his life, he was tormented. If he turned to kids, he did so with such guilt it haunted his every waking moment. He was disgusted with himself, but couldn't control it."

"That level of disgust never stopped him from causing a lot of damage."

"It didn't – but that's because he was driven. It's true. I did help him out of some trouble from time to time, and I did arrange for him to get out of some tight jams. I was in his debt. I had to do whatever I could for him."

"You make it sound as if you did Jack favors. You never did favors for anyone. You knew that if his house came tumbling down, so would yours. Your fortune was linked to his."

"Indeed it was. So was yours. It was because of Jack that you and I have more money than we'll ever spend, regardless of how hard we try. Jack provided for us more than any two women in history have ever been provided for. We must be grateful to him for that, and overlook his shortcomings."

"I am grateful to him. I showed that gratitude by letting him molest me for three long and dreadful years. When I turned fifteen, I became too old for him."

"To judge from your diary, he rewarded you well. After one of your sessions with Jack, you were given some incredibly expensive gifts. And we are not talking Barbie dolls or candy bars here. A quick appraisal of those gifts today would total in the millions. It appears that you were the most expensive teenaged harlot in history."

"I was a little girl, not a harlot. I was terrified of him. He might have been a weak and vulnerable man in the bedroom, but he was a bloodthirsty killer in the boardroom. With his clothes off, he was pathetic, but with his clothes on, he was the perfect embodiment of a robber baron. He knew only one thing. That was how to make money. He didn't care how that money was made, either. I'm sure that's why you married him. You already had plenty of money of your own, and you wanted more. A whole lot more. He was the man to funnel each of your millions into smart investments in a growing economy. As a result he made you so rich it became almost an embarrassment."

"That's what attracted me to him, I admit that. I didn't turn to Jack for sex, and he sure as hell didn't want sex from me. When I met him, his fortune was big, but not big enough. He knew that to make the fortune which we eventually acquired, he had to have access to my money too. A marriage contract seemed the sensible way at the time. Many of the great marriages of history have been contracted for lesser reasons. There are many reasons a man and a woman come together to form a union. With Jack and me, money kept us together. When he was no longer with me, he left all that money to me or to you, even though he knew you weren't his daughter. In fact, everything that went on between you two was hardly incest because you weren't Jack's blood. His money was my reward for a lifetime of having overlooked certain weaknesses on his part. As a point of honor, I faithfully kept all his secrets until you started recording them in your shitty little diary."

"He was driving me crazy. Screwing up my mind. I started keeping the diary as an alternative to going insane."

She whirled around the room, upsetting a large vase of flowers as she did. "Don't give me that crap. You were never the victim of anything. For all I know, you seduced him. You ferreted out his weakness and exploited it. Don't forget. I knew you when you were twelve going on fifty. You were like no little twelve-year-old girl I'd ever known. At the age of twelve, I was an innocent. When you were twelve, no slut from ancient Babylon could have taught you anything."

"Stop it, damn you! That's a horrible lie. I was a normal little girl. If I became corrupted, if I lost innocence, it was because of him. You know that in your heart. You can blame me for everything, but the bald truth is that I was seduced by a powerful man I feared, a man I thought was my father. A man who held the power of life and death over me. Few men on the face of this earth, including presidents of the United States, ever defied Jack Kelly. Do you truly believe that a twelve-year-old girl could have stood up to him?"

"You can justify your whorish actions until hell freezes over. But I'm not buying the act. If he seduced you, and I have only the demented rantings in your diary to support that accusation, you also seduced him. You were a Lolita from hell at the age of twelve. One of my boyfriends confessed to me that he got a full erection every time you crossed the room back then. If all your embarrassing little writings are true, both you and Jack should have found better pastimes and more interesting pursuits than playing with each other. With all the world out there to snare, neither of you were forced to turn to each other. It was a deliberate act on both your parts. If your diary is true, and I have serious doubts that it is, then I'll never forgive either of you for carrying on sexually with one another in my household.

"You could have looked. You could have seen. But not you. You were pursuing your own games. Collecting your own horde of dirty little secrets."

"I am a hopeless romantic who has always followed the dictates of my heart, regardless of where that heart led me. I'm also a woman of flesh and blood. I have desires. Often, those desires are of a carnal nature. I'm a gloriously lusty woman, I admit to that. God created me that way. I have always wanted sex, plenty of it, and I always got as much of it as I wanted. I fully intend to continue getting what I want, even if I happen to divert some of the talent you might have originally discovered. It's all fair in our game of love and war. How many men did I discover for you?" She waved her hand in the air as if to brush off any response from me. "So what if you discover some stray pieces of talent for me from time to time? Like Dino, whom you falsely and very unfairly accuse of being a Cuban. That's utterly ridiculous."

"Is he your new passion? Don't you think he's a bit young for you?"

"First, you attack Anishi's injections which have made me younger and more beautiful than I've looked in years. Now for all I know you're plotting to sabotage my relationship with Dino, who has aroused greater desire and passion in me than any other man in years. I don't think I'll ever bother to read that stupid paper David is sending over. It's just another attempt on both your parts to sabotage my life and my new plans."

"Which, I gather, include seeking immortality on the screen."

"That would really offend you. What if we made a better film than 'Kinky' ever was? You know my film appearance will be compared to your 'Kinky.' You know you'll be humiliated when you read the comparisons."

"I beg of you, I'm not lying. I seriously believe you and I are in some serious trouble. We're being stalked. I really believe that. Somebody is trying to do us in."

"I'll hear but I'll not rush to judgment." She looked at herself admiringly in the mirror. It was obvious that her attention was about to shift to other matters, and that it was time for me to go.

"The other night," she said, pausing to turn and look at me intently before finishing her sentence. "The other night I couldn't sleep. I turned on the TV. Bette Davis in 'All About Eve.' That line, beloved by all queens, about 'Fasten your seat belts...' It held up very well. Our bumpy ride isn't over yet. Before this day ends, I'll have a surprise for you."

. . .

Before dinner with Mommie that night, I had two important phone calls to make – one to Anishi, another to Vince Foster at the White House.

I couldn't delay either confrontation one more minute.

In the privacy of my dressing room, I ordered Ted to place both calls. He reached Anishi first, as Vince Foster was not in his office although a White House secretary promised the call would be returned.

Anishi had remained in Key West in case the kidnappers contacted her and had bowed out when Mia had invited her to Star Island.

"I'm back and I'm here to help," I assured her. "We'll get your boys back--I promise that."

I'm so grateful," she said, near tears. "I have been going out of my mind waiting for some word. Even a ransom note. But nothing. Not one word. This silence is killing me. I tried to sleep for a brief time last night. But I kept dreaming John and Henry were dead. That this mysterious boss of mine had put them to sleep."

"Don't even think it. I'm a very intuitive person. In my gut, I know John and Henry are okay. They're probably playing in the sun right now."

"You're trying to reassure me, and I thank you for that. But both you and I know nothing. We can only guess. Only hope."

"The moment I put down this phone, I will summon all the forces I have to find your boys. Money is no object. But I must say I'm surprised they haven't contacted you with a ransom note."

"Each time the phone rings, I die a bit. Any moment I expect to be delivered some special message from the kidnappers."

"You're to let me know the moment you get word. You promise that?"

"Of course, I will. I'm so very grateful. I'm the last person in the world you owe any favors to."

"That's true."

"But you'll stick by your word to help me rescue them? You won't let me down?"

"I won't let you down." I paused. "Does Mia know any of this? I'm seeing her for dinner tonight, and I've just had a long talk with her. I didn't mention John and Henry."

"It's amazing. The boys have been long gone, but she's never mentioned or asked about them. Actually, that isn't really surprising. She goes for days at a time without encountering them. They might live under the same roof, but they inhabit different worlds."

A gnawing suspicion came over me. I hesitated before speaking. Apparently, I hesitated so long that she asked me if I were still on the line. After all, she was used to Mia who abruptly terminated conversations.

"Aren't there some more details you can tell me about how they disappeared? I'm willing to get my people involved, but so far I have nothing to go on. How were they kidnapped? Exactly when? I really need some raw meat. Did someone break into Mia's house, and, if so, did you report it to Snake? Were there signs of a struggle? Something? Anything?"

She paused for such a long time that I began to think she might be inventing a scenario. "I know I haven't been forthcoming. It's..."

Pay dirt! She was lying. I'd caught her in a lie. I just knew it. "C'mon, I can't stay on this phone all day. If I'm to get your boys back, I need to know all the details, especially those you're about to tell me now."

"Originally, the way I'd plotted it with my boss, the kidnapping was to be a hoax."

I'm sure she detected a slight gasp escaping from my throat.

"I'm telling the truth. The whole kidnapping had been my idea--not his."

"Whoever the fuck 'he' is."

"Whoever he is. I'd been plotting this kidnapping for days. That's back when I was getting on better with the boss. Before he became suspicious of me. My scheme back then was to get Mia to put up the ransom money. Even though she doesn't like my boys that much, the way I figured it she'd be good for a cool two-million dollars. She'd do that, I felt, just for me, and not the boys. After all, the way I saw it, she wouldn't want me to get angry and cut off injections. She firmly believes these injections have not only restored her beauty, but given her a new way of life, if only with that cheap hustler, Dino."

"She's made it abundantly clear how pleased she is with the results of your injections which I can only pray haven't contained a virus."

"Nothing has been injected into her veins but my harmless elixir."

"You can assure me of that?"

"I give you my word."

"Your word doesn't mean a hell of a lot."

"I know how you must feel about me. I've cheated and lied most of my life. Now when I'm telling the truth, you must think I'm continuing to lie."

"Actually I do. I just can't trust you and this kidnapping story." I paused, as if searching for the right accusation. "From the very beginning, I was suspicious. If I really believed John and Henry were in true danger, I would have cancelled my trip to Europe. But from the very first, something didn't ring true about this."

"That was then and this is now. One night Mia told me how many threats of kidnapping she'd received when you were growing up. There were three major attempts at kidnapping you. Thank God none of them succeeded."

"What else did she tell you?"

"She said if you had ever been kidnapped, she and Jack would not have paid the kidnappers one cent. She claimed that whoever kidnapped you wouldn't return you. That they'd kill you after taking her money."

"I find this memory very disturbing. But just how does it apply to the kidnapping of your boys?"

"I looked into Mia's eyes the night she told me about these kidnapping threats. I really believed her. She was fiercely determined. It didn't take much for me to realize that if she wouldn't have put up money for you, she certainly wouldn't put up money for John and Henry. When my boss called again--I can never reach him, he always calls me--I told him what she'd said. I said the kidnapping thing was off. She wouldn't go for it. Then I'd be stuck with my story and my boys' disappearance. Eventually I'd have to bring them back and make them part of the conspiracy. After all, they'd be grilled about where they'd been."

"This is all very fascinating. But not leading to the real details about their kidnapping."

"Don't you see? I think I planted the kidnapping idea in this monster's brain. When he became suspicious of me, he decided to kidnap John and Henry but for a different reason than money. My boys are his secret weapon. With a knife at their throats, he knows I will do his bidding."

"Then you've become a lethal weapon around Mia. You may be forced to inject her with the virus. You've placed me in a position of having to protect her from you."

"I promise I'll not inject her with the virus." There was a long hesitation. "At least for forty-eight hours." Her voice became strangely threatening. "That's it! You'll have forty-eight hours to rescue John and Henry. If you don't succeed by then, I can't be responsible for my actions."

"You are--in fact--issuing an ultimatum."

"I hate to put it this way. You've been so kind. It's true. It's an ultimatum. I have to be completely frank with you. I can't trust you on your own to bring John and Henry back to me. You owe me no favors. You've only met my boys once. They mean nothing to you. But since Mia's well-being might suddenly depend on you getting my boys back to me, I feel you might become a lot more receptive and a hell of a lot more cooperative."

"You've got that right. I want your boys back. But my main concern is Mia. Nothing must happen to her. Nothing. Do you understand that?"

"I understand perfectly, and with your help there is a good way out of this." She became suddenly businesslike. "My boys wanted to go to the beach right near Mia's house. They've gone there before. I didn't see anything wrong in letting them go."

"As if boys that age need permission to go to the beach."

"I sheltered them. They ask my permission to go anywhere or do anything."

"That's obvious."

"When they weren't back for dinner, I went to the beach. They were gone. I asked everybody I saw. No one had seen them that day."

"Has it ever occurred to you that they might have run away? Just to escape you."

"Everything occurs to me, but I'm sure they were kidnapped. They would never leave me. They are devoted to me."

"Is this all you have to tell me? Not that it wasn't enough. A kidnapping hoax. Now the real thing. It's all hard to take, but I'll pull something off. I always do."

Ted motioned for me that the call from the White House had come in. Vince Foster was back in his office. "We'll be in touch later," I said, putting down the phone. Like Mia herself, I wasn't much for phone good-byes, not with Vince Foster on the line. I sucked in the air. I really needed more time between these two calls. I'd wanted to be clear-headed, cool, calm, and articulate when I talked to Mr. Foster--not the agitated, confused, befuddled actress I was at the moment. I took the receiver from Ted. "Vince, my darling man, at last we speak in person. Up to now, I thought you were after Ted and not me."

. . .

"Ms. Kelly, in the flesh, if only over the phone." It was Vince Foster.

"Let's drop this Ms. Kelly stuff. It's Sherry to you. Or Sherry, baby, if you and I decide to let our hair down."

"I'd like to let my hair down with you anytime, but Bill saw you first."

"What on earth do you mean?"

"He saw 'Kinky' first. Then called me for a second showing later that night. He claimed he liked the second showing even better than the first."

"How flattering. Did Hillary see it, too?"

"No, she was out of town--or otherwise Bill wouldn't be watching 'Kinky.'"

"Do you think Hillary will ever get around to watching it?"

"Definitely not! Contrary to talk radio, Hillary is not a lesbian. I personally can vouch for that."

"I see." I decided not to pursue that one.

"I can't believe this. Here I am, Vince Foster, a little barefoot boy with cowshit on his feet, talking to the very beautiful Sherry Kelly. I should also add the very rich Sherry Kelly. In Arkansas we're impressed with big money. We spend most of our lives trying to bag the big one. Often we have to get involved in some pretty wild schemes on our way to paradise. Regrettably, we rarely get there."

"I can understand that. Well, not really. I never pursued

money in my life. It was all given to me. I never did a damn thing."

"That's the way to live."

"It has its drawbacks."

"Such as?"

"I never know if a man is in love with me or my money."

"Do you really care? I mean, as long as they deliver."

"You're right. I don't really care." I lit a cigarette. "I know what a busy man you must be, and I'm sure you didn't call me to talk about my money. Unless, of course, this is a solicitation for a loan."

"We'll discuss your giving me a loan another day. Setting me up as a CEO of one of your big companies. That is, when I leave the White House." As an afterthought, he added, "If I ever leave the White House. My salary here doesn't equal your monthly restaurant tab."

"A deal. Anytime you want a job, you come to mama. Give Bill a big wet one and fly off to your Sherry pie."

"How you talk!"

"Dammit, I'm trying to talk Arkansas dialect. No one ever heard of the damn place until Bill became president. I hear you raise pigs. Shit like that."

"That's about it. But we're mighty proud of our little state."

"I prefer my villa on Como – that is, if I could ever get there."

"You must be running around a lot."

"A lot." I puffed furiously on the cigarette, like Bette Davis in "Now Voyager." "Life is rough. Maybe you and I should escape from our responsibilities."

"That sounds like the stuff of dreams."

"I had Ted show me a picture of you after you called. You know, you're not bad looking. Much better looking than Bill."

There was a slight gasp on the other end of the phone. "Coming from you that not only makes my day, it makes my life. Sherry Kelly thinks I'm good looking. That's reason enough to continue to live. What better judge than you?"

"How do you know that?"

"I've read the tabs."

"What better source? I have one here in my dressing room. Its headline is emphatic. Says I've been cloned. I'm a *faux*

Sherry Kelly. The real one has been abducted, and right this very minute is being raped by aliens from outer space as their craft circles the world."

"Bill and I read shit like that every day. He's trying to get used to it. But do you ever get used to crap like that?"

"Believe it or not, you get used to it. Or else learn to ignore it. Bill's had it rough. I read that the reason he initially endorsed gays in the military was because he himself was the biggest cocksucker in Arkansas. Now, Washington."

"That was said. It's not true, of course. But he's an expert at licking pussy. Nobody in Little Rock was any better. Or so I've heard."

"After Nixon, and some of the others, it's good to have a man back in the White House who likes pussy. It's good for the country. But I don't think you should get too hetero up there. Personally, I believe all men should take it up the ass a few times in their lives. It'll teach them humility."

"That's a dubious pleasure I've never had."

"I can arrange it for you."

"I'll take a rain check on that. I have another far more intriguing – at least to me – arrangement I'd like to make with you."

"Fire away."

"This is awkward for me."

"I'm not bashful. Shall I say the words so you won't have to?"

"That would make it a hell of a lot easier on me. At times – like every minute – this White House job sucks."

"Boss man wants a date?"

"How did you guess?"

"Many people who saw 'Kinky' fell in love with me. That's understandable. Why wouldn't they? Let's face it: I'm god damn gorgeous. And, as you know by now, I'm blonde all over unlike Marilyn. No bleach has ever touched that special part of me."

"You made that easier for me. Thanks. But all this is so very unfulfilling for me."

"What do you mean?"

"Arranging something for Bill. After this brief talk, I'm in love with you myself. I don't want Bill to have you. I want you just for me. Especially now that I know how good looking you think I am. I'll tell you something of a confidential nature, too. I've got Bill beat by at least two inches. At least!"

"I'm sure you have. Sometimes those extra two inches make all the difference in the world."

"Hot damn!" Forgive me for saying that. But that's how everybody talks in Arkansas."

"You're forgiven. Let's put the bread on the table. What's the pitch?"

"Bill is flying to Miami."

"I heard it over the news."

"Miami is very close to your retreat on Palm Island. After his speech when the reporters think he's gone to his suite, Bill would like to fly by helicopter to your Palm Island place. He wants to meet with you personally." He paused. "To thank you. After all, you were one of the biggest contributors to his campaign, and he's very grateful."

"He wants to express his gratitude?"

"You might put it that way."

"Fine with me. I'd like to meet the president. But I'm sure you're aware of all the dangers involved. I don't want us to end up on the front page of every tabloid in the world."

"You wouldn't believe this from what's reported in the press. But we can be discreet around here. Even Arkansas boys."

"I hope so." I crushed out the cigarette. It was funny how we'd avoided the other thing. "Vince."

"Yes, your attorney called."

"I have many attorneys. You mean David Miller?"

"A lawyer I respect and admire. I knew he had to make the call because you demanded it. But this whole conspiracy thing. You know, of course, we hear about ten of those a day."

"But you only need one to be the real thing."

"True, but we've checked this out. We even know you went to Gstaad to see Dr. Euler. We also know you've stashed him at your place in the Azores. Dr. Euler is a harmless eccentric. Funny in a perverse kind of way."

"But he does perform lobotomies."

"He does. Legitimate ones. When he's not performing lobotomies, he's a conspiracy buff. He's told people that forces have contacted him to perform lobotomies on Kohl. On Thatcher. Why not add Bill to the list now that he's president?"

"None of this crap checked out?"

"None! It's a game with him. You've met him. Don't you think he's perfectly harmless?"

"I don't think any man who performs lobotomies is that harmless."

"Believe me, if I thought someone was a potential threat to Bill, I'd be at their throats in a second. Trust me on this one. We're still new here, but I think we're a bit more experienced than you are in these matters."

"I'm sure you are," I said.

"When Bill meets with you, he'll be heavily guarded. But, of course, we'll have to keep it quiet."

"Naturally, but I'll agree to the meeting only if you think no harm will come to the president. I wouldn't want to be a party to that at all."

"I understand. I can't give you an exact time. Can I call Ted and make all the arrangements? Can you be flexible about the timing?"

"I can be as flexible as you want."

"You've been a real sport about all this. Hell with Bill. When can I meet you?"

"I'm involved in a Big R right now. And you're married. But as soon as both of us are free, let's get together."

"Don't make it too long. I'm an impatient man. Hate to wait."

"It's worth waiting for."

"I bet it is! Goodbye, love of my life."

"Goodbye. I'll give you a full report on Mr. President."

"Lucky man. You sound like a little darling."

"I work at it. Love and kisses." I put down the receiver.

For some reason, I felt I'd just taken part in a bit of madness. So, the White House is a bit crazed. So what? Why should it come as any surprise to me that they're as looney-tuned as anybody else?

. . .

The wind was blowing through my hair as I waited on the Kelly helicopter pad on Star Island. Snake had agreed to fly here from where he was located: a motel in Marathon along the

Keys. At the rate I was paying him, he would gladly board any plane to answer my summons.

"Pretty Miss," he said as he disembarked, a little wearily I thought.

"Glad you could come here on such short notice for our brief little chat."

"Brief little chat," he said, smirking. "Now who's kidding who? When I figured you had business with me that couldn't be conducted on the phone, I knew what you had up your sleeve. That this was a job for Snake Jr. I went right into the bathroom of that motel where my men reached me and washed it real good and clean from its previous duties. Took a lot of soap."

"I'm sure it did. But that's not why we're here. Something even more urgent."

I took him by the hand and led him into an enclosed room which Mia had built to protect her coiffure while she was waiting for a helicopter to arrive. Ted had thoughtfully arranged for some brandy and glasses. I offered him a generous pouring which he accepted almost too eagerly.

"This sure ain't rotgut whiskey, is it?"

"Not at all. I'm glad to see that you're a man with a discriminating palate. Each jigger is worth fifty bucks a shot."

"This is the most expensive liquor I've ever had in my life. When we were kids, we used to make our own on the Keys. Good as it was back then, it sure didn't taste like this high-priced stuff."

"Someday when we have more time, we'll taste various brandies. But I summoned you here for more urgent matters." I took his hand and stood real close to him, looking him in the eye. That way, I hoped to detect a slight glimmer of either shock or else mendacity when I informed him of my news.

"Anishi's boys, John and Henry--you know of them--have been kidnapped. Do you know anything about this?"

Without a flicker of an eyelid, he returned my stare with a certain steely glare. "Not a god damn thing. When did this happen? Why wasn't I informed at once? After all, I am the chief law enforcement authority in Monroe County. I assume it took place in my own little briar patch."

"On the beach. Near Mia's house."

"Show me the ransom note. There's always some clue in the ransom note, woman. This isn't my first kidnapping, you know."

"I'm sure you've been involved in many a kidnapping," I said enigmatically. "But in this case there is no ransom note. Not yet. The kidnapping took place right before I flew to Europe. So it's been many hours."

"That's very strange to have no word from them."

"The whole thing is strange. Anishi thinks her mysterious boss is behind it. I'm sure you know something about him."

"Yeah, I do. We've got his voice on tape. After the shooting, I ordered Mia's phones tapped, as if you didn't know."

"I want a copy of that tape. Agreed?"

"Agreed. If I know you, you'll turn it over to that lawyer lover boy of yours, David Miller."

"After hearing what's on it."

"I've been so busy I ain't heard the damn thing myself yet. But at least we'll know what his voice sounds like. A Spanish accent, they told me."

"I must have that tape. When you fly back, put a copy of that tape on this helicopter and have it flown back to me. Don't hold out on me like this. You wouldn't want to take a cut in pay, now would you?"

"That I wouldn't want at all. I'm very happy with our little...shall we say, financial arrangement. It's what I've been looking for all my life. That way, when I retire as a public servant, I'll have a little nest egg to retire on. I certainly can't retire on a sheriff's pay."

"Retire later. Right now you've got work to do."

"I also have a major clue. I hadn't told you about this before because I didn't think it was important."

"Spill the beans."

"About six weeks ago, Anishi rented a house in a remote area up in Key Largo. I didn't think anything was unusual about that. I figured she needed to escape from Mia some times, and wanted a place for her little love nest. She came and went there only a few times. Always alone. My men never saw the house occupied. Then a few days ago two Jap men flew into the Key West airport. They rented a car and drove directly to this house. They're living there now, at least I think they are."

"You're as suspicious of Anishi as I am. You think she may have staged this kidnapping and stashed John and Henry in Key Largo. She admitted that was her original intention. Originally she was going to try to bleed the money out of Mia. But Mia, she learned, doesn't pay ransoms."

"If we find John and Henry in that house, we'll know that Anishi is a liar. Some big revelation that will be. If we don't find the boys there, then maybe we'll have to believe her current story. That her mysterious Spanish boss is somehow behind all this."

"At any rate, we need to find out what these two gentlemen from Tokyo are doing here. They're obviously tied in with Anishi. What does she need them for? It may be some other scheme of hers, having nothing at all to do with her Spanish boss."

"That's what I'm thinking. Well, I've got to be off. You are seeing to it that I certainly earn that paycheck."

"As I plan to."

Rushing up the walkway from the gardens beyond, Ted was racing to me with an urgent message.

As he came into our waiting room, Snake glared at him. "Sucked any big nigger dick lately?"

"A few," Ted said, without missing a beat. "But I hear that you're the only man in Monroe County who can satisfy a size-queen like me."

"You got that right, you little faggot. But you can only dream about it. You'll never get your chance." He looked over with a leer at me. "Unlike Pretty Miss here who can have it any time she wants."

I took the message from Ted. It had come across on my confidential fax that I gave to virtually no one, having made an exception to Anishi in this case. She told me she'd received the ransom note. It demanded three and one half million dollars in small unmarked bills. The kidnappers claimed that if the ransom money weren't delivered in twenty-four hours, the heads of John and Henry, enclosed in ice blocks, would be sent to Mia's estate in Key West.

I handed the note to Snake, after blowing Ted a kiss and thanking him for the delivery.

Snake was a slow reader, but he finally got the message. He

looked at me with sad eyes. "I always have a gut feeling about these things. My gut tells me there will be no happy ending to this story."

"But you'll talk to Anishi. You'll demand she give you the ransom note."

"I'll do all that. But first I'm leaving you and this good brandy behind. I've got an unscheduled stopover in Key Largo before going on to Key West. If I find John and Henry at that place in Key Largo, I just might arrest that slanty eyed pussy."

"We'll talk about that later."

"I'm not going to let you down. You haven't seen Snake Sr. in action, and you certainly haven't see Snake Jr. in action."

"Later, later." Taking his arm, I directed him toward the waiting helicopter. "Just one more thing. The president of the United States just might be paying me a secret visit to Palm Island. This is completely top secret but I want you to summon extra men to that area. They're not to interfere with the Secret Service, of course. This is to be a major operation. Utterly hush-hush. I'll fill you in on the details as soon as I'm told of the president's plans."

"Hot dog, hot damn, and hot pussy. You sure like to keep me busy."

"Stick around. More fun and games on the way." I stood in the wind blast of the pad watching the helicopter take off in the garish pink sky, like cotton candy, heading out on his mission impossible.

If anything I was developing a fondness for him. I felt tonight could be the beginning of a beautiful friendship.

As I dressed for dinner, Ted had turned on the news for me, since for several nights in a row, I had become a regular feature on prime time, and not just Entertainment Tonight. Tonight, mercifully, I was not on the air waves.

He came back into my boudoir to tell me that Mia wanted to speak to me on the phone.

"Yes, Mommie," I said, picking up the receiver, although, as always, bracing myself for whatever news she had to reveal.

"Just for tonight, I've segregated our house guests and put them in separate dining rooms. I fear that all of us assembled together in one room wouldn't properly represent family values."

"What are the arrangements?"

"I've hired two male strippers to serve faggot pie to Ted and Maxie."

"I assume you mean tuna and macaroni casserole?"

"You've got that right. Anybody who's been to Fire Island knows that's all they ever eat there, anyway. Now, for the various menageries of ethnics we have in residence, I will have an Italian specialty, veal Marsala, with pasta, made for Dino. For Rafael, roast pork, black beans, and yellow rice."

"Sounds perfect. What about me?"

"A simple, dietetic salad without dressing. I want you to dismiss your various lovers and entourage from the Sodom you've been maintaining since you were eleven. Tonight I want to dine *en famille*. Just us. The immediate family. As a party favor, I will reveal my surprise. Be ready at nine and don't make yourself up too much. I am at my most spectacular tonight, and you couldn't compete with me anyway. So why bother?" With that, she slammed down the phone. She never said hello or goodbye.

. . .

Promptly at nine, I appeared in Mommie's private dining room directly below her boudoir, where she'd encountered many of those fabled lovers of yesteryear, or at least those visiting Dade County. Tonight, I'd worn a shocking pink gown cut very low. I resembled Monroe doing that "Diamonds Are a Girl's Best Friend" number in "Gentlemen Prefer Blondes." Mia always became infuriated at me when I wore pinks or reds, since in her view, she owned these colors by divine right. I'd decided to defy her tonight.

"What a ghastly outfit," she said as soon as I appeared. "Go back and change right away."

"Can't Mommie. I've just returned from a difficult trip and this is all I have to wear."

"It clashes with my gown." Tonight, she was a vision in various shades of red, almost as if she'd dressed to look like a femme fatale waiting at the gates to hell.

"If you wear any more red," I told her, "and put any more rubies on your fingers, and paint your face with any more scarlet, you'll explode in flames. But in my little pink number, I'll cast a soft, forgiving glow on your fire."

"A symbolism under which you've always lived. Even though I've been harsh with you from time to time, I feel sorry for you. Having me as a mother has made you feel inferior, and rightly so." It was only then that I realized that Mommie was completely drunk. She managed to hold her liquor well, but she slurred a word here and there, just enough to give away her state of intoxication. When she began one of her long rambles about her beauty, power, and fascination, versus my own "ordinary little mousy look," I knew it was the drink talking. It certainly wasn't reality speaking.

If anything, I looked eighteen times more gorgeous than she did tonight, but if she couldn't admit that, I didn't want to force the issue.

As I seated myself opposite her, I wished I still owned the Capetown Diamond. Only the Capetown could compete with her masses of rubies, which included a stunning necklace that she claimed had once been owned by Catherine the Great. Upon her death, she'd promised the necklace to me, but I didn't know the current status of her will. Neither did David. I doubted very seriously if Anishi were even mentioned in it.

"Why did you decide not to invite Rafael? It's rude to withdraw an invitation at the last minute."

"I spoke to him on the phone. He'd much rather watch a soccer game on TV and have his food served on a TV tray. Trust me. It would be better if he were not here tonight."

"So what's the surprise?" I asked abruptly. "You know I hate surprises."

As if to answer me on cue, a light tap was heard on the door.

. . .

Dino, more spectacular than he'd ever looked in his life, stood in the doorway, until Mia summoned him inside the room. The only person in the world who'd ever looked better-- and I'm only guessing here--was Rafael at the age of eighteen.

In white pants two sizes too small for him, and in a white shirt unbuttoned practically to the waist, he smiled faintly at me and went over to give Mia a good evening kiss. Did I detect a flicker of tongue up one of her nostrils?

"It's my house and my dinner party, and I'm laying down some ground rules," she announced to Dino and me. "First, there will be no name-calling. Each of us has known each other rather unsuccessfully, I might add--for a while now. There have been the usual betrayals, blackmailing, cheating, stealing, and slander, not to mention double-crossing and perhaps murder attempts, but all that is part of life. What we've done in the past was predictable. Part of the game." She slammed down her liquor glass and snarled, "Now it's time to act civilized." She then reeled off a list of household do's and don'ts in her most matriarchal tones.

After listening to her rules of the game, I sat down gently in the chair opposite Dino, biding my time for the moment. I didn't think it appropriate to challenge Mia on her assertion that the Star Island mansion belonged to her when it clearly did not.

"Welcome to our happy little cottage," I said sarcastically. "I will do a daughter's best to make dinner pleasant for you."

"It's already pleasant," he said in his most velvety hustler voice. "What could be more pleasant that surrounded by the world's two most beautiful women?"

She downed another large gulp of Scotch or whatever it was she was drinking. "You bet your sweet ass you are. At least *one* of the world's most beautiful women."

"Might I add what a pleasure it is to gaze upon the second most beautiful male in the world," I said.

He looked miffed. "Just who is the first?"

"Rafael."

"Your Rafael is already developing a wrinkle or two. I have perfect skin. My lashes are longer. My skin not as rough. I'm at the peak of my beauty. How can you dare sit there and say he is more beautiful than me?"

"Now, now, my children," she cautioned. "We must play by my house rules tonight. No cat-fighting. Agreed?"

"Agreed," he said, looking dejected. "But Sherry here really should watch her tongue. When we tell her the news, I don't think she's going to put me down any more. Not after tonight."

"Just what delectable bit of news do you have to share with me?"

She smiled as enigmatically as the Mona Lisa. "Dino and I are going to be married."

I slammed down my drink. Instead of congratulating them, I blurted out, "You're going to make him sign a pre-nuptial agreement, of course?"

He glared at me.

I flashed her an uncertain smile, turning from him. At least she had a sense of realism about the man she planned to marry.

"Now come on, baby. We don't need agreements."

Ignoring him for the moment, I leaned closer to her. "How much?"

"One-hundred thousand dollars," she said, slurring her words. It was as if she'd never spoken of such a small amount before. After all, that was usually what she'd pay during a day's shopping or for a weekend vacation.

"I find that hard to believe," I said. "So much? Of course, Doris Duke pulled that on Rubirosa at the last minute. Her pre-nuptial agreement called for twenty-five thousand dollars."

"That was 1947," she said. "Haven't you heard of inflation?"

"Duke should have agreed to pay more," I said. "After all, Rubirosa was compared to a peppermill, but this pathetic little boy is hardly worth one-hundred thousand dollars."

"My darling daughter. Don't put him down. You may have cast him off for Rafael, but I have found much hidden talent here. Perhaps--oh, could it be?--that I discovered greater assets here than were known to the famous flasher herself?"

"That's right," he chimed in. "I held back on you. Mia, on the other hand, gets all of me. I love her."

"The tabloids will be cruel," I said. "I'm warning you. If they attacked me as a cradle-snatcher, what will they say about you?"

"I know exactly what they will say," she practically hissed, leaning in toward me. "That I stole a young man from my own world-famous sex-siren daughter. The entire planet will know that he prefers me to you."

During the awkward silence that followed, a handsome waiter arrived and poured some Chivas Regal in her glass.

"After our marriage," she said, "I suspect that most of my energies will be spent keeping your hands out of Dino's very tight pants." She downed another slurp. "My darling," she said to him, "your pants are very tight. I, on the other hand, believe in leaving something to the imagination."

"I never did," he said with a certain authority as if he were secure enough in the relationship that he could start to defy her.

I remained stonily silent although furious about this marriage announcement. Finally, I could restrain myself no more. I leaned over to him and gently rubbed my hand across his smooth cheek before giving him a gentle slap.

He pulled back, stunned. She seemed unaware of my action.

"If Mia forces you to sign that pre-nuptial, just how do you propose getting her money, which is what this marriage is about, anyway?"

"This marriage is about love," he said, blowing a kiss to a drunken Mia. He smiled at the waiter, and ever so slightly ran his finger across the waiter's hand when the young man handed him his champagne. Although it was just a flicker of a touch, I recognized at once that he planned to audition the waiter later in the evening in lieu of going to Mia's much-used honeymoon suite. She'd be too drunk by then to notice his absence.

The waiter poured me champagne in a tulip glass. His eyes met mine with a twinkle. Obviously, he'd prefer going to my bed tonight instead of to Dino's, but being from the working class, he had to make a living. In olden days, I would have walked off with the waiter just to make Dino furious, but I had something better waiting for me in some other part of this house, or at least I hoped I did.

I raised my glass in a mock toast to Mia and Dino. "May I offer my heartfelt congratulations to the soon-to-be newlyweds? I know both of you will be supremely happy. Sounds to me like a marriage made in heaven."

"Don't be sarcastic," she said. "Dino and I have a very active agenda. I've got the money, and I want glory. He's got no money and wants glory. My money will buy him glory. Once he gets glory, we'll share it. Won't we, darling?"

"Glory," I said flabbergasted. "What in hell are you talking about? Glory? You want to be saints."

"We're talking about becoming the god and goddess of the

silver screen," he said. "Mia is going to appear in *Butterflies*. With me as the male lead. After the wedding, of course. With all the publicity the film will get with our marriage, it's bound to make millions."

"It'll get publicity all right, but I don't know if that will translate into box-office power," I said.

"Look what happened to you," she said. "You were famous before you made 'Kinky.' You became even more famous after the movie. The same thing will happen to me. Everybody will want to see Mia Kelly on the screen. At the peak of her beauty."

"You keep saying that," I interjected.

"What about me?" he said. "Because of Sherry here, and that Banana Republic ad, I'm also famous. A younger crowd will flock to see me."

"Dream on, my sweet children." I got up and walked to the edge of the terrace to breathe the air. A nightmare was unfolding in front of me, and I wanted to wake up. As I neared the edge of the patio, I came to an abrupt halt. Knowing Mia's fondness for cannibalistic vegetation, I feared I might be devoured on the spot by some woman-eating plant.

As I stepped back, I noticed Ted rushing across the patio with a message for me. When he spotted Dino, he came to a dead stop, his eyebrows extending to his hairline. "Dino, you naughty girl, haven't seen you in my bed lately. What's the matter? Can't get that big old thing up any more?"

"Ted Hooker," he said. "I thought you died of AIDS."

"I'm still around. Like AIDS, I'll still be around to plague the hell out of you. I'm waiting for you to become really big, maybe even bigger than Brad Cruz. Then I'm selling my story for thousands. In some way, I really want you to become a movie star. That way, my expose will sell for really big bucks."

"Give flasher here her message and get off my terrace," Mia barked, not quite certain if Ted had actually bedded Dino. "This is strictly a family gathering."

"Here," Ted said, looking dejected at Mia's curt dismissal. Before leaving, Ted said nothing else to Mia but turned to Dino again. "Maxie's here."

"Who's Maxie?" Dino asked.

"The one and only Maxie," Ted said. "He's right under this

roof tonight. Dying to talk to you. Catch up on old times."

"Tell him to forget it," he said. "I've got no time for antique faggots like that."

"Get out!" Mia screeched at Ted. "We've got important business to discuss."

The first message was from Anishi. She'd heard again from the kidnappers of John and Henry. They had upped their ransom to ten-million dollars. The second message was from Vince at the White House. After our phone conversation, he'd reported to the president, and the date was definitely on. All arrangements were being made. Vince was still uncertain of the time. I promptly ripped up both messages before seeing there was yet a third message. It was from David. The lawyers of Cruz had decided not to settle. He was suing me for one-hundred million dollars. I ripped that message up with even greater fury.

"I suppose you don't want to share your dirty little secrets with us this evening," Mia said.

"Very personal. However, I'll share one secret with you, providing you tell me one of yours."

"What's that?" she asked, downing another gulp of Scotch.

"With Dino here getting only one-hundred thousand dollars in the case of your untimely death or divorce, and with a few billion in some bank vault somewhere, who's getting the rest?"

She rose in her chair to her most stiff-backed position. "You, daughter dearest, pride of my loins. Except for a minor percentage of the whole, which will be divided among various charities, you're getting it all."

I was stunned, having feared she'd left me out of her will.

"With your own billions," he said, "and one day with Mia's billions, that would make you the richest woman of all time. The Queen of England will be hitting you up for a loan. You'd no longer have to flash tits and ass on the screen to earn a buck or two."

"Now out with your dirty little secret?" she said.

"It was from Bill Clinton at the White House." I made it sound like a joke. "He wants to discuss a matter of domestic policy with me."

"Not bloody likely," she said. "I played the game fair. I told you my secret. The heir to my fortune bit. You didn't carry through with your part of the bargain, though. Tell the real truth. What was the message?"

"I told the truth." As an actress, I read the line to make everyone think I was lying.

It was then that I looked into Dino's face. Unlike Mia, he actually believed me. That had not been my intention. Underneath those adorable curls, whatever little brain power he had was working overtime.

Not wanting to keep him from his rendezvous with the waiter, I walked over and placed both my hands on Mia's shoulders, half supporting her in her drunken state. "Thanks for what you just told me. It really does mean a lot to me. It means the world to me. Your love."

She looked up at me in tears. "Give your old Mommie a big wet one and take her to bed. I've got to sober up."

I turned to Dino. "Now, listen, daddy. You don't mind my calling you that? Just imagine! Dino Paglia my new daddy. You thought that if you could get Mia to marry you, you'd end up as sole heir. Didn't you?

"I'll admit to no such thing."

"I'll see that you never get your greedy hands on one Kelly cent--not even the one-hundred thousand dollars promised in the pre-nuptial. If you ever fuck with me, I'll tie you up in the courts forever."

"I'll outlive you, bitch."

"My estate will carry on for another five centuries. Longer than even you'll live."

"You might destroy me. But you might also end up getting destroyed. I'm not stupid. You're not coming clean with everything. There are forces out there plotting against you. That shooting of Cruz was no accident. There are people out to get you. I don't know who they are. But they're after you. You might not be around to interfere with my plans."

"You just may be right."

"Let's call a truce," he said, reaching for my hand which I didn't offer. "I mean, Mia, you, and I are going to be family now. "Maybe it's not the ideal family, but a family."

"What about Rafael? How does he fit into this little family portrait?"

"Don't start that shit about Rafael being Dino's father," she said. "I'm not in the mood for it." She looked at him. "You wouldn't lie to me, would you?"

"Mama, I'd never lie to you. I won't cheat on you either. When we get married, it'll be for keeps." He took her in his arms and kissed her long and passionately. Then he helped her up and together they made their way across the patio.

The handsome waiter returned to retrieve the champagne glasses. "Dinner is ready," he announced.

"The guests had to leave," I said with a smile to him. "Why don't you serve me? I'll dine alone."

"A beautiful woman like you should never dine alone."

"It's just for tonight."

"I'm booked up for tonight," he said. "Another commitment. How about me and you tomorrow tonight?"

"Thanks anyway. But I've got an engagement."

"Too bad. It would have been nice."

"Nicer than what you're facing tonight. You'd better lubricate yourself real well. You'll be serving table bow-legged tomorrow."

"It's just for the money. It's not what I really want. I don't like it that way. I'd rather be the fucker."

"He's definitely a top. But I assume you've discovered that already."

"Painfully," he said.

"Okay. Forget that god damn diet salad Mia ordered for me. Bring me a thick steak. Cooked rare."

CHAPTER TEN

Even though Rafael was in the next room eagerly demanding a blow-job, Ted felt it was vital I take an urgent call from Jerry. It was about Cruz. Any man suing me for one-hundred million dollars piqued my interest. For one brief moment, I almost let the only-too-eager Ted rush off to Rafael's bedroom to do my duty for me, but decided against that. He might be better at it than I am.

Picking up the receiver as I undressed, I asked abruptly, "What is it, Jerry? It's late, you know."

"I'm in a gay bar. Sorta like a private club."

"What a revelation! Why don't you call me when you're in a straight bar? That would be news."

"You don't understand. Cruz is here too. I've spoken to him. He wants to see me in a private booth. For a little chit-chat."

"So Cruz is gay? The rumors are true, after all. I was never sure."

"Honey, we gays have known that for years. He's one of us. Whenever he can, he slips away to this gay hotel in San Francisco."

"Of course, I've heard the rumors. According to gay gossips, everybody is gay – even moi. Although I've fucked half the men in the world, some people still call me a dyke. The only rumor I've not heard is that you're straight."

"Even an idiot wouldn't believe that."

"I'm really interested in what the fucker says. He's not inviting you over to proposition you. The conversation will be all about me. You know, of course, the asshole's suing me for one-hundred million dollars."

"He told me that earlier in the evening. I couldn't believe it. I'll try to persuade him to drop the suit."

"I'm sure that won't work. But you could do me a big favor."

"What's that?"

"Report back to me on everything he says. I mean, everything. That will give me a good idea of what the fucker is up to. I don't think he wants to go into court and dreads it as much as I do. My god, our attorneys will open a Pandora's box.

Not only about me, but him too. I don't think Cruz wants that. I think this suit is about extortion. Forcing me into a bigger out-of-court settlement than I'm willing to make. You find that out for me. You want 'Butterflies' made, don't you? You find out what Cruz is up to, and I'll guarantee you that 'Butterflies' will be made."

"It's a deal. But I can do better than report back to you. I have all sorts of equipment in my van outside. You know how I like to run around the country taping or recording the hot stuff. I can secretly record my talk with Cruz. You'll hear every word."

"That would be divine. Can you get away with it?"

"Are you kidding? Did you know, for example, that I've taped all my conversations with you?"

"I didn't know that little tidbit and I'm sorry to hear it."

"That shows what a clever fox I am."

"Great! If you can fool me, I'm sure you can fool Cruz. Get everything on tape. I want to hear every word. David thinks I shouldn't do some of the stunts I do. Like secretly taping people. Sometimes that guy likes to play by the rules. But when an overpaid actor is suing me for one-hundred million fat ones, what are the rules?"

"I've set the stage even better. Earlier tonight I told him that you and I had fallen out with each other. You're out of the film and no longer the backer. A role assumed by Mia Kelly."

"Stick with that story. He'll spill more if he thinks that. Hop to it before Cruz grows too old to talk."

"If I pull this off, you'll owe me one. A big one."

"I know," I said growing impatient. "Sherry Kelly always rewards cunties who do favors for her. You know that better than anyone."

"I know you won't let me down."

"Don't you let me down." I abruptly put down the receiver.

In the privacy of my toilette, I prepared myself for Rafael. That blow-job might lead to other things. Even as I stared approvingly at my full-length figure in the tall mirror, I had an ominous feeling that my call from Jerry wouldn't be the only call I'd receive before dawn.

I put on a robe and summoned Ted.

"My, you look gorgeous," he said entering the bathroom, as

always, without knocking.

"I'm going to bed now, cuntie."

"I wish you'd let me be your stand-in, at least for tonight."

"No way! If I did that I'm sure Rafael henceforth and forever more would prefer you to me. I've heard tales of your technique."

"You flatter me."

"I just wanted to tell you to stay close by the phone tonight. I don't like to be interrupted. But on this night of nights, I'm open to calls. You never know who is likely to ring me up later. Jerry. Again. Anishi. I noticed she hasn't returned my call yet."

"She left the house in Key West real sudden like. No one knows where she went. She did claim that she thinks you're infiltrating spies into Mia's house and plans to fire some of the new servants recently hired. She doesn't trust them."

"As if she's trustworthy." I adjusted my hairdo just slightly. "Vince Foster. He might call. Dr. Euler. Maybe even Bill Clinton himself."

"I've tried to reach Dr. Euler but he left the place in the Azores. Said he was going for a long walk. So far, he's not come back."

"I'm sure he'll come back." I paused.

"There is one call I definitely want to take. From Snake. If I'm asleep, wake me. I think he'll have something most interesting to report."

"You'd better get some sleep while waiting for all those calls."

"Yeah," I said a little crudely. "Now run along and put on that hideous nightgown you've worn since the 50s. That no self-respecting drag queen would be caught dead in."

"Oh, I do have one little tidbit of gossip for you."

"Make it snappy."

"Maxie, it seems, has become a spy for you."

"Better for me than someone else."

"He overheard Mia making arrangements today. Before the film and before marriage, she's driving up to Palm Beach for a few days to a spa. To prepare herself for all that filming and all those photographs. Without Dino. She doesn't want him to witness what she has to go through to make herself over."

"You mean, she's not entirely relying on Anishi's

injections?"

"That's right. It also means with her gone we'll have Dino to ourselves once again."

"How lucky we are."

"What about The Iguana?"

"If he calls, slam down the receiver."

"Will do. You know, I always leave you with a good finish. You got plenty of calls for dates. I'll reveal only the most interesting offers."

"Out with it."

"JFK Jr. Ready for a repeat performance."

"He's cute. But disappointing in bed. Turn him down."

"O.J. Simpson."

"I thought we'd heard the last of little dick."

"Madonna."

"Predictable after that kiss of ours."

"Michael Jackson."

I turned to glare at him. "Michael Jackson? He wants a date with me?"

"Right on."

"He's got Elizabeth Taylor and all those little boys. What could I possibly do for him?"

"Publicity."

"About the last thing I need in this world is more publicity."

"Are you excited by your upcoming date with Bill Clinton?"

"I haven't told you the real reason I'm meeting with the president."

"I assume it's to fuck him."

"That's what you think. My real reason is to get him to drop charges against Rafael. That air-piracy crap. Rafael is a freedom-fighter, not an air pirate."

"You wouldn't use your historic meeting with the president to ask such a personal favor."

"I'll also let him know that if he grants my little request, I'll become the biggest contributor to his next presidential campaign. That will catch his interest."

"Okay, assuming you get all that business out of the way, and Billie boy still wants sex."

"Trust me. I've handled *bigger* men than Bill Clinton. Good night."

. . .

When I pulled off my robe and crawled into bed with a nude Rafael, the reception wasn't what I expected.

"Why do you neglect me so much?" He turned over, with his back to me.

"Darling, in my heart I think of you all the time. You're always with me."

"I can't even get a good blow-job when I want one. Much less anything else."

"You know how demanding it's been lately on me. It's hard having a love affair when you're dealing with nothing but crisis management."

"You and I are going to have a crisis unless you start showing me some respect. I'm not just a top-man to have around when you want me to throw you a good fuck. As a future president, I should be consulted on things. Right this very minute I think there are eighteen conspiracies going on and I'm not in on any of them."

"Let's have some pillow talk," I said, as I ran my fingers up and down his manly, rock-hard chest with the washboard stomach. "I'll tell you everything that's going on. We'll decide how to handle everything together."

"That's more like it."

Even as I said that, I knew I never would come clean with him about everything. A suspicion had been planted in my brain, and it grew hourly. Suppose there was some Cuban-linked conspiracy? Maybe it was determined in Havana that Rafael was to hijack the plane and fly to Miami and so-called freedom. That hijacking could have been staged just for my benefit. Perhaps he was here this very minute using the pillow-talk ploy to get vital information from me.

I sucked in the flower-scented air of the bedroom. Mia always kept too many flowers around. It was like a funeral parlor in here. I decided to pretend to keep him informed about what was going on. I couldn't tell him everything – like I was arranging a private meeting with Bill Clinton. Even in Havana, the president's reputation had preceded him. Rafael would never agree for me to meet alone with the president. He'd insist on coming along, if only to discuss future American-Cuban relations.

My plan with him was to indulge in a limited hang-out. To make him feel privileged with information but to hold back the really good stuff.

Before anything got revealed, the red light flashed on the hot line.

"Excuse me, angel," I said, slipping from the bed and heading to a soundproof phone booth in the room. Mia once used this room and had had the booth installed so she could conduct her private business here without her lover of the moment being privy to what deal she was discussing.

Even though I risked infuriating him, I took the call in the booth. It was from David.

Without any preliminary fatherly greeting, he announced abruptly, "Dr. Euler is gone. Apparently, he's no longer in the Azores."

"But how? Why?"

"It's all very mysterious."

"He must be on that island somewhere. You just can't get a plane out of there on a moment's notice."

"I think he was abducted."

"Tell me more."

"There was a Cuban military air cargo plane there. I think word reached Havana that you'd stashed Dr. Euler in the Azores. After all, I'm sure your plane was being watched. When Dr. Euler didn't disembark in Miami, it was pretty obvious you'd stashed him somewhere. Out in the middle of the ocean, the Azores were the only place. You could hardly drop him out of the plane onto a submarine."

"How convenient that Cuba had a military plane there."

"That had been arranged months ago with the Portuguese government and Havana. It was all perfectly legal. It was just a lucky coincidence for them."

"Has the plane left?"

"It's flying to Havana right now."

"You've got connections in the Azores. Why didn't they search the plane?"

"A military vessel? Don't be crazy. That would have provoked an international incident between Portugal and Cuba."

"So, there's nothing we can do?"

"With Dr. Euler out of the way, stashed away in Havana, no doubt in a prison, you can at least proceed with your meeting with the president without any fear from this good doctor."

"I guess. But somehow I'm not all that confident. I'd rather Dr. Euler be under my roof than under Castro's."

"There isn't a hell of a lot we can do about that now." He paused awkwardly, not willing to ring off suddenly as we usually do.

"What is it, father?"

"It's this father thing. That and being your attorney. I don't know if we should have attorney-client talks at this hour. Or father-daughter talks."

"Maybe we'll have both. Right now it seems we've got a lot of business going on."

"That's ever so true. But I want you to know I'm here when you need me. I mean, as a father - not just your attorney."

"Knowing that helps me sleep a little easier at night."

"I love you, baby. I want you to take special care. Thank Ted for me for the almost hourly bulletins I'm getting. You must keep me informed at all times of your whereabouts. And what's up. I demand that. You have this tendency to get carried away with your schemes. You could get into a lot of trouble. Be extremely careful. Don't put yourself at risk and check with me before doing anything crazy. You're my daughter and I've got to protect you."

"I'll keep you posted as to my every move."

"Bullshit! You know you won't. But I love you any way. Except I love you alive. Not dead."

"No harm will come to me, I can assure you."

"Yeah, right. As if you had the power to grant that assurance."

"I'll cover my ass. I promise you. One more thing, is Cruz deadly serious with that lawsuit?"

"Serious. Determined. Fierce. His attorneys are unbending. Now that it's over, Cruz really knows how close he came to ending up at Forest Lawn. He's out not only for money, but for vengeance. The whole shit will come out in time. Maxie's involvement. Everything. It'll be a field day for the tabloids."

"Can't we do something to prevent it?"

"At this point, there's nothing I can do, but defend you and your interests."

"There must be something we can do other than settle out of court. Something."

"There you go, plotting one of your schemes again."

"I have no scheme," I said, lying to him. At this very moment I suspected that Jerry was recording his private talk with Cruz. "Good night, father. You have a daughter's love and devotion."

"Good night, angel. I hope Rafael is good to you."

"He is. But we're having some period of adjustment problems."

"Predictable."

As I emerged from the soundproof booth, I detected familiar noises coming from the bed. Rafael was obviously in the throes of an orgasm. I assumed he got tired of waiting for me to do my duty and was masturbating. Then I detected a head bobbing up and down on that massive cock. It couldn't be Ted. As much as he wanted to, Ted wouldn't betray me like this.

I flipped on the soft pink-shaded lamp by the bed. It was then I detected the handsome waiter Dino had tricked with. He looked as if he were gulping down the final cup from Rafael and was having a hard time swallowing it all. I should know.

After he'd finished his job, he raised his head, semen still emerging from the corner of his pouty lips.

"Miss Kelly," he said, startled and not quite knowing what to do. "I didn't even know you were in the room."

"It's okay," I assured him.

Rafael lay back on his pillow, beaming. This blow-job was staged not only for his relief but as an assertion of defiance of me. He knew that, and he knew I knew that.

Quickly I went to my dresser and removed five one-hundred bills and handed them to the waiter as he buttoned up his shirt. Although Rafael was nude, the waiter was fully dressed. I placed the money in his hand and quickly ushered him to the door.

"Miss Kelly, Rafael is even better and bigger than Dino."

"I know that, cuntie." I gently pushed him out of the room and shut the door behind him.

When I turned to confront Rafael, he was asleep on the

pillow.

I turned off the light and slipped in opposite him. Sherry Kelly did not melt down at discovering a lover getting a blow-job. When did I ever have a lover who didn't get blowjobs on the side? They all do it. Since I was plotting a little indiscretion or two myself, I couldn't blame him for this one incident. After all, it wasn't as if I'd caught him in bed with Mia. Now, that would have been a serious confrontation. I decided to forget the whole thing and go to sleep.

But after an hour sleep wouldn't come. When the red light on the hot line flashed again, I was ready to take the call. Slipping from the bed and a slightly snoring and sexually satisfied Rafael, I headed for the soundproof phone booth again.

. . .

It was Vince apologizing for calling me at such a late hour. "Typically it's been a very long loosey-goosey day at the campus."

"Did you speak at a college?" I asked in a slightly bleary voice.

"No, that's what we call the White House complex."

"That's news to me."

"Rock and roll here has replaced the middle-aged GOP formality of George and Barbara."

"I hear that when men wear ties up there now, they're funky. Women are no longer required to wear dresses. A few men wear cowboy boots, or so I was told."

"That's absolutely right. Bush wouldn't even allow beards. Now we'd even allow a bearded lady."

"I approve of all these changes. I like informality myself."

"I'm not so sure. My God, I'm still a young man and some of the staff in their 20s make arthritis jokes about me. Rock groups like U2 and the Cocteau Twins can be heard on boom boxes as these kids walk by Secret Service agents. These stiffs must long for the return of J. Edgar."

"It sounds like a fun place to be."

"It isn't. I'm not used to living in this gold-fish bowl. We've got a lot of problems here. A lot of secrets we don't want leaked."

"I'm sure that was always true."

"Maybe, but all this inexperience can lead to big mistakes. The Bay of Pigs and Jimmy Carter's downfall resulted in part from an inexperienced staff. It could happen to us."

"Let's hope it won't."

"Which brings up the subject of tonight's call. I've met with Bill again. He definitely wants that date. I won't bore you with the details which I've worked out with Ted. But the date is definitely on right after he finishes his speech in Miami Beach." He paused for a long moment. "That is, if you're still up for it."

"I'm still game." Silently I thought that my meeting with the president would be pay-back time for Rafael's exhibition with that waiter.

"I'll be really frank with you. I told Bill not to do this. It's too risky. I told him he should send me to do the job instead."

"That would be nice too but what did the president say?"

"He said you were no Gennifer Flowers. You wouldn't be calling any press conferences. If there's one thing you don't need, it's more publicity, especially after the Cruz shooting. I guess what he was saying is that you are the only woman in America he's attracted to who can be discreet. A person he can trust."

"I certainly won't be calling any press conferences and I won't be granting any *Penthouse* interviews. I've got too much to hide. I don't believe in the public's right to know."

"The public knows too much already. Especially about Bill."

"I think some things should be kept private. Call me old-fashioned."

"I like that about you. You don't seem to be one of these in-your-face feminists."

"I don't need a movement to liberate me. Trust me, I was liberated a long time ago."

"I bet you were." He paused again, a long, awkward moment. "I hope you don't think that Bill, now that he's in the White House, does this kind of thing all the time."

"I hadn't thought about it."

"He's promised Hillary that if she would stand by him, the past would be the past. Never to be repeated."

"Breaking his promise so soon?"

"Let me put it this way. He intends to keep his promise. But only after his meeting with you."

"I'm going to be his last fling, so to speak."

"That's exactly how he sees it. One last fling. A final night cap before giving up drink forever."

"I'm honored that the leader of the free world chose me. Really flattered."

"He's flattered that you would even consider a date with an old man like him after all the handsome studs you've bedded. Of course, I don't know that you actually slept with the long roster the tabloids claim."

"Oh, I probably undressed a few of them. But I never slept with Mel Gibson, Kevin Costner, Arnold, Stallone, or Clint Eastwood. Perhaps all the others. But definitely not the ones I named."

"I don't blame you, since I don't see what women see in that group of men either. But Cruz is really hot. Even my wife admires him."

"Contrary to the press, I've never slept with him either. In fact, the fucker is suing me for one-hundred million dollars."

"He'll never get it unless he can prove that you actually put a real bullet in that gun."

"I don't think he'll ever prove that. Because I didn't do it. Although after suing me, I might now be tempted."

"I'll lend you my gun."

"You keep a gun?"

"All Arkansas boys have guns. You never know when we might need one."

"In your case, I hope you never will."

"Thanks. I won't keep you any more. I know you have more important things to do. But I want to ask one last favor."

"From the president?"

"From me. When this thing blows over, and we have a quiet moment up here, I'd like to fly somewhere and meet with you. There are many interesting things I can tell you. But mainly I want to talk about my getting out of the campus. It's not my thing. I thought it would be. But I'm bitterly disappointed here. It's driving me crazy. I really have to go even though I don't want to let Bill down."

"I'd meet with you. You name the time and place."

"I appreciate that." He paused again. "You know, you don't have to go through with tomorrow tonight."

"I know that."

"Just because Bill is attracted to you doesn't mean you'd be attracted to him."

"Right you are. Actually, my meeting with the president has more to do with Mia Kelly than anything else."

"I don't get it."

"I'm tired of hearing how many presidents she's bagged. From JFK on down the line."

"Surely, not Nixon?"

"Surely not. Nor Carter either."

"Let me imagine the rest."

"Until we meet in the flesh," I said. "Hang in there. I'm here for you when you need me."

"Knowing that makes it easier. I've got to get a grip on myself. I feel I'm coming apart at times."

"I feel that way every morning, especially lately. Maybe we'll be a support group for each other."

"I like you a lot, and I haven't even met you."

"Don't worry. I think relationships in the future will all be conducted over the wire."

"You've been great the way you've handled this special request."

"When my country needs me, I'm here. Good night." I gently hung up the phone.

. . .

After the call I returned to bed with my still-sleeping Rafael, and it was then I decided that if he became president of Cuba, the United States could invade his country and he'd sleep through the entire war. I've had many nights when I knew sleep wouldn't come and I'd survived them all. I'm a real nocturnal pussy. That's why I've had so much fun. You can do more at night than during the day.

Since I knew that sleep wouldn't come, I got out of bed again and headed for my dressing room. Might as well make myself up for the day. On those occasions when I didn't get any sleep, I always applied a little more warpaint.

Once ensconced in the satiny gloss of my dressing room, I noticed the red light on the phone flashing again. AT&T was certainly making money off moi tonight.

It was Jerry and it was urgent he meet with me, regardless of the time. He'd just returned from the bar where he'd secretly taped Cruz. He couldn't wait to play the tape for me. Since one-hundred million dollars - no small change - might be at stake here, I asked him to taxi over to Star Island at once. With the tape, of course.

Another call had come in from the Azores. Not about Dr. Euler. It was assumed he was gone forever. It was about my art. It had been safely secured in a bank vault. Since the art was already stolen, I didn't want it stolen again, certainly not from me. Considering the pressure which the Swiss government had begun to apply on the art work's recovery, I was very happy to have retrieved all of it. Actually, I didn't plan to return to Switzerland again. There was always Zurs in Austria, as I've often noted. I have always felt that on some deep level, the Austrians always appreciated and valued my patronage more than the Swiss.

Ted, the man who could usually get any person - living or dead - on the phone, finally failed me. He couldn't reach Anishi in Key West. She'd just disappeared after making the call about the ransom note, and no one at Mia's household down there knew where she was.

In my brightly lit mirror, I rechecked my makeup. Even though Jerry was a faggot, I wanted to look my most devastating best for him. He was, after all, a movie producer and director who'd asked me to play a sultry if aging beauty in his film. Of course, I was providing most of the financing, but that was another matter entirely. When in life didn't I provide most of the money?

The Jerry that Ted ushered in was one I didn't recognize. He still wore his trademark black turtleneck sweater and black slacks with white sneakers and red socks, but something was different about his face. I decided at once that this was no night to call him "cuntie" and engage in gay banter. Ted wanted to stick around, but Jerry signaled me he wanted to talk privately. When Ted had gone, Jerry turned to me, his face ashen. "I've got to tell you something. I've just lived the 'Oh shit!' day of my life."

"More trouble about 'Butterflies'? Mia is bowing out?"

"Fuck the movie!" he said, raising his voice in fury. The fury wasn't directed at me, more at the world. "I may have made my last god damn film. When I got back from the bar after taping Cruz, a message was waiting for me from my doctor. I'm HIV positive. Other than my doctor, you're the first person I've told this to." He looked deeply into my eyes as if there were something that I, with all my money and power, could do to save him.

Faced with the revelation of AIDS, I realized the limits of power and money. I said nothing. I knew I had to formulate some words of grief and sorrow, which I truly felt, but nothing came out of my mouth. Shocked and stunned, I just stood there.

Over the past few years, I'd lost many friends, mainly acquaintances, through death by AIDS. I always heard about it after they'd contacted AIDS, after everybody else in town knew, or in many a tragic case, after they'd died. Never in my life had I come face-to-face with someone confessing for the first time that he was HIV positive.

"Jerry," I said, in my most soothing and reassuring voice, "I am so deeply sorry. So very sorry." Trying to recreate what Princess Di would do in a situation like this, I reached for his hand. It was important for him to know that I wasn't afraid to touch him, that I wasn't going to treat him like a leper. "There are things that can be done. Treatments. They may not work, but let's give everything a try."

"You'll save me?" He held onto my hand too aggressively, almost crushing my palm. It was as if he didn't know his own strength. He was like a man holding onto the one hand that would save him as he dangled precariously over a 10,000-foot drop, like me on that mountain in Switzerland the day I lost the Capetown Diamond. My face indicated he was causing me pain, and as he realized how strong his grip was, he released my hand.

"I'm sorry. I feel so desperate. You are the only person in the world I could turn to right now. I know if there were any treatment on earth, legal or illegal, that would save me, Sherry Kelly will get it for me. You will, won't you?"

"I'll do anything, I promise. It's the least I can do. You're too young and too wicked to die. We'll save you yet, fucker."

The relief and joy that swept over his face convinced me that he believed me. Only I seemed to know I was lying. Right at this moment, my intuition told me that he would be dead in two, maybe three years. But he couldn't face that, at least not now, and I didn't want him to. Of course, I planned to carry through on my promise. I would secure for him any "cure" for AIDS that was being peddled in the world, even though I knew at this point all cures were fake.

Whatever I did for him would give him hope, and I wanted to instill hope in him right now. I didn't want him to sink into a deep and morbid depression over his upcoming death. To accomplish that, I wanted him to feel that we could continue to do business as usual. We wouldn't talk about AIDS, at least not until tomorrow. As I kept reminding myself, Scarlett was right. We'd deal with that problem when tomorrow became another day.

"I want you to continue with your work and your life," I said. "Continue, with my help, to make films."

"That's what I really want to do. What's the alternative? Sit around and think about dying? To think of all my old buddies like Rock who died of AIDS?"

"You and he were an item once, right?"

"Very briefly. Both of us foolishly subscribed to the theory of 'so little time, so many men.' It all seems so stupid now."

"Now, perhaps, but not back then. Things are different now." Like a bolt, a sudden fear came over me. "Forgive me, I don't mean to pry into your sex life. But I must ask you a question. It's about Dino."

He gently touched my arm and looked reassuringly into my eyes. "There was no exchange of body fluids, if that's what you're asking. A lot of fondling and masturbating if you must know. He even posed for pictures. From the waist down only. That boy is no fool. He wanted to entice me but didn't know where my ass had been the night before. Don't worry about Dino. He knows how to protect himself."

"That's a relief. My fear was that he might get AIDS and pass it on to Mia. I think in the case of those two there has been some exchange of body fluids."

"I know there has been. But then, she has more money than I do."

"At least he convinced you to offer him the role of Numie in 'Butterflies', opposite Mommie playing my part."

"He talked me into it for forty-eight hours. I have these momentary infatuations. Just ask any actor in Hollywood. Then my real business brain takes over from my prick. You see deep down behind this blond white WASPy facade, I'm very businesslike - stone-cold sober about money and the bottom line. Actually, my parents were successful Jewish merchants - that's where I learned about money."

"I didn't know you were Jewish."

"I'll pull out my cock and show you it's cut if you want me to prove it."

"Cut the crap. Most WASP boys are cut, at least in America."

"A bad idea. A mutilation perpetrated by their mothers as an act of vengeance on the male organ. Violence against males after women have endured the pain of childbirth."

"So you're Jewish? I never think of such things. Jew, Christian, all these tribal religions bore the hell out of me."

"Anyway, the bottom-line Jew in me woke up yesterday morning and decided that the idea of casting Mia and Dino in 'Butterflies' was one of my dumbest. Who knows if Mia can act?"

"Have you told them they're out of the picture?"

"Not yet, and I fear I don't have the balls. Do you want to see them just to show you they're not big enough for the job?"

"Keep them in your pants. I've got balls big enough for the two of us."

"I want you to tell them before announcing the real stars."

"Who might they be?"

"Sherry Kelly and Sean Nielson. 'Butterflies' will gross three hundred million around the world. It'll be bigger than 'Kinky'."

"Don't talk to me like I'm Joan Collins. My lust for stardom is waning even as we speak. I don't think I found life in the films as exciting as I wanted it to be. Right now, I'm sorry I made even one damn picture. I don't want to make another."

"I can't believe you're saying that!"

"Thanks for your confidence in Sean and me. But you'd

better go back to Mia and Dino in the cast. After all, she'll provide the rest of the financing and I won't have to."

"Are you sure? Do you absolutely mean that?"

"I'm sure. Let Mia and Dino have it."

"Okay, but I'll agree to that only if you won't change your mind."

"I'm the Rock of Gibraltar on the subject."

"I'm real disappointed."

"Let's forget it for the moment. We've got a lot of other business to concentrate on. Your health at the top of my agenda. But, first, let's hear this tape. Is it any good?"

"It's hot - and not at all what I expected it to be."

I settled back on my chaise longue after giving him a glass of freshly squeezed Florida orange juice.

He put on the tape for me.

. . .

He fast forwarded the tape, as he knew I wasn't interested in all the gay chit-chat. The sound for me came on when he reached the good part.

BRAD: My first night in the hospital I woke up with this odd sensation. I wasn't aware of what was happening at first. Then I knew. One of the male nurses was going down on me. He was pretty good at it too.

JERRY: Until I saw you here at the bar, I wasn't sure you were one of the fraternity. I'd heard the usual rumors.

BRAD: The only fraternity I'm a member of is the Brad Cruz fraternity. I like variety in my sex life. Who doesn't? Pussy one night. A little boy-ass the next night. A blow-job in the afternoon. With blow-jobs, it really doesn't matter who is doing the servicing. Man or woman. A mouth is a mouth. I've found men are often better at this than women.

JERRY: I wouldn't know, having never tried a woman. That's one dubious pleasure I can truthfully say I've never had.

BRAD: You haven't missed all that much. Sex is sex. More and more I've come to think it doesn't matter the source of the sex, only that you get it and get it a lot. I'm oversexed myself. Can't get enough. I've got a virtual erection all the time and I fear it's going to get me in big trouble one day. It seems that half of America - male and female - is throwing themselves at the feet of Brad Cruz wanting to get fucked.

JERRY: You are one lucky man. I've had my share of the good times since I'm a movie producer. But nothing like what you must get.

BRAD: Nobody gets as much as I get. I really believe with the right seduction technique I can have anybody I want in America. Even straight guys. I've propositioned guys with the straightest credentials. They never said no to Brad Cruz. Naturally, as I was plugging them, they loudly asserted they wouldn't let their ass get invaded by anyone but me. I always view that as a joke. They probably got so turned on by the experience you'd find them tomorrow night in a gay bar searching for someone to plug them.

JERRY: I'm sure you're right. You're one good-looking mother-fucker.

BRAD: Read that line good-looking mother-fucker with a big dick. Which brings up the subject of tonight's discussion.

JERRY: Count me out. I'm not that big.

BRAD: Forget it! I'd let you play with it and feel me up if you want to slide over here. But that's as far as I'd go with you. You're just not my type. But I'll tell you who is my type.

JERRY: Name names.

BRAD: Dino Paglia.

JERRY He's everybody's type. For him, even Bill Clinton would turn gay. I know Jesse Helms would.

BRAD: I think you're right. He's the sexiest guy I've ever seen.

JERRY: I'm surprised. Sherry told me she introduced the two of you. She claimed you didn't seem to strike it off. No significant bonding.

BRAD: That shows what a good actor I am. I was deliberately cool. I didn't want to give myself away. The truth of the matter is I was salivating. Let me ask you something. Is what I saw in his tight pants for real? Or was he padded?

JERRY: Trust me. I've played with it.

BRAD: I figured you had.

JERRY: It's for real. It's not a dick. It's a fucking log.

BRAD: I want him. I want you to arrange it. I don't expect favors for nothing. I might even agree to appear in one of your films. Not "Butterflies." I think that's nothing but bad luck for me. But a film some time in the future. Right now I'm committed to an action film. With....and you're gonna shit. Sean Nielson. Sherry Kelly's secret passion.

JERRY: That does surprise me. With you out of 'Butterflies', Sean was talked about as your replacement.

BRAD: I know. But Sean has gotten derailed in the meantime, among other things.

JERRY: Dino himself wants to do the movie.

BRAD: That's okay with me. But only after I audition him. To make sure he's big enough for the part. I'm sure he'll fill out that bikini better than I ever would, and nobody ever called Brad Cruz Princess Tiny Meat. There are too many sore asses walking around Hollywood who know better.

JERRY: I think a rendezvous with Dino is only a phone call away. I'm sure he would jump at the chance to bed down with Brad Cruz. He is, after all, the star fucker supreme. You know he may get married.

BRAD: I've heard rumors. To Mia Kelly. She must be out of her mind. Read that her super-rich, super-cunt mind. You don't marry the Dino Paglias of the world. You fuck them. You leave them with a memory. Or, as I suspect in the case with Dino baby, he leaves you with the memory.

JERRY: You can say that again. Write down the number at your suite. I'll get back to you within hours with the time and place of your date with Dino. This is a sure thing for me to arrange at my private sex pad on the beach. I just know he'll say yes.

BRAD: What else?

JERRY: Just one more thing before I bid *adieu*.

BRAD: What's up?

JERRY: Just why are you suing Sherry? I thought her offer of an out-of-court settlement seemed pretty generous. Especially since it wasn't really her fault.

BRAD: Bullshit! I'm not sure it wasn't her fault. I mean somehow I think it was her fault, if only indirectly. I woke up my first morning in that hospital and I suddenly realized that the world's greatest male star might be in some funeral parlor right this minute getting penetrated by every rich necro in America. Just imagine what a funeral parlor could have made off me with all the necros. You know they do things like that, don't you?

JERRY: I've heard stories. Judy Garland and everything.

BRAD: Exactly. It could have happened to me. I'm leading a glorious life. At the top of the heap. The world's sexiest man. Forget this JFK, Jr. The most sought after animal on the planet. One bullet from her gun could have snuffed out our brightest star.

JERRY: She was innocent.

BRAD: I don't believe that for a moment. Ms. Sherry, even if she didn't put that real bullet in the gun herself, knows who did it. I want vengeance. Let's face it: I'm the ultimate narcissist. Do you know the worse thing you can do to a narcissist? Try to kill him.

JERRY: The lawsuit would be very messy indeed. A lot of things come out in a lawsuit. Things you might not want revealed.

BRAD: Things Sherry Kelly might not want revealed, you mean.

JERRY: That too. But it could backfire on you. I've got to warn you. That rich pussy plays rough. She's not going to lie back and take this gracefully. She determines who is going to fuck her and when. You're playing with one formidable cunt here. She and her mama control the world's money supply. You may be a rich man yourself, but your total wealth wouldn't buy one of their mansions.

BRAD: I'm not afraid of super-cunt and her money. The whole world will know that Brad Cruz fights for his rights. I read somewhere that Doris Duke killed her lover or her interior decorator if you believe some stories. She got away with murder. Settled for $25,000 or less. Shit like that. I'm not going to be bought off for even twenty-five million. You've got to understand my motive here. I grew up poor. Real poor. I want money, and I see this gun shot as the best thing that ever happened to me. Now that I've survived the wound. It's my chance to really accumulate some big bucks without having to make a film. Besides, the bitch won't go to court. She's got too much to lose. My attorneys fully expect a massive out-of-court settlement, far greater than anything she's offered to date.

JERRY: It won't work. Even though she and I are no longer speaking, I know her. She won't let you get away with it. If she thinks someone is after her, she'll stop at nothing to prevent them from getting to her snatch. You've got to believe me on this one.

BRAD: Fuck that! I know what I'm doing. Now if you want me to do you one big favor one day, now if you want to ingratiate yourself with Hollywood's biggest star, you set up that date with Dino. I'm starting to get hard already.

JERRY: Let me cop one feel.

BRAD: Feel free. You'd hardly be the first.

JERRY: My, oh my. You are impressive.

BRAD: I told you. But not as impressive as Dino, right.

JERRY: Even God isn't that impressive.

BRAD: You've got me salivating, Jerry boy. Do your duty. Set it up.

JERRY: Your wish is my command.

BRAD: Get back to me real soon. I'm a star who doesn't wait. No one in Hollywood puts Brad Cruz on hold.

JERRY: I'm off to do my duty. And thanks for letting me feel you up. It's a memory I'll carry to my grave. My early grave.

BRAD: Not early grave. You mean-assed mother-fuckers live forever. Just like me. I'm eternal. I even survived Sherry's attempt to assassinate me.

JERRY: But can you survive her vengeance at what you're doing to her?

BRAD: I can survive anything that rich bitch throws at me.

JERRY: Good night, my darling. And enjoy Dino. You've got good taste. Even Sherry went for him, and she goes for only the very best.

BRAD: In this case I would agree with you. Even though I'm a bigger star than she will ever be, I'd go for her sloppy seconds any day.

He turned off the tape. Saying nothing for a long moment, we sat looking at each other. A scheme was forming in my overtaxed brain.

. . .

"Jerry," I said, taking his hand, "I'm getting an idea. I need your cooperation to pull it off. Naturally, there will be a pot of gold in it for you as a reward for your help."

"I'm all ears."

I led him to the terrace where I hoped to think more clearly in the cool breezes of early morning. Too much had been going on around this household. I felt I was coming unglued.

"You're up to something. You're plotting. That tape inspired you. I can tell."

"That's true. Right now your health concerns must be the all-important issue between us. But I want you to keep working. I want you to direct a projected TV series about some Cuban high schoolers in Miami."

"But 'Butterflies'. I want to shoot that first."

"It will take awhile to get the series launched. You'll have time to shoot 'Butterflies' before the TV series. I think this series will make millions. You'll be rich, though not as rich as me. But then, who in the whole fucking world is as rich as me?"

"I may be rich but will I be around long enough to enjoy it?"

"That is the question, my dear boy."

"I've heard about the series. The buzz is out. Some think it'll be hot. Others claim it'll bomb. Same old story. Nobody knows. I know one thing. The series needs a sugar daddy right now."

"Look at sugar mama. I want Dino to star in it. The series will make him America's leading male sex symbol. It already has a leading female sex symbol as personified by moi."

"That could be done, even with Dino. He's got the sex all right. All I'll have to do is create the symbol."

"You can do it. I can count on you."

"Why Dino? I know you dropped him. That Rafael must be even better hung, if that's possible."

"It's possible. I'm going to ask Dino to do something for me tonight. If he cooperates, and I fully expect he will, I'll owe him a favor. The lead in the series will be his generous reward. Don't worry about his becoming a sex symbol. You won't have to work too hard. Before the first episode is shot, Dino will not only be a sex symbol, but a household word in America."

"How do you plan to accomplish that?"

"With your help, and I'll owe you a big favor too. I'll get your treatments. Any treatment. We'll find a cure. In the meanwhile, we'll have you directing a hit TV series. Of course, I'll have to call David right away and tell him my plan. I think the producers already have a director signed for the project, but you know in this business, last-minute changes are inevitable."

"Then it's not a done deal?"

"Trust me, it's a done deal. It's just that the producers don't know about it yet. Tomorrow morning will be plenty of time to break the news to them."

"What's this favor you want?"

"Before the evening is over, we're going to make a porno film."

"You know I'm not in that business any more, although I'm damn good at it. I called my super-lavish, rock-hard production company Chi-Chi Presents. I just do porno flicks these days for fun."

"Do you still have access to that penthouse suite on South Beach?"

"Do I ever! My good buddy owns it. I mentioned it to Cruz already."

"Rent it for me for a day. Fifty-thousand dollars."

"Do you mean that?"

"Do I talk money when I don't mean it? Rent it! Is it still set up for filming?"

"State of the art. We've even got sound. Whatever sound track we've recorded in that penthouse has always been perfect. I like sound with my porno."

"So do I. Sound is very important, especially in this film I want shot."

"We've enticed some of the biggest stars who come to South Florida up to that penthouse. Don Johnson. Uncut and parlor size. Burt Reynolds. I should have put a magnifying lens in the camera. Those boys, and many others, thought they were alone in the boudoir with the hottest piece of female ass on South Beach. We arranged a hot harlot for them. What they didn't know was that their action was being taped. Someday, I'm going to sell those tapes. Release them around the world. Jerry Wheeler's biggest hits. Reputations will be made or lost in Hollywood."

"Cool that idea for the moment."

"Who's going to star in the latest episode?" He looked at me and smiled. "As if I didn't know."

"The two parties haven't been informed yet. Before the night is over, we've got to arrange it."

"You should have set this up earlier."

"Sometimes, sexual liaisons are best arranged on the spur of the moment. This porno movie has got to have great clarity. I want it shot and developed all within twelve hours."

"Why the rush? The parties can't be that hot."

"I just might distribute the film to every major TV news network in the world. They'll forget all about that Rob Lowe tape when they see this one. Now here's my plan."

. . .

Long after Jerry departed on the mission I'd asked him to accomplish, I sat thinking about my latest scheme. I was also perplexed that Ted had been unable to reach Anishi, and Snake had seemingly disappeared in the sky with the helicopter.

I could see the lights in Mia's suite. Apparently, she had risen early after her drunken debauchery and was now getting her wardrobe assembled to be driven to a spa. I'd heard she was going to Palm Beach, leaving Dino in our trusty hands which is just what I wanted at the moment. I didn't want her finding out about my latest scheme and putting a stop to it. After all, she now regarded him as her personal property.

Impulsively I put through a call to David. It would be a limited hangout conversation. Even he must not know of the porno flick I was about to shoot. Later. There would be plenty of time to tell him later.

His sleepy voice came onto the phone. "It's a bit early. But I'm used to phone calls from you at all hours. What's it now?"

"David," I said into the receiver. "I prefer to keep calling you that instead of father - or 'daddy,' don't you agree?"

"I prefer David. After all, when we were dating, some kind people thought we might be the same age. I wouldn't want to spoil the illusion."

"Don't be a bitch, darling. No one seriously thinks you and I are the same age."

"You want something? Another favor? What do I have to do now? Kidnap Bill Clinton? Or, are you already planning to do that yourself?"

"I've got more important things on the brain. I called you to talk about that projected television series you sent over to me yesterday. As a possible investor."

"You mean that thing about the Cuban high schoolers in Miami? I'm surprised. You usually never respond to such offers even though you could have made millions with some of the projects I sent over. Why this one? And why do you want to wake me up to tell me about it at this hour?"

"I'm hot for it. As you know, the whole damn country is going Hispanic. It might attract a big, big, audience."

"What's your motive behind this? You want Rafael to play the Cuban English teacher? A sort of '90s version of that Glenn Ford movie, 'Blackboard Jungle'?"

"No, I want to back the series, and I want Dino in the lead."

"An Italian like Dino playing a Cuban? The little hustler wouldn't do it. It'd be too revealing about his real identity."

"Make the fucker the star and make the paycheck right, and even Dino will go Hispanic, I assure you."

"You must owe him a big favor. Surely the kid wasn't that good. Besides, with his upcoming marriage to Mia, he will hardly be hurting for money."

"He wasn't that good. I don't owe him any favors at the moment. But I will owe him a favor. For an act he's yet to perform. Emphasis on perform."

"Daughter of mine, you're plotting again. Plots of yours always cost money and get you and me in plenty of trouble. Trouble I might have to get you out of. You've got to tell me everything. Spill the beans to papa. What are you plotting?"

"I can't tell you yet. If I did, you wouldn't let me go through with it. You're too cautious. I have to pull off my own little stunts, play my own games. Then call you and have you bail me out. That's how you and I do business."

"Sounds like another risk."

"All you have to do right now is give me your assurance that if I back that god damn Spik series, Dino will get the lead."

"You have my assurance. First thing in the morning when I get to the office, I'll make arrangements with the producers. They're desperate for cash right now, and they'll agree to anything at this point. With your financial backing, you won't even have to flash for them."

"Now you sound like Mia."

"Why not? I'm your father, and I don't like my daughter flashing it on the screen."

"I'll remember that the next time any producer tells me to drop drawers. Good night." I put down the receiver.

. . .

It was "Moon over Miami" when I heard the latest subject being summoned into my hastily erected court. But this time, the film didn't star Betty Grable. The new movie paired an even more funtime couple, Sherry Kelly and Dino Paglia in that order of billing.

Standing in the doorway in too-tight white trousers, he arrived with his flower-speckled shirt unbuttoned to reveal a perfect chest, tanned and with nipples waiting to be devoured by the hungry, starving mouths of the world. He was, after all, the most seductive boy on earth, and seemed well aware of that undisputed fact.

"Mama," he said upon seeing me, "you finally got tired of my old man and wanted a young, hot whopper for a change."

"Not exactly. But you have such a way with words."

"All my young years have taught me that when Dino Paglia is summoned at this hour of the morning, it has something to do with sex."

"It does. Maybe not exactly in the way you think."

"Since Mia was drunk last night, and is up at the moment packing, I was using the opportunity to plow that waiter. He told me that he was summoned to your boudoir last night to take care of Rafael. I gather you and papa are no longer an item."

"We're still in there."

"But obviously you've agreed to see tricks on the side. And so early in the relationship."

"Don't you worry about that. That's not why I called you here."

"Fine with me. Actually I wanted to see you anyway. With Mia leaving for Palm Beach - without me - I feared I'd be lonely. That's why I invited a special guest to spend time with me. I hope you don't mind. You'll like him."

"Him?"

"Yes, him. I can't spend the rest of my life fucking old bags. I need some young stuff too - just like you."

"I guess I'm included in your conquests of old - might we add rich? - bags?"

He moved closer to me and reached out to caress my not-altogether-fallen breasts. I took his hand and moved it down to his side, although he attempted to direct it to his crotch.

"You're not an old bag, mama. You're the hottest woman on earth. We belong together. Just you and me. You should never have rejected me the way you did. But I'm glad you've changed your mind."

"I haven't changed my mind. Things are still the same between us. I'm not getting back together again. That's that. I'm in love with Rafael."

He glanced at me, barely concealing his disgust. "With an old man? My old man? Don't you get it? The sun won't have to come up many more times before Rafael will be forty."

"I think I've been reminded of that before."

"Too old to get it up for you. You'll be at your ripest, your most demanding. He'll be wanting to watch the ball games and have a *cerveza*. With me, you'll get twenty more years of hot erect cock than you would with Rafael. When you're sixty, I'll still be going strong and can give it to you every night."

"How many times have you said this? And to how many women or whatever?"

"I have love only for you. I want to give myself completely to you."

"Thanks for your very tempting invitation, but I have a completely different offer in mind tonight. First, I want you to make your own money, and I'll help you do it. Lots of money. Second, I don't want you to get it up for me, but for someone else."

"Who, for Christ's sake?"

"Brad Cruz."

"It would be no trouble at all for me to get it up for him. He's the second best-looking man in America - after me, of course."

"Listen to my plan. All you have to do is seduce Cruz before a hidden camera in a South Beach penthouse. Put on a good show. I want the secretly filmed tape released to the networks.

They showed that Rob Lowe tape endlessly. This one, they'll show even more."

"Hell, yes, they would. With me as the star! First, I'm better looking than Rob Lowe and a hell of a lot better hung."

"They'll screen out your most vital parts, but will reveal a lot of skin."

"I'll be sensational. The hottest stud in America. I'd make myself a household word overnight. Once the TV screens of America flashed my body around the world, my fan mail would soar into the millions. Rob Lowe, eat my dust!"

"I'm glad you see what a boost this would be for your career. There's more."

"What?"

"For your cooperation, I'll star you in a TV series. *Star*, I said. About a group of Cuban high schoolers in Miami. You'll become the biggest TV star in the world. Hollywood offers will flood in once you're a hit on TV."

"Terrific!" he shouted, his eyes lighting up. Suddenly, he paused as if he'd misheard something. "Did you say *Cuban* high schoolers? Cuban? Why Cuban, mama? I don't play Spiks!"

"All the press releases will say Dino Paglia, the Italian actor cast in a Cuban role."

"I get it. But you'd better make god damn sure of that. I'm Italian. Not Cuban. You get that? You get that straight. You'd better get that straight."

"I've got it. The filming will take place early this morning. Jerry will be directing it. It's got to take place soon."

"Fine with me. The sooner, the better. I'm ready and raring to go." He checked his hair in one of my many gilded mirrors. "Damn, I look good. Fucking gorgeous. I can seduce anybody. You ever met a better looking guy than me? Confess up!"

"In all honesty, I think I really haven't."

"So you admit I'm better looking than Rafael?"

"I'll admit it. He is a very handsome man, but your looks defy belief. No one, and I mean no one, is better looking than you."

"It could all have been yours, sweet mama of mine. I'd belong just to you. When I go out that door and do what you want, star in that fucking porno clip with the Cruz shithead, become the biggest fucking star on TV, I won't need you any more. I'll be big in my own right." He turned around and looked longingly at me. "I'm giving you one final chance to have me as your own trophy boy."

"As reluctant as I am, I must say no."

"Your loss."

"Ted will arrange matters about the Cruz thing. Cruz will know nothing, of course. By tomorrow evening you'll be the second most talked-about person on TV."

"Second most?" he asked, looking disappointed. "Who will be *numero uno?*"

"Brad Cruz. Or, as he refers to himself, the biggest star in Hollywood."

He laughed mockingly. "Right you are. This will make me a star. Cruz will become the fallen star." He paused, as if a troubling thought had crossed his mind. In all his upcoming excitement, he'd completely forgotten about his commitment of marriage to Mia.

"If you're worried about Mia, don't be," I said. "I've already cleared it with her." Sometimes it pays to lie. "Except the agreement is, you're not to mention this to her before the event. She doesn't want to be informed. That way, she'll pretend complete innocence about it with a certain validity."

"I get it. She doesn't object?"

"Of course not. You know how sophisticated she is about such things."

"I've heard plenty of stories."

"Now, there are certain things that really piss her off. Like catching you in bed with me. That she would never tolerate. But walking into her boudoir and catching you plowing a waiter would be familiar turf to her. All her boy friends have done that."

"So I've heard. I'm just one in a long line?"

"But she didn't marry the others."

"True, but I'm not happy with this one-hundred thousand dollars pre-nuptial. I want a lot more money than that."

"You'll never get it from her. I think the most any trick ever got out of her was ten-thousand dollars. With her, you might be kicked out the door tomorrow. Look at her track record. You'll be lucky to get the one-hundred thousand dollars."

"I don't like the sound of this at all."

"But that's always the deal with her. That's why I'm offering you the TV series. You'll do the movie first. Then follow with the big TV series. Even if she fucks you over, as you and I both know she will, you'll be big. You won't need her or me either."

"You're a scheming bitch. But as one hustler to another hustler, I really believe you. Don't fuck with me. This had better be legit. If I'm going to do something wild, like risk my upcoming marriage, I want to be sure I've got something waiting in the wings."

"You do. Far bigger and better than anything she would offer you. The important point, it will be Dino Paglia making the big ones. As a star. Adored by millions. Not some toy boy of an aging beauty. And certainly not for one-hundred thousand dollars."

"I think you've got yourself a star. Besides, I've always wanted to plow into Cruz. Let him know what it's like to get fucked by a real stud."

"He'll walk bow-legged in his next flick."

Before leaving, he stopped at the door and blew me a kiss as gentle as the night breeze. "You'll never believe my next line, mama. But you're the only person I've ever really loved in my whole life. The only one I felt warm and cozy with, the one woman I wanted to devote the rest of my life to loving. Now the world will own me - not you."

"Nice speech. Use it on your next sucker."

"Fuck you, mama!" he shouted at me. A jerk in his throat made him sound as if he were about to cry. "I meant what I said. Every god damn word of it." At that, he slammed the door in my face.

For one silly, brief moment, I actually believed the little hustler. Me, Sherry Kelly, the most hustle-wise and hustled woman on earth, actually believed the fucker. As if to return myself to reality, I picked up an heirloom crystal vase that had belonged to Edith Wharton and hurled it and its pink flowers across the room. The whole cascade of beauty crashed against the white marble tiles of the patio.

. . .

An hour later, as I sat alone in my patio with my thoughts, Ted came to summon me to the main courtyard of the villa. Mia's limousine was waiting but she wanted to have a cup of coffee with me and a final farewell.

When I got to the courtyard, she was seated at a table, hidden behind monumental sunglasses even though it was still not dawn, and wearing a turban as if her spa treatments had already begun.

"I hope I didn't wake you up at this hour," she said.

"I was awake. I haven't been able to sleep all night."

"With a sex-crazed maniac like Rafael in your bed, I'm not surprised."

"It wasn't that."

"With you, my dear, it's always *that*."

"Don't sell me short. I have other interests, other pursuits."

"I'm sure you do." Her voice was condescending. "We'll talk of them later. I summoned you here at this ungodly hour to issue a warning. I have grown tired of your fun and games. I'm going away for a brief while and I want your assurance that you won't be restaging 'Gone with the Wind' around here. We truly have had enough, and it's time for you to settle down. Become more demure if that's possible."

"You have my guarantee. Nothing will happen. It will be 'All Quiet on the Western Front'."

"I want to believe that. I also want your assurance that you will look after Dino and see that he doesn't get into any trouble."

"Again, you have my guarantee. But while you're at this spa, would you also reconsider this marriage? Do you think this is a bright idea?"

"It's not bright. But I've protected my ass. I'm doing it for a lark. The film too. I just want to shake myself out of the rut I've been in for the past twenty years. Do something new and different before I pass on to my heavenly reward. Imagine me in heaven? All my lovers wearing saintly robes will be lining up to fuck me when I reach the Pearly Gates. Those robes will go flying to the wind."

"And what a pile of them there will be."

"Don't be catty. You can't afford to cast stones."

"Before you go, I have some bad news for you."

"Oh, no, let me have it. I can always count on you for bad news."

"I had nothing to do with it. John and Henry have been kidnapped. They're asking millions for ransom. We can't reach Anishi."

She sipped her coffee without missing a beat and then turned and stared at me. At least I thought she was staring at me. I couldn't tell where she was staring because of those monstrous sunglasses. Suddenly, she burst into hysterical laughter.

"Anishi is up to her old tricks again." Her voice was mocking. "Don't tell me a street-smart pussy like you fell for her old kidnapping hoax again."

"I was skeptical. But I think I believe her."

"Did she tell you the kidnappers were threatening to ship the heads of her kids frozen in ice blocks if she didn't come up with the money?"

"As a matter of fact she did."

"That's it! You fell for the old decapitated heads in an ice block trick, did you?"

"You are making this out to be a total joke. I had no idea she'd ever tried this stunt with you. She let me in on a secret: she said she thought of pulling the trick with you but chickened out one night when she heard you say you didn't cave in to kidnappers. Not even if the ransom money was for me."

"She didn't chicken out. She went through with it. I just didn't buy it. A few days later and properly chastised, the bitch showed up with her kids. John and Henry were perfectly safe, as I am sure they are right this moment. Don't put up one cent. I absolutely forbid you to do it under threat of disinheritance. A threat I now permanently plan to hang over your head."

"I believe you. Anishi is such a liar. As soon as I confront her, I'll expose this. That is, if I can find her. Ted keeps calling and calling your manse in Key West. She's never there. None of the servants know where she is."

"She's not there because I kicked her out. On the one chance that you may be right, I decided to give her the boot. Besides, I'd grown bored with her and her kids. We were fighting all the time. Then you got me scared. Maybe she was putting something into those injections. Maybe I am in some kind of danger. I'll be thoroughly tested at the spa to see if anything has gone wrong. I wanted to make sure I was pure and clean before going to my marriage bed."

"Getting rid of her is one of the better things you've ever done. She's dangerous. The fact she tried to extort money from you over this fake kidnapping shows how frightening she is."

"You know how quickly I bore with my latest toy. My own daughter had deserted me to flash for the silver screen. I turned to her. But that was then, and this is now. Today I have Dino. The film. There will be other offers. At my age, I have to keep myself amused. What am I to do all day? Attend charity benefits?"

"But you'll grow bored with Dino the way you did with Anishi and all the others. It's your way."

"You're right about the others. But with Dino, I don't think I'll ever grow bored. At least not for years. We're going to do films together. I may just be able to make this Big R work until the millennium. That's all I want. To live until the millennium. I mean, really live. After that, I don't give a fuck. All of us must die sometime. Even you, my darling. Although it's difficult to imagine you turning old. Ever."

"I'll probably die young. I've always feared that."

"Who knows? But I don't want to die without having lived life to the fullest. That's why I'm daring to take some chances now. Another marriage. To a kid young enough to be my grandson, although in bed he is no kid."

"You don't need to tell me. Been there. Done that."

"Don't remind me. Can't you see? I want to do everything in my power to convince myself I'm alive. I feel I've been dead, and I'm about to embark upon a splendid new renaissance."

Ted appeared in the patio, informing her that if she were to keep her early morning appointment with the doctor, she'd have to leave at once.

"Goodbye, darling," she said to me, getting up suddenly. She didn't seem to see well in the dimly lit court and behind those sunglasses. He took her by the arm and guided her along.

"Did you say goodbye to Dino?" I asked, calling after her.

"Couldn't find the little devil. I wrote him a love note. Left it on my bed. I'm sure he'll find it because I told him to sleep in no bed but mine."

"That's one promise I know he'll keep. Goodnight, Mommie

dearest."

When she'd been ushered out the door and into the limousine, I turned and headed toward the garden. The first pink streaks of dawn were beginning to cut through the pitch blackness of the Miami sky.

. . .

Not since so many nights ago had I wanted to wander alone in my garden. That night, someone had been stalking me, maybe with an intent to kill. Tonight, more than I did back then, I felt that a lot of unknown forces wanted me dead. Even so, I felt safe in this Florida garden, as I had doubled the security after I feared I was being stalked. The house had good security before that, although that security - at least that one night - had been breached. Daddy Kelly always insisted on good security, especially when Miami shifted its population from Jewish/WASP to Cuban. Daddy had once been robbed at gunpoint in Bogota, and he never got over his fear that all Hispanics were armed bandits.

He'd predicted that with the Cuban invasion, Miami would become one of the most dangerous cities on earth. Time proved him right. Thank God he never lived to see me shacked up with a Cuban, a former Communist at that. Daddy Kelly might judge other men harshly, but he wasn't without his flaws. What if the world had known his secrets?

An image of my real father entered my mind. David, my dad. What a juicy headline that would make in some tabloid. We'd been lovers too. How many of my future biographers would come across that tidbit of information? I hoped none. There are some secrets best left unprinted, notably such tidbits as the night Jacqueline Onassis confided to me that she'd been in love with Robert Kennedy, and had in fact loved him far more than Jack, and with far greater passion.

At the boathouse, memories of my teenage days came back to me. It was at this same spot that I'd auditioned so many beachboys of yore, or fended off the advances of aging playboys. Peter Lawford had put the make on me here, but I'd turned him down. I'd brought many dates here, including those old teen throbs I'd shared a moment or two with.

Fabian (remember him?) didn't have what it took. Sal Mineo (remember him?) came on strong with eight inches, but later confided to me over drugs that he'd rather take it up the butt.

Of them all, the one I most clearly remember from the boathouse was David Eisenhower (five and a half inches). Grandson of the famous general himself, David was no conqueror of women. In fact, it turned out that I had been his first. The kid had a lot to learn, and I taught him a few tricks to improve his technique. Actually, he didn't have a technique, unlike his brother-in-law, Edward Cox, who has David beat by at least three inches. Maybe that's why they call him Cox. At least David was a more experienced soldier by the time he'd reached the tender bed of that Nixon daughter. What was the child's name? Julia? Tricia? Tricky? Who gives a fuck?

As unexciting and unfulfilling as those days were, I still missed them. They had their moments and being real, real young was a lot of fun, especially if you're so rich you don't know how much money you have.

As the moon over Miami faded in a golden glow, giving way to an early dawn, I felt like a goddess, and there weren't many of us left any more. Goddesses have a rough time in life and get a bad press, but that's the cross we bear.

I closed my eyes and wished I had a drink. Better than any liquid refreshment, I wanted company, and at this moment, only the presence of Rafael would do. I needed him and decided after a minute or two alone at this deserted boathouse, I'd go and join him in bed, snuggling into his arms as if they would give me momentary protection from the world.

Slowly, very slowly, a chill came over my body, beginning with my arms, but creeping up to my brow. I had the clear feeling I was being stalked again. Someone in this garden was observing my every move. I had to get out of here at once.

I jumped up from the chaise longue and headed back toward the house. Almost out of nowhere, a dark figure blocked my path. He seemed to emerge from a cluster of hibiscus bushes. Before I could scream, run away, or defend myself, I felt the cold steel blade of a knife at my throat.

Gasping for breath, I stared into the face of my assailant. He wore a stocking mask which made him all the more ominous and frightening.

"Say one word, make one sound, and you're dead meat, puta!"

The voice was oddly familiar. It was a voice I'd heard before. His calling me puta triggered my memory. It was Geraldo Martinez, Castro's former henchman, the murderer of Tricia Navarro, and now perhaps my own assassin.

"Let me go," I said softly, almost a whisper. "I'll give you anything. All the money you want."

"You'll give me more than that. That one-hundred thousand dollars of yours just gave me a big appetite for more. You've got it, bitch. More than you need, and all that I need. I want your money, your jewelry, your gold. But not until I've had you."

"You must be out of your mind. I don't even know how you got in here." I felt the pressure of the knife intensify against my throat. "You'll never get away with it. I've summoned someone from the main house. A servant will be here any minute."

"Stop lying, bitch. I've cut off the power to the boathouse. Me and you are ready for a little honeymoon. I'm going to fuck you. I've been thinking of doing nothing else since I first saw your tail. You're the kind of woman a Cuban man dreams about. Especially one who's had nothing but Cuban or nigger boy-butt to fuck lately. I want the real stuff and I'm going to have it. You'll give it to me or I'll kill you. If I kill you, I'll still have you. Dead or alive."

I felt I'd stumbled into hell, and no one could help me now but myself.

Pressing against me, he forced me to edge back toward the boathouse. Once inside, he shut the door behind us. He forced me down onto a sofa lit by pink streaks in the sky pouring in from the picture windows.

At this point, he ripped off his stocking mask. Even though the room was semi-dark, I felt I could see into his black eyes. It was the closest and most intimate contact I'd ever had with true evil. This man had killed without remorse. I fully expected after his rape of me, he'd plunge the god damn knife into my heart. That would be the ultimate rape, the final penetration.

He ripped off my thin dress. I was wearing panties but no bra. He took the knife and ran it along my breasts, its cold blade threatening my nipples as if he planned to cut them off.

"I'll tell you only one more time, and then I won't tell you again. Let out one scream and you're dead. The knife goes into you. You won't be the first woman I've killed."

"Tricia Navarro, among others?"

"Another puta bitch like you. I always like to fuck them before I kill them. I want a woman to know the greatest sexual pleasure she'll ever thrill to before I plunge the knife into her. The way I see it, even a *vaca* about to be slaughtered deserves one final thrill."

"You won't get away with it. It won't be just prison this time. It'll be the electric chair. You'll fry, you bastard."

"Shut up, cunt!" He pressed the knife into my belly before falling on my breasts and attacking them with his tongue and teeth. The assault was savage. I wanted to cry out and scream with pain. But I felt he told the truth. The moment I did that, I'd know the sharp edge of that knife.

He bit into my nipples as if he wanted to tear them from my body. The nipples were being chewed like raw steak. Finally, when I thought his attack would never end, he removed his slobbering mouth from my breasts.

"That did what I wanted it to," he said, rising up over me, but still pressing the knife into me. "It got my dick all worked up. You're about to feel the full impact of the Geraldo Martinez hard-on. What will make this a really exciting fuck for you is that I don't practice safe sex. Not only that, but I've got AIDS. Got it from a god damn nigger mariposa I used to fuck."

My situation appeared hopeless. I was desperate. At this moment, I hated Rafael for sleeping through all this. If I ever survived this ordeal, I'd fire my entire security staff. There was only one weapon I had at my disposal. I'd used it once before in Saudi Arabia when an oil sheik tried to rape me. It had worked then. Maybe it would work now. It was my only hope.

"Okay, you bastard," I said to him. "If this is going to be the last fuck of my well-fucked life, I'm going to get into it and enjoy it. If I live from the fuck, I'll die of AIDS. If I don't live, I'll get to know the feel of a knife in my gut. I'm going to give you the fuck of your life. I'll be like a woman ordering her last supper. You haven't been fucked until you've been fucked by Sherry Kelly. My final joy is knowing that no woman will ever satisfy you again. You'll always remember this fuck. The rest of your rotten life will be downhill."

He seemed to like that talk. He got off on it, as I hoped he would. I even thought he believed it, which would make him an even bigger fool than I suspected.

"Go on, puta, talk some more like that." He ripped my panties down and with his free hand - the one not holding the knife - plunged his fingers into my vagina. Removing his fingers, he licked them. "Tastes good. Pure honey. Just like I thought. The best god damn taste I've ever had in my life."

"Let me guide you in," I whispered into his ear, becoming the movie goddess. "Let me feel you. Play with your balls before I guide you to my honeypot."

He allowed my hand to travel to his groin. I felt his throbbing penis. Then I burst into uncontrollable laughter.

"What's so god damn funny? Why are you laughing?"

"I'm laughing at you, you little Spik runt. That's no cock. What happened to the rest of it? Someone cut it off? You're no man. Rafael Navarro is a man. I've seen nine-year-old boys with bigger dicks than yours. What a mariposa!"

All the time, I held his small penis in my grip, slowly applying pressure.

"Let go of me. I'll kill you for this. You've laughed at me for the last time."

He raised the knife to plunge the blade into me. As he did, I jerked my knee and sent it crashing into his tiny testicles. He screamed and jumped back in pain. Yelping and doubling over, he moved the knife menacingly toward me. I grabbed his wrist and with a power, force, and intensity of strength I didn't know I possessed, I sent it downward. The razor-sharp knife severed his penis. I raised my knee again and sent it crashing once more into his groin. He screamed even louder in pain. It was a blood-curdling scream from deep within his throat, a scream quite unlike any I'd ever heard before, like some sex slave of ancient times feeling the bite of the castrator's knife. The sound of the knife hitting the floor was music to me. Kicking the wounded bastard off me, I raced toward the pool, pulling my panties up around my legs to keep from tripping.

I let out a scream that no Tarzan or Carol Burnett could equal. With all the speed I could muster, I raced toward the house.

In less than five seconds, floodlights were switched on throughout the garden. A siren sounded. At last the security force was awake and on the job.

Without ever looking back at the boathouse, I fled into the patio of the mansion and in through the back door. A maid rushed to meet me. Seeing my nude body, she raced to get me a robe. The security force fanned out across the garden.

I heard Rafael shouting down from my bedroom window on the second floor. The sound of Ted's hysterical voice came from the hallway along with his footsteps.

Over the intercom sounded the booming voice of Dino. "What in fuck's going on?"

"He tried to kill me," I shouted at the maid. "He's in the boathouse. Tell the guard to get him."

Ted was the first to reach me, and I clung to him desperately. The maid had run screaming into the garden.

I must have passed out at this point. When I regained consciousness, I was in my bed. Rafael, Ted, and Dino hovered over me.

As I opened my eyes, I looked into Rafael's kind and gentle face, so unlike that of Martinez. "Did they find him?"

"No. The scumbag got away. There was blood everywhere. You must have stabbed him. We'll get him. Can you describe him?"

I felt a creeping nausea come over me. "It was Geraldo Martinez."

CHAPTER ELEVEN

After a sleepless night, I searched for something to wear for a day I fully expected to be hand-delivered from hell. David heard the full report about the attack from Martinez and my severing of his penis, but decided this was the last story he wanted to bring to the police and especially the media.

"It would make Second Coming Headlines," he'd predicted. "He tried to rape and murder you. You gave him the unkindest cut of all. Maybe we'll call it a draw on this one, since both parties were injured. Instant justice. Except now you must beef up security as never before. He might try to get back at you. In fact, I can almost predict that. He's a psycho. But I don't want to alert the police unless we have full disclosure here, which I'm against."

At times like this, he was not reassuring. He played by the rules too carefully, although bending them a bit now and then as when he didn't want to call the police. I much preferred the solution of a raging Rafael. With the help of his Cuban supporters in Miami, he wanted to track down Martinez and kill him. In spite of my rage, my ultimate good sense took over and I tried to cool Rafael's passion.

As he showered, Ted, the eternal message boy, barged into our bedroom with yet another message. It was from Anishi. She left word Mia had kicked her out of the Key West manse, but I already knew that. She couldn't give us a number where she could be reached, but she informed us that she'd be in touch real soon with details of where I was to deliver the ransom money, all in small unmarked bills.

"How convenient," I said to Ted. "With that much money at stake and in small bills, I'll need two armored trucks to deliver that kind of loot. I love how she just assumes I'll put up the money."

Ted made the final wardrobe choice, selecting a pink dress with a red Hermes scarf, although I secretly suspected that's what he'd like to wear himself. Most definitely I'd be wearing large dark sunglasses. This was one day I wanted to hide from the world.

Another message came in from South Beach. This one,

according to Ted, was from Jerry's assistant. I was assured that Chi Chi Presents was at this moment filming the world's hottest love scene starring Brad Cruz and Dino Paglia. Cruz might be one of the most famous tops in California, but this morning he was discovering the bottom side of his personality. Madonna would approve. Every top needs to become a bottom at least once a season. Madonna and I definitely agree on such matters.

Heading for the terrace I picked a flower and placed it on the coffee table for Rafael. I was like a maitre d' getting ready for the arrival of a special guest. After last night's episode with Rafael and the waiter and my attack from Martinez, I didn't think I owed anybody any favors, but I decided to be my most charming self anyway. If word got out of my attack on Martinez, no man would ever get it up for me again. I'd be known henceforth and forever more as the world's most famous castrator.

Even now, I couldn't believe I had done what I had done. But I had to convince myself: I did it to survive. Which was more important? My life or the tiny little penis of Martinez.

The ever-faithful Ted appeared on the patio. I thought he was bringing another urgent message from someone. But instead he carried a small glass jar.

"We found it!"

"What in hell are you talking about?" I demanded to know.

"The little thing in this jar. One of the guards found it in the grass near the boathouse." He held up the jar for my inspection.

Instead of screaming, I gasped. The jar contained a tiny, pathetic piece of flesh which I assumed was once the erect penis of Martinez. I shuddered and turned away. "Please take that thing out of here. At once. I think I'm going to throw up."

"What should I do with it?"

"How in hell do I know? Preserve it in alcohol." I slammed down my coffee. "No," I shouted. "Put it in the freezer. Freeze the god damn thing."

At this point and in dramatic contrast to what was resting in that jar, a fully erect Rafael walked nude onto the patio. Fresh from his shower, he was toweling himself.

Ted screamed in sheer delight when he spotted Rafael's rigid erection. He'd seen the treasure in limp condition before, but never fully aroused as if ready for plowing. I know, of course, this erection wasn't entirely sexual. He always got an erection when showering.

"I've died and gone to heaven," Ted said. "Rafael - not that blasted sheriff - is the real snake."

"Run along now, my little mariposa," he said affectionately. "As a kid, I used to perform in a few Superman shows in Havana just for fun. But I don't do that anymore. So fly away on gossamer wings. Sherry and I are about to do some serious bonding."

"Ted brought something to show me," I said looking toward the jar and turning away in disgust.

"What have we here?" he asked, taking the jar and examining its contents.

"That used to hang on Martinez," Ted said.

"What a trophy!" Rafael said, his erection gradually diminishing. "I wish I had his severed head instead."

"It's not much, is it?" Ted asked, looking first at the contents of the jar and then at Rafael.

"I knew he didn't have much. Men like him always talk big. Some stud! But I still think we've got to get him before he strikes again at us. The guy's a maniac. He won't let this alone. He'll be out for revenge. He'll want blood."

"I'm afraid," I said.

"Not with me here to protect you. I won't let you out of my sight."

The buzzer from my boudoir sounded, and Ted rushed to see what was the matter. Surely it wasn't Bill Clinton at this hour.

Ted was gone for just a minute. When he returned to the patio, he was visibly shaken. "It was Snake. He wants you to fly at once to Key Largo. Take the helicopter. You've got to get there soon. He's going to have to make an announcement to the press some time this morning."

"What in hell is the matter?" I asked.

"He won't say, although he predicts it'll make headlines around the world."

"It's John and Henry," I said. "He's found them murdered."

"I don't know what it is," Ted said. "He won't tell me. He said you've got to get there at once before the press does."

"I'm going with you," Rafael said, taking my arm. "We'll leave at once."

"Darling," I said, "not before you put on your pants."

"Not before that." He gave me a soft brush of his lips on mine. He turned to Ted and then looked at the jar. "For God's sake, get that god damn thing out of here. Don't frighten Sherry any more with it." He headed at once for the bedroom to get dressed.

"I'll call the pilot," Ted said. "Can I go too?"

"Of course, you can. I'll need you."

"Should I tell anybody where we're going?"

"I don't want anybody to know. But I did want Mia to know about the Martinez attack. Her own life could be in danger, even if she's at the spa. You don't know what weirdos are working in spas these days."

"I've tried to get through to her but she's not in Palm Beach yet."

"Then reach her in her limousine."

"I've tried that. She's en route to Palm Beach all right. I'm sure of that. But she's not picking up calls in the limousine."

"Keep trying. We've got to get in touch with her. Have two security guards waiting at the spa. They are to guard her constantly from the moment she arrives."

"Do you think her car will be hijacked on the way there?"

"The idea didn't occur to me until you brought it up. Any more pleasant goodies like that to share with me? You know I'm half out of my mind already."

"I'm sorry. But it's something to think about."

Rafael, fully dressed in slacks and a T-shirt, came back onto the patio. "Let's get airborne. Let's see what sort of surprise Snake has for us."

. . .

Snake was waiting as our helicopter came to a landing in Key Largo. Rafael helped me down from the plane. This wasn't the first helicopter ride I'd taken with this pilot, recalling that mountain in Switzerland and the long-lost Capetown Diamond.

"Sorry, I didn't get back to you right away, but I've been real busy," Snake said. "You'll soon see why."

"It's John and Harry," I said with rising panic. "They're dead!"

"Two people are dead. But it's not John and Henry."

He ushered me into the back seat of his sheriff's car and almost shut the door on Rafael. Snake seemed to treat him like my toy boy - not the future president of Cuba. I'm sure when Rafael became president of Cuba, he'd break off relationships with Monroe County for this oversight.

As if competing in a Grand Prix, Snake hit the road with tires burning.

"Where are you taking us?" I demanded to know.

"Do you have to go so fucking fast?" Rafael asked.

"Got no time to spare," Snake said. "I'm taking you to that house that Anishi rented up here on the Keys. We've checked it out. Those little Jap boys of hers had been stashed here. At least they'd been stashed here until a few hours ago. Someone came and got 'em."

"So the kidnapping was a hoax after all," I said. "Mia warned me."

"I think the kidnapping and the ransom notes were a hoax until now," Snake said. "Now I think they're real. The boys have gone. I don't know where."

"Maybe Anishi has stashed them somewhere else to throw us off the trail." Rafael smiled at me, as if proud he could speak English like that.

"I don't think so," Snake said. "After Anishi was kicked out of Mia's, she checked into the Vista Linda Motel. I was told she didn't make any phone calls all night."

"Where is she now?" I asked.

"This morning she rented herself a car, and one of my deputies is discreetly following her up the Keys. Naturally, he's driving an unmarked car. At last report, she's north of Marathon. We expect she'll be here within the hour."

"You're taking us to the house where her two friends from Tokyo are staying," I said. "They were holding John and Henry."

"They were - that's true," Snake said. "But sometime this morning those Tokyo boys passed into mortality. They won't be kidnapping anybody else anytime soon. At least not on this earth."

"They were murdered?"

"You might call it that. I'd call it butchered."

I shuddered, huddling closer to Rafael for whatever protection he could offer.

"I want you to see for yourself before I call in the news cunts," Snake said.

Recalling my own act of recent violence, I didn't think I could hold up to view one more gruesome scene. At first I was tempted to tell Snake about my encounter with Martinez but decided to withhold that news for the moment.

All too soon we were at the rather nondescript Keys house. It evoked an assembly row development house. It looked so lower class, so suburban. Driving by, no one would believe that anything sinister could go on here. It was the house of the faceless millions who sit around watching sitcoms at night.

But in spite of the harmless look of the dwelling, I felt a sinister aura as I entered. I was ushered into the house by one of Snake's deputies. The sheriff was issuing orders to his men about what they were to do when Anishi pulled up in the driveway.

The living room looked undisturbed. No sign of struggle anywhere. A small TV was flickering as if someone had been watching the screen all night before retiring to bed and forgetting to turn off the set.

Rafael took my hand and squeezed it hard before permanently clasping it to his side. He didn't want to let me go, and I appreciated that. I was so happy he was here for me now.

Snake came into the house and ushered us toward the back. "I want you to come to the bedroom." He paused in the hallway and turned to glance back at me. "Have you had breakfast this morning?"

"Breakfast?" I asked in astonishment. "How can you think of food at a time like this?"

"I wasn't thinking of food. I just wanted to make sure you hadn't eaten. Because if you had, you would throw up at what I'm about to show you." He turned away and proceeded to lead us down the darkened hallway.

Holding Rafael's hand, I followed along reluctantly.

Snake paused at the door to a bedroom. With trepidation, he opened the door into the brightly lit room. He motioned us to enter.

Rafael headed in first with me trailing behind. I paused at the doorway, taking in the scene before me. Then I let out a blood-curdling scream. Rafael put his arm around me as I averted my eyes. I crushed myself into his shoulder as if to blot out what I'd just seen.

Two nude Japanese men lay in a river of blood on the cement floor. Both men had been decapitated. In one brief second my eyes revealed to me that each of them had been castrated. Their mutilated genitals lay between their legs. It was then I realized Martinez had done this.

I staggered back into the hallway followed by Rafael. I had seen enough. "I can't look."

Snake came back out of the bedroom and led us down the hallway and into the kitchen.

"One of my boys made some coffee," he said. "What would you say if I offered you some?"

"I'd like that. I need some coffee. I need something."

"What a brutal murder," Rafael said. "Whoever killed those men didn't want to just take John and Henry away. It's like he wanted to leave a calling card."

"Did he ever," I said almost spitting out the words. "He'll strike again."

"Exactly," Rafael said.

"I wouldn't go so far as to say that," Snake said. "It's probably a onetime thing. A random bit of psycho violence. You can trust old Snake on that. This ain't no serial killing."

"What are you going to do now?" I asked.

"I'll have to call in the press for a chat. But first we're waiting for Anishi to arrive. Me and you both had better have a talk with that yellow pussy before I call in anybody."

"Are you going to arrest her?" Rafael asked.

"I could. I've got plenty of charges. Not about the murder. The fake kidnapping. I don't think she had these men murdered. I don't think she even knows they're murdered. They were her support group. She wanted them alive to do her bidding while she collected millions."

"I dread your press conference," I said. "What are you going to say? You won't bring me into this, will you?"

"Hell no! Do you think I'm some kind of fool? You're the

boss lady. You're the sweet pot where the honey comes from. I'm not going to do anything to jeopardize that."

"Thank God."

"Depending on how our talk with Anishi goes, I may not even bring her into this. Not right away. Because that would alert reporters about her connection to Mia."

"Oh, God," I said. "Mia will just die. She'll blame me."

"She's got a right to blame somebody. I'm going to have the most limited hangout press conference I've ever had - and I've had quite a few."

"Just tell them a little bit of it."

"That's right, Pretty Woman," Snake said. "Just enough to whet their appetite. To tell the truth, I don't know a lot about this myself. We'll confine the press conference to the murders. No story of any kidnapping. No Anishi. No early morning visit by you to this house. Who in the world would ever believe that the rich Sherry Kelly would visit a modest little place like this anyway?"

"You want me here when Anishi arrives?" I asked.

"If she arrives," Rafael said. "She could be driving to Star Island."

"I think she's heading right here." Snake turned to me. "I want you to talk to her first. Of course, I'll be eavesdropping but she might tell you more than she tells me. Don't worry. I'll hear every word."

"I certainly want to talk to her," I said. "Do I have questions to ask her."

"It'll take awhile for her to get here," Snake said. "In the meantime, I have some more entertainment for you."

"I think I've had enough entertainment for one morning," I said.

"This is by special request from you," Snake said.

"What do you mean?" I asked.

"That tape I told you about," he said, looking put out with me that I didn't recall at once. "The last phone call from Anishi's boss. I've got it all on tape. Every word of it. Why don't you listen to it while you're waiting for her? It'll shine a little light on this mystery. I've got to check something out front. When she gets here, I don't want her to know that anything's wrong. I don't want her to suspect anything. See you later, alligators."

When he'd gone, Rafael turned to me, a puzzled look on his face. "Why did he call us alligators?"

"It's just an expression. A very old expression. But Snake is a very old-fashioned kind of guy."

"You Americans. I think I'll never understand you. Why alligator? Why not crocodile?"

At this point one of the sheriff's deputies came into the kitchen carrying some equipment. After a brief glance at us, he said nothing but placed the equipment on the kitchen table. He turned on the tape for us.

. . .

The moment we heard the first words, "Puta Bitch," Rafael and I knew that Anishi's secret employer was Martinez, even if she didn't know that herself.

The first minute of the tape wasn't clear. We made out only a few words, having entirely missed why Martinez exploded in anger and denounced her. We could only gather that she'd not carefully carried out his instructions, or was moving too slowly to achieve a plan he'd set out for her.

Suddenly, the sheriff's recording came in so loud and clear I felt I was in the same room with Anishi and Martinez, a daunting prospect.

MARTINEZ: Forget what was said before. We've got a new time-table. Why can't you get the cunt to Montego Bay like I told you? We have everything set up at Round Hill.

ANISHI: She agreed to go for a week. Then she met this hustler, Dino Paglia. I know it's sick but she wants to marry the creep.

MARTINEZ: Dino Paglia! Who does the scum think he is? Dino Paglia! That's Rafael Navarro's son. I don't blame the kid. If I had a turncoat like Navarro for my papa, I'd change my name too.

ANISHI: I'm trying to talk her into going to Montego Bay for her honeymoon. She's more or less agreed.

MARTINEZ: What about the trip to Havana?

ANISHI: She knows how easy that would be. I told her she would be welcomed personally by Castro to Havana. But she's balking at the idea.

MARTINEZ: What's her god damn problem?

ANISHI: She's worried about media coverage. She's afraid that by entering Cuba through the back door the State Department might take away her passport.

MARTINEZ: Bullshit! Have you told her how many Americans go to Havana illegally and nothing bad happens to them? Have you told her that, bitch?

ANISHI: I've told her! But she claims she's no ordinary American. If she goes to Havana, she thinks Jesse Helms will denounce her on the Senate floor. Make a big deal over it.

MARTINEZ: We think we might have that idiot killed anyway. It's time the old dinosaur died. He's caused enough trouble for one lifetime.

ANISHI: She can hardly count on that.

MARTINEZ: But the goodies Castro is offering her. Like a sugar daddy with candy for a kid.

ANISHI: She definitely wants her mansion returned. The one she had built with Jack Kelly in the 50s.

MARTINEZ: I know the fucking house, bitch. I've slept there.

ANISHI: If she goes, she'll want more than her house back. She's got a long list of demands. She wants an audience with Castro personally. She had her lawyers compile a list of properties confiscated in 1960. She wants all her companies returned. Jack Kelly went to his grave denouncing Castro. Those companies belonged to Mia and Jack Kelly. She wants restitution.

MARTINEZ: Shit! Some of those companies don't exist any more. That child-molester husband of hers exploited my people. It was the sweat and blood of the Cuban people that made her rich.

ANISHI: Not just Cuba. A lot of other countries too.

MARTINEZ: I don't give a god damn about other countries. I want what's right for my own country.

ANISHI: I can't make her change her mind. I can only report to you her demands. Her list is long. She wants everything back.

MARTINEZ: Fuck! She's got more money than she'll spend in a million lifetimes.

ANISHI: When you're rich, you want to be richer. You know that.

MARTINEZ: I know nothing of money. I've never had money.

ANISHI: Can't you just promise to give her anything she wants? The point is, entice her to go to Cuba. Once she's in your hands, can't you deal with her then? I know you have very effective ways of doing that.

MARTINEZ: You can tell her anything. Promise her anything. But get her ass on that plane to Jamaica. Then to Cuba. Did you show her the pictures?

ANISHI: She's thrilled with them. She says her house looks better now than it did the day she left it.

MARTINEZ: Do you know why? We took money from the Cuban people. Money the government doesn't really have to spend, and Castro took that money and restored the house of this rich bitch. A woman who has houses she hasn't even counted yet.

ANISHI: But it was her house.

MARTINEZ: The sweat of the Cuban people paid for that house. It belongs to the Cuban people.

ANISHI: That's not how she sees it.

MARTINEZ: You're wasting my time, bitch.

ANISHI: I'm sorry you don't think I'm moving fast enough.

MARTINEZ: I don't think you're moving fast enough at all. Here's what I really think. I think you're not carrying out our plans.

ANISHI: I've followed all your orders.

MARTINEZ: Like hell you have, you dirty yellow puta bitch. We've got Mia Kelly staked out. We don't think you've shot the virus into her blood. We think you've lied.

ANISHI: But I did. I did! I gave her three injections of the damn stuff.

MARTINEZ: I don't believe you. She'll have herself tested soon enough. Especially now that she's fucking little Desi Navarro. We'll be able to get our hands on those reports. Once we get them, we'll know if you're lying. If you've lied to me, you're dead.

ANISHI: I've never lied to you. I've always told you the truth.

MARTINEZ: As a little baby, the first words you ever said were a lie. You've lied from that day on.

ANISHI: That's not true! Wait and see. I'll get Mia to Havana. On her honeymoon. I will. You just wait and see. Once in

Havana, she's all yours to do with as you like. If you think you can get her to sign all those companies over to the Cuban people, as an act of supreme generosity, that's up to you. That's Castro's job. With her mind going because of AIDS she might sign them over. That would prevent future claims from her heir, Sherry. My job is to get her to Havana. I'll do that. Then I'm through. In Havana she can die of AIDS. You can figure out how to take her money.

MARTINEZ: I can always tell when a bitch is lying. You're lying now. What if I tell you I already know that you've chartered a plane to fly you and your faggot boys to Chile?

ANISHI: That's not true! How could you possibly know that? It's not true!

MARTINEZ: Just in case you are thinking of leaving sooner, I have to warn you. That pilot would never make it to Chile. He'd have an unscheduled stopover in Cuba before that.

ANISHI: It's not true! I wasn't planning to do that.

MARTINEZ: You must think you're dealing with fools.

ANISHI: What are you going to do? With me?

MARTINEZ: Never call you again.

ANISHI: You mean our deal is off?

MARTINEZ: Our deal is off.

ANISHI: You won't call me again. I'm free to go.

MARTINEZ: I won't call you again. The next time I talk to you, it will be in person. You'll get to see me at last.

End of tape.

At the kitchen table I sat staring at Rafael. There was so much to talk about. To analyze. But at this moment Snake came into the room.

"Anishi is on the dirt road leading down to here," he said. She'll be in the driveway in about two minutes. Come into the back room. Here's what I want you to do."

. . .

Since it was a small house, we could hear Anishi turning the key and entering the front living room. For some reason, Snake had asked us to be seated in the Florida room. He'd concealed himself in the utility room nearby where he could hear every word said through the cardboard-like walls.

She was shouting something and calling out but it was in Japanese. Suddenly, she discovered the locked door where her two murdered cohorts still lay in a pool of blood.

We could hear her pounding on the door. Then in English she shouted through the door, "Open this door, you bastards! I know you're in there, you god damn child molesters! John! Henry!"

She raced toward the back of the house where we sat at a glass-covered table on this bleak morning. Apparently, she was looking for some instrument to beat in the door. As she ran out into the Florida room, she spotted us. A startled gasp came from her throat.

"Sherry," she shouted in astonishment, completely ignoring Rafael who must be getting used to such treatment. "What in hell are you doing here?"

"To what in hell do we owe the honor of your visit?"

"I don't know."

"Don't know? You scheming bitch. Why are you calling for John and Henry? You said they were kidnapped."

"I got an anonymous tip they were being held here."

"You did? So you came to rescue them completely unaided and unarmed."

"That's it. I'm here to rescue them."

"But weren't you supposed to bring the ransom money?"

"I don't know. I think they wanted me to see that my boys were alive before they went through with the ransom pickup. I think." She turned and practically spat at me. "How in hell do I know what their plans were?"

"How did they contact you?"

"They called me at Mia's."

"One second ago it was an anonymous tip. Now they called you at Mia's. You forgot. You've already left word with me that Mia kicked you out."

"They called me at Mia's before she kicked me out."

"Not bloody likely. The sheriff has tapped all of Mia's phone lines. No call came in for you."

"You've got me so confused I can't remember. I checked into a motel. The call came in there."

"How did they know to reach you at the Vista Linda Motel?"

"I think they followed me there."

"Snake staked out the Vista Linda. Your phone there was tapped. No calls came in for you there either."

"It wasn't exactly a phone call. It was a note slipped under my door."

"Do you still have the note?"

"I tore it up."

"You tore up such a vital note. That's hard to believe."

"I've been so upset I don't know what I'm doing. I'm half out of my mind."

"So you drove here at the demand of the kidnappers?"

"They wanted me to come alone. I wasn't supposed to alert the police." She looked frantically around the room. "Where's John and Henry?" She practically lunged at me but Rafael blocked her. "What have you done with my boys?"

I handed the key to the locked room to Rafael and indicated that he, as agreed with Snake, was to go and show her the bodies in the bedroom. "Rafael will unlock that bedroom door."

She screamed, "If you've done something to my boys, I swear I'll kill you!" She raced toward the bedroom door beating him there.

I turned my back to the hallway. It was more than I could handle.

A scream came from deep within her throat. "They're butchered! Where's John and Henry?" She rushed back to the patio to confront me. "They're decapitated."

"Tell me something I don't know."

"Do you know who did it?"

"Geraldo Martinez."

"Who is that?"

"In case you don't already know, it's your boss. The one you've been taking orders from for God knows how long. Perhaps even before you came to live with Mia."

"I swear I didn't know his name."

"That I can believe even though it comes from your lying mouth. Martinez doesn't exactly leave calling cards, other than your two murdered friends."

"Then he's got John and Henry?"

"We can presume that. But why I don't know."

"It's obvious. I've told you before. As long as he has John and Henry, he can make me do what he wants."

"You're forgetting one thing."

"I'm forgetting nothing."

"You were useful to Martinez only when we were under Mia's roof. Now that she's kicked you out, you are of no further use to him. He doesn't know that right now, but he'll find out soon enough."

"When he finds that out, my boys will be of no use to him either."

"You've got that right. He'll either let them go to come back home to mama or he'll...."

She interrupted me. "Any friend who would butcher two men like he did this morning won't just release them."

"I'm convinced." I paused. Another scheme was forming in my mind. "We could suddenly make their lives valuable to Martinez."

"And just how would you propose to do that at this late hour?"

"We could distribute circulars in the Cuban community in Miami. With pictures of John and Henry. Call them runaways. I'll offer a million-dollar reward."

"You think that would work?"

"How in hell can I be sure? But it's better than sitting on our ass. Letting them die."

"I'll try anything."

"Ted can have those posters on the streets in just two hours. Of course, Martinez will not show up in person to claim the reward. He'll have some innocent party show up. Probably a Cuban who doesn't know a damn thing about anything."

"It might work. Anything to get my boys back. They could be dead for all I know."

"You should have thought of that before you staged this kidnapping in the first place. It was you who put the idea in that creep's head."

"I know that now. But I didn't think straight. This kidnapping seemed my last chance. Especially with Mia kicking me out. I thought I could extort money from you and flee the country before Martinez had me killed. With all that money, I planned to start life all over in Chile. With my boys."

"What a foolish dream. I don't know how you thought you'd get away with it."

"It was a chance. It might have worked."

"My distributing these posters and offering a reward might work too. The alternative is to let the hours go by and let Martinez kill the kids."

"Please, help me!" she said, grabbing my hand. I'll do anything if you'll get them back to me. Anything you want."

"I'll ask only one favor."

"What's that?"

"If I get your boys back, would you take them away? Out of my life. Out of Mia's life. Just go. Disappear."

"I will. I'll make no more trouble for you ever again. I promise."

"It's a deal." She sat down in a wrought-iron chair opposite me. Rafael brought her some black coffee which she tasted tentatively then put down.

I turned to her, meeting her black steely eyes with my baby-blues. "One more thing, Mia is not going to Jamaica on her honeymoon. And certainly not to that reception you guys were planning for her in Havana."

"I know that now." She picked up the cup again and sipped at the coffee. "All my get-rich schemes. This morning I know that none of them will work. I will die poor. Nothing is going to work. I'm not only afraid for the life of my boys, I'm afraid for my own life. Martinez will have me killed. I just know it. Some horrible death. He's a monster. I dare not imagine what he is doing to John and Henry right now. Sodomizing them for sure."

"He's most definitely not doing that. I've got to get to work. I've got to get David on the phone."

At this point Snake came out of the utility room.

Upon seeing him, Anishi placed her face in her hands. "You've been here all along. You've heard every word."

"That's not all," Snake said. "I even know you're the tenant of this house. You stupidly paid for the lease with a check. I've even got the cancelled check."

"What are you going to do with me?"

"I could bring charges. Faking a kidnapping is old hat in Miami. But south of the border here in Monroe County, we view that as serious business."

"Don't take me in now," she pleaded. "Let me stay free long enough to see that John and Henry are safe."

"I just might do that," he said, "providing Pretty Woman here agrees."

"I agree," I said. "Take her to my place at Palm Island until we get news about John and Henry."

At this point, Ted came into the room with a private message from Jerry. I read the note quickly: "It's in the can. Hottest sex scene ever filmed. Cruz is still at my apartment. Waiting for Dino's promised return in the afternoon. Need further instructions."

Snake looked at the note with a pang of jealousy. He didn't like notes passed in front of his eyes without his being privy to the information.

"Pretty Woman," he said, turning to me. "I want you to get on that helicopter of yours with this Cuban boyfriend of yours and fly your hot piece of tail to Star Island. You've never heard of Key Largo for all I know."

"But it was a movie, wasn't it? Before my time."

"It's likely to be a movie again if we don't hush up all the juicy details of this story. I've got to announce the murders. But I'm telling very little to the press. Very little at this point. I'll have one of my deputies drive this Jap bitch to your place." He looked with disdain at Anishi. "I'll be down later for some questions of my own. Sherry asked you a lot. But she's not a professional like me. I'll ask the really tough ones."

A sheriff's deputy came into the room. "He's here, Snake."

"Good," Snake said, motioning with his hand for Rafael and me to get out of the house.

Out of curiosity, I turned to him before heading for the door. "Just who is here?" I asked.

"This fag hairdresser from Key West. I've flown him in. I'm not as young as I used to be. I need a little touch-up before facing the news cameras."

"Fine." I looked at Anishi. "I'll do my best. No promises. You got your own boys into this. You tried to extort money from me. You're responsible for endangering their lives. I have no sympathy for you at all."

"I know, I know. Don't rub it in!"

As I raced up the hallway, Rafael trailed behind me. "If I ever get a minute alone with you, you've got a lot of explaining to do. I keep thinking a lot is going on around here that I don't know about. You're not letting me in on things."

"I tell you everything. At least I'll tell you everything when I get a moment."

"That moment had better come soon."

"It will." The helicopter pilot reached down and hoisted me aboard. Rafael didn't need help.

Airborne, I snuggled up in Rafael's arms en route to Miami. "I've got to leave you for a brief time this morning. I've got an appointment in David's office."

"Can't I come too? I don't want you out of my sight."

"That would be lovely. But I want you to write that poster - in Spanish, of course - and direct the operation of getting it distributed through the Hispanic community of Miami."

"I can do that. At last you're beginning to see that I have some organizational ability."

"I do indeed." I settled back into my seat for the final minutes of the flight. At this point I wasn't even sure myself how to proceed through the morning, but an idea was occurring to me. Cruz, or so I was told, was still resting in an apres-fuck environment on South Beach. Perhaps he'd welcome a call from Sherry Kelly at that same love nest.

. . .

Sex, lies, and videotape. They seem to go together. At Star Island later that morning, I got into the back of my limousine accompanied only by Ted and a security guard in the front seat, plus the chauffeur. I lied to Rafael about where I was going. I certainly wasn't going to sign papers at David's office, as I'd said. I had quite another mission.

As Jerry well knew, I was going to that South Beach apartment still occupied by Cruz waiting for Dino who would never return. After his film session, Dino would be coming back to Star Island, with firm instructions not to tell Rafael about his recent porno job. Rafael would surely get the idea I was trying to corrupt his son.

Rafael, along with Dino and his mysterious guest who had

yet to arrive, had been invited to Palm Island where Anishi was now stashed.

Word had reached me that Mia had checked into her spa at Palm Beach, and I'm sure she would be demanding to talk to me as soon as she'd fully digested the news of my knife attack on Martinez. Although it wasn't going to help her beauty treatments at the spa, Ted was also instructed to tell her about John and Henry and Anishi's failed attempt at the kidnapping hoax. Mia was even to be informed of the two decapitations. I know I'd promised to keep it quiet while she was gone, and she hadn't been away but for a few hours, and I obviously hadn't kept any of my promises, but was I to be blamed for all that had transpired?

Somehow I felt she would blame me although I don't know why. Events were spinning out of control. The only thing she wasn't to be informed of was that her future husband had just made a porno tape with America's most popular actor and if that stuck-up star didn't cooperate and drop his one-hundred million dollar law suit against me, that video might be broadcast around the world. With all the other news she had to digest this morning, I didn't think Mia needed to know about the video tape too.

She was supposed to be having a rest at the spa, although I feared all this news might drive her back to Star Island. I certainly hoped not. Having her away served my purpose right now. I had also invited Maxie to Palm Island because I felt he, too, needed a rest after all those betrayals of me. Presumably he was on my side now, and I wanted to keep an eye on him. I certainly didn't trust him completely after what he'd done to me, but I didn't want him to get away either. It was no telling what he might do. He'd wanted to come with Ted and me on all our misadventures, but I no longer included him in our schemes. I was still covering up the news about his putting the real bullet in that gun that I'd fired at Cruz. If that lawsuit-proned actor learned that a trusted member of my household had put the actual bullet in that gun, I feared it would look bad for me, even though I wasn't personally implicated. I just knew if it could be proven that Maxie did it, I'd lose a few more million to Cruz. I was a victim of the circumstances, but in most cases I always ended up paying.

Ted had secured the keys to the secret apartment from Jerry. I was just going to let myself in, and walk right in on Cruz. Surely he was resting after that session with Dino. Even though I was intruding without an appointment on his privacy, I felt he really needed to know that we'd secretly captured his performance on tape.

David, of course, would not approve. Incidents like this one had come up in the past. He took the position that one should not blackmail people to prevent them from bringing lawsuits against you. I think he said it was actually illegal, but I'm not sure. It's very hard to determine what is legal in this country. I'm sure the concept changes from day to day, especially now that Clarence Thomas sits on the Supreme Court.

Once we reached the South Beach condo complex, Ted got out of the limousine first. Jerry was waiting in the hotel nearby to give him a copy of the film should Cruz not believe that I had taped him. The security guard followed me into the building where Jerry had arranged for my clearance.

Once at the door of the apartment, I told the guard to wait outside. This had to be a private meeting between Cruz and moi. The guard gave me a knowing smirk, seeming to think I was cheating on Rafael, and planned to fuck the actor.

I instructed him that if I pressed the emergency alarm system I carried in my purse, he was to use the spare key, enter the apartment, and rescue me at gunpoint if necessary, although I hardly expected we needed to strong-arm Cruz. Under no circumstances except a mortal threat to me was he to fire at the actor. Shooting Cruz one time could be forgiven by my public, at least I hoped so. Being involved in a second attempt on the actor's life, even if he threatened me, was a definite no-no.

The guard nodded that he understood, but I always wondered if these trigger-happy private cops could really be trusted. They certainly hadn't done a good job protecting me. I was going to fire all of them and get a new batch from Chicago. I'd wanted to do that before the arrival of the president, but there had been no time to train new ones, with all the excitement going on.

I smiled faintly at the guard, a nervous smile. I was afraid to enter the love-nest, but I turned the key and barged in anyway. The time had come for me to find out what surprises awaited me here.

. . .

The sound of running water coming from the bathroom alerted me that someone was in the shower. Singing, no less, obviously remembering a happy experience. If I recalled, Dino always left you satisfied. I arranged myself artfully on the sofa, crossing my legs and trying to look as seductive as possible. Then it occurred to me. Why was I trying to look seductive? I was here on a different mission. Blackmailers don't need to look seductive.

As time went on, I tapped my nails against a glass-covered table. Cruz seemed to be a menace to the South Florida water supply, but perhaps he had a lot to wash off. At last the water was turned off. It still seemed like an eternity before he finally came into the living room. Buck-naked, he was toweling himself off.

"What in hell!" he said upon seeing me. "How in the fuck did you get in here?" He made no attempt to cover his nudity, but then he'd once appeared nude in an early film and didn't seem at all shy displaying his cut tool which was still dripping wet.

"I have a key. I also have some business to discuss with you. Of a non-sexual nature."

He stood in front of me provocatively drying himself, deliberately spending more time in the genital area than I'm sure he normally would.

"If it's about the lawsuit, forget it! I'm going through with it unless you settle on our terms. Get it, *our* terms." He leaned over me and practically spat the words in my face.

"I get it!" I said, noticing that his arm was still bandaged from the gunshot wound.

"If you're here to get fucked by the Cruz Missile, that's another thing."

"How unusual!" I said sarcastically. "I thought you were the bottom."

"What in the fuck is that supposed to mean?"

"Cut this macho shit with me. It doesn't play, big boy. I know you take it up the ass!"

"Rumors. Rumors. Every big star in Hollywood is the victim of shit like this. Even Sherry Kelly. I hear you are, in fact, muff-diving with Madonna."

"And Hillary. Barbra. Cher. Even Jane. It depends on which paper you read."

"Brad Cruz is the fucker. Not the fuckee."

"Is that so? Before we go farther with this charade, I have to let you in on a secret. You were taped taking it up the ass. A big ride from Cowboy Paglia."

He looked startled. Slowly he sat down on the sofa. "You slimy bitch! You god damn scumbag rich cunt from hell."

"I've been called worse. Do you want to see the film? Do you doubt I have it?"

"I don't doubt it for a minute. I know you have it, you cunt."

"It's all yours if you drop the suit. I'll call David Miller. He'll be here in about forty-five minutes with papers for you to sign."

"Does he know about the film?"

"I suspect he'll find out all about it. No doubt conduct private screenings at his firm for interested parties. You have a lot of fans out there. You might even get a featured spread in *Playgirl*. I understand you refused a centerfold for them."

"But I noticed you accepted *Playboy's* offer. Or was it *Penthouse*?

"It doesn't matter. If you don't agree to drop the suit, I'll go public. CNN would love to show it. Of course, they'll censor it like they did the Rob Lowe film but the public will interpret the action."

"You're bluffing, bitch. You won't do it. Dino is set to marry your mother. She'd disinherit you. You're trying to prevent me from getting some of your millions. Millions I deserve, incidentally. But if Mia Kelly disinherits you, who would be the big loser here? You think about that, cow."

"Mia is a woman of the world. All her lovers have engaged in gay sex. In her world, she just assumes that all men do that. In your case, I'm sure she's right."

"Men might do that. Getting shown on CNN is another matter. Like I said, I think you're bluffing. I don't think you'd do it. In trying to ruin me, you'd make her the laughing stock of America. I don't think you'd do that to dear mom. Humiliate the woman from whom you'll inherit a few billion." He got up from the sofa and walked over to my chair, his cock practically dangling before my mouth. "I think it's a risk you don't have the balls for. Unlike me." He reached down and shook his balls at me. "See these balls, dyke bitch. Those are Brad Cruz balls. They're ballsy enough to call Sherry Kelly's bluff. I want that settlement. I'm going to get it. All the threats, blackmail, and cajoling on your part aren't going to work. You're going to pay up, cunt. You almost killed me. You're going to pay for that."

"I'm warning you. I'm not going to sit here pleading with you. We rich pussies are too proud for that. Here's my final offer. You'll get all the millions you would have gotten if you'd appeared in 'Butterflies'. Withdraw the suit, and you'll also get the tape. I'll guarantee in a document that it will never be shown, and if it is, I'll agree in advance to a huge settlement. I think that's a fair offer considering that I was not responsible for putting the bullet in that gun. How about it?"

He looked at me with contempt, moving back a few steps. "You'd like that, wouldn't you? Arriving unannounced at this apartment with your dirty little film stashed somewhere with one of your faggots."

"How right you are. The faggot is Jerry Wheeler. He got to film you after all."

"The bastard! I'll see that he never works another day in Hollywood."

"You don't have that kind of power. I'll see that he keeps working for as long as he wants to."

You'd buy jobs for him?"

"I would."

"What about all the millions you've already invested in 'Butterflies'? What do you think this tape will do for Dino's career?"

"I think it will make him an overnight sensation. For God's sake, he's playing a hustler. His role will be type casting."

"If you show that god damn film, it could ruin me."

"That's because you've always played the all American boy. You're the Stars and Stripes. The Red, White, and Blue. You're the untainted hero. The Boy Next Door. This film will destroy that image. So that's why I know you're going to take my offer."

"I'm not going to take your offer and walk away from the millions I'm entitled to. I've always taken chances. This is one risk I'm going to take. I don't think you'll go through with it for reasons cited. Your coming here is just a feeble attempt to intimidate me. I don't intimidate easily. I didn't become the world's biggest star giving in to intimidation. I've been through this scene before."

"What are you talking about?"

"Early in my career. Little shits tried to pull this stunt with me. When I was sixteen, I posed for some stuff I wished I hadn't. I was fucking starving to death. That's something you rich pussies wouldn't understand. A sixteen-year-old with a big dick starving to get some rib-sticking food in his gut. They threatened to release the pictures to the media unless I gave them five-million bucks. At the time, I didn't have five-million bucks. I refused. I said no. Have you ever seen those pictures? I ask you. Have you ever seen those pictures?"

"Not that I recall. I'll have to ask Ted about them. He knows crap like that."

"He hasn't seen them either. I think they shipped them to one or two publications. Nobody, not even the *National Enquirer*, was interested. Fucking CNN might look at your silly tape, but they won't show it. Neither will any other station. If they do, I'll deny through my press agent that it's me. Do you know how many guys in America are dead-ringers for me? I'm a god damn type. A lot of good-looking guys in America look like me. Lucky bastards they are."

"So you refuse my offer?"

"The negotiation is over." With a violence, he wrapped the towel around his waist. The show of the Cruz genitalia had just ended. "See that door, bitch. Why don't you get your ass out of here?"

From the bedroom came the sound of a man's voice. "Brad! Brad! Where in the fuck are you? Is someone there?"

"Just the maid," he called back. "Giving us fresh towels."

"Get the fuck in here," the man called out. "I'm awake and raring for action again. It's sticking up all the way to the ceiling."

"Coming, baby, to claim my reward." He whispered to me.

"Now get out, bitch."

Grabbing my purse, I headed to the door. But he ran behind me and clutched my arm. "No, don't go. I have a surprise for you. A final lesson I'm going to teach you. You think he wanted your honeypot. We'll see. But when Brad Cruz offered his ass, the fucker came trotting to my door in heat."

"What in hell are you talking about?"

"Come with me, slut. I'll show you." He yanked my arm, practically pulling me to the doorway to the bedroom. He threw open the door.

There in the bed with the sheets tossed aside lay a Viking God, fully erect and demanding immediate attention.

It was Sean Nielson.

. . .

"Go ahead, bitch," Cruz said. "You know you want it. You've told everybody in Hollywood you want it. Go, girl, go!" He pushed me toward the bed.

I stumbled and practically fell on Sean.

"Oh, man, I'm so fucking hot!" he said, taking my head and guiding it to his groin.

Without caring or thinking what either man thought, I moved surely and swiftly. My eyes closed, I sucked in the taut-swollen apple-sized cockhead. My tongue flicked wantonly around the fiery red knob which emitted a clear fluid. Caressing, tickling, teasing, my lips slid along his rigid thickness. He was pushing me ever downward. Deeper and deeper was his penetration into my throat. Finally, he released me for air. I looked up at him. He seemed in the spasmodic bursts of an impending orgasm.

But ending it this way wasn't what the director of this film had in mind. Cruz yanked me off Sean and began ripping at my dress, tearing the front. I tried to wriggle free but with one lunge he tore the summery dress from me, unsnapping my bra. With his long deft fingers, Sean had already pulled down my panties and was fingering and exploring.

In rapid tempo I descended again, my lips compressing tightly around Sean's powerful shaft. My throat muscles bathed, squeezed, and caressed until I had the entire surface saliva slickened. His big, oval balls squirmed and moved as if denied attention too long. I lathered one, then the other.

With his big, strong Viking hands, Sean reached for my shoulders and gradually pulled me toward him. His tongue darted into my mouth, tasting his own juices. He licked these juices from my lips, then stuck his long tongue in my mouth, as if trying to penetrate my throat with it.

A sensation of great joy surged through my body, as my tongue savored the salty taste of him. I could feel his fingers exploring me once again. Then he was entering me, penetrating me to a depth that only Rafael had reached before.

Cruz's fingers were smearing me with fluid. He inserted a finger in my tight opening. I spread my legs and braced for his assault. When he entered me from the rear there was a moment of searing pain. I didn't think I could take it. He bit my neck. Real hard. I think he drew blood. That new pain served its purpose: it so distracted me that I seemed to open up to him and allow the total penetration of his lust-enflamed cock. His prick plunged and explored through the relaxed sphincter and anal canal. He was jabbing his way through the tight inner sphincter.

I was moaning. If the sound would come, I would have screamed.

"I'm gonna blow your brains out with my load, bitch," Cruz threatened as he continued to bite into my neck.

Sean said nothing. His tongue was too busy. He pounded into me with a ferocity. It was as if both men were fucking each other, their long pricks meeting somewhere within me. The sensation was unbearable. It couldn't go on. White heat like this didn't last.

Suddenly Sean gasped loudly. A moan, at first soft, then growing louder, gurgled up through his throat. He jammed the full length of his erupting prick into me. Gushing spurts of hot cum shot into me, and his tongue probed deeper into my mouth. He was in the delicious throes of orgasm, and so was I. I clung to him at the same moment I reared upward to take the long strokes of Cruz's cock which pounded with ever more forceful lunges. I buckled and quivered, ready to receive each thrust. My hips gyrated and pushed back to meet him. Equal force to equal force. I could feel him pumping me full with rapid-fire spurts. He buried the full length of his ejaculating prick into me. His loud moans and sobs became quiet sighs. He collapsed on top of me.

Somehow I managed to ease out of this sandwich. Rising on unsteady feet, I grabbed my panties and bra and headed for the bathroom. As I looked back Cruz was buried between Sean's legs, as Sean lay back on the bed reaching out to light a cigar. He seemed proud of himself.

Cruz raised his head only slightly. "Don't tell the world, and I don't know why, but what Brad Cruz likes more than anything else is to lick clean a dick after it's just emerged from a slimy pussy."

I shrugged and shut the bathroom door behind me. Thank God there was a phone there. I dialed the desk clerk. "Is there anyone on duty who'd like to make five-hundred bucks?"

"Try me, lady," he said. "I'm ever ready."

Suddenly, I realized he thought it was a solicitation for a fuck. "Not that. Some other time. Could you run over to that store across the street? Buy me a summer dress. Size eight and get it up here real quick. I've had an accident with my present one."

"I'm not into drag, and I've never bought dresses before, but for five-hundred dollars, I'll put it on my MasterCard."

"Fine. I need the dress right away. When you get here, I'll give you a thousand-dollar bill which should cover your cost and the cost of the dress."

"In that case I'll get something real cheap."

"Get anything! But get me that god damn dress."

I quickly headed for the shower that Cruz had only recently vacated. Perhaps I stayed a little longer than usual but I wanted a thorough cleansing as if it could erase all signs of any passionate lovemaking. I just hoped there weren't teeth marks on my neck.

After the shower I found a terrycloth robe and put it on. I put a towel around my head, looking rather like Lana Turner in the 40s.

When I came into the living room Sean was sprawled out nude on the sofa. Having cleaned the groin area, an also nude Cruz was now busy delivering the toe-sucking of a lifetime.

"Sherry," Sean said. "Come on in. I really enjoyed that.

Perhaps I should explain why I'm here."

"I think I understand why you're here."

"It's not what you think. When I heard you weren't going to let me replace Brad in 'Butterflies', I got real mad at you. When I was at my most furious, a call came in from Brad. I was really surprised. He's offered me a co-starring part in his upcoming movie. It was originally slated for Travolta. But he backed out. Wouldn't do the nude scene. Claims he's too fat. But I'm not afraid of the nude scene. I've got nothing to hide."

"I can see that."

"This part will make me a big star. Up there with the likes of you and Brad."

Cruz interrupted his toe-sucking to confront me. "Sean means up there with me. You're no fucking star! You never will be. A lot of people like you make one movie and are never heard from ever again. Not Brad Cruz. I have staying power. I'm true Hollywood royalty - not you."

"I'm sure you are, at least until tonight at six o'clock when CNN goes on the air. That will be the end of your career. Final chance to accept my offer."

"What in the fuck is she talking about?" Sean asked Cruz.

"She's bluffing," he said. "A feeble attempt to blackmail me."

"It's no bluff." I looked at Sean. "Better find yourself another co-star for your buddy movie. I doubt seriously if it'll be Brad Cruz."

"What does this mean?" Sean pulled his hulking body up on the sofa to take better notice of me. Unlike Cruz, he seemed to believe me except he didn't know what I was talking about.

The doorbell rang. I grabbed my purse, plucked out a thousand-dollar bill, and made for the door. The security guard was there but also the desk clerk. I nodded to the guard that everything was okay before handing the clerk the bill. I grabbed the box from him and raced toward the bathroom.

Without really noticing what I was putting on, I slipped on the dress. It was purple with large pink flowers. I quickly did my hair and tried to look as alluring as possible for my farewell.

Back in the living room, I put on dark sunglasses, hoping no one would recognize me in this dress. "It's been fun, boys."

Cruz had apparently grown tired of toes and was now

making a massive tongue assault on Sean's hole which was causing the actor to rise again like a skyscraper.

"Actors!" I said.

"Aren't we fun?" Sean called out to me, his legs up in the air.

"A blast." I opened the door, shutting it quickly behind me. I didn't want the security guard to see the action on the sofa. For all I knew, he might be a secret spy for the *National Enquirer*.

As I climbed into the back seat of my limousine, Ted screeched when he saw me. "Darling, that dress has got to go. I didn't know you were going shopping. If that's your taste, you'd better take Maxie along next time."

"Shut up. Let's get back to Star Island at once. I want to get out of this dress before someone spots me."

"What happened to the chic one you entered with?"

"Cruz liked it so much I let him wear it."

"You look a little rough for wear."

"My time with Cruz didn't go well. Do you have the film?"

"I can't wait to see it."

"Good, you've got it. Get David on the phone. It's about time we told him of our up-and-coming release. He won't like it but I'm determined. I'll threaten to fire him unless he cooperates."

"David will be pissed."

"I know, but Brad Cruz, Hollywood Royalty, is about to be dethroned."

CHAPTER TWELVE

With the ever-loving Rafael at my side, my caravan of limousines headed down the Florida Keys toward Palm Island. In the back seat of the limousine, I was ready and raring for action, with five telephones and three television sets. I hadn't slept all night, and I didn't think David would get much sleep the following night. He was completely opposed to my airing of the Cruz tape.

"Daughter of mine," he told me earlier. "I believe in playing hard ball, but this is a bit much. Don't do it!"

I'd pulled rank on him. I told him I was determined to go through with this regardless of his advice. There was just the slightest suggestion that if he didn't cooperate fully, many other law firms would be interested in taking over my representation. That had done the trick. He'd agreed to follow along wherever my schemes led me.

He could arrange virtually everything, and he'd be the perfect choice to deal with the networks. As if to compound matters, he was also against my meeting Clinton on Palm Island. "If you want to meet Clinton, or, more to the point, if he wants to meet you, do it at a big dinner and invite eighteen other guests. And never for one minute be alone in a room with him. You could end up on every front page of every newspaper in the world."

Good advice, I suppose, although I often ended up on the front page whether I liked it or not.

The first call came in from Jerry, and I had to be discreet about this one. Rafael didn't know that Cruz was about to make film history with his son. I had told Rafael, however, about Dino starring in a new TV series to be financed by me. David had arranged that even before eight this morning over the objections of the reluctant producers. What did they know? I knew more about stars and star quality than they did. I'd have to send them kicking and screaming into success.

"It's ready for the networks," Jerry informed me, "and is it ever hot! Makes me want to relaunch Chi-Chi Presents. I'm good at this porn stuff. Once this film hits the networks, the Cruz career is over. The networks will have to censor it. But they can show plenty. That Cruz is a real sword-swallower. I don't know how he does it."

"Experience," I said. "Years and years of experience."

"The film will be delivered to David's office at three o'clock this afternoon. He'll view it personally along with some key members of his firm. Unless you issue different orders, copies of the film will be released to all the major networks at six o'clock tonight."

"It's a deal. Now start thinking about that upcoming TV series."

"I am thinking about it. I'm thinking about 'Butterflies' too, but I'm also worried out of my mind. About every thirty seconds of every day, I'm thinking about AIDS. About dying."

"There's a lot of hope yet. We'll come up with something." Rafael was looking at me too suspiciously so I decided to put down the phone after thanking Jerry and giving him an affectionate goodbye.

As the image of Dino and Cruz making it flashed through my mind, I settled back into the comfort of the limousine as it sped to Palm Island. I wasn't worried that the sheriff would have us arrested for speeding.

I held Rafael's hand all the tighter. I don't think he fully realized what a dangerous game I was playing. David did, and had issued so many warnings his voice had gone dry. I knew that everything I was doing would cause some unknown forces to strike back at me. I didn't know when and how they'd hit. I didn't want to sound paranoid, but I knew they were coming to get me. Perhaps Clinton and I should meet after all. I had much to tell him.

As if reading my mind, a call came in from Ted, who for purposes of discretion had been stashed in a limousine trailing me. "Sherry," he said in that sweet, plaintive voice of his, "I've talked to Vince. After a few changes of plans, it's definitely on. Clinton can't wait. I don't know how he does it, but he'll slip away after his speech and fly secretly to join you. Vince will call again with exact details. You owe me one for this. Don't you remember your promise?"

"The football player. Another offer for David to make."

"Where do you plan to stash Rafael during all this excitement?" he asked pointedly.

"My overtaxed brain is working on that right this very moment. So far, I haven't a clue but somehow I always manage to come up with an idea."

"You'll have to get rid of the jealous stud, although why you'd trade in a dick like Rafael's for Clinton is beyond me. If only for a night."

"Some day I'll explain it to you."

"Turn on your TV in about two minutes if you want to hear Snake's press conference."

"I want to hear, but on the other hand I don't want to hear."

"Good luck." He rang off.

Rafael turned on the news program for me. A spiffily attired Snake, with a to-die-for coiffure from that Key West hairdresser, faced the news camera. True to his word, it was definitely a limited hangout. He reported few details of the murder, but included the forced entry of the rented villa on Key Largo. The motive, at least according to Snake, appeared to be robbery of rich Tokyo tourists.

Snake was very clever the way he manipulated the news people. He immediately tied in the murders of the Japanese tourists with it being another "bad day at Black Rock" for tourism in South Florida.

"This is an act of random violence," he told the reporters. "Yet I know every member of every foreign press will use it to attack our safety record here in South Florida."

He was carefully sending a message to the reporters as to how to play this story. It would be headlined as another threat to the tourism business. People who read papers in South Florida or watched the TV news were far more interested in their pocketbooks than in the murder of two Japanese "tourists," and Snake knew that. By focusing on how these murders might lead to thousands or even millions of dollars in lost revenue, he steered the spotlight from the actual murders themselves.

He left out a few details in this press conference, although it was just a matter of time before more juicy little bits leaked out. He revealed that the two traveling men from Tokyo had been stabbed, but specifically didn't mention decapitation and genital mutilation, although how long he could suppress those details remained to be seen. Obviously when the bodies were flown back to Tokyo, a bit of a fuss would be made about this.

Apparently, his grilling of Anishi had gone well. She was not mentioned as the holder of the lease on the house. Fortunately, her involvement with the murdered men and her connection with Mia hadn't been brought up either. At least for the moment. But I knew to stay tuned.

Also there apparently had been no connection made between the missing John and Henry and the murdered Japanese. Although flyers were circulating through Miami, John and Henry had been revealed only as two runaways. They'd not been identified as Japanese. From the flyer, they appeared to be two runaway boys, obviously from some rich family, presumably white, who was willing to put up one-million dollars for their safe return.

On TV Snake was bidding "so long" to the press. Its members no doubt would summon him back before the cameras when more details of this gruesome case became available. I hoped the hairdresser was available.

Even before he'd gone off the air, another call came in from Ted's limousine. "We bought some time with that press conference. I hate Snake but he can be strangely effective at times. Right now one of his deputies called. The flyer thing has paid off. The sheriff's office has been swamped with calls. Everybody in Miami wants that cool million. But he says one is strangely legitimate. He thinks it's from the guy who's actually holding the kids. We've got to move fast. Snake's heading right to Palm Island to work out the details with you."

This time I decided to let Rafael in on the details. No need to exclude the future president of Cuba from everything. "Snake thinks he's found John and Henry."

"Thank God. I hope you carry around a million in your purse."

"Call Snake back and tell him we'll be at Palm Island in minutes," I told Ted.

"The way he drives he'll beat us there," he said.

"Oh, the money. Call David and see where the nearest bank is. I mean, the nearest bank where he can get us one-million dollars. I mean, like now."

"Who do you think you're dealing with? Pigs? I've already

done that. It's in Tavernier."

"I know the place. I hope this is handled discreetly. I don't want the paparazzi shooting me removing a million bucks from a bank in Tavernier."

"The bank manager has been promised a generous commission for keeping this quiet. Your reputation has preceded you. David vaguely suggested to the manager that you had to pay off a trophy boy to keep him from causing trouble. The implication is that the boy might be a bit young, and his parents might make a fuss."

"How thrilling!"

"The manager claimed he was quite familiar with your record in this area, and would keep a tight lip. In fact, in his exact words, he said loose lips sink ships."

"How charmingly World War II." I put down the receiver, as the limousine was making its final descent to the boat-landing dock where we'd be taken to my own little private retreat, although Mia still insisted it belonged to her.

I leaned back and closed my eyes, gripping Rafael's hand tightly. I wanted to ride the rest of the way in silence. Somehow, I thought that going back to Palm Island would change my life forever.

. . .

"Howdy, Snake. Should I say hello down there to Snake Junior, too?"

The sheriff was waiting for me in the living room of my Palm Island home. "Both of us are doing just fine, ma'am. Just fine. We're both overworked with the demands made on us."

"I'm sure you are. That's what you both get for being so good at your job."

"You might put it that way."

"But of course, we're not here to discuss you or Snake Junior today, are we?"

"No, Pretty Woman, we're here to get back those boys, John and Henry, and I think I can do it."

"I think you can indeed, and I'm very proud of you."

"I don't sanction kidnappings in my little briar patch of Monroe County - except in the most extreme of circumstances."

"Like, give me a for instance."

"In case you ordered one for whatever reason you thought necessary at the moment."

"I see."

"I know you rich pussies are entitled to change your mind, and I was sure wondering if you are still up to giving that one-million reward."

"We've been in touch with my attorney and can pick up the money at a bank in Tavernier."

"That's a lot of money, ma'am. Since I had to take all those phone calls from every Spik in Miami, don't you think it would be fair if I get half a million of that for my efforts? That's more money than Snake Junior and I have ever seen."

"Not this time," I said, eying the gardens outside the windows which were really mine although Mia also claimed them.

"That comes as a great disappointment to me. I was hoping with the money to have some special condoms designed for me. Some that would actually fit - not the tight shit on the market today."

"In time, in time, my fine man. You'll get everything coming to you." I walked over to pour myself a strong vodka. While at the bar, I poured some bourbon over ice cubes and passed it over to him without really asking what he drank. From watching the movies, I knew all southern sheriffs drank bourbon.

Sitting down on the sofa in front of him, I let my dress deliberately ride high. Then I cast a soft smile, a sort of Marilyn Monroe come-hither look. "Would you say that we are up to date in our transactions? In other words, I don't owe you anything. You don't owe me anything."

"I'd reckon we're pretty even at this point."

"Fine. I wanted to clear the air on that, and I also want your complete cooperation with the presidential visit. Sorry I don't know the hour."

"Your faggot secretary has kept me abreast of all the developments. You can count on Snake here to keep everything hush-hush. Like I did at the press conference this morning. Did you catch it?"

"You looked terrific. But it's only a matter of time before

more news and more details leak out."

"We'll deal with it when it happens."

I pressed a button to summon Ted, who in minutes flounced into the room carrying a fax from David. As he spotted Snake, and the sheriff saw him, I braced myself for their encounter. Their dialogue with each other was always the same with small variations.

"Fairyboy," Snake said. "That's the brightest red color I've ever seen hair dyed. Why, it's so red, it's tangerine."

"It's not dyed. This is my natural color."

"There's nothing natural about you. I hear you're a regular bitch in heat."

"And I hear you have the biggest dick in Monroe County. Is that really true? So many men exaggerate. Why don't you whip it out so we can judge for ourselves?"

"Not on your life. You can see it in your dreams - that's all."

"That's the way I want to keep it," I interjected, taking the fax from Ted. "Please excuse us, love. Snake and I still have some negotiating to do."

Ted left the room as Snake whistled in mockery after him.

"Please, please," I said. "No sexual harassment of my staff."

I read the fax from David. "A million dollars in small unmarked bills is waiting at the bank," I told the sheriff.

After Snake had read the fax, he looked up at me with the suspicious eye that only a southern sheriff who'd seen it all could possess. "Everything looks in order here. You're not bullshitting."

"Thanks. Now how do we proceed? If you pull this off, there will be a reward."

"Considering the fees you pay, you can have Snake or..."

"Snake Junior," I said, filling in the rest of his sentence.

"You've got that right. Both are ready and rarin' to go."

"That's comforting."

He looked sad and didn't say anything for a long moment. Finally, he gazed over at me, as if he wanted forgiveness. "There's a problem here that I haven't been able to solve without messing you up in it." He hesitated as if fearing I was going to rain damnation on his head. "It involves putting you at a certain risk."

"Exactly what are you talking about?"

"The kidnapper claims he's got a gun pointed at the heads of John and Henry. He wants you personally - no one else - to show up with the ransom money. He then wants you to get into a car and drive with them to Miami. He will release you and the boys only when he thinks you're not being followed."

"This is a risk. He could kill all of us and still make off with the money."

"You're safe as long as you're in Monroe County. I'll see to that. But my authority ends at the Dade County line. Anything could happen to you up *there*."

"What a piece of shit this is."

"I know and I hope it's not going to lead to you firing me. But it was the best deal I could pull off. I'm dealing with a Spik fanatic."

"Have you told Anishi any of this?"

"Not a word. I don't want that Jap pussy to know any details until we pull this one off. After all, it was Yellow Tail herself who got us in all this deep do-do."

"Do you know where John and Henry are?"

"I don't but the Spik said he'd call the sheriff's office in about half an hour from now. Supply us with the point of contact."

"Rafael is not going to like this."

"My deputies could detain him."

"What do you mean?"

"Get him involved in some phony police work where we need his assistance. Make him feel really important. I don't know. We could come up with something to distract him. The question is, will you take this risk? The guy's a fanatic. I really believe he'll carry through on his threat."

"Then I'll do it. Set it up. Let's go for it."

. . .

Within the hour, Rafael assured me that he'd return some time after lunch. He explained that he'd been asked to perform a mission of such vital importance to law enforcement in Monroe County that only the sheriff knew the exact details, none of which he could share with me. At giving him a long, lingering wet kiss, I promised like a dutiful wife I'd be waiting for him to return. I lied.

Snake had made contact with the kidnapper holding John and Henry. He was still threatening to execute the boys immediately if his instructions weren't carefully followed. His final sign-off was, "Don't fuck with me." At least he spoke English, perhaps taught the language by Raphael in Cuba.

It was back to Key Largo again, but at a different address this time. Anishi wasn't the only one who could lease houses at Key Largo. The landlords there, I assumed, would also accept money from Martinez.

Snake allowed me to go part of the way in my air-conditioned limousine with a security guard and my always faithful Ted who was nearly hysterical. One mile before the house I was to visit, I had to bid him farewell and get into a plain black car that looked a bit rundown and mud splattered. Fortunately, I knew how to drive although I'd been chauffeured around most of my life.

Snake came over to the car and handed me a suitcase with one-million dollars in small unmarked bills. "I hate handing over so much money to a Spik kidnapper, Pretty Woman. But I guess that's how we're going to play the game. Good luck and don't take any chances!"

"Don't be an idiot! Don't take chances! What in the fuck do you think I'm doing driving to the home of some psycho! I'm certainly not doing this for that bitch Anishi. It's to save those boys. Their minds are already fucked up, but they deserve a chance at life."

"You're being mighty brave."

"Like hell. If anything, I'm scared to death. A hero I'm not."

"Don't worry. We've got the house staked out. It'll be completely surrounded by my deputies."

"That's comforting. I'll be inside with a psycho with a gun. A lot of good your men are going to be for me."

"It's all we can do playing by these rules." He leaned over to whisper something confidential. I smelled whisky on his breath. "I've got a much better plan."

"For God's sake, what is it? If it's a better plan, then why in hell are you risking my life with this dumbass scheme?"

"I say we storm the house. Guns blazing in all directions. We could break in on the fucker and fill the Spik full of Gringo lead before he has time to shit out his beans."

"He'd probably shit his pants all right - just after he'd blown off the heads of those two boys." I started the car, speeding off toward the house where I'd been directed.

Through my rear-view mirror, I saw him disappearing in the coral dust left by my spinning wheels.

I was on a mission I never thought I'd find myself on. Mia always told me that if you lived long enough, everything would happen to you. I was about to find out what she meant.

. . .

I stood in front of the door to a modest little bungalow house. For a moment I hesitated, wondering whether I should ring the doorbell or not. I didn't know protocol in matters such as this. It was certain I didn't need to announce my presence. From the moment I came down the road in clear view of the house, I knew my presence was seen.

The door opened suddenly and I was jerked inside. I could feel the butt of a gun pointed at my temple. "Shut up, puta, and do what you're told," came a voice heavily accented in Spanish.

If Rafael were the English teacher of this man, he didn't do a good job. His voice sounded like a bad imitation of Martinez.

"Did you bring the money?"

"All in small unmarked bills. One-million dollars and not a cent more."

He pressed the butt of the gun even harder in my temple. "You lie to me, bitch, and you're dead."

"I'm not lying. It's all there. I didn't count it but the bank assured me it's all there."

"Counterfeit. Maybe it's counterfeit."

"Bullshit. It came directly from the bank."

"I don't take your word for it. I count every Yankee dollar."

"That will take a bit of time." I nervously glanced around the tiny living room. "Where are the boys? I demand to see them."

"Your demands don't mean a god damn thing, puta bitch. A gun's at your fucking head. Who gives a shit about your demands?"

"Where are they?" My voice was growing more frantic by the minute. "I must see them!"

He threw the suitcase of money on the table in the middle of the living room, then half pulled, half shoved me toward a courtyard that separated two parts of the small house. In the center of the courtyard someone had crudely tried to build a fountain out of coral and rock. The fountain didn't work. It was like the house itself which looked strangely unoccupied.

"You want to see the mariposas?" It wasn't really a question. "I'll let you join them while I count the money. If the money's not here, and if it's not good dollars, the three of you will never leave this casa alive."

He removed a key from his pocket and opened the door to a utility room. I was pushed inside. The hot air was unbearable and there was only one small window letting in the fierce Florida sun. I heard the sound of the door being locked.

John and Henry ran to embrace me as if I, not Anishi, were their real mother.

Considering my tastes and proclivities, I have spent few moments of my wasted life in the arms of Japanese boys. With all the Italian stallions and Norse Gods roaming the earth, Austrian soldiers and British airmen, there was no need or desire for Japanese. Just as you get locked into a mind set, along come John and Henry. In spite of their names, which sounded like English monarchs to me, they were very Oriental, their skin a dusky yellow and not the olive or golden brown Asian skin sometimes is.

I'd only met the boys once, but you would not know that by the way they clung to me. It was as if I were offering them shelter from some dreadful storm, which I probably was.

"Are you okay?" I asked John when he finally let go of me. Henry still clung to the vine.

"We're afraid," John said. "But now that you're here, I'm not afraid."

Henry broke away and looked pleadingly into my eyes. "We had only Luis to look after us. Please, take us away from that one. He's very crude."

Fortunately for Henry, Luis was away counting money.

"He didn't harm you in any way, did he?" I asked. Among his many talents, Luis could be a child molester, for all I knew.

"He didn't hit us or beat us if that's what you mean," John said. "It's his tongue. He says terrible things to us. Mocks us. Makes fun of us."

"In terms of the world, my dears," I said, "it is Luis who could be ridiculed. A villain from a B movie. But let's not get into that just yet. More time later to deal with Luis."

"Luis did tell us what Anishi was planning," Henry said.

"Exactly what was that?" I asked.

"She wanted you to think we were kidnapped," Henry said. "She was going to get a lot of money out of you."

"That's right," John chimed in. "We were really thrilled you'd put up ransom money for us, and you don't even know us...*yet*."

"With the money, she was going to build a big house for us in a place free from earthquakes," John said.

"Earthquakes?" I asked. "Until now, I was unaware that earthquakes were a big problem in South Florida. But who knows for sure these days? I used to think New York was immune from earthquakes."

"In Japan once, we were in an earthquake," Henry said. "Our whole house just came tumbling in right on us."

"Why weren't you killed?"

"We were in a far corner of the house that just gently slipped away from the rest of the building," Henry said. "It was like a rail car wreck. We were in the only part of the house that was spared."

"We huddled with Anishi in the corner of that little room until they came for us," John said. "But that took hours. The three of us...we just huddled in that corner."

"Any minute we thought we were going to die," Henry said. "It was awful."

"Sounds that way to me. I've been in earthquakes in California. What fun!"

"Anishi vowed that if we ever got out of that old quake alive," John said, "she'd build us a fancy house one day to protect us. In a place far from quakes."

"How convenient," I said. "With my money."

John looked me right in the eye. Although the son of the world's greatest known liar, he looked as if he were telling me the truth. "We're very sorry that she planned this fake kidnapping."

"We are," Henry chimed in. "Very ashamed. We'd never do that to anyone. Certainly not to a nice lady like you."

I was only slightly bitter at the thought of her extortion. "One small correction. Don't ever use the word 'nice lady' to describe me. Maybe forty years from now. Almost no one ever calls me a nice lady."

"I think I know what you mean," Henry said. "Luis has another name for you."

"What's that? Or should I ask?"

"Puta."

"He must have heard that from someone. Thanks for telling me. I'll owe him one for that."

"I never know what 'owe him one' means in this country," John said. "Does that mean you'll actually pay him money for calling you a puta?"

"It means I'll get back at him." I gently patted John's cheek.

"Right now I'm not sure how to do that. This is no fake kidnapping. With Luis, it's the real thing. When he comes for us, watch my every move. My every facial expression. What I do with my hands. Everything. I might be trying to send you a signal. If there's any way I can overpower him and escape with you guys, I'll do it. Don't cry. But we're in real trouble. He's going to force us to drive with him to Miami. We're his protection. But since we don't know what he's going to do with us in Miami, we've got to try to overcome him before the end of the line."

"When can we go home?" Henry asked, clinging to me.

"There is no home to go to. I own half the mansions in the world, and I don't have a home to go to. Neither does Anishi. After all this blows over, we'll find a place for you on Palm Island. A place that's a real home. Far removed from quakes."

"You promise?" Henry asked. "I love Palm Island. We've been there."

"Were you all right on my little island? I mean, was it a happy time for you?"

"It's quite wonderful," John said. "Very romantic. Your Palm Island is nice. But Little Palm Island was even nicer."

His remark surprised me. I knew why I found Little Palm Island romantic - in fact, that's why I built a hideaway house there - but I didn't understand why John would find it romantic.

"We always wondered why you built the big Palm Island house for yourself as a retreat," Henry said, "then built a smaller version of the same house on Little Palm as a retreat from a retreat."

"Back in those days, I was one young lusty broad. I needed many places to hide. I reserved Little Palm for doing things I wouldn't feel safe doing on Big Palm. Besides, I could run around nude. A true Garden of Eden for whatever Adam happened to be romping with me at the moment."

"I can understand that," Henry said. "I agree with John. We've been caught up in the romantic mood of the place too. Just like you."

"Exactly what does that mean?"

"It means that Henry and I have gotten tired of waiting around to meet some girls. We don't meet any girls. Ever. We don't meet anybody. We got so tired of waiting, we decided to begin our sex lives without them."

"You mean, I can only assume, with each other? I've heard of such things."

"I bet you have!" John said with a smirk. His remark was a little too hip for my ears. He might not be the innocent child I'd suspected. I looked both boys in the eyes. "How's it going? Give me a report."

"It's going great!" Henry said. "I'm the bottom. A natural."

"I'm the top," John said.

"That much I could assume from what Henry said. Do you find it fulfilling?"

"The most satisfying thing in the world," Henry said. "We're only sorry we waited so long. I've always loved John. But now I know what loving him really means."

"I love Henry too," John said with slightly less conviction. "Luis caught us while we were going at it. I mean, I was really plowing butt..."

"Skip the details."

"Luis claimed what we were doing was disgusting," John said. "I told him it was an act of true love. He called us a lot of names. Mariposa. Shit like that. Said we were involved not only in incest, but in sexual perversion. Is that true? Do you find us disgusting?"

"It's incest, and no, I don't find you disgusting. I've never been accused of upholding family values in this country."

"Are you going to make us cut out what we're doing?" John asked.

"Not at all. Full steam ahead if that's what you want. But I suspect that this adventure will end one day when you go out in the world and meet other people. Naturally, you turn to each other. Who else have you ever known?"

"I think it's more than that," Henry said. "I want to spend the rest of my life with John. If he ever leaves me, especially for a girl, I'll kill him!"

That was followed by a long silence. A chill came over the hot air of the room. I felt Henry really meant that. I smiled awkwardly, first at Henry, then at John. "Perhaps there is more passion and commitment here than I ever realized. In that case, and when I'm thoroughly convinced, I will throw a Japanese wedding with all the trappings, on Palm Island. Right in the main house. Not on the secret island. I'll instruct Ted to set it up. He'll love it."

"We know that some people, especially that Luis, will think it's wrong for me to marry my brother," Henry said. "In my case, there's no other way."

Again, he said that with such power of conviction that it frightened me. It sounded like the beginning of a dangerous obsession. "If you're that committed, I guess not," I said, trying to sound matter-of-fact about the whole subject. A nervous laugh came out instead. "Considering how good-looking and sexy I am, I bet if I had a brother or sister, either one would be chasing and panting after me day and night."

"I bet they would," John said. "I've even had wet dreams about you myself."

"John!" Henry said like a stern housewife admonishing her husband for staying out drunk all night. "I thought I told you there would be no more talk like that."

"Okay," John said, looking sheepish. "Okay, that's the last time."

"And the last thought like that," Henry commanded, as if seeking an absolute guarantee over John's brain signals.

"And the last thought," John said, as if reluctantly giving in to these new terms in their relationship.

All that caused me to wonder who the real topman was.

"Will you let me wear a bridal dress?" Henry asked, turning to me and smiling, as he took my hand and gently caressed it. "White?"

"White as the snow on an alpine peak," I said, as a pang of regret over the loss of the Capetown Diamond swept over me. "I'll have it made just for you. With sequins, no less. Lots of lace."

"That's great!" Henry said.

"It'll be a wonderful wedding." Straightening up, I sighed. "Right now, boys, I've got business to attend to."

"What are we to do?" John asked.

"Figure out how to stay alive. Remember, watch my every move. We must seize every chance. With the combined brain trust of America and Japan, we can surely overcome Luis without getting killed doing it. He can't be that smart, even if he's the one with the gun."

"You won't let anything bad happen to us, will you," Henry asked. "Like it did to Anishi's friends from Tokyo?"

"I won't let anything bad happen." Even to my own ears, my promise sounded like an empty one.

"You know what Luis did to Anishi's friends?" John asked.

"I know, I know. Don't speak of it."

"Thanks a lot for coming for us," John said. "I really love you." He reached out and, to my surprise, kissed me right on the lips. Real hard. Henry preferred a light peck to my cheek instead of confronting the talented and succulent blood-red lips of the world's most notoriuos puta.

We heard the key turn. With his gun pointed at us, Luis threw open the door. "Come out, bitch. We're gonna have a little talk. Just you and me." He glared menacingly at John and Henry. "You mariposas are staying locked in the closet." With the gun still pointed at my head, he stepped back to let me pass. In a pretend move to brace myself, I gently unlocked the door, hoping he didn't see me. Holding the door, I looked back at John and Henry, signaling them frantically with my eyes. They could see the door was unlocked.

"Come on, puta!" Luis shouted at me. "I don't have all day."

I quickly slammed the door hoping he wouldn't check it. Then I stood in front of the door looking pleadingly at him. "We're better to you alive than dead," I said. "You asked for only one million. I would have easily gone for two million. One million on each head."

He'd forgotten the door, looking at me in astonishment. "That much for mariposas? Get into that living room, puta. We've got a lot to talk over before running from this house."

I could almost feel his greed as his excitement mounted. He didn't touch the door or even look back.

. . .

Luis shoved me into the living room where he virtually tossed me onto the sofa. "The Yankee dollars are all in that bag. Every single one of them. But now it's a new deal. I want that other million."

"That will be more complicated. I sat up on the tattered sofa adjusting my dress, which was very similar to the one I'd worn in 'Kinky.'"

Luis sat in a chair opposite me, pointing the gun at my head.

"I mean, we'll have to go to a bank. The bank will have to be notified. Shit like that. You just can't walk up to a teller and demand one-million dollars."

"I bet you could, cunt."

"We'll work it out. Another million dollars is nothing to me. I've spent that on dinner. Naturally, I had a few guests."

"You rich bitch! Fidel is right about you Kelly cunts."

I leaned seductively forward which gave him a great window for viewing two state-of-the-art breasts. "My main concern is that the boys and I get out of this mess alive. What assurance do I have that once you get the money, you won't kill us?"

"You've got no guarantee of nothing. You gotta take that chance. You ain't got no choice."

"Just what is your silly scheme?"

"As soon as we work things out, we're going to get into a car and drive north to Miami. If a cop tries to stop us, you're dead. A private plane is waiting for me at the Homestead airport. We're going to fly to an island in The Bahamas. It's an island controlled not by those idiots in Nassau but by our men.

We need it from time to time. Once we land and I'm safe, then I'll send you and the mariposas off in a boat. You'll be safe and I'll have the money. But I'm not going to no bank to get the fucking money."

"What do you propose? That I print it myself?"

"Don't you fuck with my mind, puta! A woman like you can get on the phone and call her secretary. The fucking secretary can get the money and deliver it here before I blast your fucking head off. If you don't know what I can do, you can ask the sheriff what happened to those Jap friends of Anishi. That yellow vaca."

"I know what happened to them. In fact, I actually saw how they ended up. Not a pretty sight. You don't have to pull any rough stuff to convince me what a bloody killer you are. I know you can kill."

"Then you'll listen to me and follow my orders?"

"Like in the army."

"Good. What about making that phone call? Will you do it?"

"Of course, I will. Give me the god damn phone."

"No monkey business. Monkey business and you're dead, bitch."

"No monkey business." I scooted over on the sofa and reached for the phone. Frantically, I dialed Ted who was in my limousine.

"Sherry," he screamed hysterically into the phone when hearing my voice. "We've heard nothing. We thought you were dead. Snake was about to have his men storm the house."

"For God's sake, don't let that happen! We'll be dead for sure."

"What's the matter? What can I do?"

"A big, big favor. Call David. Have him contact that bank in Tavernier. I need another million dollars. All in small unmarked bills. You are to pick up the money. Deliver it here. You got that?"

"But, I'm afraid. If I bring the money there, the guy inside might kill me too. I couldn't do it. I'd be so shaky I'd drop the money."

"Cut the shit! Grow some cajones. You can do it. I always thought you were more of a man than you pretended to be."

"You're right about that. Once a long time ago I was a top.

But only for one night."

"You've got to do this."

"Enough! Enough!" Luis was shouting at me and pointing the gun at my head.

"I've got to go. Get here as soon as you can. And make sure all the money is there. My friend Luis here likes to count every Yankee dollar. He loves the feel."

"Are we going to get out of this alive?"

"We truly are. Trust me." At another wave of that gun, I put down the phone and settled back on the sofa.

Even as I'd issued instructions to Ted, another scheme was forming in my fertile brain.

He lit a cigarette and blew smoke rings into the air.

"You wouldn't have another one of those cigarettes, would you?"

"I've got plenty. For that extra million, I guess I owe you a cigarette. No monkey business."

He lit it for me and got up, gun still pointed at me, and handed me the cigarette. After that, he seated himself across from me.

I smoked the cigarette like Bette Davis in "Dead Ringer." Leaning back, I sighed. "It's going to be a bit of a wait. You just don't get one-million dollars delivered in five minutes." Sprawled on my back, I crossed my legs. I deliberately hadn't worn panties. It was just like my scene in "Kinky". "Who's going to get all these millions?" I asked, knowing where his eyes were concentrating.

"I'm taking it all for myself. I'm also taking the risk of my life. Geraldo turned the boys over to me. His orders were to behead them and ship their heads in ice blocks to your home. I would have done it too until I got this call from my girlfriend in Miami. She'd seen your flyer. We decided to go for the money. Get the big Yankee dollars and flee the country. Run from Geraldo. After this double cross, he'd have us killed for sure. Not just killed. Geraldo never likes to just kill until he does some torture. Fidel always sent the most difficult prisoners to Geraldo. Even the most tight-lipped son of bitch talked when Geraldo got hold of him or her."

A chill went through my body and a vision of Tricia, but I still didn't shift my position. He didn't shift the focus of his attention either.

"God, I'm hot," I said. "In more ways than one."

"You are the puta Geraldo said you were. A real bitch in heat."

"Luis. Luis. Oh, Luis. You might be threatening to kill me, but you have the most succulent looking mouth I've ever seen on a man. I bet you have one satisfied girl friend."

"I can take care of women."

"I adore Cuban men as lovers. Dino Paglia. Rafael Navarro. Even Geraldo Martinez."

"He's fucked with you? The bastard!"

"He's fucked with me too."

"That asshole. You're getting me hot, bitch. I'm getting hard."

"God damn it. So am I. God I want you to fuck me. Stick it all the way in. I bet you're a real man. I bet you can take care of a woman better than Martinez ever could."

"I'm much bigger than him."

"You can still hold that damn gun on me, but at least take it out and play with it. I want to see it. Real hard."

"God damn you, bitch. You've got me so hot I feel like I could blast off." He unzipped his blue jeans and pulled out his respectable looking uncut cock already fully erect.

"Pull back the skin. I want to see the head."

Even though he held the gun - or rather both guns - he complied with my instructions.

"That's a beauty. So big. So thick." I started fingering myself, using both hands. I wanted him to see everything. "You've got to put that up in me."

"It's a trick. I know." He was shouting.

"If you won't put it up in me, and you know I'm dying for it, at least come over here and eat me. You can still point the gun at me while you eat me out. I've got to have a man. Right now."

"Okay, bitch, I'm coming over there. No monkey business. I'll eat your cunt but I'll have that gun pointed right at your belly. Monkey business and you're going to feel hot lead in your gut."

"Stop talking! Put that tongue to work. I need your tongue in me. All the way. Stuff it as far as you can. If you won't give me that big dick, give me your tongue."

On his knees in front of me, he devoured me like a man who hadn't eaten in weeks. "Oh, God!" I shouted as loud as I could. "You're the best ever. It's thrilling. When you finish, I want to suck that big Cuban dick of yours. Lick those cajones. I'm so hot I'd like to stick my wet pink tongue up that asshole of yours. Does your girlfriend do that? I would if you belonged to me?"

He was murmuring his approval but he was working his tongue so fast I couldn't really hear what he was saying.

I started moaning and groaning although Luis actually did nothing for me. It wasn't even a sex act to me. It was all play-acting.

Gently, ever so gently, John crept into the room. He was carrying a large stone from the fountain. I signaled him to move forward and very carefully encased my attacker's ears between my creamy white thighs.

As John stood only a foot from Luis, I suddenly wrapped both my legs around his head, virtually imprisoning him although knowing he'd think I was in the throes of orgasm.

The rock came down with such a thud I was sure John had killed Luis. He fell from me onto the floor, dropping his gun. John quickly retrieved it.

It was only then I spotted Henry at the door. "Quick," I called out to him. "Run out the door. Get help. The sheriff's men will see you."

He bolted to the door and ran out into the yard screaming for help.

I slowly got up off the sofa.

John stood over Luis with the gun. He wasn't moving. For all I knew he was dead.

Both of us were suddenly fascinated by his erection which was gradually retreating.

"What are you thinking?" I asked John.

"Damn it! I wish I had a dick that big. If I did, Henry would be walking bow-legged day and night."

. . .

Safe on Little Palm Island, John and Henry were having a

family reunion with Anishi. I'd instructed the household, especially John and Henry, not to tell Rafael of our most recent adventure. I knew he'd be furious with me for going ahead with the plan without him and not seeking his advice. No doubt he would have viewed himself as an expert on how to handle such matters. My instructions were to pretend that Snake had rescued John and Henry at a house where they were abandoned unharmed on Key Largo.

"That Snake is an amazing man," Rafael said. "With a guy like that in charge, I feel really safe in Monroe County. He won't let anything bad happen to us here."

"I'm sure you're right about that."

"All this police work I've been doing has made me horny." He indicated with his eyes to follow him to the bedroom.

Although my mind wasn't exactly in the mood for sex, I followed him reluctantly, anxious to get it over with. We were in bed for about an hour before he'd had his fill and rolled over. I eased out of the bed gently and headed for my bathroom, hoping to pull myself together to face further excitement this day.

I needed a few moments by myself to sort things out. Completely exhausted, I sat in front of my mirror repairing my face. Rafael had fallen asleep in the bedroom. A pattern had emerged with him. I noticed that before his late afternoon siesta, he liked to get very oral, so he could go to sleep with a satisfied smile on his lips. It was later in the evening that he went into heavier, commando tactics in bed.

Frankly, I was glad that he was asleep. I didn't want him to see the TV stations broadcasting the six o'clock news of his son fucking Cruz. I'd rather explain all that to him later. Even as I thought about this upcoming embarrassment, I realized I should have consulted him. After all, Dino was his son, and he had some rights in this matter. If nothing else, the future president of Cuba deserved that much respect. Although I hadn't told him yet, the thought of becoming First Lady of Cuba no longer thrilled me.

What I really wanted was to leave Hollywood in my dust and become Sherry Kelly again, the real one. A private person. Stashed away somewhere in one of my many mansions, away from the world and away from cameras and prying eyes. I had the money to ensure myself that kind of privacy, and that's what I wanted more than anything. I was just too tired of appearing on the front pages of sleazy tabloids around the world. How could Princess Di live with that day after day and not go completely crazy? I'd have to ask her sometime.

The taste of Rafael still with me, I thought I'd go and gargle. What darling Rafael didn't seem to realize when he got carried away was that a human mouth and a human throat could only expand so much. Once that maximum expansion was achieved, it was sheer torture after that. On the other hand, I decided I'd never let him in on that secret.

Just as I rose from my chaise longue to go to my beauty spa bathroom, Ted discreetly knocked on my door and entered, no doubt bearing news from Vince of yet another change in the President's plans.

"I know how excited all of us are about watching Dino's debut on the six o'clock news. But you have a guest in the meantime."

"Tell them to go away. You know I don't receive guests."

"I thought you'd like to see this one. What a doll!"

"Who is it?"

"The boy who posed with Dino in that Banana Republic ad we're all so crazy about."

"What a surprise."

"Dino has pulled off all his clothes and jumped into your pool. He'll be right up. But his friend, Angelo Carmona, is ready to see you now." He paused. "If you don't want this one, please toss him to me."

"Show the kid in. Tell him to wait in here. I'll be out in a minute."

Slut, harlot, Jezebel, and puta that I am, I could not have that gorgeous boy meet me looking as disheveled as I was now, *apres* blow-job. I certainly had no desire to pursue him, but I also knew that meeting Sherry Kelly was a memory he would carry in his brain forever, and would fondly remember on the day he died in 2065.

Wanting to make it good for him, I slipped into a shocking pink bikini and adorned myself daintily with a see-through lacy cover-up. I applied scarlet-red warpaint to my lips, reworked the eyes with just the right shading, and eventually transformed myself into the world's leading sex goddess. Not a bad job, and I didn't even need Maxie to help with the make-up. Just as I was preparing my descent upon Angelo, the phone rang. "Yes," I snapped.

Ted again. "Maxie's just got here. He'd like to have a drink with you."

"Fine. Stash him in one of those guest bedrooms by the poolhouse. You know that blond pool boy I hired from Key West."

"You might say I know him *very* well."

"Tell him to go give that old sod a massage. All of us will meet later over a family celebration dinner. A sort of Dan and Marilyn Quayle evening to celebrate family values."

"Sounds peachy." It seemed another call had come in. "David's on the phone. Line one."

I pressed the button to hear that familiar voice.

"Everything's ready to roll at six o'clock tonight. CNN, CBS, NBC, ABC, you name it."

"Good, that's just what I want."

"Are you sure? Are you absolutely sure? You know, these things have a way of backfiring."

"Full steam ahead."

"As your lawyer, I felt I had to protect you."

"What do you mean?"

"My agreement with the TV stations is this: I have retained the right to withdraw the tapes as late as 5:55pm Eastern Standard Time. After that, the networks say it will be too late to alter their programming. They're going on the air at six even if we change our minds at 5:59pm. I've established various hotlines with the networks. Ted will keep open a hotline to you. You can still change your mind - even as late as 5:54pm. If you're not on the phone by then, Cruz's career is history. God knows what Mia's reaction is going to be to this. Her future husband is involved in case you need to have your memory jostled."

"At this point, I feel very strongly about my commitment to destroy Cruz."

"Your call. I don't think I would have done it this way. But you're the client. You're also my daughter. I don't want you hurt from the fallout on this one."

"I understand." I paused. "Thanks..."

"For what?"

"For being here when I need you."

"I'll always be here for you. As we say down south, you're my blood. I love you, sweetheart."

"I love you too." I put down the phone.

With one last look for reassurance, I checked myself a final time in the mirror before throwing open the bathroom door and navigating my way through the rooms and corridors leading toward my upstairs living room. It was showtime.

Angelo jumped up from a wicker chair. "I'm dreaming."

Attired only in a pair of blue jeans and a simple white T-shirt, he bore an amazing resemblance to Dino, as if he were Dino's brother.

"Dreams sometimes come true," I said. Eerily, my introduction to Angelo evoked my first meeting with Rafael and his reaction to me. Maybe it was a Latin response.

"No woman on earth can look that gorgeous. I mean, I saw 'Kinky.' But this is the real thing...the real thing, man. And banks filled with lire she hasn't counted yet - I mean, the banks, not the lire."

"Angelo," I said, extending my hand. "I can see why your mamma mia named you that. You are indeed an angel. Botticelli would have liked to have painted you."

"Or do something to me, I'm sure. But even Leonardo would have given up trying to capture your eternal beauty."

"And even he would have needed the glow of dawn. Sounds like an old Nat King Cole song. I'm quite familiar with the portraits of Leonardo. I think he would have insisted I wear less makeup."

"Maybe, but you don't want to look plain-faced, now do you?"

"I couldn't possibly look like that." I motioned for him to sit down. I gracefully glided into a chair in front of him, crossing my legs so seductively that even Grable and Monroe, much less Dietrich, could never have captured so seductive a move.

"I recognized you at once. You're the boy in that Banana Republic ad."

"Man," he said, "I'm twenty-two."

"You don't look it."

"I'll drop trou if you want to see that I'm fully mature," he said, his hand moving provocatively to the fly of his tight jeans. "I don't have what Dino's got, but then, who does?"

"That won't be necessary. I'll take your word for it. Why have you appeared so mysteriously on my doorstep at a time like this?"

"I got a call from Dino. He wanted to set up housekeeping with me while Mia is at the spa."

"You obviously agreed."

"At first, I said no. I mean, Dino and I did that for a month or so with the girl in that Banana Republic ad. I think it's more his thing than mine. Frankly, I like to be with just one person at a time."

"I note you said person. Not man or woman."

"Oh, I don't discriminate about which sex it is."

"I thought so. At any rate, you accepted his offer."

"It was more than that. Dino held out the hope that you'd promote me for the part of Ricky in his new TV series. I'd do anything to get that part. I'd be great at it. If sleeping with Dino - or *whoever* - is part of the deal, that's cool."

I noticed that when he said "whoever," he looked enticingly in my direction. "You mean, if I want you for myself, the deal with Dino is off."

"I mean, if you want me, I'm ready to move in now. This very second, I'll take you to the bedroom over there and show you what I can do. I've gone to bed with older women before. A lot older than you. In fact, I'm attracted to older women - but only the gorgeous ones - more so than to anything else coming down the pike. Women say I make them feel good. Real good."

"Just like a kid again," I said, perhaps too sarcastically. "I'm sure you're good at your work. Right now, I'm not shopping for a boyfriend."

"Too bad. I was real disappointed when you called Dino after that Banana Republic ad came out. I wish you'd called me instead. But then I figured it was size you were after."

"Not at all. I just thought he looked cute. So do you. Both of you are about the cutest tricks in America. Even though I'm not demanding sack time with you, I'll definitely see that you get the part of Ricky in that series."

"Great!" he said, jumping up again as if he wanted to rape

me on the spot. "You don't even know if I can act."

"When a boy...man, is as cute as you are, they don't have to act."

"Do you think the director will agree?"

"Jerry Wheeler? My dear child, when Sherry tells Jerry you've got the part, it's no more questions asked. In your case, the director will adore you. But no sex with him without condoms. Promise?"

"I promise. Sounds like he already has AIDS."

Although I remained seated, he moved closer to me, his fly dangerously close to my face. "Take a look," he said. "There's definitely expansion going on down there."

With my trained eye, I glanced briefly at his jeans. He was right.

"Our deal's concluded. I got the part. But there's something else I need, and I need it real bad. I've got to have some relief. Not with anyone. It's got to be you. I don't want to have to force you, but I can't stand here and keep myself under control any longer. Don't put up a fight. Just give in and enjoy it. We'll both have the hottest time of our lives. I got technique, man."

His fingers went for his fly, this time for real. Perhaps my reputation had preceded me. Who knows what Dino had told him. At the sound of a light tap on the door, he jolted back, half unzipped.

Ted entered with a naked Dino toweling himself dry.

I leaned back in the chaise longue as Angelo retreated. I felt it was time to call my kindergarten class together in time to watch the early evening news at six.

Angelo took no notice of the nude Dino. His undraped body held no mystery for Angelo, as it was a sight I'm sure he'd seen many times before. Too many times. If anything, he seemed bored with Dino and was itching to chase after bigger game. Namely, moi. At least I applauded his good taste. In many ways, Angelo was more mature than Dino, certainly a whole lot smarter.

When I quickly grew tired of the flashing, I addressed Dino in a softly modulated voice. "All of us in this room are familiar with the sight of a naked male body. All of us have seen and fondled human genitalia in our time. But now that the exhibition is over, perhaps we could put on a minimum of clothing. A pair of skimpy shorts, at least."

"Oh, mama," Dino said, "you're such a prude."

I, star of the controversial "Kinky", gave him the bird.

While checking out Dino's merchandise for one last appreciative glance, Ted reluctantly handed him a towel.

"Here I am about to appear nude on TV screens across the world," Dino said. "All at your suggestion, and you insist that I walk around this beach house on some almost-deserted private island you own and wear clothing too. Figure that."

"Exactly. And that's why I became rich and famous."

Angelo and Dino looked at me in almost the same state of bewilderment. Had they heard right? I smiled enigmatically, like La Giaconda now safely ensconced in Austria, not in Paris. My young guests wanted to be rich and famous, and they also desperately wanted to understand exactly what I had meant by my remark. I chose not to divulge any more secrets. The stark truth was that I was born rich and famous. These children could only aspire to my status. Actually, I'd long ago determined I was a dying breed. With my passing, some fifty-five years from now, no one would ever again attain the vast wealth of the Kelly family. How could they in these times?

With Dino clad in a pair of shorts and a horny Angelo still seeking sexual relief, I took each of them by the hand and directed them to my living room where Ted had arranged first-class seats for us in front of a giant TV screen.

After all, I was the producer of tonight's news, regardless of the channel. I noted that he'd installed a desk with a phone, the hotline to David, in case I still wanted to withdraw the film from the air at the last minute. After Ted spoke to someone on the phone, he placed the receiver off the hook, letting it rest on the desk. I glanced at the nearest clock. It was now 5:47pm. My option for withdrawing the tape was about to run out, and I was fiercely determined to go through with it.

Draped in a giant beach towel, which they shared, Angelo and Dino occupied a wicker love seat. They were obviously playing doctor under that towel.

Ted rushed about, hysterically adjusting TV sets. I decided to watch CNN on the largest of the TV screens, although Ted had turned on the other major networks on satellite TVs he'd brought into the room.

He murmured something into the phone on David's end of the line and turned to me. "You have just sixty seconds to cancel. Otherwise, all networks are ready to roll."

I remained stonily silent. He knew what that meant. No one else in the room was aware of my option, and no one asked for clarification. Dino and Angelo seemed engaged in some sort of mutual masturbation, which was probably not a bad practice in these horrible black plague days of AIDS. I decided to call the surgeon-general tomorrow and have her recommend it to America's youth.

After what seemed like an hour, but was only a matter of seconds, Ted said, "Run it," to whomever was on the other end of the line.

The time was now 5:55pm. I was growing edgy. The children around me seemed to view the events about to unfold as part of a day's work. It actually was providing sexual excitement for them. I've found that models live in a world entirely their own, and I didn't want to invade that murky head space.

It was amazing to me how casually Dino was treating this incident which surely would change his life, although in what way I wasn't exactly sure. I was overcome with a sudden panic, fearing I couldn't go through with this. I had to cancel the program.

When not overseeing the action under the beach towel Ted glanced at me. With his eyes he signaled it was too late.

Suddenly, a fiery ball of flaming fuschia, with red high heels and scarlet hosiery, stood in front of me. It was Mia in a rage. Like a vindictive goddess, she'd emerged seemingly from out of nowhere.

I looked at her, then my eyes darted to the TV screen.

May Day.

CHAPTER THIRTEEN

"What in the hell is this?" Mia screeched, one hand placed aggressively on the hip of her well-publicized figure. "A fucking TV showroom?"

"Mommie, dearest," I cried out to her, fearing what was about to be flashed across the television screens of America. "This is not the best moment for you to arrive unannounced at my house."

"The last time I checked Jack's will, flasher, this was my own little island, right down to the last coconut falling from the last blighted palm. I'm ordering you and your sick nut crew off the island at once before I'm forced to call Snake."

"It's my house, bitch. I have the deed. Everybody in this room is staying until ordered off by me." My voice, usually a sex-kitten Marilyn purr, sounded like an angry fishwife, even to my own ears.

Mia with growing irritation glanced at all the television screens. "What in hell is so exciting? Clinton and Hillary in a double assassination? Your entourage is usually too busy fucking each other - in various combinations - to watch TV." Ignoring me, she spotted Dino. "My darling lover boy. Where in hell have you been swinging it? Not in my direction, I can assure you. Why are you hiding on the sofa there under that towel and not rushing to give your mama a big wet one, you adorable child you." Moving to a position in front of the sofa she yanked the cover from him. Not only did she expose her nude lover but also Angelo fully erect. "What the fuck?" She looked as if she'd died, been suddenly reborn, and was trying to stand on new and wobbly legs, much like a colt. She studied Angelo carefully. "A Scotch!" she cried out to no one in particular. "My kingdom for a Scotch. Straight. A triple."

Although she'd commanded the drink from no one in particular, Angelo after zipping up was by her side in just moments with the Scotch. Forget Tom Cruise in that movie about cocktails. Angelo would have made the greatest bartender of all time. That child was one speedy stud. I hope not in all departments, however.

Without looking at him, she took the drink offered and belted down a hearty gulp, as if she desperately needed the booze to fortify her. For the first time, she gazed into his face. She was so used to being offered drinks by the Ted Hookers of the world that a young man like Angelo seemed to have taken her by surprise, as did everything she'd encountered in the past minute.

"Mama, I can explain," Dino said, rushing toward her, with a towel loosely draped around his nudity.

She brushed him aside as she stared intently into the face of Angelo. "This creature before me happens to be the second most beautiful human being inhabiting the planet. Except for moi, of course. But then, I'm legendary."

"I'm Angelo."

"You are indeed, my darling. An angel descended from stud heaven." Her eyes went from his big feet all the way up to his hairline. "You are a big boy. That must be a size thirteen shoe you're wearing, if you call the things you kids wear today shoes. You're not Cuban, are you?"

"No, Italian. People who get to know me call me 'The Italian Stallion'."

"Good," she said, casting a disdainful eye at Dino. "As dear Dino knows, I can't stand Spiks."

Ted deliberately turned up the sound on the TV. It was CNN. "We interrupt this program to bring you a special bulletin from Miami. The subject of this news broadcast is deemed unsuitable for children. In an unprecedented move for CNN, we will hold the announcement for one minute so that parents who wish to hear the news can remove their children from the room."

That made me immediately think of all the children around American watching TV without their parents.

In disbelief, Mia looked at the announcer. All the while, I sat nervously on the sofa, my back stiffly arched as if I might take flight from all of this at any minute.

"CNN - I just know it - is going pornographic," Mia said. "It was bound to happen." She turned toward me, her face accusatory. "Flasher, are you in the news again? Whatever is going to be broadcast on that blasted channel - whatever it is that is making parents across the land usher their kids from the room - you are behind it. I just know it. Parental discretion is advised every time the camera is turned on you."

"That's not true and you know it."

CNN had certainly captured the attention of America with its announcement. Of that I was certain. Phones were probably buzzing from here to Nome, as friends called friends to tune in.

A world-class drinker, Mia once drank Sinatra under the table. She told me she'd regretted that because later he couldn't get it up in spite of all her time-tested techniques for arousal. She appraised Angelo once again. He stood within inches of her, and she made no motion to shoo him away. He wasn't the kind of boy you shooed away. Even a straight man would want to plow into a bubble-butt like that. If a straight woman met him, the world was hers.

Dino, in spite of his discomfort, had no intention of leaving the room and missing his film debut upon the world's screens. I was certain that he'd even worn body makeup for the scene, probably smearing Cruz with it.

The announcement began: "Brad Cruz has been called the greatest of all American movie stars and the only actor left in Hollywood that is certifiably straight. Now after viewing this film, there is reasonable doubt about the straight credentials of Brad Cruz, who over the years has played some of the straightest arrows ever shot out of Hollywood. In this heavily censored film clip you are about to see, Brad Cruz plays out a scene with Dino Paglia, the underage future husband-to-be of Mia Kelly, the world's richest woman. Mr. Paglia was a former boy friend of Ms. Kelly's daughter, Sherry, who recently turned screen actress in the film, 'Kinky'."

Even I, who'd seen a porno flick or two in my time, felt a pang of embarrassment watching Cruz and Dino on TV. The censors had been effective, but the action was unmistakable. In one clip, Cruz was clearly demonstrating his circus ability as a sword swallower. In the clip that followed, he was writhing in ecstasy as he took those long, thick, penetrating inches up the butt. I could empathize with Cruz. I knew what they felt like. Dino photographed beautifully. A quick look in his direction confirmed that he liked his appearance on the screen, in spite of the various acts he was performing, which to some of America, would appear perverted. In contrast to Dino, Cruz was merely grotesque.

No one, especially Mia, said anything. I glanced at the other TV sets. ABC had switched from Clinton's boring speech to the pornographic video. So had CBS and NBC. All channels were showing Jerry's masterpiece. Except each channel had begun the clip at a different time. That meant that various stages of the act of seduction were being flashed across the screens.

I looked into Mia's face. At first it revealed complete bewilderment. That look shifted rapidly to an agonized acceptance. The face seemed to say that if you lived long enough you'd get to see everything. Surely that day had arrived for her, as she watched her boy friend - now quite obviously her former boy friend - flashed across the television screens of the land. Surely, the BBC would greet morning audiences in London with some version of this clip over their morning cuppa.

Having shown the film, all channels broke for a spin on the news. Various commentators came on the air. No one in our room - not even Mia and certainly not Dino - had found anything to say yet. However, Jerry Falwell was on CNN denouncing Cruz as a pervert and announcing that he - "like all decent moral-majority Americans" - was calling for a boycott of his films.

The biggest trooper of all of us, Mia herself - mourner at the grave of thousands of friends and lovers - was the first to rally herself. She looked at me, and that glance said it all. Somehow she knew I must be responsible for the events flashed across the TV screen. No words were exchanged now. I knew that would come later.

She bolted down the rest of that drink Angelo had offered and threw the crystal across the living room, sending it crashing against the wall in a hundred pieces. The goblet had belonged to Madame du Barry. "I think I'll go to my room," she said to no one in particular.

The ever-eager Angelo responded as if the invitation had been directed at him. It wasn't specifically an invitation, but "go to my room" meant only one thing to him. "I'll help you, Ms. Kelly."

"My sweet angel," she said, "I think I'll need your help." She glanced with disdain at Dino, as if discarding a rotten piece of meat from her platter.

He looked dumbfounded. It must not have been easy for him just to stand here and watch a multi-billionaire mama walk off with his best friend, now obviously former best friend.

Angelo took her by the arm and directed her toward the hallway. Before leaving the room, she turned and looked back. "I'll have talks with all of you later, especially you, flasher. As for you Dino, why don't you put on your clothes for a change and get the fuck out of this house?" Supported by Angelo, she left the room.

Swaddled in his towel, Dino came toward me. I wasn't seeing clearly at this point. It was to be some sort of confrontation, I feared. But I wasn't ready for it.

His showdown with me was suddenly interrupted by the appearance of Rafael in jockey shorts at the top of the steps.

"Sherry," he yelled down at me. "God damn you. I know you're behind this. I've seen it on TV. I've had it with you. With America. With this whole shitty mess." As if seeing Dino for the first time, he looked at him as if he wanted to kick his butt. "Be Dino Paglia. Don't worry about anyone thinking you're Cuban. You won't have to deny me as your papa. I deny you as my son."

"Papa," Dino yelled. "I didn't want to do it. Sherry made me do it."

Rafael wasn't having any of either of us - not me and certainly not his turncoat, lying hustler son.

"Get away from me, Dino," I shouted, brushing him aside. "Go on. Be a big TV star. But get out of my way." I raced toward the stairs, no longer hearing or even caring what the TV commentators were saying. I'd had enough TV for life.

For the first time, I realized how much I was in love with Rafael. I couldn't let him leave me. I'd hold onto him at all costs - even if it meant calling the security guards to detain him at the gate. I rushed down the hallway toward my bedroom. No, *our* bedroom. It was our bedroom now, and I wasn't going to let him leave it ever.

Rushing to our bedroom, I threw open the door just as he was slipping into a pair of jeans. I stared into his eyes, and they told me what I most feared. He was definitely going to leave me, and nothing I could say or do would stop him. Not even the security guards at the gate. This Cuban guerilla fighter would be more than a match for any security guards I might use to detain him.

When I'd rushed to the room, I thought this was going to be some angry confrontation scene, perhaps on the level of E. Taylor battling R. Burton on and off the screen in such locales as Gstaad or in such films as 'Who's Afraid of Virginia Woolf?' But seeing him in all his hurt, pain, and vulnerability convinced me this was going to be no fiery blast. "I love you," I said to him in a voice so alluring it was guaranteed for male meltdown.

Instead of rushing to my arms, he resisted. "You don't love me. You don't love anybody. Nothing. Just your own reflection in the mirror. You've been told this before, but it's still true. You're self-enchanted."

"That's not true. I reached out. I care for others. I love you."

"I too am part of your reflection in that mirror. A handsome stud with a well-stuffed crotch. A trophy. Bigger and better than his son. But then, aren't you always pursuing something bigger and better?"

"I've never viewed you as a trophy."

"That's how you view all men. In that regard, you're just a pale reflection of Mia. From what I've read in one of those biographies, she went for the really big game. Men like John F. Kennedy. You couldn't have him - a little before your time - so you bagged John F. Kennedy Jr. instead. Besides, your mama had already beaten you out in the Kennedy Sr. sweepstakes."

"You've been reading that pulp crap written about Mommie and me. There's not a word of truth to it. They make up all that shit."

"Do they?"

"Of course."

"Did Mia have an affair with Kennedy?"

"Over a period of years."

"Did you have an affair with John F. Kennedy, Jr.?"

"A very brief fling."

"Then it's true."

"That one tiny bit of it might have some truth in it. But those books have pictured me having affairs with just about everybody: Madonna, Tom Cruise, Mel Gibson, Kevin Costner, Arnold Schwarzenegger, Sylvester Stallone, Richard Gere, even granddads, Paul Newman and Robert Redford. Can you imagine? For one thing, all the people on that list, including Madonna, have small dicks, with one exception, and he doesn't go for me at all."

"Isn't getting the big one part of your trophy gathering?"

"It used to be. Not when I met you. I'd love you even if you weren't hung like a horse."

"I doubt that."

"It's true. I really love you."

"You don't know the meaning of the word. I loved my wife - that was real love. I never loved my son. He was my Desi but I never got to know him. He's become somebody I don't understand or relate to. I thought I loved you, but I'm not really sure."

"You do love me. When we go to bed at night, you tell me so in a thousand ways."

"That's lust. That's passion. That's not love. At night, I can control and dominate you. During the day, you treat me like one of your maricones. Ordering me to get a drink. To get someone on the phone. I'm a proud man. You can't make me one of the little boys flitting about your various mansions. I thought I told you this."

"I never meant to."

"With all your billions, with all your power, you're so used to commanding people to do your bidding, you don't even know you're doing it. It was the way you were born."

"I've had so much on my mind lately. I don't know what I'm doing half the time."

"You'll never change. You'll grow old, counting all those billions. The studs will come and go. They'll get younger. Take Mia, for instance. She used to sleep with big and powerful men until she became too old for them. Today at her age, she's sleeping with Desi. She could be his grandmother, but has taken him as a lover instead. At least until that TV broadcast. That's probably the end of that affair."

"I should have involved you in my plot with Dino. I know I should have. I should have asked your permission."

"I would never grant permission for my son to do something like that on TV. I want to be president of Cuba. If the Cubans find out Desi is my son, it would ruin my chances of ever becoming president. I'd be disgraced. Cuba is a very macho society."

"Is that what you're thinking about? Your presidential ambitions?"

"It does cross my mind from time to time. I'm not blaming you for corrupting the kid's morals. I think he never had any morals. He doesn't take after me. He'd fuck anything if it served his purpose."

"Wouldn't you?" My words stabbed the air. Suddenly, I felt like Martha in 'Who's Afraid of Virginia Woolf'? Her character was beginning to stir within me. I was becoming the screeching harridan I so dreaded. "Haven't you been using me as a meal ticket? Didn't you want me to finance your stupid presidential ambitions? Isn't that what it was all about?"

"No, baby," he said, turning on me with Latin fury. "I don't need you or your money." He groped himself. "I've got cojones, woman. I'm a man and I can go out and get what I want in life without the help of a woman. Without her money. Wait and see. Some day, I'll invite you to the presidential palace in Havana. You're looking at Castro's replacement. You're also looking at a man who's got hopes and dreams. I'm going to hit the streets of Miami and start making those dreams come true."

"I wish you luck."

"I'll need luck and a lot more."

"Goodbye," I said, fighting back tears. "I wish you a long and happy life."

"I wish the same for you, too." He turned his back to me and began packing to leave.

I didn't want to see that. Too much had happened in the past half hour, and I felt dizzy. I headed for the next room since I didn't want to hear him slamming the door as he left.

. . .

Lying in bed, too weak to get up, I felt numb all over. It was as if some dentist had injected novocaine throughout all parts of my body. As I lay prone, Rafael was leaving the island right now. I was doing nothing to stop him, and I could hardly believe that a control freak like me would respond like that. Did

I secretly want him out of my life? Was he too much man for me? Did I actually desire a man I could manipulate and who, like all the boyfriends before him, would be only too willing to do my bidding? I knew none of the answers to those questions, and was pissed off at my brain for asking them.

Where would I find him again? He was heading for Miami - that's all I knew. I breathed a sigh of relief. My handsome Cuban pilot was still facing charges of air piracy from the Federal Government. He'd have to make an appearance in court at some time, perhaps not represented by David any more, but by some Cuban lawyer. I'd have David find out about that appearance. The moment Rafael showed up in court, I'd swoop down like a giant bird of prey from the sky, rescuing not only him, but getting him freed of those ridiculous air piracy charges.

I sat up in bed. A plan was evolving in my ever fruitful brain. I'd work a deal with Clinton. Surely he wanted something from me other than the obvious. I'd agree to fund his re-election campaign in 1996. If his womanizing ever got him into trouble with some trailer park bimbo, I'd secretly pay his legal fees, which could run into millions.

Hillary and Bill, or so David told me, were poor and practically homeless on the streets of Little Rock. They didn't even own a house. David also told me that as governor of Arkansas, Clinton earned about $35,000 a year - or some such obscene figure. That was the cost of one of my gowns. I'd never been to Arkansas, but I decided it must be one poor state if that was all it could pay its governor a year. Actually, to tell the truth, I wasn't sure where Arkansas really was. Was it the south? The Middle West? Actually, I didn't care. Although I've traveled the world, America, to me, consists of Florida, New York, and California. I never felt a compelling reason to go anywhere else.

I did, however, end up one night in a backwater in Kentucky. I wasn't exactly sure how I got there, or what my companion's name was. When I woke up the next morning in some dreary motel room, I demanded to know where I was. I'd never spent a night in a motel before. I think it was called Day's Inn or some such shit.

Although my companion looked like a horse at least in one

department, this horse breeder didn't appear all that enticing in the morning sun. He needed, among other things, massive dental work. When I learned I was in Kentucky, I nearly screamed. Sherry Kelly in Kentucky! If the locals found out, I feared they would lynch me. Dropping two-thousand dollars on our shared double bed, I decided to abandon any of my clothing and other possessions I wasn't already wearing. I fled to the reception desk. Here, I encountered a snaggle-toothed hag who told me I owed her twenty-six dollars for the night. Imagine! Can you believe there are still places in modern America that charge only twenty-six dollars for a double room for the night? I tip the doormen who call me a limousine one-hundred dollars. I tossed five-hundred dollars at the bitch and told her to keep the change. I demanded a taxi at once. This hillbilly (they do have hills in Kentucky, don't they?) informed me that they didn't have a taxi service in this hellhole. Eying the five-hundred dollar bill, she said her husband would drive me to the nearest airport forty miles away. "For a tip," she added.

Husband was asleep in the adjoining room where they apparently lived. It took massive persuasion and threats of death and penile mutilation on her part, but the Kentucky cow finally aroused her derelict husband. He was no bull. He looked like one of those rapists from the film "Deliverance". Remember Burt Reynolds of the even-if-he-gets-it-up, who-can-find-it school?

Smelling of horse shit, her lunatic husband hauled me away from that motel in a mud-spattered pickup truck with a bad muffler and two monstrous dogs into deep French-kissing. After paying off this Kentucky swine, I arrived at the airport and chartered their most expensive plane to fly me to Miami.

The day wasn't a total disaster. Unlike the retard who'd driven me here, the pilot looked like some gay guy's fantasy of a blond stud. He not only flew me to Miami and civilization again (if you can call anything in Miami civilization), but he even accepted my offer to "come fly with me."

After the day spent with him, certain parts of my body felt like Hiroshima after the bomb fell from *Enola Gay*. I wonder if being around all those horses in Kentucky inspired the men there.

Those thoughts aside, I got up and walked over to the glass doors leading to the balcony. Opening them, I stepped out on the terrace to breathe the air. I couldn't believe my own mind. My lover had just walked out on me. I was scheduled to entertain the president of the United States, and I had no idea what creditable conspiracy theory I could mount to convince him the Republic was in peril. What was I doing? Thinking about one stupid night spent in a state no one's ever heard of.

The persistent ringing of the phone by my bed interrupted me. Normally, I don't answer phones, but this was the inner house hot line. That meant big trouble.

Or maybe no trouble at all, but good news. Thinking it might be Rafael calling from the front gate, I rushed over to pick up the receiver. "Yes."

"That you?" It was Mia's distinctive voice.

One word from me and she knew perfectly well who it was. My voice is far more famous than hers. "What is it?" I said coolly, fearing anything she might have to say to me. I was going to deny any involvement - regardless of how remote - in that film clip.

"I thought I should catch you up on the news here at my Palm Island retreat," she said with a bit of unconcealed glee in her voice.

"What news?" Haven't we had enough damn news for one day?

"Dino has left my room only ten minutes ago. I had Ted go to the safe and give him ten-thousand dollars to stay away from me for the rest of my life. Imagine? Ten-thousand dollars. That's the cheapest I ever bought anyone off before. He said you'd promised to make him a big TV star, and I could take all my billions and shove it. Sweet child. He claimed he'd be making so many millions he didn't need any of mine. What a relief."

"What about Angelo?" I asked, not really caring.

"Darling Angelo is right here in my boudoir right this minute. Massaging my feet. It feels so relaxing to have such manly hands on me. The child really knows how to give a good massage. You haven't had him before me, have you, bitch?"

"I just met him."

"Good. I'd like to try someone you haven't already sampled.

The dear child has even taken off his shirt so I can admire his physique. That physique is definitely made for silk pajamas, or perhaps no pajamas at all."

"Enjoy."

A loud crash sounded in the background. She screamed before she dropped the phone. Angelo yelled something. A struggle was going on. I shouted into the phone, but no one answered. Suddenly, the line went dead.

I ran from my bedroom and down the stairs where we'd watched TV. All the sets were dead. The living room was strangely silent. I imagined I heard a sea gull outside the window.

A movement in back of me caught my attention. As I whirled around, I stared into the face of Martinez. He had a gun, and it was pointed right at my heart.

. . .

"I'm the one with the weapon now, puta cunt," Martinez said. "Before this day ends, you're going to wish you were dead. Before this day ends, you will most likely be dead."

"Then shoot me now." I stood defiantly before him. "Get it over with."

"You'd like that, wouldn't you?" he taunted me. "It won't be that easy for you. Ever since you castrated me, I've thought about nothing else but our meeting again. I have fun and games planned for you that will make your mind explode. Just like my mind blew up in my head when you cut off my dick."

I closed my eyes briefly and prayed that my Rafael would suddenly appear and rescue me from this nightmare.

"Do you know what a man feels like when he loses his dick?" he asked, the question not necessarily directed at me, but at the air around him. "You wouldn't know that, would you? Women don't have dicks, so they can't know. Later, I'll cut off your nipples, or maybe slice each of your nice big breasts off your body completely. I'll also do surgery on that pussy of yours. But with all my cutting into your flesh, nothing will equal the cutting off of my dick."

"You tried to rape me, you bastard."

"That's right, puta bitch. I tried to rape you. You stopped

that rape. But we're going to finish it now."

"I don't understand." How could he possibly rape me now? As if I hadn't realized before, Martinez was completely deranged. He'd do anything.

"Walk down that hallway," he instructed me in a voice as cold as the Arctic night. "Walk very slow. Don't make any wrong moves or you're a dead pussy. Head for that little tiny room downstairs, the one painted green. I've got it set up for you."

Not knowing what else to do, I obeyed him. There had to be some way out of this. But what? I knew Martinez wasn't on the island alone. His guerrillas had probably taken the entire island now, and had overcome my security guards. Rafael had probably left the island only minutes before the Martinez forces had arrived. They'd no doubt invaded by boat. J. Paul Getty had been right in warning Mia never to live close to the water.

At the foot of the steps, two armed guerilla fighters stood near the green room. They were only slightly less sinister versions of Martinez. Each one looked as if they'd kill you without a moment's hesitation. They'd probably make it easy on you and shoot you in the head, whereas Martinez would mutilate you. As I stared into the eyes of each man, I knew each of these so-called soldiers had killed before.

One of the guerillas, looking no more than eighteen, opened the door for me after a signal from Martinez.

"Get into that room, puta bitch," Martinez barked at me.

I entered the darkened room as if going to a death cell. Martinez came in behind me, shutting but not locking the door. The two armed men stood guard outside, and I didn't have to be told they'd break into the room on a moment's notice at the sound of a struggle.

I shuddered to think what fate Martinez had envisioned for me. I feared mutilation, even my own death. Yet I remained remarkably calm, at least on the outside. I was afraid but not hysterical. I didn't think plea bargaining would work with this killer. He obviously knew I had all the money in the world. If I didn't own all dollars, at least I had most of them, and what I didn't have, Mia did. Like me, she was probably his prisoner too. That explained the sound of the struggle in her room when I was speaking to her on the phone.

"Pull off all your clothes and lie down on the bed!" he commanded like a drill sergeant with a recruit.

"What?" I asked in astonishment.

I stared at him in the darkened room. Even though I couldn't see too clearly into his piggy eyes, I knew his command was meant to be obeyed. For one brief moment, I debated with myself to resist him. I'd lunge for him. Try to get his gun. Kill him even. Then shoot it out with the guards who would most definitely burst into the room firing at me. The more I thought about that, the more ridiculous it sounded. I'd seen too many Rambo movies. On the other hand, I thought it also foolish and ridiculous for me to strip and lie down on that bed to endure whatever torture and mutilation Martinez had in store for me. He'd killed Rafael's first wife, Tricia. God knows what he'd subjected her to before mercifully letting her die.

Not knowing what else to do, I stripped off my clothes and stood completely naked and vulnerable before his eyes. I am not a modest person, and my nudity has been flashed on screens around the world. This was the first time I'd ever felt embarrassed to be nude before another human being. Unlike most men, he wasn't looking at me with the desire a man has for a woman. He was, however, absorbing every inch of my nudity, but it was almost the way a surgeon might view a patient upon whom he was about to perform a critical operation.

"Lie down on that bed, puta bitch," he barked at me. Reluctantly I lay down, turning over on my side.

"Lay flat on your back, puta bitch, the way you've done for thousands of men. The way you did for that slimebag, Rafael Navarro. We can't find that son-of-a-bitch anywhere. Where is he?"

"He's gone. We had a fight." For the first time since I'd encountered Martinez, I was glad Rafael had gone to Miami. I shuddered to think what horror Martinez would inflict upon him.

As if reading my mind, he said, "We're going to get him. Bring him back here. Right in front of you. I'm going to cut his dick off and stuff it down your throat. Make you eat every inch of it."

With his gun still pointed at my heart, he opened the door to let in the two security guards. The eighteen-year-old, seeing me nude, let out a whistle and said something in Spanish.

"You should be flattered," Martinez said to me. "I'll translate what he said. He said you are one hot piece of ass. He'd like to fuck you in the mouth, in the cunt, and up the ass, and then start all over again and fuck you again in the same three holes."

I remained stonily silent. Although Martinez had his gun still pointed at me, the men carried their weapons in their holsters on their thighs. The two men had brought rope into the room. They proceeded to tie me up extra tight. First, my hands. I wanted to resist but thought better of it. Martinez would probably pistol-whip me in the face if I did.

When the two men had tied my arms, they tied my feet. Martinez then sent them away. I was now exposed and helpless for the next stage in this drama he'd written for both of us. He knew his role, but I didn't know what part was to be played by me. I dreaded each minute of this script as it unfolded.

He looked at me with a cruel smirk, as if he were about to achieve some sort of satisfaction he'd been dreaming about. "The rape is about to begin. Be patient, puta bitch. You'll get my gun up that hot cunt of yours. Just be patient."

For one brief moment, I felt I hadn't mutilated him after all. But his severed penis had been found on the grounds.

In front of my horrified eyes, he stripped off his shirt, then slowly lowered his pants. When his pants fell to his knees, he slipped down his jockey shorts. "I had the bandages removed this morning, just so you could see my dick."

I didn't want to look. Something told me not to look. Yet I felt compelled to do so. I stared at the short stub of his penis. It extended for a half inch or so from a mass of black pubic hair. The end of his penis was still bloody and covered with scar tissue. I averted my eyes to the ceiling.

"You've turned me into a woman," he shouted at me. "A god damn puta! One of my guards saw me taking off the bandages. When he looked at my dick, or what's left of it, he said he'd seen women better hung than me. I picked up my gun and blew his brains out."

I began to cry, softly at first, but more and more the tears came from deep within me. Those tears ran down my face and onto the bed pillow. I closed my eyes tight and waited for his next move, which I feared would be a blade, although I'd seen no knife in the room.

Very, very slowly, I felt a hard, blunt instrument being inserted into my vagina. Still I didn't open my eyes. Ever so slowly the instrument moved deeper within me.

"This is the only gun I have to fuck a woman with now," he said. "Thanks to you." Almost erotically, like a man in passion with a woman, he moved his gun back and forth within me.

I cried out. Like a fully erect penis, the gun went into me as deeply as he could insert it. He rode back and forth, back and forth, imitating sexual intercourse.

"Wait until this gun comes, puta bitch," he shouted into my face, peppering me with his saliva of hatred and contempt. "Just you wait. When the gun blasts off, you're going to have the climax of your life. What a blast-off. You think Navarro spews a hot load into your cunt. Wait until your cunt takes the lead from my gun."

A loud rapping at the door and the sound of a guard screaming in Spanish interrupted him. He abruptly withdrew the gun from me, and angrily stormed toward the door, pulling his pants up to cover himself as he did.

He threw open the door and barked something in Spanish. Dismissing the guard, he turned to me. "We have a little surprise for you. Someone tried to get away from us. But we caught them."

I closed my eyes and cried softly. I knew they'd captured Rafael.

"You're about to have a visitor. Me and you will continue our fucking later. Right now, I want you alive. We not only have the visitor we've captured, but we know President Clinton is planning a visit here. To fuck you. We got all the details we didn't know from Ted Hooker. It's amazing how much that mariposa told us when I took my cigarette lighter and heated up his tiny little balls."

"Let me go," I shouted to him. "Untie me."

"All in good time, puta cunt. I have big plans for you. Also, big plans for Mia Kelly. I also have plans for your friend we've just captured, and I definitely have plans for the president of the United States."

It seemed like hours that I waited in that room, my torture chamber. At any minute, I expected Martinez to return with his act from hell. I'd lost all sense of time, until finally, a tough-looking Cuban woman came into the room. She looked like a guerilla fighter, which she probably was, or else had been. Dressed in army fatigues, she had a pistol strapped around her waist, but did not remove it from her holster.

Eying me nude and tied up, she muttered something in Spanish, and very slowly, and rather professionally, began to untie me. First, she loosened the ropes binding my feet. Then she untied my wrists. I sat up in bed, massaging my wrists. I had a splitting headache, and I certainly knew why. Seemingly displeased with my nudity, she tossed me my dress. Feeling sore all over, I rose slowly from the bed, and quickly slipped into my dress. I didn't know where my panties were, and didn't care at this point. Vowing never to go nude again, I just wanted to cover myself from the world's prying eyes, especially from this guard and most definitely from the leering gaze of Martinez.

At the sound of a loud rap at the door, the guard went over and opened it. I fully expected Rafael to barge into the room and save me somehow. To my complete surprise, Anishi entered the room. The guard stood back to make way for her, then stepped outside and locked the door behind her. That left me facing her.

At first, when I looked into her eyes, she said nothing. Nor did I. I almost didn't know what to say. If she felt like I did, her future was too much in doubt to want to talk about it.

She looked like she'd been recently tortured. No longer some exotic princess in expensive silks, she wore a simple little frock dress that was torn and filthy. Circles like black rings appeared around her eyes.

"I have no idea what Martinez plans to do with you," she said. "With me. With Mia. With anybody. If I did, I'd let you know. I'd tell you the truth." She paused, a touch of melancholy in her voice. "The truth - that's something I've never told you before."

"Everything you've said to me has been a lie," I said, merely confirming what we both knew. She nodded her head in agreement, knowing I didn't expect an answer. Although I didn't know what she'd been through - and probably never would - I feared she was too beaten to talk.

"The kidnapping of John and Henry?" I asked. "At first a hoax, then hell?"

"A clumsy attempt on my part to extort money from you for my boys. I wanted to provide for them. I believe Martinez is going to have me killed. Sooner than later."

"That doesn't surprise me. But you worked for him."

"Let me tell you the truth." Her voice grew stronger, and in spite of her frail condition, a masculine strength emerged from her. "You might call this a gallows truth. After a lifetime of concealment, I have nothing to hide anymore. I've never worked for Martinez or anybody else. Certainly not Mia. I only worked for myself. As a child, I saw how evil the world really was. I wanted only to manipulate that world so that it would not manipulate me as it had done. I've never had respect for the world or anybody in it. That includes you and Mia."

"What you felt toward me was always evident. You didn't bother to conceal it."

"I wasn't really interested in you at first. I saw you as an obstacle that prevented me from getting Mia's money. You became interesting to me only when I thought I could extort money from you. I paid you a compliment. I thought you were decent enough to put up money to rescue my John and Henry."

"For a clever woman, you've been very foolish."

"I know. I could manipulate Mia. I could never manipulate you."

"Why should you? You had nothing I wanted. Nothing to dangle in front of me. At least with Mia, you could hold up the false promise of a Fountain of Youth. Not with me. I know that one day - sooner than later - everything's going to sag. You couldn't use any of your bag of tricks with me. You were reduced to using your children as bait. Which you did rather shamelessly."

"I have no shame," she said, almost at the point of tears. "Any woman who at the age of three was forced to perform unspeakable acts in front of old men, any woman like that could have no shame ever again. Whatever I did, I did to survive. I'd do it again."

"Many people have survived without resorting to your ways."

"It was more than survival, and you know that," she said, almost accusatorially. "I wanted fame and fortune - nothing approaching your status. But I wanted to be up there at the top - respected, powerful, rich, even alluring. And I wanted to achieve that in America, not Japan."

"What do you have against Japan?" Considering the challenge, and knowing Japan as I did, I realized her answer could take all day.

"I was used there. Used by sick old men for their own pleasure. It is never the pleasure of the woman in Japan, only that of the man. The country is worthless. It's without sophistication. Completely shallow." She sucked in the air of the hot, stale room, as if desperate for breath. "Fame. Money. Power. All that meant America for me. When I saw how stupid people of fame could be, I wanted to reach far beyond them."

"Search for bigger game? I don't think Mia - and especially me - have any power right now. Martinez has the power. The power of the gun. We're in a jam and all the money in the world can't bail us out."

"I used to think money could do anything, buy anybody out of any trap. With Martinez, I know that's not true. With him, it's different. I've just talked to him. I don't think he can be bribed. He wants something else from you, and I don't know why. He wants you to experience the ultimate humiliation, and his feeble little killer brain can't seem to come up with anything that would be that humiliating to you or that satisfying to him."

"Mutilation?"

"Perhaps that. He did seem to want to mutilate you before killing you. I'm not sure I understand such hatred toward you."

"It had to do with something I took from him."

"For God's sake, for the sake of all of us, give it back."

"I can't. What I took is gone forever."

"A fine mess that makes for all of us. I wish I could provide you with even the tiniest clue that you might use to save us. But I know nothing that's going on here. Except I fear something terrible is about to happen."

"It is, but I don't know what."

"Will my sons be all right?"

"I'm sure they will be," I said without conviction.

"Can't you think of some way for us to escape? To rescue them?"

"Hell, no. We're trapped."

My eyes darted to the door at the sound of a key unlocking it. For one brief moment, I felt a sense of hope. Someone has come to rescue me. When the door opened, I faced the cold, black eyes of Martinez boring into me. I felt he'd come to escort us to our executions. Brandishing his pistol in the air, he commanded us to leave the room at once.

I desperately held onto her hand as we were marched down the hallway and into an open patio. Four armed guards stood here with attack weapons pointed at us. In one corner of the twilight-lit patio, two guards were restraining John and Henry.

. . .

At the sight of Anishi, John and Henry tried to break free and run toward their mother. Two guards held them back. As Anishi moved to rush to the aid of her sons, Martinez stuck his pistol into the back of her neck.

"No fucking family reunions," he barked at her. "I've got other plans for you shits."

She turned to me, still squeezing my hand in a death grip. I felt she'd break my bones. "He's going to kill us," she said under her breath, the words not aimed at me exactly, but as a statement to herself.

I feared she was right. She and I were cows at slaughter-time. Would Martinez also kill John and Henry?

With his gun pointed at my heart, Martinez stood in front of me.

"Why are you doing this?" I asked. "Why are you trying to kill everybody? Doing so could only mean the end of you. You'd gain nothing. If you'll let us go, you know I'll see that the world will be yours. Everything you've ever wanted."

"Do you know what I want more than anything else in the world?" he asked, his lips moving so close to mine that he peppered my face with his spittle. "I want my dick back. Can you get my dick back, puta cunt?"

I couldn't bear to look into his twisted face. Glancing briefly at Anishi, I saw that she didn't understand what Martinez meant. How could she know?

"You're right about one thing," he said. "The world is going to belong to this dickless wonder. You're going to make that happen for me. I have plans for you. When I have plans for someone, they live." He turned like an executioner to Anishi. She trembled with fear. "When someone has outlived their usefulness, I tell them adios." He looked back at me. "This Jap pussy has outlived her usefulness. She not only knows too much, the stupid cunt has tried to sell what she knows to the enemy camp."

I looked at her for confirmation of what he was saying, although I didn't exactly know who the enemy camp was. For that matter, I didn't know what camp Martinez represented, either.

"I didn't mean to," she said, pleading for her life. "I needed money for my boys. Those men you speak of came to me. They made me an offer. I listened. But I didn't take it."

"Shut up, you lying cunt!" he said. "You were going to take every penny offered. When we caught you, you were holding out for a higher price. You were going to reveal all our plans."

"I wasn't!" she screamed. "I wasn't!"

Even I, who didn't know what she was talking about, understood that she was lying.

Martinez did too, slapping her face so hard he drew blood from her mouth. Henry screamed for his mother until a guard kicked him in the stomach. The boy fell over in pain on the patio, whimpering in agony.

Martinez looked at me. "Have you ever been an eye-witness to an execution?"

"No!" I said, filled with dread. "And I don't want to be."

"Sometimes, Miss Rich Bitch Movie Star, we have to attend shows we don't want to see."

Anishi looked into my eyes. Tears were falling down her cheeks. "Minutes from now I'll be dead. No more Anishi. You owe me no favors. But if you survive this one, and John and Henry come out of this alive too, please take care of them for me. Give them the love I would have given them."

I didn't think she would ever make me cry. But she did. I started to cry real hard, something I rarely did. Right now I wanted to be delivered miraculously out of here and into the arms of Rafael. That was but a dream. This awful patio was the here and now. Reality. Biting reality. How I hated every moment of it.

My voice seemed to have escaped me. When I first tried to answer her, no sound came out. Finally, I muttered, "I will. I will. I promise you."

"Cut the crap!" Martinez barked at us. He grabbed Anishi by the hair and made her walk to the center of the patio. This time, both John and Henry screamed out for her.

"Good-bye, my children," she called across the patio to them. "Anishi loves you. Anishi will always love you. Everything I did, I did for you. Take care of yourselves. Love each other like I taught you."

Martinez slapped her mouth to shut it. "If one more word comes from your rotten fucking yellow face, you'll watch your boys die before you."

Slapping her thighs with his pistol, he forced her to her knees. Then he placed the pistol at her right temple. "I once saw a newspaper photograph of some Vietnamese shithead executing someone like this," he said, apparently addressed to me. He pressed the barrel of his gun deeper into her temple. "A lot of people thought that was one of the most horrible photographs of the Vietnam War. I got off on it. Hung it over my bed and beat my meat looking at it every night. That's when I had meat to beat, you bitch!"

I knew what was coming. My piercing scream resounded across the patio, as Martinez pressed his pistol even deeper into Anishi's temple and fired one bullet.

Without saying a word, she collapsed in death on the hot, steamy patio.

There were no screams or even cries from John and Henry. Only soft, almost strangled whimpers.

Martinez signaled the guard to remove her body from the patio. He motioned for another guard to take me away.

As a Cuban guard approached me with a gun, I looked into his eyes. He was a handsome boy who looked like he should be in high school, not on the death squad of Martinez. He waved his gun at me, and signaled me to start walking. Out of hearing distance of Martinez, he whispered into my ear in heavily accented English. "Miss Kelly, you're my favorite movie star. I saw 'Kinky' eight times. Let me have your autograph. Please!"

"What is your name?" I asked the young guard when he'd returned me to the room where Martinez had terrorized me. Although I didn't look my most seductive best, I tried to be as alluring as possible.

"Juan Garcia, Miss Kelly," he said, sounding very respectful. His English, in spite of that accent, was quite proficient. For all I knew, he'd gone to school in Miami. He'd probably never been in a room before with a woman as gorgeous as I was. Certainly not one as rich.

"You are one good-looking man," I said. "I guess you've read in the newspapers that I like Latin men."

"I didn't read that. But I read about you and that Italian boy, Dino Paglia. Me and him are the same age. What a lucky prick he was."

"I've grown tired of Dino. I've had it with Italians. What I've never had before is a Cuban."

"But I heard you were making love to Rafael Navarro. He's as Cuban as black beans and yellow rice."

"Rafael was just a bodyguard. Nothing more." I looked around the room as if expecting to find the woman guard I'd met previously. We were alone. "As you can see, Rafael wasn't a very good bodyguard, or I wouldn't be trapped like this."

"If I'd been your bodyguard, I would never have let Martinez capture you." For the first time, I noted what a husky voice the young man had. Or had his voice grown huskier since entering the room alone with me?

"What is that bastard Martinez going to do with us? With Mia Kelly?"

"Nobody knows what Martinez is going to do. Sometimes I wonder if he knows what he's going to do. He's a psycho. Especially now that he's lost his prick. You may not have heard about that. Someone cut off his prick. We don't know who. He was one mean bastard with a prick. Without a prick, he's from hell."

"I didn't know that," I said, lying. Considering what I had in mind for Juan Garcia, I didn't want him to think I was a woman who went around cutting off pricks. Au Contraire.

"He knows Clinton is coming here. That's all I know. He's going to do something to Clinton."

"Assassinate the president?"

"I don't think so. Something about an operation."

"You mean cut off the president's prick? Something stupid like that?"

"I just don't know. I heard something about an operation. Something with a doctor involved."

"That makes no sense to me." It made a lot of sense, as Dr. Euler's image flashed before me.

"It doesn't make any sense to me either," he said, as I moved closer to him. "My job is to guard you. I don't know anything else going on around here."

"Could you get out of here if you wanted to?"

"Even I am guarded. Except the shithead guarding me has found your supply of liquor and wine. He says they're the greatest in the world. Nothing cheap. He'll be asleep by early morning."

"Then you could swim ashore and escape."

"I guess I could. I couldn't go through the gates, though. They're heavily guarded. Martinez won't let any guard out until we finish the job here. I think he is growing more and more loco."

"Juan," I said, moving even closer to him. "I know Martinez plans to kill me. That is, when I do what I'm supposed to do with the president."

"I think you're right. He's already shot that Japanese mother. He's killed many people in the past. He'll kill many people in the future before someone kills him."

"Why is he doing this?"

"I don't know, and I don't even have a clue as to his long-range plans. All I know is his plan for right now, and I don't even know very much about that. He's going to kill the people in your house. At least some of them. He wants to terrify you into cooperating with him when Clinton comes here. Do you understand that?"

"Sort of."

"I think he believes that by killing most of the people around you, you'll come through for him. But after you do whatever it is he wants, he'll kill you, too."

I moved as close to him as I dared. After all, he was supposed to be guarding me, and his pistol was still stashed in his holster. "I learned something. Something you need to know. I know why Martinez is having you and all the others guarded. He's using you right now to guard us. But when he's through with you, when he no longer needs you, he'll kill you just like he plans to kill me."

As he looked into my eyes, I realized what one of world's wealthiest and most beautiful women could do in the presence of a young and impressionable man. I might even be telling the truth. It was a guess, but I bet I was right.

"He'd shoot me?" He looked at me in disbelief. Disbelief quickly turned to rage. "The fucking lying bastard. He'd do that, wouldn't he?"

"You know Martinez better than I do. Of course, he'd do it, and you know it! He's killed many people who knew too much. Look at what he did to Anishi. See what he does to people who work for him and who know too much."

"I see, I see a lot, Miss Kelly."

"It's Sherry for you, baby. Sherry. All yours."

A fierce determination came over his face. It was the look of a young man intent on his own survival. But also a sexual passion was there. He wanted to get laid. Sooner, rather than later.

This time, I moved so close our bodies were glued together. I brushed my tongue across his lips. It wasn't a kiss. Only a tantalizing flick of the tongue. He sighed in response.

"Juan," I whispered into his ear. There went that talented tongue of mine at work again. "You must escape. But be safe. Make it tonight when the guard thinks you're asleep. Get help for us. Martinez will be killed. I'll transfer twenty-million dollars to your account. I'll put up ten, Mia Kelly another ten. I'm sure dear Mommie will think ten million a cheap price to pay for her life. Do you know how much money twenty million dollars is?"

"Shit! I bet even Castro hasn't stolen that much money from the Cuban people. That's drug lord kind of money."

"It can all be yours. All you have to do is swim the short

distance to the shore. Rush to the nearest phone booth. Call the sheriff. His name is Snake. Tell him you work for me. We're being held prisoner on Palm Island. Also tell him to have the Dade County sheriff's department bring Mr. Navarro with them. If I come out of this alive, I want Rafael at my side."

"You said he was only your bodyguard - not your lover." He sounded a bit petulant. Was it jealousy of Rafael?

"I know, but after what happened to me, I don't want to ever be without a bodyguard again."

"You won't have to be. I'll be with you."

I could feel his sweet, young, Cuban breath on my lips.

"You'll have twenty-million dollars - maybe more. You won't need to work as a bodyguard."

He put one arm around me and pulled me close. "I'm talking about being your lover. Not your bodyguard. Forget that Dino Paglia. I've just replaced him. What you need is a real man."

At this point, my tongue went into his mouth and washed it thoroughly. My experienced hand unzipped his trousers and soon he had a full, uncircumcised erection. An erection that was being skillfully manipulated by an expert. "I've never felt anything so good in all my life," I said, lying. "I want you inside me." Right then, I actually meant that.

He sighed in pleasure. I could have grabbed his pistol at this point. But I didn't. His escaping and getting help for us was the only way. Still, I had to firm up the deal in some way.

"I want you inside me more than I've ever wanted anybody inside me," I said. "It's too risky right now to get on that bed. Stand with your back to the door and listen. I've got to taste you."

"To taste me?" he asked, not seeming to understand. When I feel to my knees and in one gulp devoured him, practically sucking in his balls, he not only understood, but took both of his hands and held the back of my neck in firm position.

I sucked for dear life, because in some way, I felt pleasing him and bringing him to a spectacular climax would save me. It was as if my life force lived within this young man, and I wanted to connect with it. He loved my tongue lashing, and I loved satisfying him this way. My whole life and the lives of others depended now on this young man I'd known for only minutes. I didn't want him to go away with what could be empty promises. I wanted him to feel me and my love and the promise of my life. If he wanted it bad enough, he'd come back for more.

After far too short a time, his entire body was almost in convulsions. I suspected it'd been the climax of his life. Before he'd even recovered, I stood up facing him. My lips met his, and we both enjoyed a taste of his offering. Even though the threat of death hung over both our heads, it was one of the most erotic moments I'd ever known. I'd never tasted anything as sweet and thrilling as this young Cuban.

He was almost completely mesmerized at this point. I took his left hand and put it up my dress. "There it is," I whispered in his ear. "Just what you saw in 'Kinky'. But this is no movie. It's real. Feel it. Enjoy it."

I trembled in ecstasy as his inexperienced fingers moved inside me.

The young man had found the love of his life. His eyes told me that.

"Promise me," he said, never taking his hand away. He kissed me passionately. "Promise me that if I get out of here alive, that you'll let me have you every day for the rest of my life."

"I promise," I said, without hesitation. I think I meant it. "With all my heart. I promise."

"I believe you're telling me the truth." He looked into my eyes with a longing I'd never seen in any man. "You belong to me now. It's a promise I'll hold you to."

At the sound of footsteps in the hall, he straightened up and zipped up his pants. I moved to the far corner of the room.

The unmistakable voice of Mia was heard up and down the hall. She was a raging bull. The door was suddenly thrown open.

. . .

"Flasher!" Mia screeched at me. "You've got us into a pile of shit so deep, we may never crawl out."

"Mommie, are you okay?"

In her red dress, she looked as if she'd been roughed up. "I've been manhandled before. Lyndon Johnson, Martin Luther

King, Jr. And that maniac, Prince Philip. But never before by a bunch of young Spiks with such bad manners."

"Did they hurt you?" I asked, moving to comfort her.

She backed away, as if not wanting to have anything to do with me. "They pushed me and shoved. Me, Mia Kelly. With all my power and money, I was pushed and shoved. That darling boy, Angelo, who indeed lives up to the promise of his name, came to my rescue, but was knocked out with the butt of a gun."

"I'm so sorry."

"And well you should be. I just know you're responsible for bringing this down on our heads." She looked at me as if she were the tribunal at Nurnberg evaluating the deposed leaders of the Gestapo. "And who in hell is Geraldo Martinez?"

"A Cuban terrorist. Henchman for Castro. He was the shithead I castrated in Miami when he tried to rape me."

"Oh, my God. Now I know we're in for it. In case your Mommie never taught you this before, men don't like to lose their little dicks. For some reason, the bastards think they're important."

"I know," I said impatiently. "He was going to rape me, and he bragged he had AIDS."

"I know you did what you had to do. In the old days when men tried to rape me, I gave in to it because I didn't want to get roughed up and smear my makeup. Even while getting raped, a woman wants to look her best. I figured the better I looked, the faster the bastard would get his rocks off and get out. But in this day of the AIDS crisis, rape can mean death. A girl has to protect herself."

"Mommie," I said, abruptly changing the subject. "Did you know that Anishi was secretly working for Martinez?"

"That Jap bitch! Wait till I get my hands on her lying throat!"

"Too late. She's dead. Martinez shot her. Gun to the temple. Right in front of me."

She shrieked, grabbing hold of me, scratching my arm in her desperation. "Don't you know what this means? If Martinez killed Anishi, he plans to do away with all of us."

"I know that. I'm desperately plotting ways to save us."

"They're going to kill us! I just know it! We're going to be lined up and shot. One by one." She was crying, but when I offered her comfort, she jerked away.

"There is no point in killing us," I said sharply, slapping her face to keep her from becoming hysterical. "We are the two richest women in the world. Dead, we are nothing to them. Alive, we represent money. Great money. They won't kill us until our money's been transferred to them. Maybe we are the bankrollers they need."

"But how could they possibly get us to transfer our billions into their coffers?"

"They have their ways." I didn't like the ominous sound in my own voice.

"I think you're wrong. I think they're going to take us out and shoot us now."

"It won't be that easy for us."

As if both our prophecies were coming true, we heard the sound of boots in the hallway and a rattling at the door. When the door was thrown open again, Martinez was standing here. The gun he was holding was aimed directly at Mia. The two Cuban guards who followed Martinez into the room grabbed her, shoving her toward the door. In an uncontrolled fury, she slapped one of the guards. But Martinez intervened, jabbing his revolver at the doorway to her mouth, bloodying her lip. Sighing, she relented, her whole body seeming to sag. Slowly, with the barrel of a gun pressed against her spine, she preceded the guards to the door and headed down the corridor.

"Mommie!" I screamed after her.

She didn't look back for one final goodbye. That hurt me more than any rejection I'd ever known from her. Just one more time, I wanted to see her beautiful violet eyes and make contact with them.

With his revolver, Martinez motioned for me to stay in the room. Without saying another word, he stormed out of the room, slamming the door behind him. I heard the lock turn. I was a prisoner in this awful room once again. If I were ever to get free, I vowed I'd have this room torn apart and rebuilt. The recent memories of what had happened here would live with me forever, even if forever had become a series of minutes.

I felt I'd never see Mia again, at least alive. She'd been right, I feared. Martinez planned to kill her, and then, no doubt, the bastard would shoot me too. With all our money, I thought I could buy him. Certainly, we could transfer more money to him than his present employers, the faceless one, regardless of their bankroll. My new reality suggested Martinez couldn't be bought because he was insane. To buy off someone, that person had to be sensible enough to appreciate the great amount of money likely to be offered. In the case of Martinez, money might not matter to him anymore. Perhaps he figured that after his emasculation, life wasn't worth living. If not that, he'd surely succumb to the AIDS virus, which meant that all the money in the world would be of little use to him. His employers might have already come to that conclusion before they'd hired him.

Daddy Kelly had always warned me about kidnappers. I lived in fear all my life that I'd be abducted and held for ransom, all tied up somewhere. Even when a ransom was paid, I feared killers would rape and murder me. Mia had the same fear. Right this minute, I felt that day - so long dreaded - was now upon us.

Strangely, I wasn't hysterically clawing the walls in a battle to escape, but what chance did I have? I'd only end up getting shot that much sooner. I was just waiting. An endless wait to see what would happen to me. Any minute now, I expected them to come for me and do what they would. Probably the same thing they were doing to my poor Mommie right now. A torture session followed by a bullet in the head. Martinez usually preferred to shoot inside the head instead of the heart.

Like me, what chance did Mia have right now with a gun pointed at her? Beg for her life? Offer lots of money? Both might work on a sane person. Martinez would be more amused than impressed.

I thought I'd be crying. My eyes remained dry. I felt I'd come upon the entrance to a long, dark tunnel. A strange void loomed before me, one that nothing could fill.

It was about to be over. I'd come to the end of my wasted life.

For all I knew, Mia was now dead, her body growing cold. I'd soon follow her to the grave. I was staring into my own future and realizing it didn't exist. The thought made me feel numb. My brain sent no signals about how to escape. How to survive. There was no time now for Juan Garcia to swim ashore tonight and get help for us. Clinton, as is his way, would be late. If this were truly the end, I wanted it to come quickly.

I didn't want to stand here stupidly, like some prisoner on death row waiting for a call from the governor. Susan Hayward had already played that part, anyway.

Before I could get lost in a death-row depression, a guard - not the darling Juan Garcia I so wanted to see, but a new and different one - came to unlock the door. He entered the room. Instead of young Juan, this was an old and bearded relic of some guerilla battles in the jungle. He looked like a bad movie villain. Some Hispanic thug from central casting.

"Puta!" he yelled at me. He'd obviously heard Martinez call me that. Waving his rifle, he motioned for me to leave the room. Offering no resistance, I did as I was told. A defeated and broken Jew being led into a death chamber.

As I walked down the long, breezy corridor, every touch of my feet on the flagstones was like walking barefoot on hot coals. Frantically, my eyes darted around, looking for any avenue of escape, regardless of how remote. I wanted to make a break for it. But there was no way out. Anything I did would get me about five bullets in the back.

The guard forced me back onto the same patio where Martinez had assassinated Anishi. Her blood was still drying in the twilight. In the oncoming night, the patio lights had been turned on.

There in the center of the patio, Mia had been tied to a hospital bed, the same one once used by Daddy Kelly when he'd suffered through a long illness. Her mouth was bound. She looked up at me with such panic in her eyes, I had to muffle a scream at her plight. She was desperate and there was no way I could help her.

Never in my life had I looked at her with such love. Knowing she was about to die made me realize that in spite of everything that had happened in the past, I still loved Mommie. I wish I had told her that long ago when there was time. When it would have meant more than it did now. I wished we hadn't spent most of our lives feuding.

The Cuban woman guard I'd encountered earlier when I was nude glared at me. She stood guard over a helpless Mia. Her eyes darted about like a wild animal waiting for the inevitable slaughter.

Martinez came onto the patio. In spite of having no dick, his macho walk made him the biggest stud on the island. He had a weapon much more powerful than his little penis ever was: A revolver. Who knows how many people other than Anishi had been killed by that revolver? It was obviously his most prized possession since I'd removed his other most prized possession. Since that was likely to be my final bitter revenge against Martinez before he killed me, I was glad I had chopped off his dick. At least the gaping wound would be something left behind for him to remember me by.

As Martinez approached me, my guard dug the barrel of his rifle deeper into my temple. In his left hand, Martinez carried a needle and a vial of fluid. He handed it to the woman guard. Without any preliminaries and as if giving a routine injection, the guard took the needle, jabbed it into Mia's arm, and depressed the plunger.

Even the gag couldn't wipe out the sound of her pain. After her flesh was pierced, she didn't pass out. She remained fully alert, her eyes darting recklessly about. Then, suddenly, she fell back on the hospital bed, as if giving up. The mysterious contents of the vial were already coursing through her blood stream, and she seemed to have accepted the inevitable, the hopelessness of any further struggle.

"Puta bitch!" were the only words heard on the otherwise soundless patio. In the distance I could hear the crash of ocean waves.

I didn't need to be told who was calling for me. It was Martinez. Looking first at Mia, then at me, he appeared triumphant, as if he'd just won a major jungle battle and now was ready to amuse himself with his captives.

"Your mama has spent years donating money for AIDS research. Campaigning for AIDS funding to save the world's mariposa population." He spat in my direction, his virus-laden wad narrowly missing my face. "Now the bitch - just like me - has something that might be even worse than AIDS."

Even though her mouth was muffled, I could hear the scream trying to escape from her throat.

Maybe it was the long day itself. I passed out.

. . .

When I woke up, I was in a different room, one I didn't recognize. I suspected I was still on Palm Island. I often didn't recognize rooms in houses I owned, since I rarely visited entire wings of any house I occupied, only the rooms I wanted to live and love in. This place looked like the stainless steel storage room for a kitchen, although most of the equipment had been removed except for a gas-fired oven in the wall. On seeing it, I thought in horror that Martinez was going to force my head into that oven and asphyxiate me.

My hands were tied behind my back, and I struggled to move and get to my feet until I realized they were tied too. I had been bound and dumped in a corner of this awful hospital-antiseptic room. The gag in my mouth was choking me, as I struggled for air in the stifling hot room. The temperature felt like it had hit one-hundred and five degrees.

Suddenly, the door was swung open, as Maxie was shoved into the room by the same two guards who'd come for Mia. His face was badly bruised, as if it had been gun-whipped. His withered old body was encased in a pair of tattered shorts and a soiled T-shirt. He was barefoot, his hands tied behind him.

"Sherry!" he called out. "They've got you too? They're killing us one by one."

I tried to answer him, but only muffled sounds escaped through my gag.

"Martinez has Ted right now. He's torturing his genitals, and Ted can't stand the slightest bit of pain. Genital torture, an old technique of Castro himself."

He stood helplessly in the middle of the room, waiting for whatever horror was about to descend upon him. His face told me he knew it was going to be a nightmare, the worst he'd ever known. Maybe his last nightmare.

At this point, I thought Anishi had been lucky. She'd been allowed to receive a bullet in the head without a torture session. With that virus going through her blood stream, Mia had not been tortured in the traditional sense of the word, but sentenced to a slow, horrible, and painful death, the same agony she'd seen so many others experience as she tried to help them. It was all in vain. In time, if she ever survived this day, she'd join the afflicted she so fervently wanted to rescue.

Since I couldn't answer him because of my gag, Maxie kept talking. His mind seemed to have already left his body. He wasn't really speaking to me at this point, but having a half-dazed monologue with himself.

"All my life I've been beaten up by someone. Being bashed by Martinez is familiar turf to me. I couldn't walk down any street anywhere in the world without some blokes pouncing on me. They always knew I was different. Of course, dying my hair mauve when I was thirteen and walking through the toughest neighborhoods in the East End of London was a definite guarantee that I was going to get the shit beat out of me. I didn't care. I was flamboyantly defiant. The very next night, I'd cover up the bruises with lots of cheap makeup, keep the same violet hair, maybe this time add some flaming red lipstick, then go out on those rough streets once again. I didn't always get beaten up. At least not at first. Sometimes men wanted to make love to me. It wasn't actually love. Raw lust, really. After their appetites were satisfied, they often beat up the subject of that lust. Namely, *me*. With the money you were going to give me, I was actually looking forward to retirement. I'm tired of walking the streets, especially at my age. And in any event, who or what could I possibly pick up today? I wanted to locate some genteel boarding house down in Bournemouth, settle in there quietly, and read all those books I didn't read during my youth when I was out cruising the streets. I'd tell everyone there I'd lost my wife, but had eight grandchildren. I even planned to mail letters to myself from those offspring. Even though I'd written them myself, I'd have shown the letters around the boarding house. I'm great at faking handwriting. I'd even produce photographs of my grandchildren. Of course, my fellow borders would sense that I was a bit of a puff. But many non-puff Englishmen act like puffs, so it wouldn't really matter or arouse undue suspicion. No one would think much of my frilly mannerisms. I'd just be considered eccentric, especially my mauve scarves. I've always been addicted to mauve scarves. Mainly, I'd be respected, something I've never been in all my life. I'd live well, eating English food in all its overboiled glory, the way I like it. Forget this raw carrot stuff you Americans indulge in. With the money you were going to give me, I'd buy presents at Christmas for the fellow boarders. Nothing too elaborate. Tasteful, though. When I couldn't stand any more of such respectable behavior, I'd take a train trip up to London. A bloke I know there will always hire me to stand at the door to a drag joint in Earl's Court, impersonating Queen Mary and collecting (with perfect manners) five-pounders from all the studs who wanted to see the show. That way, I could stay in touch with the real world before retreating once again to Bournemouth when I couldn't stand all the tawdry decadence of London."

Even though I couldn't answer him, my eyes met his. They told him I understood.

One of the guards had turned up the oven to full blast. The heat spewing forth from it made the room almost intolerable. Sweat poured from both Maxie and me.

He'd stopped talking. It was as if he knew something was about to happen. Somehow, words didn't matter anymore.

Martinez came into the room. This time, his revolver rested dangerously in a pouch by his side. He carried some long object wrapped in a beach towel. He stood in front of the oven and dropped the beach towel. I couldn't see the object he held in his hand. Opening the oven, he placed the object inside, just above the gas flames.

As he slammed the oven door, he glared at me before motioning to one of the guards. The guard pulled out a knife. Upon seeing the knife, Maxie closed his eyes right after he'd bid me a soft goodbye. He braced himself for the stab wound he obviously felt was inevitable.

Instead of knifing him, the guard cut his shorts from his body. Maxie had been given no underwear, so he now stood nude in the room except for the soiled T-shirt. I looked away from the sight of his withered genitals. I didn't want to see anything. Both Maxie and I knew at this point that stabbing, or even shooting was out of the question. It would be death by torture, a favorite sport of Martinez.

The guards grabbed hold of Maxie and threw the old man to the floor. Each of them firmly grasped him by the ankles, which they hoisted into the air. This ancient legs-apart veteran knew very well the position he was being forced into. The guards spread his legs even farther as if to open up his anus all the more. Was he going to be gang-raped? Certainly not by Martinez.

He stood in front of me. "What you are about to see was inspired by something I learned in class from Rafael. In Havana, he once taught Shakespeare. As well as a lot of English history. I became very excited during one history lesson. I had to excuse myself and go to the men's room and beat my meat. That is, back when I had meat to beat." At the thought of his castration, he kicked me with his boot. "It was about the murder of an English king. One of the Richards. Or maybe it was an Edward. Who in hell remembers? All those faggot English kings sound alike to me. I liked the way this faggot died. I always wanted to kill someone like that myself. Divine justice, I say." He turned from me and looked at Maxie spreadeagled before him, his ass sticking up as if ready for penetration.

"You old mariposa," Martinez sneered at Maxie. "How many times have you taken it up the ass? No doubt, five thousand. Ten thousand? Well, prepare yourself for the hottest fuck of your miserable, faggot life."

He moved over to the oven and put on a protective glove. He reached into the oven and withdrew the object.

"Mama!" he shouted. "Is this mother-fucker hot!" He brandished a four-foot long, fiery-hot poker in front of Maxie's face.

At the sight of it, Maxie - still held down by the guards on the floor - screamed out his fears. "Don't! DON'T! Shoot me! KNIFE ME! Kill me any way. But not that! Don't kill me that way. Please. Please! PLEASE! His screams turned into a pleading, whimpering blur, as he braced himself.

Martinez looked down at Maxie with utter contempt before inserting the tip of the glowing red poker into the entrance of the old man's anus. As the hot metal met flesh, Maxie let out a blood-curdling scream. The smell of burning flesh permeated the air. With its entrance secured, Martinez rammed the poker as far into the bowels of Maxie as he could, then violently twisted the shaft within its agonized channel. A sound not quite human came from Maxie. As blood spurted from his mouth, he collapsed in death onto the floor.

I closed my eyes. I'd seen enough. Whatever was going to

happen next, I had surrendered to it. Let them come for me too. Get it over with. I couldn't take much more.

There was the sound of footsteps. Body movement. Maybe Maxie's body being hauled off. I didn't know. I didn't want to see. After what seemed like an eternity, the kitchen storage room was shut and locked.

When I finally opened my eyes, the room was eerily empty. It was peaceful and serene, as if no violence had ever occurred there.

Maxie's body had indeed been removed.

Still bound and gagged, I was mercifully alone at last. Until they came for me.

. . .

I don't know how long I'd slept, but I must have passed out from the heat and the horror of watching Maxie die a hideous death. When I regained consciousness, my bound and gagged body, combined with the stifling heat of the room, made me feel faint again. My parched throat desperately needed water, and I struggled to sit up.

It was only then that I became aware of Martinez sitting in a chair in the center of the kitchen storage room, staring at me. "Puta cunt," he announced. "I was letting you get your beauty sleep. I want you to look real beautiful tonight for Clinton."

For the first time, I became aware of the lengthening shadows in the room. It was dark. Bill Clinton was due to arrive in a few hours. Or was he? I was out of touch with everything. I didn't know who was dead or alive, much less who was coming to visit.

He got up from his chair and walked slowly toward me. What new horror was he planning? At this point, I almost wished he'd kill me and get it over with. He reached down and ripped the gag from my mouth. I gasped for air.

He stood menacingly over me. "Know what? Even without a dick, I can still piss. Imagine that! Would you like a demonstration? Better shut your eyes and mouth real tight, 'cause my urine is filled with the AIDS virus."

He unzipped his pants. In seconds, urine was raining down on my head. I closed my eyes and mouth as tightly as I could until this stinking bath was over. I jerked my head several times, hoping to shake away every drop of him. When I reopened my eyes, he had thankfully zipped up his pants and was sitting again in the chair in the middle of the room.

"What do you want with me?" I cried out to him. "With Mia? With all of us? Why are you killing us one by one? This is madness. You'll never get away with it."

"So what if I'm caught? I'd die of AIDS before I come to trial."

"Are you doing this for the sheer sport of it all?"

"That too. I'm enjoying it. Sticking that poker up Maxie's ass was thrill enough to make me get my rocks off." He glared at me. "If that was still possible. I wanted to get even with you for what you did to me. I also have a mission. Remember that TV series, 'Mission Impossible'? That's what I have. Except my mission is very possible."

"What horrible assignment is that? Coming from you, I expect the worst."

"You'll get it! It has to do with Bill Clinton. When we found out Clinton is due to visit you tonight, my bosses concocted a plan."

"Who are your god damn bosses?"

"I don't know - and that's the honest truth. I don't know who they are, and I don't know what their grand plan is. I only know what they want me to do. Do you think Castro ever told me his grand design? He only told me to carry out my role in the grand design. In other words, it's like making a big quilt. I'm sewing together only one piece of it. I don't know what the final quilt will look like."

"Fool that I am, I actually believe you."

"It's true. There's no need to lie to you at this point in our love affair. We're all coming to the ends of our lives. Don't you appreciate getting to be a servant in someone else's grand and intricate plan? It adds meaning to our lives."

"I don't know what this fucking grand plan is. I only know that I don't want to be a part of it."

"But you are a part of it. In fact, you're the second stage of the plan. There will be many stages to this plan. Stage one has already been achieved."

"What, pray tell, was that?"

"The taking of this house. The discipline of some of the household. A little respect for Geraldo Martinez. The shifting of power around here."

"Okay, so you have the god damn power. What next?"

"You got it, sweet pussy. Me and you, baby, have been called in for stage two of the plan. Don't ask me what stage three is. We're not involved in that. In other words, someone else has written most of the script. I doubt if me and you will even be around when the entire script is read. But this rotted carcass called America will be. And it won't even know what happened to it. One morning, all you dumb bastards will wake up and there will be a different America."

"None of this sounds very realistic."

"Why should it? The whole world has never made any sense to me. All of the stunts I've been called upon to perform - carrying out some fucker's grand design - have all failed. Everything I did for the Soviets failed. Everything I did for Castro failed too. A total wash-out! Even this god damn crazy shit I'm involved in now will probably fail. Failure is something I'm used to. That's why I take my pleasure whenever I can find it, puta bitch!"

"Then you admit what you're doing now is crazy?"

"I admit it. Why shouldn't I? It's party time in the asylum. Every assignment I've ever done has been lunatic, especially the top-secret missions. You wouldn't believe some of the things we Cubans did for the Soviets. You just wouldn't believe it."

"If you were involved, I could believe it."

"Shut up, you smart-ass bitch!"

"What do you want from me?"

"Bottom line?" He smiled to himself. "Aren't you shocked by my command of English? I told you I had a very good teacher. Rafael Navarro. Remember him?"

"Very well."

"He's still alive. Somewhere in Miami. I don't know why he left your honeypot. That I've got to find out. My bosses don't give one god damn about Rafael. But I do. I'm going to track him down and kill him. For my own sport. It will amuse me."

"Let him alone."

"You're hardly in a position to give orders. I'm giving the orders right now. My new orders are that I'm going to take you on a tour of this property. We'll visit a room or two in this fine house. After our visit, I'm going to ask you to perform a service for us. If you don't, some truly terrible things will happen."

"Terrible things have already happened. Anishi. Mia. Maxie."

"A mere preview of coming attractions." He reached down and untied my feet, although my hands remained bound. "Now get up, bitch, and start walking. You'll want to visit some other members of your household. Those I haven't already killed. I've got plans for them." He looked ominously at me. "And do I ever have plans for you."

. . .

With my hands still tied behind my back, I had no choice but to follow him on this journey to hell. Feeling weak and dizzy, I longed for Rafael. Although I regretted the death of Anishi and Maxie, particularly the brutal ways they were murdered, I did not mourn them. Both of them had worked against my interests and had betrayed me. Their going left a void, but no real pain.

That, I reserved for Mia. Throughout the afternoon, I'd flashed upon her dying a slow and painful death. Anishi and Maxie had mercifully died quickly, but Mia's death would undoubtedly be slower and more agonizing. I still held out hope that a virus was not in that vial whose contents had been injected into her arm. Perhaps it was another substance not harmful to her. Maybe Martinez was just bluffing, trying to force us to cooperate in his latest scheme. It was a hope at least, though dim and faint.

A pot-bellied Cuban guard stood at the entrance to one of my guest bedrooms. At the approach of Martinez, he opened the door for us. Reaching back for me, Martinez shoved me inside the brightly lit room. All the previously dim light bulbs had been removed and replaced with heavy wattage instead. The bedroom looked more like a surgical unit than a romantic lair.

I gasped when I saw a nude Angelo spreadeagle on the bed, his hands and feet firmly tied. He was gagged. The Cuban woman guard I'd encountered earlier stood over him. As Angelo whimpered and moaned, she soothingly ran her fingers over his smooth olive skin. Although she was being very gentle with him, he reacted to her touch as if her fingers were on fire. He obviously knew something I didn't.

"There he is!" Martinez said proudly, as if displaying a trophy he'd bagged. "Your former lover, Dino Paglia. Son of Rafael Navarro. Would you believe it? Even after a little torture, he denied he was Dino. Even after I had five of my guards brutally rape him while I looked on, he still denied he was Dino. Or, more to the point, Desi Navarro. Claims he's someone called Angelo. That he's Italian. Not Cuban. As if Geraldo Martinez wouldn't know a Cuban boy when he saw one."

"It's not Dino!" I protested. "It's someone else. Let him go! He's not involved in any of this. A perfect stranger who'd just arrived at the house before you took it over with your thugs."

With his usual ferocity, Martinez turned to me and slapped my face really hard. "Right! Let him go. Just untie him, tell him to put on his clothes and get the hell out of here. Why don't we just drive him to the nearest sheriff's office? What kind of idiot do you take me for?"

As if in a world of her own, the guard continued to lovingly fondle Angelo's smooth skin. Her touch was exceedingly erotic, but under these circumstances, it hardly aroused passion in Angelo. The guard ran her fingers up and down the length of his body, paying particular attention to his arms, chest, and legs. She didn't touch his exposed genitals.

Martinez walked over and slapped the guard on the arm, signaling her to back away. He looked almost lovingly into the eyes of the struggling Angelo, the way a seducer might view the object of his passion. It was an eerie moment. It was as if Martinez intended to make love to Angelo. He ran his fingers through his black curly hair and, as if imitating the guard, fondled the boy's chest. Perhaps it was a mirage, but there appeared a certain tenderness on the face of Martinez.

That look quickly disappeared as he raised his eyes to confront me. "You may wonder why this young boy is struggling so desperate to escape our touch." His face grew even harsher. "I'll tell you why. Dino here is experiencing some discomfort because we've already told him what we plan to do with him." He looked admiringly at the guard. A sudden hunch informed me that the guard might not be a guard at all. But a nurse. Perhaps a doctor.

"This ugly, sadistic, blood-sucking vampire is an expert in her field. For Castro in Havana, she's performed her services on some three-hundred victims. She makes that Nazi Bitch of Buchenwald look like Shirley Temple."

"What are you talking about?" I demanded to know.

"You see," Martinez said, staring triumphantly at me, obviously taking pleasure in the revelation he was about to make. "She's an expert in removing the skin of her victims. Slowly. Ever so slowly. Inch by inch. Long before she's finished, her victims cry out for death. When she actually starts removing the skin, she'll take the gag off Dino and we'll record his screams, his pleading. You'd be amazed at what comes out of a victim's throat when the skin is removed. I've listened to dozens of them."

At the sound of those words, Angelo struggled to break free, but was hopelessly bound. Martinez looked down at him, all love gone from his face. His laughter was demonic. "Look, the kid wants to keep his skin. Imagine that! My only regret is that Rafael won't be here to watch the procedure. I wanted Rafael to watch the operation and to know it would be but a prelude to what I have planned for your personalized Cubano stud."

"This is not Rafael's son!" I screamed. "He doesn't even know Rafael. It's not Dino Paglia. This boy is an innocent kid."

"Shut up, bitch!" he shouted at me. "I don't need you to tell me who Dino Paglia is. I saw his picture. Someone showed me that Banana Republic ad. This is the same boy."

"But there were two boys in that ad. This is not Dino. It's the other boy in the ad."

"I know perfectly well who Dino Paglia is. All it took was a cigarette lighter burning the tiny balls of Ted Hooker. He told me right away who Dino Paglia is. That's good enough for me."

"Under torture, Ted would confess to anything. Even killing President Kennedy."

"Castro was responsible for that."

The guard picked up a revolver and pointed it at my chest. She looked as if she were ready to assassinate me now.

"Against the wall," Martinez barked at me. He was used to

commanding. He shouted something at the guard in Spanish, then looked back at me. "If you even move during what you're about to see, if you take just one step toward the bed to rescue your lover, you're dead. Just look into the face of this ugly cunt here. Do you think she'll hesitate one second before pumping lead into you and through you? Consider how many victims she's already killed."

As instructed, I looked into the guard's face. Martinez was right. This vicious woman would kill without hesitation.

I did as I was told, bracing myself as best I could against the wall. An incredible dizziness came over me, and I had to struggle just to stand up. I wasn't prepared for another of this lunatic's demonstrations. I prayed to God Martinez wasn't going to order Angelo's skin removed in my presence.

Ever so gently, Martinez ran his hand down Angelo's chest until he reached the boy's pubic hair. He tugged at the hair gently. Then his hand descended even lower and enclosed Angelo's penis. A peculiar look came over Martinez. It was as if by fondling Angelo's penis, he remembered and regretted the loss of his own. He gently stroked the boy's organ, failing to arouse it at all. If anything, it seemed to recede. Still holding the penis, he looked up at me. "I had one of these once. Before it was cut away from my body. It was the greatest source of pleasure in my life. I had big plans for my dick. Before I died of AIDS, I was going to fuck three-hundred young boys and girls, the younger, the better. Each time I climaxed inside them, I would have the added thrill that I was sharing my AIDS with them. It would make my orgasms all the sweeter."

Using more force now, he reached down and tugged roughly at Angelo's generous foreskin. "Once, I had a covering just like this unfortunate kid's. You stupid Americanos cut off your children's foreskins, unlike us Cubano fathers. It desensitizes the dick. A dick with a foreskin has a more sensitive head. At least, that's my theory. Maybe my dick wasn't as big as Dino's here, but I had as much foreskin as he has. Now it's all gone. Not only the foreskin. But the dick as well." He pulled hard at Angelo's penis, causing the young man great pain. He struggled to free himself, but remained hopelessly tied and gagged. Deep moans came from behind the gag. The way he struggled, it was as if he sensed the skin removal was about to begin.

In a lunge like an animal darting to ensnare smaller game, Martinez descended upon Angelo's penis and chomped down on the foreskin. He began to chew it voraciously, like a lion tearing into fresh meat.

Angelo was screaming, but what came out from behind the gag wasn't quite a scream.

I tried to avert my eyes, but I felt compelled to look. Not as a voyeur. I needed this final proof to convince me forever that Martinez was a complete maniac. Death awaited all of us if I couldn't devise a plan to escape. Time was running out.

I could no longer look at the mutilation occurring before me. I seemed to have momentarily lost touch with reality. A voice was calling to me, but it seemed to originate on some far and distant shore. Suddenly, the reality of the situation came crushing in on me again.

"Puta cunt!"

I didn't need to be told that Martinez was addressing me. I looked into his face. His head was now raised over Angelo's body. The face was demented. Blood was dripping from its teeth. I looked at Angelo's genitals. He was bleeding profusely.

Licking his bloody lips and savoring the last bit of skin, Martinez stood up. He'd eaten the foreskin. "I got carried away there. I admit that." He turned to look at the guard. "Of course, what I just did is nothing compared to what this scumbag plans to do. I took only an inch or so of skin. She wants a whole lot more."

I looked at the gagged Angelo. He'd passed out.

It seems I have circumcised your pet. But it doesn't matter. Considering where he's heading, he won't need a dick." His eyes narrowed as he focused intently on me. "Come on, sweet pussy. We have another visit or two to make before Clinton arrives."

. . .

Martinez didn't show me where Mia was kept. If he'd injected her with a deadly virus as I feared, that meant he wasn't going to kill her the way he'd murdered Anishi and Maxie. Martinez obviously preferred Mia to die slowly.

Although I feared, as reported, that Ted had been subjected to genital torture, I just knew he was still alive. Martinez needed Ted, at least until the meeting with Clinton tonight was over. Ted was the liaison man.

Still handcuffed, I was led to my library, where I was shoved inside and told to wait. Martinez slammed and locked the door behind me. A few minutes alone, away from this psycho, was like a holiday in the Alps. I didn't know if I could endure much more of this. In my situation, I wondered what comforts the damned were offered.

I stood looking at all the books I'd bought and never read. At this tragic point in my life, I wondered if I should have been reading these books instead of pursuing men who, as the years went by, had less and less to teach me.

I was just getting used to my solitude when the door was unlocked and thrown open. A short man was shoved inside. The door was quickly slammed and locked behind him.

At first, I didn't recognize the visitor.

"Ms. Del Lago," he said. "We meet again."

The moment he called me by that assumed name I'd used at the now-destroyed clinic in Switzerland, I knew it was Dr. Karl Euler. He'd disappeared when I'd shipped him off to my villa in the Azores.

"Fool that I was to ever trust a little prick like you!" I said, glaring at him.

He looked awful, as if he'd only recently been roughed up by some of the goons who worked for Martinez. He'd also lost a lot of weight on a body that had few extra pounds to spare.

"Apparently, I didn't buy you off," I said. "You're working for them again."

"You don't understand. I was kidnapped. I went to that hideout of yours in the Azores, just as we agreed. But there was no security there. Someone tipped them off about where I was. They came for me. They flew me to Havana, then to Florida. I've been held prisoner on some island near here. It was completely uninhabited except for three guards and myself."

"I have no idea if you're telling me the truth or not." I sighed in my despair. "I'm not even sure if the truth matters anymore."

"If we ever get out of this hellhole alive, we can discuss that philosophic point at your home in the Cayman Islands. The place you were going to send me before I was kidnapped."

"I'm afraid we'll never live to get there." My voice grew stern. "Why are you here?"

"It's exactly as I told you. They are going to force me to perform a lobotomy on President Clinton tonight!"

"Why don't they just assassinate him and get it over with?"

"They don't want him dead. They'll only end up with Al Gore. They want Clinton to function as president, but with a slightly altered brain."

"I don't understand. If the president is subjected to a lobotomy, then he'll be removed from office anyway."

"No, it's more complicated than that. I have perfected a very special operation for the brain. I've performed this operation successfully on several victims..I mean, patients. The brain is altered but ever so slightly."

"But when the operation is discovered, word will get out. He'll be removed from office."

"Surely, you're not that naive. No one in his close circle is going to announce to the public that Clinton has had a lobotomy. Haven't you ever heard of a cover-up?"

"I invented the term. But it seems to me that a lobotomized president will be obvious to anyone."

"Not at first. For two or three months following the operation, the brain will function normally. Then one day, and for no apparent reason, the president will start manifesting a different behavior pattern. It will begin slowly but rather dramatically. For example, he might slap his assistant, that cute one, George something. I must examine that little one someday. Sometimes, big things come in small packages. The slap will be in front of witnesses. After that, the behavior will get worse. He'll invite three of the most prominent female journalists in America into the Oval Office for an interview. Don't ask me to name them. I find American dyke names hard to remember. In the middle of the interview, he'll drop his pants and invite each of the sluts to take turns fellating him. On another occasion, he'll go up to every member of his Secret Service and privately ask each of them if he can 'taste' them. He'll then reach for their crotches and start unzipping their trousers. No doubt, since he's the president, most members of the service will comply. Perhaps a minor protest here and there."

"What is all this erratic behavior supposed to lead to?"

"As the weeks go by, Clinton will cease being a naughty boy and turn into a political devil. Anything might happen. Perhaps, say, at a press conference one day, he'll suddenly launch into a blistering attack on the readiness of the U.S. military, of which he is commander-in-chief. Obviously, by this time there will be a major revolution in the land against Clinton. Screams for his impeachment."

"But you're still stuck with Gore, even if Clinton goes. As you said, your bosses don't want Gore."

"They don't want Gore or anyone else of the ilk. That is tomorrow's problem, and I'm sure they are working very hard to solve it even as we speak. The final solution - don't you just love that term? - for Gore is not part of our agenda. They will probably have killed us long before then and disposed of our bodies - no doubt subjecting us first to medical experiments. I, of all people, know how painful medical experiments can be. I've performed enough of them."

"I'm sure you do," I said sarcastically. "But I don't understand where I fit into this scheme."

"What do your American fishermen call it? Oh, yes, the bait. You're the bait. It's necessary that you give Clinton a certain drink I will have prepared for him. With my ability to mix drinks, I could have been a cocktail waitress. I mean bartender. The drink will knock him out. That's when I come into the room. With guns pointed at my head, of course. I will take over then and perform the lobotomy. You will be free to go at that point."

"Right. Free to go indeed."

"We have no choice but to do what they tell us. If you don't carry out this beast's orders, he'll have all of us killed. Believe you me, his thugs have tortured me into revealing methods of slow and painful death that are nothing compared to anything these Castro henchmen with their limited intellects have ever devised."

"I don't know what to do."

"Do as you're told! You've always directed the script. Probably written the script as well. You've always ruled from a position of power. For once in your life, just follow orders. There is no guarantee that harm won't follow. But every minute, every hour we delay, we might save our lives. You and Mia Kelly are very, very rich. At least half a million people out there want to take some of that money from you for some reason or another. Probably eighteen lawsuits were filed against you today alone. All those thousands will not let the world's two leading vaginal types go undetected for long. I suspect that if you're out of contact for just a few hours or more, your blood-sucking attorneys will send attack dogs to hunt you down. They'll find out what happened to you. Time, believe me, is on our side if we can hold out for a few hours longer. After I perform the lobotomy, I am - how do you say? - dead meat. A problem I've always had."

"We'll see." I thought of my recent love, Juan Garcia, and hoped that he'd soon be swimming across to the mainland to inform that god damn Snake what had happened to us.

"Will you cooperate with them?" Dr. Euler asked. "If you don't, it'll mean a sudden end for us."

"You've given me a script I can play. Everything is out of my hands now. I'll do what they want in hopes that will save me. Save us. Or, at least, what's left of us."

"That's a relief to hear. The tortures we'd be subjected to before they killed us could only have come from the brain of a demented genius."

"A man such as yourself?"

"A man such as myself. Or at least, my old self. I've done things I'm not proud of, but I've vowed that if I survive this, I will become a new and better person. I will turn my genius to good."

"We'll talk about that later. Much later."

At that, there was a sudden sound at the door. The door to the library was thrown open to admit Martinez. I knew from the look on that face that this nightmare film in which I was starring was about to begin.

CHAPTER FOURTEEN

"Pull off all your clothes," Martinez barked. It was an hour later, and I'd been delivered to the luxurious Roman bath of my own bedroom. The female Cuban guard had just departed after running a bath for me.

"Go on!" he snapped at me. "I've seen your tits and pussy before. The whole god damn world has seen everything you've got."

Without hesitation, I removed my thin dress. I wasn't wearing panties or a bra. I quickly jumped into the sunken bathtub.

With a gun pointed at me, he seated himself on an upholstered stool a few feet away to oversee the action.

I tried to be as unsexy as possible in my bath, but it was obvious that I was getting Martinez excited, although what there was to excite in him I didn't know. I avoided eye contact with him, and concentrated on my bath, which I welcomed after a long, sweaty day and a urine soaking. Sinking low, I submerged myself in the sudsy, cleaning waters.

"I want you smelling real nice for Clinton. That boy thinks he's going to get a chance to eat the world's most high-priced pussy tonight. He's a pussy-eater, you know. But is he ever in for a surprise. Sometimes we don't get what we bargained for."

I closed my eyes and for one brief moment tried to imagine I was in the room alone, that I'd never met Martinez.

"Tonight, as your crooked president, Nixon, used to say, I want to make something perfectly clear. In a little while, we are going to give you complete instructions as to what to do when Clinton arrives. From the moment Clinton and his Secret Service enter the grounds, one of my men is going to take a pistol and point it at the head of Mia Kelly. The moment you don't follow my orders, that's the very moment that your mama's brains will be spilled all over her bedroom."

I gasped at the prospect. He looked at me as if he knew he'd just won my cooperation.

He leaned back on the stool and glared ominously at me. This time, I made eye contact with him. It was like looking into the demented eyes of a thrill killer.

"Your choice is clear," he said. "I always like to give my victims a choice. Either Mia Kelly loses her brains - not to mention her life - or else Clinton has his brain slightly altered to make him a bad boy. Even badder than he already is. There's a very curious thing about this operation of Dr. Euler's. As he told me, the lobotomy won't make Clinton behave or do nothing different from what is already within his heart. In other words, the surgery will just free him to act on impulses he already has. The brake that Clinton's brain holds on him will be gone. He'll say and do things that he really wants to do anyway. That will be bad politics for him."

I sat up in my bath and looked at him with utter contempt. "You mean, if all his life he's wanted to molest Chelsea, but held back because he knew it was wrong, after the operation he'll feel free to act on that impulse?"

"You got it, puta cunt!" he said, arching his back and standing up. He pointed the gun at my head and fondled the trigger.

I scooted back in the tub, almost wanting to submerge myself, as if that would protect me from his bullet.

"Now get out of that bath and dry yourself off," he shouted, releasing his finger on the trigger. "Pay special attention to drying your pussy. I never did like wet, sloppy pussies."

I did as I was ordered, emerging from my bath. But I didn't understand his remark. What difference did it make to him how moist my pussy was? This dickless wonder could hardly handle me. I wrapped a large fluffy pink towel around my nudity as he forced me into my bedroom. Here, I encountered four of his Cuban goon squad. The leering men gaped at me, as I embraced myself for the inevitable. A gang rape, probably in the same style poor Angelo had been subjected to.

Martinez ripped the towel from my body, and the guards grabbed me, throwing me down on the bed. I was spreadeagled. Two guards pinned my arms to the bed, and the other two locked their hands around my ankles like handcuffs.

At the foot of the bed, Martinez removed his shirt, leaving only a soiled underwear top. Surely he wasn't the one who was going to rape me. I was thankful when he left his pants on.

"I want to go first," he said. "Before Clinton. As I told you, I don't like sloppy seconds."

With the ferocity of an animal, he threw himself on me, burying his head between my legs. He began to lick me and penetrate me with his tongue. I'd never known such oral passion before. It was as if all the sexual power that might have resided in his penis had been miraculously transferred to his lips and tongue.

He didn't try to hurt me or bite me, the way his teeth had so savagely mutilated Angelo's penis. It was more an act of worship, as strange as that might appear. Even though I tried to resist him and to struggle to free myself, I finally gave in to him. It was the easiest way out for me.

I'd been serviced by experts. Rock Hudson (believe it or not), John Lennon, Elvis Presley. The son of a president. No, not that one: He doesn't go that route. But never in my life had I been so thoroughly devoured by such a skilled oral seducer as Martinez. His love-making seemed to go on for hours, and even though I at first tried to resist him, I found myself approaching climax. I found it unbelievable that he could arouse any emotion in me other than fear and loathing.

I felt totally under his power and control. He dived deeper for the final moments and left me gasping. Even when it was over, he didn't remove his lips and tongue from me, but gave me little flickerings and gentle, ever so gentle, kisses.

When he finally raised himself over me, he looked tenderly into my eyes. "I'm in love with you. I've loved you and desired you - only you - ever since I saw you in that movie, 'Kinky'. That's why I tried to rape you that night. I foolishly thought that once I made love to you, you'd fall under my spell and love me back in spite of yourself."

"I'd never love you, shithead!"

He slapped my face. Real hard. "That's what you say now. In time you'll learn to love me." He reached for his shirt. "After this thing with Clinton is over, me and you - along with all your money - are going away together. What we just did on this bed we will do again and again. In the morning. In the afternoon. And at night. I will make such tender love to you that eventually when I enter a room, you will start getting hot for my love and kisses. One day, you'll be so much in love with me you'll beg for my tongue in your mouth. Then I'll know you'll have truly fallen for me."

"Dream on, asshole!"

He slapped me again. Harder than before. "I'll break you yet, puta cunt! In the meantime, me and you have a date with the president of the United States."

. . .

As Martinez hovered in the background with his pistol pointed at me, I surveyed the results of my own make-up and hair styling. People had always told me that if I didn't have billions of dollars, I could always get a job as a hair stylist or make-up artist. Judging my own creative statement, I appeared camera ready. In spite of all the pain, suffering, and lack of sleep I had endured, I'd never looked more glamorous.

In the last few minutes, I'd agreed with myself to do whatever he wanted me to do. At this point, I didn't have either the stamina or courage to defy him. It was Clinton who had foolishly placed me in this position. I'd never desired a meeting with him. Or had I changed my mind and solicited a meeting after all? I just couldn't remember. He's definitely not my type - ghastly legs - but neither was any president of the United States beginning with George Washington. I, of course, had never heard a report about how Rutherford B. Hayes performed in bed. But I tended not to go to bed with men named Rutherford.

While I was making myself ready to receive Clinton, Martinez gave me detailed and surprisingly precise instructions about what I was to do before and after my meeting. Without Clinton or me, but with a different cast of characters, it was obvious to me that he'd played a similar political game before. He was just too good at it. I could almost bet that he'd set up some hooker to entice a visiting dignitary - maybe even the president of some country - on an official visit to Cuba. Who knows what incriminating photographs were hidden in secret vaults inside Castro's Cuba?

"Do everything like I told you," he said, interrupting my reverie.

I'd almost forgotten he was here.

"Clinton is already being a bad boy even before Euler's

lobotomy, which will guarantee that he'll be nothing but a bad boy in the future. The president is arriving with only three members of his Secret Service, and not telling the rest of the boys where he is. Pulling the old Kennedy stunt slipping off to meet Monroe. The Russians might be launching missiles against the East Coast, but Kennedy wanted a piece of dyed blond pussy. Having just three members of the Secret Service on hand makes it a lot easier for us. Can you believe it? Out of all the Secret Service, there are only three guys Clinton can trust with his dirty secrets. But Castro always said that if you can find even three men to trust, that's a lot. I've never trusted anybody."

"What about the rest of the Secret Service guarding Clinton?"

"From what we could gather, the other guys will think the president is asleep at a private villa in Miami. Your private villa on Star Island. The same god damn place where you removed my treasure. They'll think you're in that villa with Clinton, but no one knows for sure."

I was growing increasingly nervous, agitated, and impatient. Glancing at a clock, I noticed that it was already past eleven. Clinton was supposed to be here at ten, but I understood he was always late. Imagine being late for a rendezvous with America's reigning love goddess? What business could he possibly have that would have detained him? Perhaps there was a threat of war somewhere. At this insane moment, I could almost wish for a war. Anything to free me from going through with this scheme. I didn't want Clinton or his brain damaged, or anybody injured for that matter, and I certainly didn't want a bullet to explode inside Mia's brain.

An in-house phone rang by my bed. Never taking his eyes from me, he darted over to answer it. He mumbled something in Spanish into the phone. "They're here!" he said, turning to me.

I'd never seen him this nervous. Although he appeared to have the upper hand, he seemed out of control, as if he couldn't go through with his own plan. Was he as insecure as that? Perhaps the mighty office of the president of the United States had intimidated even a thrill killer.

There was another call on the in-house phone. He answered

it, and again, he mumbled something in Spanish before putting down the receiver. "Two men from the Secret Service want to talk to you in the library before you meet Clinton."

"Where's the president?" I asked.

"He's gone to your master bedroom with the third guy from the Secret Service. Clinton wants to take a bath before meeting you, as he's all hot and sweaty. Fatso has been running around in the heat all day, pumping hands. The third member of the service is also a masseur. He's going to massage Clinton before he meets with you. To put him in a relaxed mood, or so I was told."

"I understand," I said, and I really thought I did. Even if I were president of the United States, I'd be nervous about meeting me. First of all, I have more money than Clinton. I was also a hell of a lot better looking. Perhaps he was also nervous, with all these pre-rendezvous baths and massages. Maybe he figured he wouldn't measure up to my usual standards.

"The men from the Secret Service are ready to see you now," Martinez said. "By now, surely you understand me. A gun will be pointed at you at all times. One false move, and it's twilight time. *For everybody*." He looked deeply into my eyes, moving close. "Even though I'm in love with you, I wouldn't hesitate for a moment to kill you. Do you believe that?"

I, too, stared deeply into his eyes. "With every bone in my body, I believe you." I turned and walked toward the library, throwing open the doors to greet two members of the Secret Service.

"Hello, ma'am," one of them said, stepping forward. "I'm Greg Palmer. Nice to meet you." He started to extend his hand, but seemed to think it was not the proper thing to do, and quickly withdrew it. He looked like a young Karl Malden.

"Glad to meet you," the other man said. "I'm Jeff Reggio." He was about thirty-five, perhaps Italian, a shadow version of Joe Namath (remember him?) when he was a star football hero. Jeff was less intimidated by me, and reached to shake my hand. "Forgive me for saying this, but ol' Billy boy is one lucky son-of-a-bitch tonight."

"You're from Arkansas?" I asked.

"How did you know?

"Just a guess." I turned my back to them and walked toward

the bar. "I'd like to offer both of you a drink." I moved to the designated bottles as I had been directed earlier by Martinez. God only knew what those bottles contained. As I turned around to pour them a drink, Jeff was suddenly behind me. "We can't drink on the job."

"Is that so?" I asked, rubbing my fingers along his cheek. "Who's going to file a bad report card on you?" I gently felt the stubble of his beard. "Certainly not moi. Perhaps Greg here."

"Hell, no!" Greg said, heading toward the bar. "I'll have that fucking drink. After all, Bill's here to party. Seems we're entitled to have at least one drink under these circumstances. Scotch for me. On the rocks."

I poured Greg a stiff drink from the crystal decanter. As I handed it to him, and for purposes of distraction, I kissed him tenderly on the lips, perhaps with a feather-like flicker of the tongue, if I recall. "You're a real man. I like manly men. I like a man who can take a drink every now and then in spite of company rules."

"Hell with that," Jeff said. "I can drink this faggot here under the table any night. Pour me some of that poison too."

I did as he asked, hoping that it was indeed not poison.

As I'd been told, I led the men over to the sofa, placing myself between them. "Drink up, boys," I said. "The fun is about to begin." As the men sipped their drinks, I placed my hand on each of their thighs, about mid-calf.

"Too bad the party is with Billy boy tonight. I'd much rather have a party with just the three of us."

"I'd like that a lot," Jeff said, as my hand traveled up his thigh. Not to neglect Greg completely, I turned and gave him a quick brush-kiss on the lips.

"Boys, I'll do you a favor. Finish your drinks - it'll loosen you up a bit. While we're waiting for the boss, I'll show you something you might have seen on the screen but not in real life."

"It's a deal," Greg said, eagerly downing his drink. "We watched 'Kinky' three times with the president."

"It's his favorite movie," Jeff said, belting down the rest of his Scotch.

Bolting up, I got up on the coffee table in front of them. I was wearing a white dress, which I ever so slowly began to lift above my knees. "I must warn you, I'm not wearing panties. If you can't take what you're about to see - too much heat - better get out of the kitchen."

"Go, girl, go!" Jeff said. Suddenly, his eyes looked blurred as he slumped over. Greg moved quickly to investigate, and as he did, he too crumbled over on the sofa.

Slowly, without taking my eyes off the men, I lowered my dress.

At that point, Martinez, spying on us from afar, came into the room with his ever-faithful companion, his pistol. The only one he had left after I'd finished him off on Star Island.

Gingerly, I stepped down from the coffee table, looking at the two drugged Secret Service men. At least, I hoped they were drugged and not poisoned.

"There's been a change of plans," Martinez said to me. "We can't use you as bait with the third member of the Secret Service. We've been spying on Clinton and this guy in your bedroom. It's clear to everybody he's a mariposa. It'll take different bait for him. Your charms won't work on that faggot. He's massaging Clinton right now. We can tell with the way that massage is going that this guy is definitely a maricone."

"I'm sure you've fucked enough mariposas in your day to spot one when you see one."

He glared at me, then walked over to the main door. "We've got different bait for Clinton's masseur." He threw open the door.

A guard shove a shirtless young man into the living room.

It took just a moment before I realized that it was Juan Garcia.

. . .

When we were alone in the living room, I knew I had to speak in whispers. But as I approached Juan, it was as if he and I were on an otherwise deserted island. Just the two of us.

"My one true love," he said softly to me in accented English. "The plan didn't work. I couldn't swim away from here for help. Martinez came for me. Insisted I take a shower right in front of him. I thought he was planning to seduce me, even though I'd heard from one of the guards that someone had removed it with a knife. Then he told me what I had to do tonight. If I didn't do what he wanted, he threatened to have me put to a slow and painful death."

I ran my delicate fingers across his smooth cheek. "He's telling the truth. If you don't do what he says, Martinez will have you killed. All of us killed, in fact."

"Then I must do it?" he asked, a kind of innocence in his eyes.

I lightly brushed my lips across his. "You must do what he wants. All of us have to do his bidding."

"Is it true that the president of the United States is actually here?" he asked, a kind of eagerness in his voice. "Have you seen him?"

"I haven't seen him, but I'm told he's here. He seems in no great hurry to introduce himself to me."

"Martinez said I had to spend time with one of his Secret Service men. That guy is a mariposa. Martinez said I was the prettiest boy on the staff except for someone called Angelo who's had an accident with his penis. Cut himself with a knife or something."

"Or something."

"Martinez said my body was the most beautiful male body he'd ever seen - except for Angelo. That's why he chose me for the job."

"Martinez has superb taste. You're beautiful. One of the most beautiful men I've ever seen. Even though I enjoy your male beauty more than anyone, right now I find myself wishing you'd been born ugly. That way, you might have done what I wanted. Rescued all of us."

"I'm so sorry, my sweet." He gently kissed both of my cheeks. Then he kissed my mouth. Real hard, inserting his tongue.

"The only way I can be with this man of Clinton's is to imagine your lips on me. Those few moments I spent with you were the most important of my life. In that brief time, I had the greatest pleasure I've ever know." He pulled me harder to his body, pressing against me. "I also fell in love with you."

At the approach of footsteps, I broke apart from him.

Martinez came into the room, looking suspiciously at me,

then at Juan. But that one always looked suspiciously at everyone.

"We've just learned the president will receive you upstairs in about twenty minutes," he said. "He's got a few important calls to make before he can see you."

"How arrogant!" I said, slightly miffed at Clinton. "He just comes in and takes over my house without even saying hello. It is I who should be receiving him."

"Let's not stand on formalities in view of the party we have planned for Clinton when he meets up with you," Martinez said.

"Why should I complain? This house hardly belongs to me anymore. If I didn't know better, I'd say you owned it."

"Maybe I will one day," he said, looking over at Juan. "When I found even Sherry Kelly's charms might not work on this Secret Service mariposa, I went looking for a male whore. My first thought was of Dino. I'm sure he's gone that way many times. But that boy's money-maker is seriously damaged. I had to turn elsewhere. To this beauty here." He glanced over at Juan, then looked at me. "You've had most of the male beauties in the world. What do you think of this one?"

"Exceptional," was all I said, as if totally uninterested.

"Damn right," he said, flashing fury. "Back in my day, I might have taken both of you on the same bed. While I fucked you, pretty boy here could lick me in all the most sensuous places. That was a sexual sensation I used to especially enjoy."

"Let's not indulge in remembrances of things past," I said.

He looked at me as if he could shoot me on the spot. Thinking better of that, he finally said, "Let's not. What's gone is gone."

A Cuban guard entered the room and whispered something in Spanish to Martinez, then left. He turned to me, then looked sternly at Juan. "Okay, muchacho, show the man a good time. And keep him distracted until we come for you."

"What am I to do?" I asked Martinez. "It seems I'm not needed at this party."

"Just make small talk while Juan here flirts with the man," Martinez instructed. "You won't be in the room for too long. Just ten or twenty minutes at the most before Clinton calls for you. Break the ice between Juan and this mariposa. Set the stage for the seduction. You're an actress. You can do it." He paused and looked deeply into my eyes. "The point is, keep the faggot distracted and involved with Juan." He stalked out of the room.

After he'd left, Juan moved real close to me, even though we both knew we were being spied upon. Both of us were being very indiscreet under the circumstances, but seemed compelled to behave this way anyway.

"Sherry," he said, his eyes almost pleading with mine. "I've never done this before. I don't know what to say to the man. What to do."

"I'll do all the talking at first. Just smile a lot."

From the other side of the living room, a door opened and a Secret Service man entered, wearing a full jacket and tie, even though the room was hot. Someone had turned off the air conditioning. The agent looked like Warren Beatty as he appeared in 1965. Perhaps even better looking than Warren, and minus the pimples. I used to know Warren very well. For Juan's sake, I hoped he wasn't as well hung as Warren, and didn't need as much sex as Warren did. Five times in three hours is perhaps too much for anyone.

"Good evening, Ms. Kelly," the agent said to me, although he didn't look in my direction. His eyes narrowed in on a shirtless Juan. "I'm Dick Knight. Who might this young man be. A male model? Dino Paglia's replacement, no doubt?"

My twenty-minute wait for Clinton turned out to be only two minutes. Blowing Juan a kiss and an adieu, I abandoned him to his fate with that Warren Beatty look-alike and hurried to my own trap - or rather, Clinton's trap.

. . .

"Come on in, Sherry," Clinton said, as I was ushered into my own bedroom. I felt a sense of irony at having the president invite me into my own bedroom. He was sitting in the sunken living room area of my gigantic bedroom, which occupied almost an entire wing of the house. I always liked big bedrooms.

Clad only in a pair of jogging shorts, the freshly bathed and massaged president had propped up his feet on my coffee table.

As I reached to shake his hand, I tried to avoid looking at those YMCA white, nearly hairless legs, much less that undefined chest. The man needed to work out and put some definition in that chest that jogging alone couldn't help. Only after I'd seated myself across from him did I take note of the fact that he didn't rise to greet me. Perhaps presidents don't have to get up to greet visitors.

"Mr. President," I said, somewhat awkwardly, wondering from which part of the room my every move was being spied upon. "It's an honor to have you here at Palm Island."

"We don't have to be formal with each other," he said, smiling. "Life moves too much in the fast lane for that. Let's just pretend we've known each other intimately for a couple of years and take it from there." As he looked up at me, I detected a slight charm in him, perhaps even a vague sexual allure, a hint of masculinity, a gleam in his eye. In spite of it all, he still wasn't my type. I suspected he wasn't Hillary's type either, but one must make compromises in choosing a life partner. Perhaps that's why I never had a longtime companion.

"I want to thank you for your campaign contribution. It was the most generous of anyone in America."

"You're most welcome. Perhaps I should have given more."

"That would have been nice. I wish your mama had supported me more.

"Politically, she's very confused. A social liberal, a fiscal conservative. I'm not sure what she wants for this country, or even for herself. She's definitely anti-immigrant. But Mommie changes her mind. A lot."

"Maybe we'll win her over the next time I run."

"Maybe. With Mommie, one never knows." Right now she wants to become a movie star. Like me."

"Fascinating. I hear you're having a lot of problems with your latest film."

"A lot. Someone trying to kill Brad Cruz was only part of it. My first co-star turned it down when he couldn't flesh out a bikini."

"Not too much to flash, huh?"

"That's right."

"Same thing has been said about me. Said, hell! Written for all the god damn world to read. I guess you read that article in

Penthouse."

"I didn't read it. The only magazines I ever read are those with me on the cover. Not that I'm vain."

"Good! The bitch who wrote the article didn't think it was small at the time. Said it gave her more pleasure than she'd ever known in her whole rotten life. After all, it's not the size that counts. It's the action. Right?"

"Mr. President, I think I've heard that point before."

"I know it sounds a little self-serving. You must have heard every line every man in the world came up with. Original or not."

"I've heard a few. Actually, some were very original. You'd be surprised what men will say when trying to get close to the richest woman in the world."

"I know what you mean. It's the same if a person happens to be the most powerful man in the world. You won't believe the letters that come into the White House from women. Often accompanied by nude photographs. I read some of them and look at their pictures when I get bored running the country. I get offers from guys, too. But I don't go that route."

"You don't?" I asked provocatively, sincerely believing that all men have gone that route at least once. "Never?"

"Well, it was so long ago, I don't remember..." His voice drifted off, and he looked uncomfortable.

"You didn't inhale?"

"Something like that," he said, abruptly changing the subject. He looked over at me, a stern expression crossing his face, as if getting down to business. "How does it feel to talk to a man who only recently made $35,000 a year? You, with all the money in the world."

"I'm not one to pretend that money is unimportant," I said, not really answering his question. "It's very important. Especially when you don't have any, although I don't know much about that. It's always been peachy to be able to buy anything I wanted, alive or inanimate. Yet at some point, even that thrill fades. Mainly, because you come not to want anything." I was growing increasingly nervous, knowing that I was not only talking to Clinton, but to unknown ears as well. I feared that Martinez and Dr. Euler would enter the room at any moment and take over if I didn't speed up the action in the script Martinez had already prepared for me.

Clinton seemed genuinely intrigued by what I was saying, although the subject held no interest for me. "Go on," he ordered. As uncomfortable as I was, I continued. After all, I'd been ordered to do so by the president. "I've never had much actual money with me at any given time. Perhaps ten-thousand dollars was the most I ever carried on my person. All my life, everything has been paid for me. Taken care of."

He leaned toward me. "How much money do you actually have? Maybe enough to pay off the national debt?"

"I've seen reports of how much money I have. But only in very rough estimates. I'm told that my actual wealth varies drastically from hour to hour. Minute to minute. Many things I own, including a certain painting, are priceless. So, basically, I have only someone's word that the money is there. I haven't actually seen it, much less counted it."

"But the gold. You must have seen or counted the gold."

"Daddy used to keep some gold bars around for mad money when we needed it. But I've not actually seen the gold either. I've seen diamonds. Lots of them. In all shapes, sizes, and colors."

He leaned back and seemed to relax again after the intensity he showed about my wealth. "I once bought Hillary a diamond. More than once, in fact. But the stones weren't special. The money I made as governor didn't allow for much diamond-buying."

"I can well imagine. But I don't feel sorry for you. You chose to go into politics. Both you and Hillary could have made more money and had a lot more fun if you hadn't done that. Look at the abuse you've had to take by becoming president. And there's more to come, as we both know."

"I can take the heat in the kitchen."

"Good, but I know I'm not as strong as you. I chose to become an actress. I didn't choose to become the subject of every scandal sheet in America. But by becoming an actress, I subjected myself to that. At this point, after all I've gone through, I frankly want out. I want to return to being a private citizen again, even though the paparazzi will probably be there shooting me in the morgue the way they did with poor Marilyn. Do you ever feel the impulse to want to return to a quiet, private life in Arkansas?"

"Many times since taking office. Right away, I had to take all that flak about gays in the military. It's getting worse. Just today, an underground newsletter is being mailed to thousands of people across America. In it, I'm accused of drug running, massive bank fraud, extortion. Rape. Yes, rape! Coverups. Break-ins. They must have me confused with Nixon. Bribery. Theft, conflict of interest, arson, money-laundering, insider trading, election fraud, obstruction of justice, campaign fraud. Federal witness tampering, destruction of subpoenaed documents, and adultery." He smiled sheepishly. "Well, on that latter count, there might be something to that. But tonight will be the first time that's been true since I took office."

I smiled like a coquette, marveling at the way he just assumed I was going to have sex with him, because he was the president. Certainly for no other reason. He must know I could do better.

"And, the final charge," he went on. "Accessory to twenty-one or so murders."

"Sounds just like you," I said, smiling facetiously. "Especially the murder part." I laughed weakly at my non-joke.

The president didn't seem amused.

I felt my body begin to break out in a cold sweat. Although I was ready to explode inside, I used all my limited skills as an actress to conceal it. "Mr. President," I said, following instructions previously given to me by Martinez. "Just to break the ice between us, and to keep either of us from becoming too much like a high school couple on their first date, I suggest I pour you an aperitif as a prelude to greater pleasures. A glass of the world's most expensive sherry from Sherry, the world's most expensive woman."

"Forget that. We bubbas from Arkansas don't go in for sherry-drinking."

"Or hand kissing?"

"That too. What I really want is a fat, juicy cheeseburger." He smiled provocatively at me. "Hold the onions. Along with a big thick chocolate milkshake. Lots of chocolate flavor."

I made a split-second decision. It was obvious to me, and I hoped to anyone spying on us, that I wasn't going to get Bill

Clinton to gulp down that sherry, containing God knows what drug. "We have room service," I said, getting up and heading for the phone by my bed. I didn't know if the line had been disconnected or not. When I picked it up, I found I could dial inhouse. I'm sure I couldn't make calls to the outside world for help. Briskly, I placed the president's order to a voice I didn't recognize at the other end of the line. I figured that whatever Martinez spiked the sherry with, he could also use to spike the milkshake.

When I came back to the sofa, Clinton reached for my hand. "Come sit with me. This country boy is lonesome tonight."

As I sat on the sofa with him, he reached for my hand, cuddling it like an awkward school boy. He was not the skilled seducer I'd thought. Even JFK Jr. had a smoother and more polished approach. I smiled weakly at him. Considering the circumstances and the pressure I was under, it was a miracle I could smile at all.

"Could I share a fantasy with you?" he asked.

"Sure, anything."

"I've been thinking about this rendezvous with you for a long time. I've read that when President Kennedy was in the hospital, recovering from one of his back injuries, he had a picture of Monroe over his bed. I don't know if he took the pin-up down whenever Jackie came to visit or not. I guess he decided right then and there if he ever became president of the United States, he would have her. After all, what reigning sex goddess would turn down a request from the president of the United States?"

"Sophia Loren."

He looked at me in surprise. "She turned him down?" He rubbed my hand with gentle fingers which soon began traveling up my arm. "Somewhere along the way, I decided if I ever became president, I was going to meet Sherry Kelly, the girl of my dreams. I owe Vince one for arranging it."

"I hope I live up to your expectations."

"Don't worry about that. I'm the one worried I won't meet your expectations. After all, I've heard that you go in only for the best. Who's the best ever? Tom Cruise? Was he your 'Top Gun'?"

"Not at all. Dolph Lundgren."

"Sounds Danish. I've never heard of him."

"The Schwarzenegger of the B-picture muscle films."

"Ever make it with Arnold? He's a Republican."

"I don't fuck Republicans. Besides, Schwarzenegger has muscle in all the wrong places - not where it counts."

"I see."

To return his impertinence at such direct questions, I asked, "Ever make it with Barbra?"

"Never," he said, frowning. "We thought about it. Nothing came of it."

An awkwardness came between us. It was as if he didn't know what to say to me anymore, or how to proceed. If he only knew the real drama spinning around him. A dreadful reality overwhelmed me, and I could only assume that it'd overtaken the president as well. Although he was definitely not my type, I began to conclude that I was not what he had in mind as a sexual partner after all. If I were right about this, I was hoping he'd get dressed and walk out of here. I didn't want any part of this scheme to harm the president. I wanted him out and safe, although I feared what would happen to the rest of us left behind.

An idea occurred to me. Why hadn't I thought of it before? I couldn't write a message to the president out of fear of being seen, but I could whisper one into his ear if I disguised what I was doing. I could let him know what was about to happen, and let him make some decisions about what to do. After all, in case of world war, he'd have to make a lot of decisions.

If the president could work up enough passion to screw me, I could whisper in his ear and tell him what was going on, pretending it was sexual encouragement and sweet passion I was communicating to him. In between my love messages, I could let him know what a trap he was in. That way, Martinez and his spies might not detect what I was up to. Of course, the president might lose his hard-on when I started to whisper such shit into his ear. Having decided on this course of action, I became Sherry Kelly, not only actress supreme but seducer from hell.

"Mr. President," I said in my best Monroe imitation, "I can't believe you've been seated so close to me for such a long time and haven't taken advantage of the situation." I ran my fingers up his flabby chest.

He looked at me quizzically as if surprised by this sudden transformation. The anticipation of sexual fun and games was reflected once again on his face. This was the Sherry Kelly he'd expected me to be, not the one he'd encountered earlier.

He pulled me closer to him and kissed me, our lips coming together so harshly it caused me some pain. Without wasting a moment, his rather rough tongue entered my mouth. He was like an oversexed 50s high schooler at the drive-in. No refinement. Not having much choice, I sucked on that rough tongue. After all, he was the president. Gennifer was right. He was definitely a tongue sensation type of guy. After what seemed like an hour, he seemed to grow tired of all this tongue-sucking and decided to seek other amusements. He pulled away slightly, probably in dire need of fresh air.

"Mr. President," I cooed in his ear, "for this special occasion tonight, I'm wearing underneath my dress the same outfit I wore in 'Kinky'."

He looked at me as if not understanding at first. "I saw 'Kinky'. More than once. If I recall, and I do recall, you weren't wearing anything under that dress."

"You've got it, big boy."

He smiled alluringly at me. "You don't mind if I conduct an investigation myself to see if you're telling me the truth. Presidents don't like to be lied to. I'm not Senator Packwood, but I have to investigate those things personally. A presidential probe, you might call it."

That hand that had shaken the hand of Robert Dole, and thousands of others, began its long ascent up my silky legs until he'd found the honeypot of his dreams. It was, after all, a world-class honeypot. His fingers seemed to have assumed a life of their own. It was as if Clinton had discovered a wonderful new playtoy, one his mother never gave him for Christmas back in Arkansas. He obviously liked the message his fingers were sending to his brain. His face became transformed, as if in a sexual trance.

All awkwardness between us had disappeared. He was definitely into his work. I just knew he wanted to take a dive down there, but I had other plans for him. I wanted him to enter me in the missionary position for the simple reason I needed to whisper something in his ear - not have his head buried between my legs.

The president rose from the sofa and slowly pulled down his jogging shorts. He had little potential as a male stripper. When the baggy shorts fell to his ankles, I stared face-to-face at Little Junior at full mast as if it wanted to be saluted.

"Eat it!" the president commanded.

Before I could obey any orders from the Oval Office, the door to my bedroom was thrown open. I expected either a room service waiter with Clinton's food order, or else Martinez accompanied by at least two armed henchmen. It was neither.

A calm, cool, and collected Hillary Clinton came into the bedroom.

. . .

Clinton looked at Hillary without the slightest emotion evident in his face. Little Junior had become even smaller, retreating into it's bird's nest. The president pulled up his jogging shorts to cover himself and went to my dressing room, presumably where he'd left his suit and tie.

Here I was, face to face with Hillary. I won't pretend I haven't met first ladies before. Mommie had introduced me to Lady Bird and Pat in that order, but never the one from Georgia whose name I could never remember. Mommie herself had known Eleanor, Bess, and Mamie. She also knew Nancy Davis Reagan. Only too well. She'd never introduced me to Ms. Reagan, even when all of us were once at the same party together in Los Angeles. Mommie hated Nancy Davis and had even partially financed the research on an unflattering book written about her. The animosity wasn't over politics but boyfriends. Even though I'd met all those first ladies, it was usually at dinners, receptions, or teas. Each of the first ladies had wanted money from Mommie and me for some charitable cause. Surely Hillary hadn't arrived here with her hand out.

The First Lady for the first time seemed at a loss for words and stood glaring at me skeptically.

"Mrs. Clinton, it's an honor to meet you. Welcome to Palm Island. I'd planned to invite you and the president here one day to use the island as your vacation retreat. Any time. I know how busy you guys are. After all, Truman and Bess liked the Florida Keys. Well, Truman at least."

"Bill and I won't be vacationing in the Florida Keys ever again. Offer it to Tipper and Al. They'd love it." She surveyed my bedroom like a real-estate appraiser.

"I will. Perhaps I could offer some other retreat for you and the president. The Cayman Islands. California. Colorado. Canada. Maine."

"No thank you."

"Europe, perhaps. The Riviera. Gstaad. I have a place in the Alps."

"No thank you."

"You know, if memory serves, I think Daddy left us a huge hunting lodge somewhere in Arkansas. Mommie and I never went there, but we still own it. Mommie and I never took to blood sports. How do you stand on that issue?"

"Bill has a stomach for hunting and killing, although he's no Hemingway. As for me, I go only for big game political buffalo."

"I see." There was an awkward pause. "I know it seems ironic that I'd be offering you a place in Arkansas, your home state. But I understand your real-estate adventures there have been disastrous. Perhaps you could have built a home along that river. What is its name? I was told that after you left the governor's mansion, you are now homeless in Arkansas. You need to own some home, unless you're using FDR as a role model. But even he owned that little cottage at Warm Springs."

"Bill and I are perfectly capable of finding our own home in Arkansas." She said that rather curtly, considering my extreme generosity. "We'll be in Washington for the rest of this century. Who knows after that?"

"You're both lawyers." Why don't you consider representing me after you leave the White House? The both of you. The starting salary will be one and a half million each."

"Is that per year?" Hillary asked.

"What else? That's only the starting salaries. When you add up all the other benefits, including commissions, you'll probably total five million for the both of you."

"That's per year?"

"Yes."

She paused a moment, smiling ever so faintly. I was pleased that she could manage a smile, considering the circumstances. "I'll accept the job and the two and a half annual salary for Bill. However, I have other plans beginning with the millennium. I plan to become the first woman president of the United States. Would you consider the two and a half million you promised me in salary as my first campaign contribution instead?"

"Of course." What was two and a half million dollars to me? I was probably addressing a woman who'd never seen more than half a million in her whole life. I'd heard lawyers in Arkansas hardly made enough money to live. That's why they had to steal.

"May I be seated while I wait for Bill?"

"You can indeed," I said, motioning for her to sit down on the sofa where Clinton and I had recently enjoyed some tongue action. He wasn't a bad kisser. I sat in a chair opposite the First Lady. "Forgive my manners in not offering you a seat earlier. I'm coming unglued lately. I didn't expect you, really."

"I could see that."

For the first time I had a chance to observe her closely. From some press reports, I'd gathered that she was a pit bull dyke, but actually she was rather feminine. With her red-tinted, slightly page-boyish haircut, she looked positively pixieish. I should have know better than to judge her from the press. I, of all people, knew what harsh portraits the press could paint. Her dress was a deep royal purple, exactly matching the purse she carried at her side. I'd heard that she preferred purple as much as Nancy liked red. The only adornment the First Lady wore, other than earrings and a finger ring, was a gold brooch with two angels about one and a half inches long. She fondled it once or twice as if it were the missing Capetown Diamond.

"You really should speak to your Cuban staff at the gate," she cautioned me, rather sternly, like a schoolmarm. "I've never received such a hostile reception in my life. Could you believe it? For a moment, they weren't going to let me enter your compound."

"How did you get in?" I asked, wondering why Martinez had allowed her entry. But then did he really have any choice?

"It was simple," she said. "I threatened your staff. I said if they didn't let the Secret Service - and *me* - in at once, I'd call out the entire U.S. Navy, Army, and the Marines. You may have a formidable staff. But they are no match for the entire might of the U.S. military."

"Why are you here exactly?"

"Bill just seemed to disappear. We have an emergency in Washington - a matter of national security, I can't go into it - and he has to fly back there at once. With me. When my boys on the Secret Service couldn't find him, we feared the worst. I took personal charge. We tracked him down all right. You see, because of some of Bill's past indiscretions, I now have informants on the Secret Service. I don't want him to get into any more trouble. From this day on, no more trouble with women. He's promised me.

"That's very wise. I'm no stranger to sexual scandal myself."

"I know that!"

The president came out of the dressing room wearing his traditional dark blue suit, white shirt, and a burgundy-colored tie with beige stripes that caused it to look like a checkerboard. I made a mental note to myself to send him a collection of ties, personally designed just for him. I also didn't like his haircut. For some reason, I hadn't noticed it before, taking in other parts of his anatomy instead. I'd send him a note at the White House later, offering him the services of the world's finest male hairstylist. I'd fly the guy directly to Washington to cut the president's hair anytime he wanted. After all, the president of the United States should look good.

He sat down on the sofa cuddly close to Hillary and reached for her hand. She didn't challenge him about why he was in my bedroom and actually didn't seem angry with him at all. If anything, a weary resignation crossed her face, but she quickly concealed it. She moved deferentially close to the president. With gentle fingertips, she flicked something from his shoulder, presumably dandruff. I'd alert the hairstylist to take care of the president's dandruff, too.

"We're moving forward in this country," the president said as if addressing TV land. "Hillary and I don't have a mandate from the people, but we have an agenda."

"If we can't create a new health-care system for the American people," Hillary said, "it isn't worth being president, is it?" She smiled affectionately at her husband.

"I wouldn't put it quite like that," he said.

For the first time, she flashed annoyance at him. "Would you excuse me for a moment?" she asked. "I need to use the little girl's room."

"I don't know about that," I said, "but I'll show you to the woman's toilet." Suddenly, the chance I'd been so eagerly waiting for appeared before me. I knew that Martinez and his henchmen were spying on us, but probably only in the bedroom. Not in the bathroom. At least I hoped not. I had to take that chance. Eagerly, I took Hillary's arm to guide her toward my combined dressing and bathroom. She reached for that purple purse, no doubt planning to touch up her makeup, as if she could compete with me.

"I'll join you too," I said. "I need more war paint."

The president looked sheepish, then flicked on the television news nearby.

In the dressing room, I shut the door behind us and uttered a silent prayer for our deliverance.

"I've got to pee in the worst possible way," Hillary said.

I directed her toward my gold toilet.

She turned as if to excuse herself. "I don't need an audience," she said abruptly. I'm not Louis XIV."

"Take your god damn pee," I said with growing impatience and nervousness. "You've got to listen and listen carefully. We don't have much time."

"She yanked up that purple dress and sat down on the toilet. Unlike me in 'Kinky', Hillary wore panties. I was shocked to find them purple, matching her dress. I thought they'd be white or else oyster pearl.

"You and the president are in mortal danger," I said in my most convincing voice, sounding a bit like a sincere Geraldine Page (remember her?). "My house has been taken over by Cuban terrorists. The president was lured here. Set up. A trap. The leader, Geraldo Martinez, one of Castro's henchmen, plans to have a lobotomy performed on your husband."

"You're actually telling the truth," Hillary said. "Although it sounds like you're demented."

The First Lady hadn't lied. She really did need to take a pee. Not since that elephant in Kenya have I heard so much whitewater passing. She wiped herself with my extra soft tissue. White only. Colored tissue can cause a rash.

"Several of my staff members have been killed or tortured," I said. "Mia Kelly is being held prisoner here too. They are threatening to kill her if I don't cooperate."

Jumping up from the stool, without even bothering to flush, she reached for her purse.

"Don't go into that living room," I cautioned. "We're being spied upon. They can see and hear everything. Maybe even in here, but I'm not sure."

She quickly opened her purse. "I've prepared for a day like this. I thought I'd never have to use this thing unless Rush Limbaugh tried to rape me." She pulled the instrument out of her purse and pressed down on a red button. "Now let's return to the living room," she said calmly. "Make idle chit-chat with Bill. Let's talk about health care. Are you properly covered? I can assure you that within minutes the shit will hit the fan."

EPILOGUE

Grand Cayman
October, 1995

Hillary was right: The shit did hit the fan. I don't want to sound like Martha Raye (remember her?) on a Bob Hope special, cheering for our boys in uniform. But when the armed forces of the United States, especially in an American-occupied territory such as Florida, surround an island and take it over, they do so with considerable zeal.

If this were one of those Schwarzenegger movies, or one of those films made by that awful little brat, Mel Gibson, I'd describe helicopter landings and commando activities. I'd go into minute detail about how John and Henry, and especially my beloved Mia, were rescued by handsome young men who looked like Tab Hunter as he appeared in the 50s, not as he did opposite Divine.

In such a saga, it would appear that all was lost. Each of us would be in great peril. That's when mighty Rafael would descend in a helicopter and swing down to rescue us. After all, I'd established that he was a pilot so I'd set the stage for such a scene. Not only is this no Schwarzenegger/Gibson film, it isn't even a Dolph Lundgren movie. It's real life. *My life*.

Rafael didn't show up until long after the action had passed. Actually, when I did locate him, he'd taken up with a young Cuban girl in Miami. I bought her off and sent her on her way, rescuing Rafael from this puta's clutches. So much for fidelity on his part. It seemed he was in mourning for me for only one night before he met this obscenely young creature.

The marines landed and rescued all of us alive. At least those Martinez hadn't killed. Hillary and Bill took French leave (in France, it's called English leave) and were flown back to Washington within hours. Not one goodbye from my presidential guests.

Only trouble was, Martinez escaped. Maybe he went back to Cuba. I don't know. All I know is that as long as he lives, I'll live in terror. I've increased my security guard. Before that psycho dies of AIDS, I predict he'll make a final suicide attempt on this compound and try to kill all of us.

After our escape, it was a sad time of bringing out the black from the wardrobe to attend funerals. I personally supervised the funerals of Maxie and Anishi - the first in England, the second in Japan. I was the only mourner present at either funeral. Both had left instructions that they be cremated and their ashes tossed to the wind. I carried through on this ghoulish assignment and was eager to be done with it. Funerals aren't my thing. I once turned down an important screen role because in the film, my character had to attend a funeral.

Of course, the world press descended on the Florida Keys when news leaked out about the assault on all of us at Palm Island. Snake handled the media in Monroe County. I'm not saying he deliberately misled by presenting himself as the savior of the day, but the account he gave at his news conference and truth were two entirely different matters. He portrayed himself as our rescuer. Actually, he didn't show up until all the action was over.

President Clinton wasn't exactly honest when questioned at his press conference. He used the assault on my household to suggest it was a Castro-backed conspiracy. He conveniently left out the fact that he was there at my island that night on another mission. Naturally, he made no mention of the fact that Hillary came to rescue him. But I could understand his silence on that matter. After all, Bill and Hillary have enough trouble.

I'll also tell you a tidbit to help me unburden my heart. Let me come right out with it: I was the woman who was with Vincent Foster that afternoon that preceded his gunshot wound on July 20, 1993 in Fort Marcy Park in suburban Virginia. Rumors about his death once rocked the stock market. The Internet still crackles with questions about evidence. But no one - no one in all of America - has ever connected me to the case.

After Vince set up the Clinton visit, he slipped off from Washington several times to see me. Ostensibly, the reason involved protecting the president. He demanded and got repeated assurances from me that I would say nothing or reveal nothing about Clinton's involvement that night.

I promised Vince, and I promised him some more. I don't know what it would take to convince that man. Actually, I found out our meetings and his calls to me weren't about Bill Clinton at all. Vincent Foster of Arkansas was captivated by Sherry Kelly. He was in love with me, and he'd fallen in love with me over the phone, as we'd seen each other only three times in person.

It's true the third and final time I threw him a mercy fuck. He was so uptight in his high-pressure and high profile job. Since he's not my type, I play-acted a bit, like Marilyn used to do with her tricks. I even told Vince that he'd given me the greatest Big O of my life. That wasn't true. But it inspired him to go at it again. I showed him a real good time, and even taught him a few tricks he'd never learned in Arkansas.

In the park that day, he told me he wanted to leave his wife and marry me. I repeatedly assured him that wasn't possible. He also told me that only that morning he'd learned that an investigative reporter - a Britisher, no less, not an American - had not only learned about Clinton's visit to Palm Island that night, but also knew of our affair. That idiot Rush Limbaugh was ranting that Vince and Hillary were having an affair.

Vince seemed unglued. Finally, I told him that I was fleeing the country. I couldn't stand any more press revelations or any more paparazzi. Let them write what they would, but I wouldn't be here to read it.

He became very agitated at that point, claiming I was "leaving him holding the bag." Perhaps I was. But what was I to do? I never had any intention of marrying him. I kissed him goodbye and left. It was a long, lingering kiss, and he begged me to stay. But how could I? I fled the park. I wasn't worried about being detected, since I'd disguised myself as a young Debbie Reynolds (remember her?)

That night, I learned of his suicide. Rafael and I were watching the news over TV. I burst into tears and ran screaming from the room. He tried to comfort me, and just couldn't understand why I'd be so upset over the death of "another bureaucrat" in Washington.

Since that night with Clinton on Palm Island, I've never seen the president again. He occasionally calls me from the White House, and he's still hot to represent me after he leaves the Oval Office. He's never mentioned Vince to me, and I sincerely believe he knows nothing of Vince's involvement with me.

It's pretty much agreed: Clinton is going to become my personal attorney at the agreed-upon figure. His only problem, or so he says, is that he'll have to delay the job for several months as he campaigns for Hillary for president. He may also have to divide his time between being my attorney and being First Man of the land. He didn't think there would be a conflict of interest in holding down both positions since I was "non-political."

Hillary flew to see me in the Cayman Islands during the late summer of 1994. The press mercifully didn't learn of the trip, which had some of the aura of the Alger Hiss trip to Britain. Although she never told me exact details, Bill had done something to piss her off, and she was seriously considering divorcing him. After two days of intense pleading, I urged her to rejoin Bill in Washington and patch up her marriage. I warned her that if she divorced him, her chances to rule the White House and the country herself would be very dim indeed. She seemed to agree with this, and eventually flew back to join her husband.

I, of course, had her hair redone while she was in the Caymans and ordered some clothes for her. Not a dazzling and spectacular wardrobe, as you might think, but clothes to soften her image. The press commented on this look in detail, but didn't connect moi with it. For that, I'm grateful. Anytime I don't get mentioned in the press, much less splashed across its front pages, I am grateful.

We've gone from the sad and dreary spring of 1993 to the sad and dreary autumn of 1995. Bill and Hillary have had to endure a hostile GOP takeover in Washington. It's what I called the white man's triumph up there: Long on speech and short on dicks. You know who they are: Phil, Newtie, Bob, Jesse, Sam. The list seems endless. Of course, one of their gangleaders hasn't even found his dick, not since he gave up chasing Southern beauty contest winners around his bedroom in 1907. Out in California, Assembly Speaker Doris Allen called her fellow GOPers "power-mongering men with short penises." That girl and I could talk.

Several people have suggested that even I emphasize penile dimensions too strongly. What do they know? Wake up, and instead of smelling roses, get out the ruler. All major media, including *Time*, *Esquire*, and *Newsweek*, are getting in on this penile dimension stuff. After all, one of those major media events only recently revealed that Hugh Grant measured up at six "cute" inches. I'm not charting new courses in revelations here, only following a trend. In the future, and this is a prediction, a man running for president will be asked to disclose penile dimensions along with his income tax forms. In other words, a winner and landslide victory for LBJ, but a total defeat for JFK.

Actually, I've had a change of heart on the subject of penile dimensions. Don't fall over upon hearing the news. Today, I'm far more interested in that "cute" six inches than I am in some of the dimensions I've indulged myself with in the past.

Juan Garcia has changed my view on that. I find his love-making today, with his "cute" Hugh Granter, more satisfying than that of Rafael, master of the deep probe. I can take it up front just fine, but deep penetrations of the throat and butt cause me discomfort. Rafael doesn't seem to realize that, and is unrelenting.

Juan mounts me every afternoon, but only after a tongue probe of the nether regions. I'm convinced he's better at that than Bill was with Gennifer Flowers. Incidentally, I kept my promise to love him every day, a promise I made during the siege of Palm Island. After his tongue probe, I find his missionary position love-making gentle and satisfying. He doesn't indulge in any of those "rip tissue and leave them bloody" tactics, even if he could.

In other words, he's not a guerilla fighter in bed, but a lover.

Of course, Juan is Cuban. I've changed on that subject too, no longer preferring Italian men to Hispanic. That anti-Hispanic bias was the old Sherry Kelly talking. Today's Sherry Kelly has two Cuban men for lovers, so you can see how I've changed. In spite of all this taste for Cuban men, I never developed a palate for black beans and yellow rice. I like paella, however. I also know the difference today between Cuban and Mexican food, and there's quite a difference.

Juan occupies the villa next to mine in Grand Cayman. I never gave him the twenty million promised, because he was never able to rescue us and never earned the money. Actually, he's hired at a fantastic salary to direct my security guard around our compound here. Fearing revenge from Martinez, I want to be prepared for his invasion if it ever comes. I'm sure it will.

Juan's partner on the force is Dick Knight, Clinton's former masseur and ex-member of the Secret Service. It seems that Dick actually has two more inches than Warren Beatty after all. Although I'd feared the aptly named Dick's penetration of Juan might cause him pain that night on Palm Island, I shouldn't have worried. It caused Juan no pain at all, according to reports. He loved it, and now has to have it at least two to three times a day, according to Dick.

Dick doesn't seem jealous that I see Juan in the afternoon. In fact, he doesn't seem to care how Juan gets his rocks off. Satisfying Juan in that capacity seems to be my job. In fact, several times as Juan was penetrating me, Dick entered the bedroom and penetrated Juan. That seemed to drive Juan into even more inspired bouts of love-making with me. It made him hotter. Frankly, I don't care. Whatever turns the boys on is all right with me, providing no one forgets mama and her needs.

Sometimes, when Juan has to go into Georgetown on business, Dick has held me down and raped me repeatedly. He definitely can go more rounds than Warren, although I remain opposed to rape. I view rape as politically incorrect. Now I know why Dick is named Dick.

After his first rape of me, I tripled his already bloated salary, thinking if he got enough money from me, he would cease his attacks. That didn't work. When I spotted Juan driving into Georgetown one day, I went over to their villa to deliver a message. I didn't want to call in case anyone was eavesdropping. Once there, I forgot what the message was. I'd no sooner entered the villa than Dick attacked again, ripping my thong from my body. I gave in to him, knowing how hopeless it would be to struggle with a man trained to guard a president. There is a problem I have with Dick. Do his attacks always have to be in the butt?

Incidentally, in case you're wondering. I keep my minor indiscretions with Juan in the afternoon secret. It's my way of paying Rafael back for his flirtations with that Cuban puta in Miami. Slipping off to see Juan in the afternoon isn't difficult. After Rafael demands his post-lunch blow job, he takes a long siesta, which often stretches into four hours. Of course, all that Cuban beer he consumes at lunch makes it easier for him to sleep the afternoon away.

David somehow persuaded the Federal government to drop piracy charges against Rafael. He never did campaign for the presidency of Cuba on the streets of Miami, in spite of his oft-repeated ambition. As of this writing, Castro is still in power. We don't know for how long. But Rafael expresses no interest in pursuing the job if Castro leaves or dies. "I'm happy to stay here in the Caymans," he keeps saying. If anything, I think the good life is making him soft. All that beer is certainly showing up in his gut. Unlike me, he doesn't work out. In fact, he gets no exercise at all, other than what he gets in bed with me.

As promised to Anishi, I am the new mother of John and Henry. They didn't go out in the world to seek other companions, and remain tightly glued to each other. They are right here at the villa with Rafael and me, and we see them every day. In fact, I even staged their wedding. Henry made a stunning bride. He really is a beautiful boy, although John's face is becoming a little cruder as he ages.

When they're not dining with us, or spending an hour or so by the pool in the afternoon, they prefer to be by themselves. The assassination of their mother seems to have profoundly affected them and made them even more withdrawn. I worry about them sometimes, and try to discuss their dilemma with Rafael. But he doesn't seem concerned.

"I failed as a father," he always says. "How can I understand Japanese children? I don't even understand my own Cubano son."

Desi or Dino doesn't come to visit us here. He keeps threatening to, but he doesn't show up. The TV series, directed by Jerry, about the Cuban highschoolers, is the biggest hit in America. Dino is the biggest heartthrob since Valentino. The X-rated video just enhanced his image as a sex symbol, whereas a few years ago, it would have destroyed an actor's career. With every man and woman in America throwing themselves at Dino's feet, offering their bodies, he seems to want none of them. "I could have anybody I want in America," he recently told me. "Anybody." I speak to him every now and then, since this series starring him is making me even richer than I am.

"But I'm tired of bodies," he said. "Besides, I want somebody with a better body than mine, and until that day comes, I'm not attracted to anyone." I think he spends his nights looking at himself in the mirror.

Regrettably, just when the show was at its peak, Jerry succumbed to AIDS. The only time I went back to California was to attend his funeral. I didn't call Cruz. First, I didn't think he wanted to hear from me. Second, he's made enough millions in settlement on that shooting that we can now live the rest of our lives without each other. He never followed through on his law suit demanding one-hundred million dollars for me, but settled for the twenty-five million so generously offered. His career in America seems to have hit the skids. His last two pictures bombed utterly, although I hear he's been offered a part in an Italian movie but it's not the lead.

I attempted to call that darling, Sean Nielson, but then I feared I'd disappointed him too. Although he called The Iguana's office many times about a picture deal with me, I just never had the heart for any of the projects. I wanted out. I haven't heard what happened to him. He just seemed to have disappeared, but then, I don't read *Variety*. The buddy movie with Cruz was never made.

The moment I arrived in Los Angeles, I was besieged by film offers. I am the hottest star in the world. But I've had it with film. I've made my last picture. Why not leave when I'm at my biggest demand, and not fade like Greta Garbo when she became box-office poison? I didn't want to wait around until my pictures started to lose money, or some Rex Reed bitch pointed out that first wrinkle.

Snake called yesterday and says that he "personally" guards the infamous Palm Island where the paparazzi hung out for months, hoping to snap a picture of Mia or me.

Although Snake has guards around Mia's house in Key West, she hasn't shown up there in months. Looking lovelier and more radiant than ever, she spends her time touring the country, raising money for AIDS research. She herself is the world's heaviest contributor, and is virtually a symbol of the AIDS movement today. The disease hasn't moved in on her yet to do its damage, and I pray it won't, although her doctors tell me it's only a matter of time.

In spite of all her problems, she manages to have some fun in life. To the surprise of half the world, she married Angelo, who could be her grandson. He recovered from the brutal sexual mutilation by Martinez. After intensive examinations, it was found that his penis was not severely damaged. It was as if it had been roughly circumcised by an amateur butcher. I should know. I have enough pictures of it. I urged Angelo to get a plastic surgeon to smooth it out for him and spend the rest of his life as a circumcised man.

However, he couldn't bear the loss of his dearly beloved foreskin. Dr. Euler performed a miracle of surgery over a period of weeks and was able to restore foreskin. Dr. Euler told me he knows Angelo's penis better than his own. Mia reports that Angelo is up and running again, foreskin and all. Back in the saddle. Of course, I admonished her to practice safe sex since she is HIV positive, and she assures me that she and Angelo do that, except "one or two nights" when they got drunk together and forgot. Bless them.

When not having Angelo fly in for post-operative foreskin examinations, Dr. Euler is working on a cure for the AIDS virus. He recently told me that he's about to have a breakthrough in his research. Mia found out about this from Angelo, and has sent Dr. Euler a monstrous contribution to help with his research.

"*Dah-ling*," Mia recently said to me. She is sounding more like Tallulah every day. "I want to be cured. I want to live forever. With Angelo, of course. I want to become as youthful looking as Angelo. I'm still looking for that Fountain of Youth. I'll have better luck than Ponce de Leon. I'll find it one day. I just know I will." I noted the desperation in her voice as she rang off.

My father, David, has cancer of the colon. He is representing Mia once again, but keeps threatening to resign every day because of ill health. He doesn't think he will be able to represent me until the millennium, when Clinton can take over the job and David can retire. "I'll have to retire much sooner than that," he told me only recently.

In the past few days, I've been receiving a lot of calls from JFK Jr. He's one smart man about some things, but not about women. He sent me roses for my birthday. I don't like roses, and I certainly don't want to be reminded of birthdays. JFK Jr. and I are about the same age.

He told me about his new magazine, *George*. I promised to subscribe fifty-thousand times to help boost circulation figures. He seemed grateful for that. After all, starting up a new magazine is a tough job with little chance of success. Actually, the little devil wanted more from me than that. He wanted to fly to Grand Cayman and get the "inside story" on what happened that night on Palm Island. He said he thinks the press didn't reveal the "real" story of that night. What a clever boy he is. I said I would get back to him with my final decision.

Actually, in the back of my mind, I'm considering giving him one more chance in the saddle. Maybe we were both tense our first time together. It was too much a repeat of John Sr. and Marilyn. It was as if he were restaging a historical event and not concentrating on the action at hand. Sometimes a second try will produce better results, although I'm not a "second try" kind of woman in most instances. In John, Jr.'s case, however, I'm willing to make an exception.

Esquire recently wrote that JFK Jr. used to walk around the university (I can never remember the names of universities) in tight shorts revealing an endowment greater than that of the university. Can I ever set the record straight for *Esquire* on that.

In case you're wondering why I broke up with JFK Jr. in the first place, I'll tell you. It had to do with my big mouth. No, it's not what you're thinking. I put that orifice to good use on that boy. I should have said "my tongue." One night, as I indulged in pillow talk with America's future president, I told him I'd spent a night with Nureyev.

Although he had grace as a ballet dancer, Nureyev was a different kind of artist in bed. His technique was to hop on, bang like a riveter for fifteen long minutes, then hop off. Later over a drink of the world's most expensive champagne, he told me that Robert Kennedy once came onto him. Rudy said it never went beyond the "kissing and fondling of male genitalia" stage. The ballet dancer, it turned out, was two and one half times as big as the attorney general.

Thinking it would amuse JFK Jr., I related the incident to him. He said nothing at first, as he got out of bed, put clothing over that overexposed torso, thanked me for a good time, and left. It would be a long time before I would hear from him again.

Ted recently presented me with a picture of John urinating snapped by paparazzi from the side of a boat. When I next spoke to John, I told him how sorry I was. But he didn't seem embarrassed. I think there is a streak of exhibitionism in that boy. Who else would walk nude on a beach in St. Barts if he didn't want his picture taken?

In the course of our last conversation, he revealed that he is seriously considering running for president on the Democratic ticket in the year 2000. Right away, this has placed me in an embarrassing position politically. I have more or less, without exactly saying so, promised Hillary my support in her bid for the presidency. With Clinton as my attorney, it would be awkward for me to back John.

Late at night, a different fantasy emerges. What if I agree to marry John, as he subtly suggested that night? Apparently, our time in bed was more memorable to him than to me. I'm sure I understand that. His father probably thought Marilyn was a great lay. But I'm sure Marilyn had a lot more fun times than with the Kennedy brothers.

Although DiMaggio and Arthur Miller weren't all that great in the sack, Marilyn must have had a few men who were. Just a few. Most of the men she bedded were really mercy fucks on her part.

If I would agree to marry John, I could become First Lady of the land. Of course, Newtie would have pictures of me in "Kinky" distributed across the land, and surely one of John urinating.

O.J. Simpson gave up on me. Although he'll be forgotten tomorrow, right this moment as I write this, every channel on TV is talking about this has-been football player. I have now heard of him - more than I ever wanted to know.

If it's not Newtie - that man definitely doesn't need a jockstrap - it's O.J. Only in America can you decapitate two people, including your battered ex-wife, and hope to make fifty-million dollars. The pay-for-view royalties should be staggering. Of course, all that has been reported.

But I'm amazed that one aspect of the case was overlooked.

When those semi-nude examination photographs of O.J. were flashed across the TV screen, the world got to see the athlete in his bikini briefs. What a scandal! I once saw a picture of Raquel Welch in a bikini. Miss Tejada, as she used to be known in Chicago, looked better hung than O.J.

Because of Ted's various favors to me, I carried through on my promise, and secured a different type of football player for him, all two-hundred and eighty pounds and six feet five and a half of hunkdom. An athlete without O.J.'s obvious problem. His name is Tommy Long, and he is known in the locker rooms of America as "The Longest Yard." After one libidinous night with Ted, I was assured that both Tommy's nickname and surname are deadly accurate. Actually, by the time Tommy flew to Grand Cayman, I felt his football career was coming to an end. He looked a little worse for wear, as if he'd been hit on the head a lot. When we were talking about visiting Europe in a few months, he asked if France were in Italy. I realized then those football injuries must have been brutal. Tommy has taken to the lifestyles of the rich and famous, preferring it to whatever happens on football fields.

One day by the pool, I asked him, "How are things between Ted and you? After all, Ted is such an older man. You're not really gay, at least I don't think you are. And, if you were gay, you could have almost anybody. Even a pretty face."

"Things are just fine," he assured me. "Ted is a little faggy for my tastes, but I like it here. I want to stay."

"You're welcome."

"The way I figure it," he said, "all I have to do is go up to that little room." He nodded his head in the direction of a tower room in the distance. "I pull off my double-X boxers and lie back on the bed. Ted's decorated all the walls with nothing but tit pictures. I just lie back, watch those tits, and get serviced by an expert. That's not exactly hard work. It sure beats playing football for a living. After all, I'm getting a little long in the tooth to keep playing on those fields. Besides, my contract wasn't renewed, and I didn't save my money."

Later, he had to excuse himself to visit Dr. Euler, which he does every afternoon for a complete one-hour physical examination, which the good doctor demands.

Dr. Euler seems a happy man these days. He no longer

works on brains. In fact, he spends every afternoon in his lab examining the bowel movements of both Tommy and Rafael. Rafael is also subjected to an intensive one-hour physical examination every day. Although both rugged men appear to be in the finest of health, Dr. Euler insists on examining their daily bowel movements for reasons I don't fully understand. He explained to me that it was an early detection system, his way of spotting a potential illness in advance. Surprisingly, he doesn't examine the bowel movements of anybody else, including moi.

I've written Dr. Euler off as a harmless eccentric, although he is of use to me from time to time, particularly because of a skin cream he's perfected. I've been using it, and I'm growing younger by the hour. For the next remake of 'Heidi', I'm sure I'll be sent the script. Who knows what's in that skin cream? Considering what's in his laboratory, I'm afraid to ask. But it's powerful stuff. I can't market it yet. The way I figure it, each bottle of the stuff costs me two-hundred thousand dollars.

The best for last.

The Iguana, sad to report, was arrested, tried, convicted, and sentenced to five years in a Federal prison on a charge of income tax evasion. Money he extorted from me. His money is all gone, but all is not lost, however. When he gets out of prison, I have offered him a job here - "the dumb butler part," von Stroheim to my Norma Desmond, although I'm much too young at this point to play the diva role.

I'll save money because The Iguana must own the world's largest collection of red jackets. Once, when he was escorting me to a restaurant in Los Angeles, two women came up to him, and, mistaking him for the maitre d', asked him directions to the women's room. The Iguana will look good scurrying about the premises in those red jackets, even if they're dated. That is, if that one could ever look good.

Life is a little boring here, and that's why I'm considering the First Lady prospect. I probably won't go for it, however, but it's something to think about. No doubt, I'll stay right here on Grand Cayman. No one seems to want to move off the island.

I'm looking out over the patio from my library window. All my men are there sunning themselves by the pool. Tommy, Rafael, and Dick are wearing almost see-through bulging bikinis. Juan is more modestly clad in boxer swim trunks. John and Henry are showing a perfect concave in their conventional trunks and are cuddling, cooing, and kissing on a chaise longue. My crew looks like one happy bunch.

Missing is Dr. Euler, who's in his lab creating who knows what concoction to spring on an unsuspecting world. But he'll be joining us for dinner.

Also missing is Ted, who almost never appears in bright sunlight, claiming it will age him too quickly. He's got a point. I recently saw him in bright sunlight, and it has brought devastation to his face. He'll look older than Maxie if he doesn't stop aging. I'm trying to convince him to start using some of my skin cream. He refused. It seems he spied on Dr. Euler and knows what the ingredients of that skin cream are. He told me, but I refused to believe it, and will not disgrace Dr. Euler even more than I have by reporting Ted's slander. Ted, too, will be joining us for dinner.

I've decided to do the cooking myself tonight. Moi. Of all people. As the only woman in this happy household, I have to keep the menfolk fed. We're having rare steak with baked potato slathered with butter, sour cream, and freshly chopped chives. For dessert, it's going to be crepes suzette, just like I used to have with Daddy Kelly before things turned rotten and dirty between us. I try not to think of that anymore, except late at night when a memory will come back, whether you want it to or not. Oh, and a fat shrimp cocktail to begin the meal. Just thinking about whipping up all those nourishing dishes fills me with a warm and cozy feeling. It's like I'm some great earth mother, and these men by the pool are my adorable children, each and every one of them. I love each one of them. But my feelings for each varies. It's still called love, though.

As reluctant as I am to admit it, Dan Quayle was right: There is something to all this "family values" crap after all.

CELEBRATING THE 20TH ANNIVERSARY OF
THE PUBLICATION OF
BUTTERFLIES IN HEAT
With a HUGE new printing!

You're invited to preview
Darwin Porter's Cult Classic of the 1970s
Once again available in bookstores everywhere!

Twenty years ago, gay readers across the world made *Butterflies in Heat* their number one best-seller in those "Boogie Nights" (and days) of the Seventies.

Yes, IT'S BACK! The original *Midnight in the Garden of Good and Evil*, with characters once denounced as too controversial but who have now become mainstream icons in fiction and film: The Blond Hustler, the Narcissistic Drag Queen, the Rich John, the Aging and Profane Duenna, the Relentless Prosecutor, the Society Matron, the 300-pound "Gin Mamma," the Gucci Carpetbagger, and a host of flamboyant and corrupt characters the likes of which haven't been seen since *Midnight Cowboy*. (ISBN-1-877978-95-7; $12.95 U.S.)

. . .

On the pages that follow,
FLF Press/STARbooks Press
is proud to bring you excerpted scenes from
Darwin Porter's classic
Butterflies in Heat:

"Take off those wet jeans," Ralph commanded.

"What else is on your mind?"

"To see the jewels."

The jeans were peeled from his legs. He stood proudly, meeting Ralph's penetrating stare. "Do I pass inspection?"

"Triple A."

"Before we get down to business," Numie said, "I want to look around."

"Okay, I'll be your guide," Ralph volunteered, "but that's not why I brought you here."

Numie paused. Just once in his life, he wished somebody would invite him somewhere without his having to sing for his supper.

For the next hour, Ralph revealed the hidden spots of beauty. A nest of blue-red orchids. A place where water was the color of crystal. A field of thick banana trees, bearing fruit that only wild things ate.

Ralph charted the way back to the beach. "I have a big map at home with all these islands drawn in," he said. "I named this one after myself. I don't really own it, but I feel like I do."

Numie remained silent. As he surveyed the island, his thoughts were different from Ralph's. He felt this oasis should belong to no one in particular, but should be used by anyone wanting to get away and escape – at least for a while – the real world.

He put his hands on his hips, spread his legs, arched his spine, and tossed his head back, enjoying the fresh air.

Ralph's body trembled. He looked down the beach, squinting his eyes to keep out the glare. Then he leaned over quickly and kissed Numie on the lips.

The gentle movement met no resistance. But the kiss was not returned. Even so, it stung. Numie instinctively reached to rub his mouth.

"Are you strictly trade?"

"If you want to call it that. I'm not a kisser, but I throw a pretty good fuck."

"You can't prove it by me." Ralph's eyes glowed with an overpowering hunger.

Numie's body moved over him.

"Make it hurt," Ralph whispered. His low moans were the only sound heard on the island.

. . .

Slowly Numie unbuttoned his shirt and then stepped out of his jeans. He was used to stripping in front of men, but this was different. His clothes gave him an extra sense of protection, but that was now peeled off.

He was sweating heavily. The only light was from an exposed electric bulb overhead. His clothes off, he was standing in the middle of the room as Yellowwood stalked in.

The sheriff's beady glare began at his feet and traveled upward, lingering long over his middle. The same appraising look Numie had seen back at the hotel room.

The fact that the sheriff was displaying such an interest in his nude body remained Numie's only chance.

Hank was searching his jeans. From the back pocket, he pulled out a marijuana cigarette enclosed in tissue. "Just what I thought. He was carrying illegal drugs."

"I thought you told me you were clean," Yellowwood accused, shooting Numie a surgical stare.

Numie said nothing. He could only watch like the hypnotized victim of the coiling threat of a viper.

"Blue wrapped," Dave said, examining the dope." I thought De la Mer was the only person in town who smoked blue-wrapped marijuana cigarettes."

"Tell the guys in number nine they're gonna have some company," Yellowwood said.

Hank and Dave left the room.

Now, Numie's chance. "Sheriff, I can explain. Surely we can work something out. Just the two of us." He leaned forward slightly so that his legs strayed wider apart. Suddenly, the sheriff's billy club was smashing into his wrist. Numie fell back in pain.

"You read me wrong, boy. *Way wrong.*"

Dave was back in the room. Following, Hank was putting on a greased rubber glove.

"Bend over," Yellowwood commanded.

Numie hesitated until the sheriff moved menacingly toward him with that club again.

Reluctantly Numie turned around, bending over.

"Pry those cheeks apart," Yellowwood said.

Numie complied, feeling like a slave on the auction block. Utter humiliation.

In one quick move, Hank's long finger was jabbing inside Numie, deliberately trying to hurt. "Got nothing in there," Hank said to Yellowwood. "Not even a turd."

"Take him to the cell," Yellowwood snapped.

"Can I put my pants back on?" Numie asked, humbled and stripped of any pride.

"Hell, no!" Yellowwood shouted.

"I'm entitled to at least one phone call," Numie protested. "I know my rights."

"Fuck your rights," the sheriff barked. "Take him out."

Completely nude, Numie was pushed down the corridor.

The smell of urine was everywhere. On both sides the cells were filled with men leering at him.

"Hi, honey," a young black called out in a falsetto voice.

"You giving that away for supper tonight?"

"There's enough meat there for the poor," another yelled.

At the end of the corridor, Numie faced a tiny room with a small barred window. Hank was placing handcuffs on him. Then Dave shoved Numie into the darkened cell——so hard he stumbled and fell on the concrete. Face down. His nose was bleeding.

Gradually as his eyes became accustomed to the darkness, he spotted two men sitting on the lower bunk of a bed.

One of them was staring at Numie with glee.

*****

He slipped out of his jeans, tossing them on the white carpet.

Moments later, Lola was back. "Wow!" she yelled, squealing with delight. "I wonder if I could lose weight dieting on weenies all week." She was wearing nothing but pink panties, red Joan Crawford fuck-me shoes, and that platinum wig. Though it sagged in parts, her body was actually like a girl's: tiny breasts forming contours on a slender frame that was emaciated. Her mouth was painted a turkey red. She wiggled her hips over to the bed.

"These white satin sheets are a little much," he said, patting them invitingly.

"Men perform better on satin than cotton," she confirmed.

"Let's give it a try." He grabbed her, cupping her tiny breasts and pinching the nipples until she screamed.

"You're hurting me," she protested.

"And you love it!"

Her only response was a soft moan before plunging her mouth onto him. Suddenly, she jumped up. Her back to him, she lowered her panties, revealing her buns. Then she fell on the bed, butt up. "A five-alarm's fire's raging in me," she said.

"Let's put it out," he said. He never saw her front part, and didn't have to look into her eyes as he did his work. Deeper and deeper, he took the plunge. Lola screamed once, but it was mostly moans reaching his ears. He rode in further, exploring more.

The bedsprings were rusty and creaky——providing just the kind of rhythm he needed to do his job. She'd brag later about having had him——he knew that. But the joke would be on her. She'd never really have him. He gave them sex, but he'd never give of himself. Not to Lola. Not to anyone.

The rhapsodic sound of her voice, the way her body was turned on, the way she needed what he offered——everything blended to make him a man again after that nightmare in jail. Riding to his finish, he was the one groaning now.

Immediately recognizing the signs, Lola started to protest, "Don't, don't, lover man. Make it last all night."

Yet her contracting and pulling only goaded the inevitable. Soaked with sweat, he tensed——holding back as long as he could. But his release was violent, spasm after spasm. His energy drained, he collapsed on top of her.

She turned her head around, wanting to be kissed.

Ignoring her at first, he started to pull out. His job over, he'd earned his supper. After all, he didn't kiss fags. But the compelling hunger of her eyes——unlike the desperation in Ralph's——told him he'd better satisfy her in that way. Pressing toward her, his mouth met hers. He was quick and efficient. But also thorough, competent in his job. Kissing her was no more unpleasant than many duties he'd been called upon to perform.

The nails of her right hand dug into his back. "I need you!" she cried. "No man has ever made me feel like that. *No man.* Don't ever leave me, *please*."

"Fuck, Lola," he said, slowly pulling out of her body——even though her muscles were fighting his going. "Who's gonna leave? I'm gonna stick around a while."

. . .

Numie was deliberately stalling, not wanting to face Lola. He wished he could be by himself tonight. He didn't want to have to relate to anybody. But that would be freedom – and he'd never known that.

Taking the long way home, he stopped off at the gaudy Victorian bus station. The beer seemed to have gone through his system in minutes.

A few sailors, a Cuban and his heavily made up girl friend, two elderly tourists, and an old fisherman waited in the lobby for the final bus in from the mainland for the night.

Numie hurried by – heading for the men's room.

Inside the marble floor smelled, and the long porcelain urinal had long ago yellowed.

Sighing in relief, Numie splashed noisily. Eyes closed, he allowed this moment to help ease the tension that had been slowly building since he left the Cuban restaurant.

Finished, he started to zip up, but stopped short. His attention shifted to the lone booth. Someone had chiseled a hole in the partition, and an eye was clearly observing Numie. Underneath the raised partition two booted feet rested.

Still at the urinal, Numie started to shake himself. After all, a customer was a customer. He certainly needed the extra money.

The eye was staring intently.

As his cock hardened, Numie edged closer to the hole.

The eye withdrew.

A shuffling inside sent a note of alarm through Numie. Zipping up quickly, he rushed out the door.

The station master was just coming in. "Hope you gave the

sheriff a good show," he said.

Numie stopped in surprise. "The sheriff? You mean, that's Johnny Yellowwood in there?"

"Sure, I've got to summon him now. He's wanted on the phone. Emergency downtown."

"What did you mean, a good show?" Numie asked.

"Kid, you're naive," the station master said. "The sheriff likes to look at guys take a leak. Been hanging out in that very booth ever since he got back from the Korean War." The station master walked in the toilet. "Johnny," he called, "you wanted on the phone, bubba."

Down the deserted street, Numie glanced back at the steep-roofed towers of the Victorian station.

He didn't know why he was shocked, but he was. More by the station master's bland acceptance of the sheriff's perversity than by anything else, he guessed.

In minutes, the sheriff's car——siren blazing——whizzed by, heading for downtown.

. . .

"Hi," David replied in a high-pitched voice. He looked at Numie intently before his nervous eyes darted away. Turning to Lola, he asked: "What does your young man have in mind?"

This question only increased Numie's discomfort. David wasn't even giving him the dignity of making up his mind. Eying a rack of slacks, Numie started to say something, but was interrupted.

In one quick move, Lola crushed out her cigarette right on the tiled floor. "We're going out tonight with Ned and Dinah. I'm sure you remember Ned, don't you?" She cocked her head and turned her most accusatory gaze upon David.

David was flustered. "I'll never forget him," he muttered.

"As you know," she went on, "Ned always shows basket. I want Numie to do the same." She glanced imperiously at Numie, challenging him to defy her.

The look was familiar, an obvious copy of Leonora at her most haughty. "Hey," Numie protested, "don't I have something to say about this?"

"Child, I happen to be paying the bill," Lola said sarcastically. She feared her position was being seriously threatened in front of David. "When you get enough bread to pay the bill, then we'll welcome suggestions, I'm sure."

Numie swallowed hard. He'd had his fill.

"Don't you understand nothing?" Lola asked. "I can't have Ned putting on a better show than you. You just can't get it that I'm not only doing a favor for you, but for the whole mother-fucking white race."

"Some favor!" Numie said.

"A well-built man like you shouldn't be embarrassed," David added. Eyes narrowed, his lips set in a sheepish smile.

The man's coyness not only made Numie uncomfortable, but added to his increasing anger. "I'm not embarrassed," he said. "That's not the point. I don't like being ordered around like this."

"It's okay," Lola assured him. "With David, you can let it all hang out." This was said with such authority she hoped to end all argument.

"I understand what you're looking for, Miss La Mour," David said, moving quickly. "Something nice, slim, and snug. I have the exact item. Bet it'll fit without alterations."

"It had better," Lola said. "Got no time for alterations." She wet her lips, then, looking into a full-length mirror, decided she needed more lipstick. She'd have to coat it on heavy to compete with Dinah. Opening her purse, she noticed her watch. "We're practically due at their place right now."

"What's your waist size?" David asked.

"Thirty," Numie said, sighing.

It was a signal to Lola that he had decided to cooperate.

"Better check that," David said, his lips curling in anticipation. From a nearby counter, he took a tape measure, wrapping it around Numie's waist. "Right you are. And now the inseam." Dropping to his knees in front of Numie, he placed his hand inside the seat of his crotch.

Instinctively Numie withdrew at his wet-fingered touch, then stood firm.

"Watch and make sure you take the right kind of measurements," Lola said, hawkeying every move.

Numie tensed. The bald man clearly repulsed him——too

many echoes of his past.

Getting up, David buzzed to the back, returning with a pair of white slacks. "Try these on."

Looking around for a dressing room, Numie asked, "Right here?"

"Sure," Lola said, "we ain't got no time for formalities."

"I'll draw the blinds up front," David said, hurrying to the door. But he was back in a moment.

Lola was boring her eyes into Numie.

Sucking in his breath, he started to strip. Tossing his shirt aside, he slowly unbuttoned his fly, sliding out of his jeans. He wore no underwear. Kicking his sandals aside, he stood straight. He grinned nicely, but it was one of defiance.

Lola was enjoying exhibiting him. It showed David the kind of white man she was capable of attracting.

David, though, was nervously mopping beads of perspiration from his forehead. His thin lips were twitching.

"The pants, man," Numie finally said.

"Oh, yes," David managed to say, his Adam's apple bobbing up and down.

Numie squeezed into the pants. "They're hardly my size," he said.

"Go on, try them on," Lola ordered.

The fabric clung so tightly it was all Numie could do to zip them up. "They pinch like hell," he said, grunting.

"Those pants do just what I want them to," Lola said. "I'll show that Dinah a thing or two." A snarl of dark jealousy consumed her face. She applied even more make-up, as if to cover it.

"Even the length is perfect," David said, mincing forward.

. . .

The minister shook his hand, a firm grip. "Glad to meet you, too."

Numie liked Roy Alberts at once.

"Aren't you the 'gay pope'?" Leonora asked, her voice smooth as cold steel.

The reverend frowned. "I hope not."

Numie instinctively backed away. He was beginning to learn

when Leonora was preparing for the kill.

"Yes," she continued, "I think I've heard you called that when you're not being referred to as the 'gay Billy Graham'." A nerve tugged at her left wrist. She really didn't know why she was insulting this kindly man. These unexplained impulses took over now and then. However, now that she'd launched the attack, she was determined to see the battle through.

"I resist labels," Alberts said softly. "I believe that God didn't limit love to jocks and bunnies."

Numie was surprised at his use of those words. This man didn't talk like any minister he'd ever met. He smiled to himself, wishing his own mama had the pleasure of meeting Roy Alberts.

"That's why I gladly accepted the Commodore's invitation to perform the wedding ceremony." Alberts went on.

Leonora searched his face carefully, her eyes probing it like a needle after a splinter. She was determined to find one weak and vulnerable spot. She focused on his mouth. It was petulant. Now she knew why she instantly disliked the man. She positively loathed petulant mouths. "But I read that a bishop suggested calling these gay marriages a 'celebration of commitment'. Why not that?"

"That's up to the individual," the reverend said. "If Miss La Mour and the commodore want to be joined in the eyes of God, then it's my duty to help them achieve that union."

She glanced ahead at the shadowy figures in the bar, but they were too dim and her eyes too weak to make out any distinct features. However, she could sense that all eyes were on her. "But they don't believe in God," she said, raising her voice. "I happen to know both of them are devout atheists."

"A devout atheist," the minister said, "is about the same as a true believer."

"Frankly, dear heart," Leonora continued, "I'm attending this so-called wedding because the commodore is a business associate of mine." She moved closer to Alberts, although his cheap shaving cologne offended her sensitive nostrils. "Confidentially, I disapprove mightily of homosexuality. It's a disgusting perversion!" She stepped back to survey the damage she'd caused. Indeed, the reverend's face showed his anguish. "I, myself," Leonora went on, "was married to a most delightful creature, a darling man named Norton Huttnar. I loved him so much I've never been able to look at another man since his untimely death at the age of seventy-eight."

The minister's back stiffened. "Miss De la Mer," he said, "I don't understand you at all. You know I'm a self-admitted homosexual, yet you insult me by calling my love a disgusting perversion." His hand trembled. "The commodore and Miss La Mour represent a new style of family. Disgusting to some maybe, but so is hatred of all things we don't understand."

The heat of the morning was causing her to see spots. She'd have to go inside and quickly. "But this flamboyance," she protested. "Even my chauffeur here called it a spectacle." Her eyes wandered around in search of Numie, but he was off somewhere talking to a drunken bum.

"Maybe it is," the reverend said, "but I prefer flamboyance to *closet queens*."

Leonora's fingers began a crawling descent down her costume. "I beg your pardon."

"Between us, *dah-ling*," the minister said, effecting a mincing, high-pitched voice, "in that rose number, with a diamond stalk coming out of your head, you're the biggest drag queen here."

"My God," Leonora said, "I've never been talked to this way in my life." Motionless, she stood at rigid attention.

"If you don't want to attend," the minister said, resuming his natural voice, "you don't have to. To me, this is a serious ceremony of two people pledging fidelity to each other as abiding friends——husband and husband or husband and wife, whatever you want to call it. You can either enter into the spirit of it, or else *leave*. Good day, Miss De la Mer."

"The vicious swine!" Leonora said to Numie, now at her side.

. . .

"You are, in fact, Haskell Hadley Yett?" an attorney was asking. "Not Lola La Mour."

Lola crossed her legs and checked her hosiery for a snag. "One and the same," she answered, holding her head high. "Lola La Mour is my professional name."

"And what kind of profession is that?" the attorney asked, settling back in a leather chair and lighting a cigarette. "That requires you to dress, act, and talk like a woman?"

Lola licked her lips, knowing that made her sexier. "I'm a cabaret entertainer," she said, adjusting her black dress. "My fans expect it of me."

The attorney fingered his mustache and moved uncomfortably in his seat. His white shirt was soaked. "Who are these gentlemen with you?" he inquired.

Lola started to answer, but Ned interrupted. "I'm her business manager here to protect her interests."

As if threatened, the attorney sat up rigidly. "Her interests are well taken care of, I can assure you."

"I'm the driver," Numie interjected, hoping to stay out of this whole affair. In the far corner of the room, he had refused even a seat. Cast in the servant role, he was determined to play it through. Aimlessly his eyes wandered, taking in the termite-eaten Cuban wicker furniture, the thirsty plants, and the bamboo ceiling. His head was dark today, and sounds had a hard time reaching him. It was some kind of hell he was hearing, but he was a long way from it.

"As you know," the attorney said, turning to Ned, "Mr. Yett was Commodore Philip's sole heir."

"Heiress," Lola corrected. She smiled demurely. "I'm known by my professional name." Trying to appear casual like watching a fly, she glanced at Numie in the back of the room. That white boy infuriated the hell out of her. He didn't seem to be impressed that she was an heiress. And that had been the one thing she knew would impress him. It didn't make sense, unless Numie was playing a game. Holding out for higher stakes.

"I'm sorry, *Miss* La Mour," the attorney said, trying to catch her eye. "Whichever term you prefer is acceptable to me." He settled back again. "The commodore has a close relative."

The word sent a shiver racing up Lola's spine.

"I think one sister is still living in New Orleans," the attorney continued.

Memories of the banquet and the call from Sister Amelia flashed through Lola's head.

"She's not mentioned in the will," the attorney said. "I had warned Phil to at least mention her. Now I must warn you: I expect his sister will contest the will."

In spite of running eye shadow, Lola tried to appear as confident as possible. "I'm not worried," she said.

She flung herself back in her peacock chair like a limp dishrag. No need to appear tense. The bars on the windows caught her eye. The office was like a goddamn jail, and she was not going to be the prisoner of white men for much longer. Sitting up rigidly, she was ready for business. "Exactly what does the commodore's estate consist of?" Her words hung heavy in the air. From the open but barred window an aroma of honeysuckle wafted across, only to be smothered by the attorney's cigarette smoke. "He never talked to me too much about his property on the mainland."

"It's quite large," the attorney said. "You're going to be a very wealthy... person."

A tingle began in Lola's chartreuse-painted toe, traversing her hosiery-encased legs, settling for a brief moment in her little honeypot, then traveling up her breasts, lodging finally at her temples, streaked with pancake makeup. "I know he had boats," she replied, again trying to sound as casual as possible. "He used to bring his yacht down from time to time."

"Yes, I know that," the attorney said. "He owns four, including the yacht. I wouldn't exactly call them boats. They're more like ships."

Her temples practically exploded. Then the tingle began its downward descent, this time anchoring permanently at the honeypot.

. . .

Every now and then, he'd turn and look over his shoulder. The two men were still there, and they exchanged friendly glances with him, but nothing more.

That beer that the bartender kept placing on the counter in front of him was beginning to take its toll. Glancing only briefly at the two men, Numie headed for the men's room in the back. He wasn't quite sure, but sensed that either one or else both of the men were trailing him.

Opening the door to the foul-smelling toilet, he spotted three urinals. He hesitated only a moment before taking the urinal in the middle.

He was so familiar with this scene that he knew exactly what was going to happen next. The two men from the bar placed themselves on his left and right. They made no move to unzip, but stood looking down at Numie.

Slowly, very slowly, he unbuttoned his jeans. He knew this was showtime, and it gave him a thrill. It'd been so long since he was the object of anyone's desire, and it was a welcome feeling returning to him. He pulled out his cock and pissed noisily against the porcelain. He heard one of the men sigh. Even when he'd finished, he still held it out for their inspection, shaking it several times. Under their appreciative eyes, it began to harden and take on a life of its own. He feared he might not be able to get it back into his pants if that happened.

Removing both hands, he allowed the men one final inspection before he tucked his hardening cock back into his jeans.

He turned and left the toilet, leaving the men standing at the urinals. By the time he reached the bar again, the men had joined him, inviting him to their table. He accepted the invitation, and was placed in the middle of their booth between them.

Also available from FLF Press/STARbooks Press...

Ken Anderson's
THE INTENSE LOVER
a suite of poems by the renowned Georgian writer

*"Few poets write with as much wit and candor," raves
Jon Hershey, author of "The Old Red Kimono."*

Ken Anderson, an Associate Professor of English, has been a
consultant for a finearts journal and a gay men's literary quarterly. His
poetry and fiction have appeared in such journals and anthologies as
*Alabama School of Fine Arts Poetry Quarterly, The Alternate,
Anthology of Magazine Verse and Yearbook of American Poetry,
Barely Legal, Bay Windows, Beloit Poetry Journal, Changing Men,
Chattahoochee Review, Connecticut Poetry Review, Cotton Boll: The
Atlanta Review, Dangerous Boys, Dekalb Literary Arts Journal, Delta,
Discourse, Fag Rag, Falmouth Review of Literature, Finished Product,
FirstHand, Four Elements, Gay Review, Gay Sunshine, Georgia State
University Review, GPU News, Higginson Journal of American
Poetry, Insatiable/Unforgettable, Insight, International Poetry Review,
Iris, The James White Review, Local Storms, Lullwater Review,
Mississippi Review, Mouth of the Dragon, Off Peachtree, Old Red
Kimono, Poem, RFD, Runaways, The Smith, Southern Review, Spoon
River Quarterly, and others.*

Permanent Gardens, his first book of poems, was published by Seabolt
Press, and his play, *Mattie Cushman*, has been produced twice and
aired often on cable television. His novel, *Someone Bought the House
on the Island*, is scheduled for release soon.

The Intense Lover (ISBN 1-877978-80-9, $9.00 U.S.) at bookstores
now. FLF Press and STARbooks Press titles are available at fine
booksellers throughout the world and distributed in America by
Bookazine., Alamo Square, Koen Books, Baker & Taylor and
Bookpeople and in the U.K. by Turnaround and Australia by Stillone
PTY.

DEJA VU

Chunky, red-haired, hard, you held me
in your eyes. I reflected your stare
like glass. But then you turned away –
a handsome blind man lost
in a bar, someone who simply
couldn't remember
just what he'd been looking for.
So I played a little game – I talked
with a friend – and won. You said,
"I'm tired of cruisin' you." We turned
into some great pornography. In the morning
I dozed. You collected your clothes.

I didn't know what to say.

The dark-blue candle, the bottle
of amyl, the dented tube
with its little sailor's cap – these
were the props
in the bedtime story
we told each other once more
last night. But you forgot
we had played the scene. I phoned you
in the next. I had to be someone else,
I guess, before you could swallow me twice,
my friend, before you could take me in
again, some other place and time.

KEY WEST

Higgs Beach

A catch
of bathers
lay dumped
on the rickety pier, chafing
in the heat, like trout. The sun
was a match
to blue construction paper. On the brow
of the sea, small beads
of light
      flashed.

City Cemetery

A junkyard
of wrecked tombs, whitewashed
blinding white
in a wild sun,
as if a fierce spiritual light flared
from the cracks....

Plastic lilies rattled
in the rubble,
and the mad palms ripped out their fronds.

COMING IN THE AUTUMN OF 1998...

Darwin Porter's Explosive New
Psycho-Sexual Thriller

BLOOD MOON